W.H. Gregory

Egypt in 1855 and 1856; Tunis in 1857 and 1858

Vol. II

Anatiposi

W.H. Gregory

Egypt in 1855 and 1856; Tunis in 1857 and 1858

Vol. II

Reprint of the original.

1st Edition 2023 | ISBN: 978-3-38230-849-0

Anatiposi Verlag is an imprint of Outlook Verlagsgesellschaft mbH.

Verlag (Publisher): Outlook Verlag GmbH, Zeilweg 44, 60439 Frankfurt, Deutschland
Vertretungsberechtigt (Authorized to represent): E. Roepke, Zeilweg 44, 60439 Frankfurt, Deutschland
Druck (Print): Books on Demand GmbH, In de Tarpen 42, 22848 Norderstedt, Deutschland

EGYPT

AND

TUNIS.

EGYPT

IN 1855 AND 1856;

TUNIS

IN 1857 AND 1858.

BY

W. H. GREGORY, M.P.

VOL. II.

LONDON:
PRINTED FOR PRIVATE CIRCULATION,
BY JOHN RUSSELL SMITH,
36, SOHO SQUARE.
M.DCCC.LIX.

EGYPT AND NUBIA

IN 1855 AND 1856.

IT was fortunate for us that we had got out of Nubia, for adverse winds again beset us, and had we remained above the Cataracts we should have fallen victims to despondency, and perhaps, as men do in desperate circumstances, contracted imprudent matrimonial alliances, built ourselves palm huts, and allowed the *Flea* to rot upon the bank. For the next two days we hardly made any way, and our only occupation was sending one sailor to hunt another sailor, as all the wives, brothers, sisters, and relatives to the ninth degree, with which the neighbouring villages teemed, took advantage of our detention, and claimed the company of our crew to solemn leave-takings. On the first evening we had a visit, which, as illustrating a very affectionate trait in these poor people, I cannot help mentioning. Our new little boy, to whom I lately alluded as successor to Nisnas, had been duly installed, but asked permission, although only arrived the same afternoon, to pass the evening with his parents. We of course objected to his going home, as he had received some of his pay, and might be wanting if the wind lulled, but he informed us that his parents had come to him, and were now sitting on the bank. They had seen that the heavy gale from the north would interrupt our progress, and had come several miles to bid again farewell to their child. When we went on shore, they came to us and said, that their great object was to see us and to ask us to take care of their boy; he had been on one journey before, but then he had his father with him, and now he was going all alone into the wide, wide world, and he was their only one. They never would have parted with him, they added, but that they knew the Howaga were good people, and would not allow oppression or wrong in their boat. We assured them they were quite right in their favorable opinion, that we would protect their child, and see that he was invariably well treated, and we made the Reis promise in their presence that on arriving at Cairo he would look after him, and get him a good berth in some returning vessel. We thus allayed all their apprehensions, and cheered them, moreover, mightily, by assuring them that if he behaved steadily he might eventually advance to the dignity of Reis—the summit of all their ambition. It was very pleasing to see their confidence in Europeans, as well as their extreme affection and proper forethought for their child.

We were from the afternoon of the 7th till the 10th before we made Kom Ombo. It was a gay, tranquil morning when the fine temple, reared upon a lofty eminence over the river (the only Egyptian monument possessing this advantage) came in view. As we rounded the long low-lying shore on the western side, whence the waters had far receded since we passed it in our upward journey, the whole population was out and working hard to get down their melons in the fertile deposit that lay bare; and a monstrous crocodile was stretched basking on a sandy island just below the temple. The building itself was dedicated to Aroeris and the crocodile-headed god Savak, and the animal itself was held sacred throughout the Ombite district. There is a broad wall of crude brick surrounding the *enceinte*, on which a learned Egyptian traveller supposes that in former times the reptile was taken out for an airing by his attendant priests. Why the crocodile like Humpty Dumpty should be set on a wall I cannot well understand. I should have thought it the last place to suit its tastes and habits.

The temple is a noble building, although of the unfashionable Ptolemaic age, having been founded by Philometor, continued by Physcon, and completed by Auletes. From the names, however, of Thothmes III. and Amun-neit-gori having been found on a portion of the structure, it is clear that this, like most of the Ptolemaic temples, is a restoration of an older sanctuary. From the irruption of sand all round, and the size of the columns forming the portico, it has at present a squat and heavy appearance; but with the portals majestically rising right upon the precipitous bank, which sheers down into the Nile, with its double entrance and double sanctuary, it must in its great days have been one of the most imposing edifices in all Egypt. In possessing this double entrance and double sanctuary to the respective gods Aroeris and Savak, Kom Ombo differs from every other existing temple in the country.

My friend in vain attempted to destroy the descendant of the local deity, who, though he had seen plenty of Fellahs passing by, continued his siesta very comfortably, but the instant the dreaded European hove in sight, with praiseworthy caution he subsided into the stream.

Throughout the whole of this the Ombite district the crocodile was peculiarly sacred. De Pauw is of opinion that in all probability the worship of this reptile was a priestly device for enlisting the superstition of the people to keep open the canals leading to different towns, without which the holy animal would not have had access to his worshippers. In the neighbouring districts, however, the homages that were paid to him in this were amply compensated for by the abhorrence in which he was held. The people of Tentyra, which lay next to the Ombos territory, were of old famous for their skill and determination in facing and overcoming the monster even in his own element, the water. The hatred, therefore, between the reptile worshippers and the reptile killers was as bitter as theological hatreds ordinarily are; and Juvenal devotes his last Satire to a pleasant account of a furious affray that took place during his banishment to Egypt, between the inhabitants of Coptos, of the crocodile faction on the one hand, and the Tentyrites on the other. In this affair the latter considerably aggravated their offences to the deity by taking prisoner one of his votaries, devouring him there and then, and literally picking his bones, as the poet says, without any culinary preliminary whatsoever.

Sixteen miles below Ombos, is the remarkable sandstone quarry, from which was derived the greater number of the monuments in Upper Egypt. It is called Hagar Silsileh, or "rock of the chain," from a legend of the Arabs, that in former times a robber prince had taken his station at this narrow pass, and by stretching a chain across the river, compelled every boat to pay him toll, in its passage up and down. The story is clearly derived from the old name Silsilis, which from its similarity to the Arab word Silsileh, or "chain," originated the fiction. A very curious mushroom-shaped rock on the western bank, part of the ancient excavations, has confirmed the Arabs in this supposition, and they affirm, that from this the chain was passed to a similar pillar on the other side, which, however, no longer exists; and they also show holes in the rock through which it ran.

The Nile contracts at this point, pressed in as it is by the sandstone hills on each bank, and there are few places more interesting both to the scientific and the unscientific traveller, than this father of quarries. Imagine immense areas as large as London squares, cut out a hundred feet deep, as neatly, and seemingly as easily as if the material had been cork; fancy innumerable streets, passages, and openings spreading like a labyrinth throughout; extend these excavations for a considerable distance on both sides of the river, and if Thebes and the Pyramids have failed to give you an adequate notion of the industry, determination, and power of the old Egyptians, these quarries will. But to the antiquarian they are full of interest, abounding as they do, not only in monuments of Rameses the Great, and mentioning assemblies held in the 30th, 34th, 37th, and 44th year of his reign, but also of earlier Pharaohs, Amunoph III., Horus, and Thothmes I., II. All along the water's edge on the western bank run grottoes and tablets, and to the north is a rock temple, in which are gravings commemorating the triumphs of Horus over the Ethiopians. In one spirited scene, this king is seen borne in a triumphal chair, on men's shoulders; a lion is by his side; the trumpeter announces his coming; his troops march in front, followed by the prisoners. These representations are valuable, as containing the notice of a powerful and conquering king, of which I am not aware that other records exist. In fact, the whole place is well worthy of a more protracted visit than we were able to allow it. Some Bedoueens informed us that there was good shooting in the neighborhood, and a late traveller mentions that he was told by the same people, of the existence of extensive ruins at a place called El Birkeh, some distance in the interior, which I have never read of as having been investigated by any traveller.

Sir G. Wilkinson gives an excellent account of the manner employed by the Egyptians to render the sandstone not merely available for rough building, but also for the finer and more conspicuous parts of their structures, which were ornamented with colors. He says, "The earliest Egyptian edifices were principally erected of limestone, which continued in use occasionally, even in Upper Egypt, till the commencement of the eighteenth dynasty; though the Pharaohs of the sixteenth had already introduced the sandstone of Silsilis to build the walls and colonnades of the larger temples, and its fitness for masonary, its durability, and the evenness of its grain, became so thoroughly appreciated by their architects during the eighteenth and succeeding dynasties, that it was from that time almost exclusively used in building the monuments of the Thebaid. But as its texture was less suited for the reception of color than the smoother limestone, they prepared its surface with a coat of calcareous composition, which, while it prevented the stone from imbibing an unnecessary quantity of color, afforded greater facility for the execution of the outlines. The subjects, when sculptured, either in relief or intaglio, were again coated with the same substance, to receive the final coloring; and the details of the figures and of the other objects, could thereby be finished with a precision and delicacy in vain to be expected from the rough and absorbent surface of the sandstone.

"Their paint was mixed with water. The reds and yellows were ochre, but the greens and blues were extracted from copper, and though of a most beautiful hue, the quality was much coarser than either of the former, or their ivory black. The white is a very pure chalk reduced to an impalpable powder; and the brown, orange, and other compound colors, were simply formed by the combination of s me of the above. Owing to their being mixed with water, they necessarily required some protection, even in the dry climate of Egypt, against the contact of rain; and so attentive were they to this point, that the interstices of the blocks which form the roofs of their temples, independently of their being well fitted together, and cemented with a tenacious and compact mortar, were covered by an additional piece of stone, let into a groove of about eight inches in breadth, extending equally on either side of the line of their junction.

"However the partial showers and occasional storms in Upper Egypt might affect the state of their painted walls, they were not sufficient to injure the stone itself, which still remains in its original state, even after so long a period, except where the damp arising from earth impregnated with nitre, has penetrated through its granular texture, as it is here and there observable near the ground, at Medinet Abou, and in other ruins of the Thebaid. But exposure to the external atmosphere, which here generally affects calcareous substances, was found not to be injurious to the sandstone of Silsilis; and like its neighbour, the granite, it was only inferior to limestone in one respect,—that the latter might remain buried for ages without being corroded by the salts of the earth, a fact with which the Egyptians, from having used it in the substructions of obelisks and other granite monuments, were evidently well acquainted."

The dimensions of some of these excavations were taken by Mr. Hamilton, and will, perhaps, give a better idea of their magnitude, than a vague description. He first mentions the quarries on the left bank, as being 250 ft. long, 80 ft. wide, and 30 ft. high; and then describes those on the eastern bank, as on a much larger scale. He entered by a passage cut through the rock, to the length of 134 feet,

13 ft. in width, and 81 ft. in perpendicular height. The square thus entered, was enclosed on every side by the cut-away rock, to the height of 80 ft. or 100 ft., except to the south, where there is a gradual ascent to the top of the mountain. At the angles of the passages and on the opposite wall, are holes, evidently intended as purchases for the ropes used in the conveyance of the blocks down the inclined plane of the passage, towards the river. Another quarry he visited to the north of this. It is approached by a more winding passage, about 20 feet wide and 320 feet long. The area is an irregular square of 550 feet by 260 feet, and of the same height as the former.

I have quoted from Mr. Hamilton, as we had neither time nor means to obtain the proportions of this most extraordinary place; but I look forward at some future period to a longer stay, and a sporting excursion with the Ababde Bedoueens, who assured us of excellent sport—hares, partridges, and a sprinkling of hyenas; besides, the hope of being the first explorer of the ruins I alluded to, is an additional inducement.

About a mile to the north of the quarries, a small island covered with high rushes, not a usual occurrence in the Nile, presented itself; and as it looked, as a former land-steward of mine would have said, an excellent "harbinger," meaning harbourer, of wild ducks, I ordered out the small boat for a chase. A crocodile, moreover, was slumbering on its sandy extremity, but, as cunning as his fellows, sidled off as we approached. On landing, I found the island full of rushes, reaching up to the chin, with deep muddy holes in it, and a perfect colony of ducks, teal, and plover, for its inhabitants. Having shot a duck, which fell between the island and the land, where some Fellâhs were working, I was shouting to them to pick it up, when, with a dash and plunge which sent the mud and water literally over me, a large crocodile dropped into the hole by which I was standing, not a yard from my feet. My gun was discharged, and the sailor who was with me had the rifle, which would have been, however, of little use amid the mud and dirt through which the reptile made his way with far greater quickness than could be expected from such a huge lumbering brute. He had been lying there for several minutes, while I was talking to the people on shore, and it was not till the Arab came up and almost trod on him, that he took his departure. The same afternoon, I shot from the boat a large lizard that was slowly crawling along the bank; he measured three feet in length, and was skinned by the old cook. The Nubians hinted at eating him, but Hassaneen, who was now himself again, rated them as filthy gormandizers, and despite of their long-lingering, hungry looks, pitched the carcase into the water. We only saw one other large lizard, which was making his way up the rocks at Abou Simbel. Had we killed him, old Hassaneen would have had to endure the sight of seeing him devoured, with the additional annoyance of being forced to hold his peace during the repast. If the good old cook had been in the West Indies, he would not have had such abhorrence of lizard, and perhaps considered an iguana *à la poulette* as his masterpiece. The Arabs give a curious account of these large lizards; they say they are hatched from the bad eggs of the crocodiles, and are consequently half-brothers to the respected deities of Old Egypt.

During all these proceedings, our *dahabieh* had nearly advanced out of sight, and as at certain turns of the stream the wind favored us, I was amused to see the sailors act exactly like the little navigating Cupids on cameos. They held up their melayeh, or plaid, and standing in the bow of the sandal or small boat, spread it out as a sail to catch the wind, which it did very effectually; so far the resemblance was complete, but I am bound to say that here the similarity stopped—no one would have taken our Arabs for Cupids.

Between this place and Esnéh, is the celebrated El Kab, or Eilethyas, a city dedicated in former times to Lucina and the Sun. The old wall of unbaked bricks, still surrounds the town; its dimensions, twenty feet thick and thirty feet high, prove its strength; while the temples, shrines, and sepulchral grottoes, show that it was a place of considerable importance and population. The drawings on the walls of these grottoes, as being anterior in point of time to the decorations of similar places of burial at Thebes, render them curious to the antiquarian, more especially as the names of several very ancient kings have been discovered there, the placing of whom in their proper chronological positions will, doubtless, be a satisfactory operation to future Egyptologers.

I have already, in writing about Beni Hassan, mentioned the song which Champollion in this place deciphered, or persuaded himself and others that he deciphered. The scene is still visible—oxen thrashing out the corn, with certain hieroglyphical signs over the drawings. The greater part of the paintings have been mutilated and destroyed, but still many remain, illustrating different scenes of private life—the usual gay decorations of Egyptian tombs. In one grotto, the laird walks forth, with his servants following bearing his chair and his water-jar, to oversee the labourers. They are all very busy, hoeing, ploughing, sowing, reaping, gathering the grain into garners, and winnowing it when there: then come the farm stock, oxen, sheep, goats, asses. After this we have the process of wine-making, then there are fishing and fowling scenes. The lord and lady then receive various fruits, and in return for so much prosperity, make their offerings to the gods. But as business without festivity would be dull work, we have also a very pleasant entertainment exhibited—the good folks, "en grande tenue," are seated connubially on the same chair; their favorite pet, a monkey, is tied to it, but his share has not been forgotten among all the good things that are to come in for the guests. These guests are introduced by an attendant in leopard-skin livery, and are seen sitting, ladies and gentlemen in rows, all smelling diligently at the lotus-flower: not a bad way of avoiding the somewhat awkward period just before dinner is announced. Then comes the real business; servants are moving about presenting dishes and bowls, tables groan with savory meats, carvers cut up sheep, roasted whole; in short, all is bustle and good cheer. Nor is music wanting, moreover. One damsel plays on the harp (just as they distract one during dinner in German hotels); another is drawing dulcet strains from the flute; she is not aware that the goddess Minerva used the same instrument, but threw it away on seeing by the reflection in the water the ugly faces it caused her to make; other maidens, for general delectation, dance; and some pleasant ladies for whom there was probably not room at dinner, just drop in towards the cool of the evening, with the sistrum in their hands, as our own young ladies sometimes appear with their music-books, on similar occasions.

Besides, however, these scenes of festivity and

joy, there are others of sorrow and mourning. Men and oxen are seen drawing a bier, on which rests the mummy of the deceased; sorrowing women in the attitude of affliction, men with hands uplifted, and others with torches, surround the funeral train; boats are introduced bearing mummied figures, for mystic ceremonies, such as those connected with death and burial, were fitting adjuncts to remind the living of all that must follow the material prosperity and the merry-making depicted in the other representations.

It is worth while to remark the manner of dealing with flax, in these good old days. Although there is no reason why they should not, but rather every reason why they should treat flax just as we do now, still it is pleasant to see them pulling it up by the roots, carrying it off in small bundles, and then combing it most deftly. It seems quite strange they have not got a scutch-mill, so smart does the affair seem. One almost looks out for the Belfast agent in the background, waiting to buy it. You see them, moreover, weighing carefully the corn, after it is winnowed; it is this prudence and economy that enables them to give such agreeable evening parties. In short, it is time not badly spent to read these lithographed pages of an extinct race, its pleasures and cares, occupations and relaxations in times long ago, three thousand years at least, though we may see others more artistic at Gornou, others still older at Beni Hassan. I may add, that should any of the party feel that grottoes and tombs and temples are bores beyond endurance, they will find excellent wild-duck shooting about the numerous ponds in the neighbourhood, and be able to delight the heart of their antiquarian companion after all his labours with roast mallard and lime-juice, for "hemlock does not hurt goats, nor luxury philosophers."

We had bought a wild-goose, which had been slightly wounded, from a Bedoueen, in going up the river, and had taken rather an affection for the poor bird, which saved him from Hassaneen's knife when provisions ran short in Nubia. Up to this period he had been perfectly silent, but during this night, on passing the spot where he had been captured, thinking, perhaps, of his young goslings all at play, he gave vent to the most horrible noises, which awoke the whole boat, and caused us to fear that some catastrophe had happened. After that he relapsed again into his usual taciturnity. It is strange that he should have remembered his former haunts, although more than a month had elapsed since he became our guest, and it was, moreover, past midnight.

On the 12th we passed through Esnéh, in the morning, where the Ghawazi, those priestesses of Athor, seemed if possible more numerous than before, swaggering about, and infesting a coffee-house near the river, patronized it would seem exclusively by them and some disreputable-looking Arnaouts, for the natives carefully avoided it.

Later in the day we stopped a short time at Erment, where Mustapha Pacha, son of Ibrahim, had erected a remarkably fine and spacious sugar manufactory; unfortunately, however, much of the temple of the town had been used in its construction, and "Himmed," in spite of his late warmness in the antiquity line, since my refusal to scale the grottoes at Ibrim, brought us on board a cartouche of the celebrated Cleopatra, which was lying on the bank amid other rubbish. The manager of these works is French, and his wife had begged of our dragoman to procure for her dates and a monkey in Nubia; the latter part of her desire it was not possible to execute, but the dates were forthcoming, and while they were being delivered we walked through the building with the superintendent, a very civil Frenchman, who gave us every information. The crop had all been gathered in and worked off, and nothing was going on, but the machinery and the establishment were patterns of order and cleanliness. This gentleman informed us that the proprietor, Mustapha Pacha, was by no means like the vast majority of his race, a drone living on the produce of others' labour, but that he was a very intelligent, knowledgeable man, thoroughly understanding the business and the machinery, and very often coming to the manufactory and residing there for some time. He showed us very large additions to the works which were being constructed, and, to the best of my remembrance, stated that they were laid down and directed by the Pacha himself. It may not be generally known that we have borrowed our word "sugar" from the Indians, whose name for the sugar-cane is "sharkara." It was known in India and in China, and in the islands of the Pacific, from the very earliest date. From the remote East it came to Khorassan, in Persia, about the fifth century A.D. The Arabs transferred it to the shores of the Mediterranean. In 1306 it was commonly grown in the Morea, and a hundred years later it enriched Calabria, Sicily, and the coasts of Spain. From Sicily the Infanta Don Henry transported the cane to Madeira, from Madeira it spread to the Canary Islands, thence it made its way to St. Domingo, and so on to the American continent.

Our new sailors rowed to-day with such gallantry and success that we promised to look favorably on their exertions, provided we arrived at Thebes before midnight. On hearing the blissful intelligence, one of them jumped up and performed a most extraordinary dance. After a series of jumps and kicks he seized a pole and proceeded to imitate a monkey; he then threw off his cap, his shirt, but, just as we imagined the trousers were to follow, the fit subsided, and he resumed his place very calmly. The crew were so inspired by the exhibition that they rowed like lions, and with cheers and songs and choruses, we found ourselves steering to our old mooring at Luxor about half-past ten the same evening. Lights were dancing over the water from the lanterns of European vessels, and we brought to at the stern of an immense *dahabieh*, a perfect *Santissima Trinidad* to our little *Victory*. This huge boat we found to be engaged by Lord Portarlington, and on going aboard of her we heard for the first time of the armistice, which astonished us not a little, and altered all our plans, as we were both bound to the Crimea in hopes of seeing the opening of the campaign. Besides this boat there were three others: one belonging to the hospitable acquaintances we made at Esnéh; the other to a party of two Dutch ladies and a gentleman, who had taken camels and boldly started on an expedition to Cosseir, on the Red Sea; the third was in occupation of a French and two young Belgian noblemen. She was the property of Il'hamy Pacha, and by far the handsomest boat I had seen on the Nile, built of iron, and fitted up internally with leather, which gave it a most cool and luxurious appearance.

As the expedition to the Crimea promised to be rather flat in consequence of the news of approaching peace, we resolved on taking our time henceforth, and on devoting two or three more days to Thebes. We had heard a great deal, on the occasion of our last visit, of a tomb that had been recently discovered by M. Maugnier, who was working for M. Sabatier, the French Consul-General, but which had been closed to strangers by a door and padlock until after M. Sabatier had visited it. On applying to M. Maugnier, he very courteously gave us an order to visit it, and accordingly the following morning we proceeded to the spot. As we passed over the Theban plain we remarked many changes in its appearance during our six weeks' absence. The poor, half-faded, sickly little tobacco plants that were then being dibbled into the ground were now robust and vigorous, with their red flowers in full bloom; the piece of water on which we had slain divers ducks was now dried up, and had become a melon plantation; the crops that had been waving in the January breeze were now gathered in heaps throughout the plain, and being threshed out.

Our way led right up to the Gebel Assass, over the eastern shoulders of which is the pass down into the valley of the Biban-el-Molouk—the gates or tombs of the kings. The tomb lies at the foot of the perpendicular precipice, which one turns one's eyes from in descending, but to which my friend, with an artist's attention, turned his eyes far more than to the tombs and scattered relics around, for the coloring of it was, beyond description, beautiful in the sun's light—a massive wall some 400 or 500 feet in height, glowing with the hue and richness of amber; not the lemon-colored amber beloved by those curious in chibouques, but glorious, deep, unfashionable amber, darker than the orange.

Whilst we were waiting for the *gardien*, we remarked on the side of an open and now dilapidated tomb, some colored drawings that had remained unmutilated amid the general havoc around. They were representations of sacred or imperial Nile barks, and were, from the cartouches on the same wall, of the early times of Thothmes III. Nothing could surpass the beauty of the coloring and the laborious finish of these painted sculptures. There were fifty figures in one boat, which had a gazelle's head forming the prow, with the horns thrown back, admirably executed Each of these male figures had his hair arranged in symmetrical plaits, and most carefully trimmed and settled—so settled and arranged, indeed, that it much resembled a fashionable coachman's wig; and as we know that wigs were worn in old Thebes on state occasions, in all probability this hair-dress is artificial. This was one of the few monuments that I was anxious to disturb and bring home, it was so perfect in every detail, so little injured even in color, and giving such an excellent idea of Egyptian drawings, that if I had had any tools capable of sawing the block, I should have removed it, and by doing so I should have been guilty of no desecration, but merely of preserving that which will be demolished and macadamised by the first excavator.

When the *gardien* did at length arrive, we found the far-famed tomb hardly worth visiting; the drawings on it were in no way remarkable; but we heard that M. Maugnier had excavated to the bottom of a deep pit, which yawned before us, and found some very splendid mummy cases, many vases, scarabæi, and other valuable curiosities. On going down into the plain we found some of the Goornah people reducing a beautiful black granite statue of some god or king into saleable proportions. It was a sitting figure, about three feet high, and they said it was headless when they dug it up, but the fresh marks of breakage showed that the mischief had been done that day. They were quite surprised and grieved that I would neither buy a hand they had succeeded in amputating, nor yet give them a present to inspire them with courage, as they said, to dig again.

Leaving my friend to take what turned out to be a most faithful drawing of the colossi appearing in the distance through the columns of the Rameseum, I started off to have another look at the vast pile of Medinet Abou. On arriving there I found a prodigious number of Arabs busily excavating, under the orders of M. Maugnier; they had just found and were clearing a fine colossal lion-headed statue of black granite. The superintendent of the works was the shekh of the village; a very civil, intelligent fellow, and a sporting character withal. He gave me a long account of wolf-hunts and battles with hyenas, which he thought was much better occupation than rummaging after old stones. He begged of me to join him in a shooting excursion, which I was obliged to decline with much regret; and presenting him with a box of strike-lights, we parted the best of friends. The working Arabs, too, experienced the Howaga's munificence, for, having a lot of farthing-pieces in my pocket, I threw a few into the hole where they were working. All the boys were in and scrambling in a second; the elderly and more sedate kept aloof, but on seeing that I put my hand again in my pocket and pulled it out with at least sixpence worth of coin in it, they could resist no longer, but rushed down the bank into the excavation, and there I left about eighty of all ages and sizes, kicking, tumbling, jostling, and scraping, in a cloud of blinding black dust. M. Maugnier will not have been well pleased with that morning's work.

The day was calm and sultry, and, as usual on calm and sultry days, great "zobaahs," or whirlwinds, were rearing up to the sky slender columns of dust, and moved along the plain. The little Arab donkey girl and myself shouted in chorus as they approached, "Hadeed, ya meshroom,"—"Iron, thou unlucky one!"—for we knew, as is well known to all Arabs, that these were not mere natural appearances, but malevolent and rebellious genii, careering away on some uncanny errand, and that hearing the name of the metal they hate and fear, they would disperse, as they did incontinently. Such in shape and appearance, as described in the *Arabian Nights*, was the cloud of smoke that rose up aloft into the air, when the chest sealed with the seal of Solomon was broken, and the evil spirit rose up before the astonished fisherman.

My way ran by the back of the colossi, where a great tablet of sandstone lay prostrate, 36 feet long by 14 feet wide, with the inscription and name of Amunoph, he who erected these prodigious images. Before me was the temple palace of Rameses; and the eye rested chiefly on the enormous block of mutilated granite that was once his resemblance. The reflections that arise from the sight of these shattered memorials of grandeur and immensity of architecture, nowadays almost inconceivable, are so truly and eloquently described by Mr. Stanley, that I again quote his words:—"What spires are to a modern city—what the towers of a cathedral are to its nave and choir, *that* the statues of the Pharaoh's were to the streets and temples of Thebes. The ground is strewed with their fragments. There were avenues of them towering high above plain and houses. Their gigantic size still remains. One was the granite statue of Rameses himself, who sat on the right side of the entrance to his palace. By some extraordinary catastrophe the statue has been thrown down, and the Arabs have scooped their millstones out of his face; but one can still see what he was—the largest statue in the world. Far and wide that enormous head must have been seen—eyes, mouth, and ears. Far and wide you must have seen his vast hands resting on his elephantine knees. You sit on his breast and look at the Osiride statues which support the portico of the temple, and which anywhere else would put to shame even the statues of the cherubs in St. Peter's, and they seem pigmies before him. His arm is thicker than their whole bodies. The only part of the temple or palace at all in proportion to him, must have been the gateway, which rose in pyramidal towers, now broken down, and rolled in a wild ruin down to the plain. Nothing which now exists in the world can give any notion of what the effect must have been when he was erect. Nero, towering above the Colosseum, may have been something like it; but he was of bronze, and Rameses was of solid granite. Nero was standing without an object. Rameses was resting in awful majesty after the conquest of the whole then known world. No one who entered that building, whether it were temple or palace, could have thought of anything else but that stupendous being who had thus raised himself up above the whole world of gods and men.

* * * * * * * *

"It carries us back to the days when there were giants upon the earth. It shows how the king in that first monarchy was the visible god upon earth. The only thing like it that has since been seen, is the deification of the Roman emperor. No pure monotheism could for a moment have been compatible with such an intense exaltation of the conquering king. 'I am Pharaoh,' 'By the life of Pharaoh!' 'Say unto Pharaoh whom art thou like in thy greatness?' Ezek. xxxi. 1. All these expression seem to acquire new life from this monster."

Those who have been in Russia, and remember the feelings with which the late emperor was approached, may form a faint conception, but only the very faintest conception of the awe imposed on their subjects by these mighty Pharaohs. I remember hearing from one who had been long at St. Petersburg, the absolutely superstitious feeling of the multitude towards their great sovereign—the subject of all thoughts, the observed of all observers, the central point from whom all ideas flowed of social and foreign policy. I heard how at his assemblies every soul watched for the glance of that keen eye, which was supposed not to leave an individual unnoticed, unremarked; and how each man fancied that the expression was in his case cordial or severe, and was elated or depressed in proportion. But the Russians of travel and education, though subservient and slavish as the most slavish serf, must have known, that great and powerful and wise as was their autocrat, there were other nations as powerful as theirs, other wills as unbending as his, other free and uncontrolled judgments upon his words and actions, other civilizations far superior. But in the case of the Egyptian, all knowledge, civilization, learning, and religion, were confined to the valley of the Nile; there was no will, no nation known that had set itself in array and had not been overcome. Superstition added its spell. Was Pharaoh, Son of the Sun, Beloved of Amun, the same dull clod and clay as the meanest fellâh? No! Everywhere he is portrayed, though inferior in rank, yet still as the friend and companion of the gods, where he is not deciding on the fate of man. It is impossible to fancy arbitrary power more illimitable, uncontrolled, more fraught with weal or woe, as good or evil character predominated, than that which rested in the hand of these unfettered monarchs.

But we have now jogged on as far as the Rameseum, where I found my friend in company with some English gentlemen, who were taking, very successfully, photographic representations of the most remarkable portions of the building. It is impossible to overrate the value of these photographs. Their accuracy is undoubted. There is no slovenliness nor neglect to confound and drive into controversy a whole century of antiquarians. As the Nile monuments are gradually perishing, it would be well worth the trifling expense that such an expedition would entail, to send forth a competent staff of photographers to take proofs of all inscriptions and sculptures which can be reached. There is every facility in Egypt for such an undertaking that a bright sun and an unclouded sky can contribute; and though many of the inscriptions may at present be unintelligible and mutilated, yet the time may come when such fragments might turn out of the highest value, elucidating and being elucidated by other remains. A complete collection would be a document of inestimable importance to the operations of the antiquarian; he would have a certain basis to work on which would not, as in the case of copies, be exposed to the imputation of incorrectness. It would be accessible to every student of archæology at home, whose means or health or occupations precluded his visiting the originals, scattered as they are through Egypt, Nubia, and the Arabian deserts. Moreover, the constant perusal and inspection of these memorials would give the student a keenness of perception as to the collocation of letters, and the grouping of hieroglyphics, which no detached inspection of localities could confer, and would be the means of throwing far more light on these interesting relics than the copies which we have at present of some particular inscriptions. It is also to be remarked, besides the incontrovertible accuracy of the photograph, that it gives minute details which the eye altogether overlooks. The sun's glance is keener and more searching than our own, and reveals, if I am correctly informed, in many instances, the existence of older writings and sculptures which have been so much defaced, in order to make way for newer drawings, as to be altogether unperceived by the observer. I can at all events state from my own observation that many details met my eye in the photographs which were being executed by the gentlemen above mentioned, which I had overlooked, and which a copyist, however exact, would hardly have succeeded in obtaining. The expenses incidental to such an undertaking, if engaged in by any private society, might be partly defrayed by the sale of copies struck off, either of the whole or of particular inscriptions, for the use of other learned societies; but it would be more satisfactory, and more to the credit of the country, if funds could be obtained by parliamentary grant, and the undertaking be conducted at the national expense.

My guide here informed me that an Arab, Achmet by name, of great antiquarian celebrity, had procured for me four Canopic vases, of which I have previously spoken, and that he was desirous to see me on the subject in his abode—one of the sepulchral caves in the hill at the back of the Rameseum. I found the worthy man at the entrance of his fortress, and he invited me to enter and be seated, thereby constituting me his guest and friend. A more extraordinary sight than the interior of his domicile it is difficult to imagine. In one corner were piled up large earthenware antique vases; in another, fragments of coffins painted and decorated with devices; baskets full of mummy cloth, images, blue bead necklaces—in short, all the paraphernalia of interment lay scattered on the floor, and in the rear, resting against the wall, were half a dozen embalmed corpses of the former inhabitants of the land, in black shrivelled ghastly completeness, with the hands, feet, and skulls of their contemporaries, heaped as pedestals around them. In the midst of this chamber of horrors we sat and discussed the price of the vases in question, which he said he had obtained after fifteen days' hard excavating; and at length, after a deal of bargaining quite incompatible with our mutual friendship, I became the purchaser of the objects, together with two curious wooden heads found on mummy-coffins, which my companion so approved of that he brought them back with him to England. Both these heads were found in the same sepulchre: one was painted red, with the features common to the ordinary drawings of the Egyptian race on the monuments; while the other was jet black, resembling the Negro countenance in lips, nose, eyes, and form of face. They are, no doubt, the likenesses of the owner of the tomb and of some faithful Ethiopian slave, with whom, even in death, his master wished to remain united.

My friend Achmet I found quite unwilling to bring his treasures to the boat, and he alleged as a reason, that some of the authorities at Luxor, on the plea of the illegality of excavations, made it a point of plundering any of the inhabitants of his side of the water, if ever they exposed their treasures, and then resold them, or presented them as offerings very graciously, to the European visitors. I had heard something of this before, and therefore acquiesced willingly in his urgent request not to show the vases at Luxor, nor to mention his name as vendor of any article. So pleased was he with this pledge of discretion, that he folded up a number of images in two parcels of mummy cloth, one of which he requested me to present to my companion, and seizing the skull of what was once perhaps the graceful head of some young Theban beauty, the toast of the days of Rameses, he tore off a long lock of her brown hair, and handed it to me as a record of my visit.

During our former visit to Thebes we were prevented by the unfavorable state of the moon, from paying a visit to Karnak by night; but this evening about ten o'clock, we announced our intention of proceeding thither to the dragoman, and requested his attendance. He was appalled at the idea, but still more appalled when we refused to hire donkeys and a *posse comitatus* to accompany them, but determined on pulling down the stream in the small boat, until opposite the great propylæa, reaching it by a stretch across country, and returning on foot *viâ* Luxor.

The moon had not yet risen when the *sandal* slipped from the *dahabieh's* side, conveying us and the dragoman, who was in a state of ludicrous terror, literally unable to speak from fear. We had previously instructed our Nubian, Himmed, to inform him that the people in the neighbourhood of Karnak were peculiarly bad people, and the despoilers of travellers; and as we watched Himmed imparting the information, we saw at the same time the poor dragoman's dusky face becoming almost livid with apprehension. Hubert did not add either to his contentment or good humour, by advising him to fill his pockets with stones to pelt off the assailants. Mahommed rebuked Hubert by saying, that though if attacked resistance would be impossible, as the odds would be of a whole village to three, yet, that at that time of the night, and amid such ruins, it was not men alone that he was in dread of. Indeed, the night was ghostly enough: light enough to reveal objects indistinctly, but too dark to declare their real nature; still, but with an occasional breeze rustling like a fleeting spirit through the branches of the palms. Softly we dropped down stream, as if on some uncanny errand, in deep silence, except when it was broken by the scream of some evil-omened bird of night.

When we arrived opposite (as well as we could guess) to the temple, the poor dragoman vainly endeavoured to enlist one of the boatmen as a companion. They evidently liked night rambling as little as he did, and insisted that it was necessary for them both to return, in order to be able to row back the boat against the stream. Away we started accordingly, having exhorted Mahommed to lead the way. This he declined doing on the valid plea of ignorance. We were, therefore, forced to be our own guides; and after half an hour's hard walking and stumbling over doura-stalks, we perceived no signs of the great temple, which we ought long before to have reached, but were evidently on the skirts of an Arab village, from the ferocious onslaught of dogs, one of whom, in self-defence, we were obliged to immolate to discourage the others. Feeling sure we had gone far enough inland, we made a turn-off at right angles towards Luxor, and soon found the gigantic mass of the grand propylæa looming at no great distance. But the poor dragoman's fear, roused tenfold by the clamour of the wounded dog and its masters, were not yet to be allayed. My friend, who was thrown out as a skirmishing party in advance, all at once with a gesture of alarm ensconced himself behind a heap of ruins. His example was immediately followed by myself; and when the dragoman came up on his hands and knees stalking the invisible enemy, we begged of him to go ahead and demand of the five armed

Arabs under the palms why they presented arms at us. As well as we could make out from the chattering of his teeth, a positive refusal was the reply, and that, if we wanted fighting and firing, we had better go forward and help ourselves. There was no gainsaying this, so we went forward, with poor Mahommed in the rear, begging of me not to be rash, and calling on all the prophets and caliphs for protection. The intervention of these holy men was successful, for we made good our way unmolested, by the south, into the great columned hall. On scrambling down the rubbish heap which obstructs the eastern entrance, we really, this time, did see a number of figures flitting among the columns, and heard the ominous click of gunlocks. The click of our double-barrels responded; but a loud shout in Arabic arose from the interior, which was answered joyfully and courageously by our dragoman. English accents intermingled then reached the ear, and we found that the supposed marauders were an English gentleman and lady, with their donkeys and attendants, persons whom we had met before. The moon had not yet risen, so we sat down and drew forth chibouques, and lucifer matches were scraped against the effigies of Amun, Lord of Karnak, and with fresh tobacco smoke Mahommed the dragoman imbibed fresh courage.

But at last a gentle flake of light glided through the columns, and shortly after, the moon arose and tipped and gilded with silver, lotus-headed capitals and their shafts; and images of gods and kings and priests arose to view, one after another, as each deep recess was illuminated. All the abomination of desolation which the arrogant and pitiless sun lays bare to view, was hid beneath the argentine raiment which the moon in her charity had thrown over Karnak. The shattered columns, the mutilated images, the gaping roof, the heaps of rubbish themselves, all the devastations of man and time, were smoothed and chastened—I was going to add, softened, but the impression I carried back of Karnak seen by moonlight, was not that of softness or prettiness. It was akin to awe. The enormous masses of portal, the huge columns of the central hall, the colossal figures gazing stonily upon me: all these objects, upon which alone the eye can rest at night in Karnak, and cannot wander as by day,—all these objects, from their inconceivable magnitude and weight, fell like a waking nightmare upon my imagination. It was actually the sensation of size that overpowered. All beyond was shade, and recesses black as Erebus; and over all, and around all, silence, deep unbroken silence. I felt positively relieved when I rejoined the party outside; and we jogged merrily along the avenue of sphinxes, back to Luxor. As we entered the town the moonlight was gaily playing on the obelisk and pylons of Rameses, the colonnades of Amunoph, the minarets of the mosque, the palms of the gardens, and the houses of sleeping fellâhs. Watchful dogs started from dense shadows, and barked violently at our outlandish voices; other hordes rushed forth on the tops of the low houses, and threatened to descend and tear us to pieces; but a united shower of brickbats from Muslim and Christian, moderated their ardour, and drove them howling to the bipeds below. So we pursued our way across the sandy beach, to where one small light glimmered steadily over the silent gentle water, from the masthead of the *Flea*.

The next day, the 15th, my companion returned to the Rameseum to finish his sketch; and I paid a second visit to the tombs of the kings, to inspect more leisurely the famous No. 17, or Belzoni's tomb, for Sir G. Wilkinson has very considerately numbered each tomb, for the use of persons having recourse to his *Guide Book*. I was so engaged with the extreme beauty of the details of this noble tomb, that I had only time to renew acquaintance with two others. In one of these, No. 9, the tomb of Rameses V., is a very remarkable scene, supposed to refer to the transmigration of souls. Osiris, the judge of the dead, is drawn as seated on his throne, with the scales of justice suspended from a figure in front of him; further on, a pig is seen in a boat driven off by a monkey, and preceded by another monkey, who marches in front. The unfortunate defunct is supposed to have changed his appearance from that of a man to that of a pig, and in that shape to be shipped off to the world again, there to expiate in that unseemly guise, the chief offence of his past life—namely, gross and unjustifiable gluttony. In this tomb many of the very remarkable drawings refer to the soul of the deceased king, which, being mystically identified with the sun, is represented, according to Champollion, as passing successively through the twelve hours of day and night. The same idea is astronomically exhibited on one of the ceilings:—a female figure, bent so that the body, legs, and arms, occupy three sides, is a symbol of the heavens; and twelve divisions in the upper part, and twelve in the lower, represent day and night. During the day the sun is accompanied by various divinities, changing in each horary division; at night his boat is towed by them. In the hall preceding that of the sarcophagus, there are forty-two columns of hieroglyphics, containing the laudatory sentence pronounced by the judges of the dead; and there are pictures of the constellations, and devices to show their influence upon the different parts of the human frame.

We returned early in the afternoon, to get everything ready for departure, and in the evening paid a visit to a certain Thada Roos, a famed Coptish collector and vendor of antiquities, modern and old, at Luxor. We had already, on going up the river, visited his repository, but found him so utterly without a particle of conscience, that we left him in disgust, and stigmatised him by hard names, to Mustapha, our consul, who, being his friend, immediately repeated them without doubt. The epithets we applied to him had apparently softened his heart, and produced a good effect; for he sent us word, that if we would only come again, we should find him a very different person from before, and most amenable to reasonable bargainings. We acceded to the invitation, and bought a few trifles from among the multifarious rubbish collected for the benefit of curiosity-hunters as foolish as, and more opulent than, ourselves. Among other things, in a boxful of particular valuables which he displayed, we remarked a very peculiar-looking silver coin, of large size and apparently, from its oxidised appearance, of considerable antiquity. On examining it closer, there was no doubt but that the devices were old Egyptian. On one side was the sitting plumed figure, holding the Tau, or sacred emblem of truth, as in the cartouches of Amunoph the Third; on the reverse, the sacred ram standing amid lotus plants. I was much puzzled on seeing it, being aware that the old Egyptians did not, as far as we knew, employ money as a circulating medium, and being also certain that the devices were perfectly genuine and extremely ancient. We asked him where it came from; and he said he bought it from a peasant, who had found it among the ruins at Edfou; that he would guarantee its being silver, as he had cut it with a knife, the marks of which he showed; and that he thought he would melt it down, as there were more than two dollars' worth of silver in it. I was suspicious of there being something wrong, and yet the apparently ignorant careless manner of the wily Copt, quite imposed upon us; so the negotiations ended by my friend becoming the owner of the silver coin, in exchange for a golden image of Napoleon III. On returning to Cairo, and happening to meet a gentleman of considerable antiquarian knowledge, who had been at Luxor during our stay there, and who was well acquainted with Mr. Thada Roos, I mentioned the purchase we had effected. "You need not enter into particulars," he said, "I know the article remarkably well. The original of it was a cylinder purchased by Miss Martineau at Thebes. As the cylinder was very curious, I requested Mr. Thada Roos to make a cast of it for me, and this cast he has converted into a matrix, to coin such coins as you have purchased, which he oxidises, moreover, with considerable skill, for the unwary." I thought, hitherto, we had only wittingly bought modern antiques, but in this instance I am bound to confess we were done to our heart's content.

In the evening, Mr. Roos came to see us in our boat, and having hinted to the dragoman that his Christianity allowed him to drink brandy, he showed the sincerity of his religious tenets by tossing off without a grimace nearly a tumbler-full of the raw material, and then proceeded to business. He informed us in a deep whisper, that he had just got in a magnificent object of art—a sitting statue of black granite; and that, if we came up when every one was asleep, he would show it to us, and sell it to us cheap, for he dared not keep it, for fear of its being taken from him by the local authorities; in fact, so great were his apprehensions of being discovered with it, that we should have it for a mere song, and it should be conveyed to the boat that very night, before the tell-tale moon should arise to reveal the secret. Unable to resist these solicitations, we returned with Mr. Roos to his house, and after the strictest charge on his part to perpetual silence deep as the grave, and a deal of feigned fear of interlopers and spies, were conducted to an under-ground apartment, where, muffled up in a white veil, was the mystery. "Shoof!" (Look) cried the Copt, pulling off the veil with a gesture of ineffable delight; and behold a statue considerably battered elsewhere, and altogether minus its head, sat before us. We feigned great astonishment, and asked the price. Only 5000 piastres (about £43), he cried, in a lugubrious tone. We told him it was much too cheap, but much too heavy for our boat; and bade him a long farewell. He seemed grieved and surprised that we should miss such an opportunity of increasing our collection of memorable objects, especially when offered to us by special kindness at so cheap a rate; but so it happened. One more look we gave the figure, to please its owner, who now, to glorify it more, lit up two additional tallow candles; but the increase of light only manifested still more mutilations; so, leaving Mr. Thada Roos sorrowing, we made off to pay our Consul Mustapha a farewell visit, and to give him some English powder and percussion caps in return for his civilities.

After a parting pipe and mutual compliments, we hastened on board, and a discharge from the revolver gave the usual signal of salute announcing that the *Flea* had slipped from her moorings. Then burst forth such a *pateraro* of firearms of all descriptions from the temple of Amunoph, the consul's dwelling, in return to our signal, that all Luxor re-echoed and boomed again with the bombardment. One of the consul's chief functions, in his own opinion, is to perform the most energetic salutes of greeting and farewell; and as discharges quick and heavy continued as long as our ship's lantern glimmered over the Nile, I perceived too soon in what manner my poor pound of English powder was employed, which I had fondly hoped was intended for deadly combat with wild beasts among the Lybian hills.

I forgot to mention, that while sitting with the consul, a messenger came in and mentioned that a young French gentleman had been thrown from his horse, on the other side of the river, and was supposed to have broken his leg. We called at the boat on the way to our own, and made inquiries, which were so far reassuring that it was hoped the bone was not actually broken. It was grievous to think of the position of an unfortunate stranger with a fractured limb in this out-of-the-way place, with no medical attendance available, save that of some ignorant Arab practitioner relying on scraps from the Koran, or water from the well Zem Zem; so we made all imaginable haste to overtake a boat, only a few hours before us, in which we knew there was a medical gentleman, who might be of use, if only to reassure the sufferer and his friends. Their boat, however, started very shortly after ours, and in the morning we were so close that we received a visit from the Marquis D'O., a young Frenchman, and the Vicomte de D., a Belgian. Their companion, the Comte de M., was the person to whom the accident happened, as he was passing over the rough ground near the Rameseum. He was still suffering, they said, a good deal, but they were almost confident no fracture had occurred. We arrived at Kenneh about an hour before them, and when their boat came up, she was moored alongside of ours. By the noise and clamour on board of her, it was evident that something had gone wrong. The cause of the disturbance was soon made known. A regular revolt had broken forth among the crew; they had refused to obey the Reis, had throttled the dragoman, and would have garotted him, in all probability, had it not been for the armed intervention of the Europeans. For these misdemeanors the offenders were invited to visit the Governor of Kenneh, and hear his opinion of their proceedings; and, as we were desirous of witnessing Egyptian administration of justice, we requested permission to be admitted likewise to the *séance*.

After having performed a certain amount of shopping for kitchen purposes, we finished our purchases by buying some famous dates, which came from the Arabian coast of the Red Sea, *viâ* Cosseir. They are sold in drums, like figs, and are larger and more juicy than the dates we had hitherto met with in Egypt, but extremely dear and scarce; in fact, the vendor would not part with more than one drum to us, and that at an extravagant price, as dates go.

It was now time to adjourn to the governor's palace, for the *séance* had begun. The governor and our Belgian friends were sitting comfortably in the courtyard, smoking their chibouques, and the governor's Arab mares were being led up and down for our inspection, till the delinquents should have put in their appearance. The less we say of the mares the better: they had neither good points nor good breeding, and were altogether a sorry lot. The governor himself, a thin, grave-looking old gentleman, received us with that peculiarly dignified and quiet courtesy, the essential attribute of almost every Turk in authority, whether his antecedents be charcoal-burning, or barbering. They say themselves, that when Allah gives a man a high situation, he also gives him the ability to fulfil it. Without going so far, we may certainly say, that whenever Allah bestows a high post on them, he certainly at the same time bestows self-possession and dignity to become it. After some conversation about the war, in which his excellency declared that we were all brothers now, and about to eat up the Muscos without salt or dallying, he requested of the Belgians to write from Cairo, to his French physician, and tell him all the news, for that he never heard a word of what was going on, except from strangers. The words, "French physician," of course fell like manna on the ears of our new acquaintances, as they were now likely to have some one to inspect their disabled companion; and while they were promising compliance, the medico himself appeared, a little animated, clever-looking, rather untidily attired Frenchman. He seemed enchanted at the view of so many Europeans, and proffered all the resources of his art with the greatest good nature and *empressement*; indeed, I am confident he would have been enchanted to have administered on the spot a gratuitous pill to every stranger present, in order to show his anxiety to be of service.

In the mean time the culprits, headed by the

Reis, had been brought in, and were ranged before the governor. Flanking them on each side were two dispensers of justice, clothed in bottle-green, and armed with rhinoceros-hide courbashes. They were shrivelled, thin, long-mustachioed, impassive-looking men, very much like the pictures of the rats on their hind legs, in full costume, as represented in the child's story-book of the *Cats' Castle taken by the Rats*. Indeed, they seem to have grown attenuated by the strong and steady exercise of their employment—administering the bastinado. The dragoman now began, in a soft mellifluous voice interspersed with innumerable and flowery compliments, to narrate the malpractices of the sailors. The Reis, who had certainly one of the most handsome faces I ever saw on human shoulders, the perfect type of oriental beauty, was clearly absolved by his masters of all participation in the mutiny; but, unfortunately, the governor did not quite understand the explanations, or was thinking of Sebastopol, or was desirous of cutting the matter short, for he gave a signal of the hand, and in one instant we saw the handsome Reis seized by the aforesaid rats, and laid prostrate on the ground in front of the assembly. After some difficulty, the governor was made to understand that the Reis was the aggrieved rather than the offending party, and the signal was given for the others to take his place. They were three in number, ill-favoured rogues; and their punishment was summary, but lenient enough. Number one was thrown on his face forthwith, with his nose in the dust; gyves were dexterously fixed on his ancles, whereby his feet were raised upwards, and the two rats, standing on each side, administered a smart castigation on his soles, which occasioned such a bellowing and roaring for mercy on his part, as would have astonished a Harrow or Eton boy, whose honest pride it is to bear the head master's birchen courbash with Spartan firmness and resignation.

We greatly admired the style of the operation, and the skill manifested by the rats. It was not violent, main-strength, downright flogging, but a pleasant kind of flipping which, without doubt, smarted considerably, but certainly did no injury beyond a temporary inconvenience. After a very short infliction the ends of justice were satisfied, and the culprit was begged off. The same process was repeated in cases two and three; but failed in the last instance to give satisfaction, or even produce a salutary effect—inasmuch as the offender, instead of shuffling off after a profound salaam of thanks for favors received, stood boldly up and demanded that the Reis should get the share originally intended for him. On being refused this somewhat invidious request, he broke forth into very violent and abusive language, amid which the ominous word "Nazrani," or "Christian," met my ear; but whether it was applied to masters or dragoman I could not exactly make out. It was, however, answered by the still more ominous mandate from the governor of "Adrab hoo tayib" (Give it him well); and the rats administered a flipping which showed "qu'il ne s'agissait pas de badinage," in this case at all events. We thus spent a very agreeable afternoon, and as we returned we passed the beaten parties, who seemed quite as well pleased as we were, to judge by their grins and nods of recognition.

Meantime our friends retired to the abode of the hospitable doctor, who had invited us also to coffee and chibouques. These we rather unwisely declined, for on their return shortly after with their host, they informed us that they had been presented to his wife, an Abyssinian, and a very pretty woman, speaking French remarkably well. They had certainly made the best use of their time, having brought back with them all sorts of droll but somewhat unrepeatable anecdotes of Kenneh manners and morals. We were completely reassured by the worthy doctor as to the safety of the invalid, whose disaster was only a nasty sprain, which a little rest would soon set to rights.

Having mentioned this gentleman's Abyssinian wife, I may here remark, that in the East these women are much sought after as wives, not merely for their good looks, in which they far surpass all the African races, but for the peculiar quality of their skin, which always, in the greatest heat, is cool and refreshing to the touch. Our friend the doctor was the first from whom I had this information; he was, of course, excellent authority, and I have since heard the same remark from Egyptians; but I cannot myself from experience corroborate the truth or falsehood of this observation, not having, although desirous of doing so, made the acquaintance of any Abyssinian female in Egypt.

We only advanced five miles that evening, passing on the way several prodigious rafts of pottery slowly floating down the river, as they have been ever floating since the days of Juvenal, who speaks of the Nile fellâh as

> Imbelle et inutile vulgus,
> Parvula fictilibus solitum dare vela phaselis,
> Et brevibus pictæ remis incumbere testæ.

Our short stretch was occasioned by the ardent desire of my friend to become the proprietor of a crocodile the produce of his own *chasse;* and as we were now in the haunts and most favored abodes of the largest of these reptiles, he determined to dig for himself a hole, and, ensconcing himself in it at early day, to await the *siesta* of the monster, who generally retires from the water when the sun's rays become sufficiently inviting to favor a comfortable snooze. The hole was accordingly excavated over night, and in the morning he took up his position in it, armed with all the means of destruction for long range and close quarters. Not being inclined to follow his example, I thought this a good opportunity of giving our goose, the royal emblem, a constitutional which he had not enjoyed since his capture, and led him forth along the sandbank, with a string attached to his wings. It would have been a pleasant sight to friends at home, could they have seen me sallying forth on this occasion, in gorgeous blue silk dressing-gown and scarlet tarboosh, along the Nile's brink, holding in one hand the chibouque, and in the other the guiding rein of the impetuous goose, who, rejoicing in his liberty, gave his toilette a great revision, by plucking out all unsuitable feathers; and then performed a series of duckings, divings, and tumblings, all with the ungrateful endeavour to escape from his too indulgent owners.

By the time our walk was over my other companion returned in no pleasant humour, and looking as if he had just emerged from one of Mohammed's shampooing baths in St. James's Street. He said he had passed sundry most uncomfortable hours in his hole, which was hot beyond endurance, and as he could not put forth his head for fear of alarming his prey, he had not even the refreshment of an occasional puff of fresh air. Once or twice he did venture to peer forth, but there was not a sign of a crocodile on land, though several wary fellows were swimming about, just showing the tips of their noses above water: in fact, whatever sporting travellers may say, it is very seldom that a crocodile is bagged. I could only ascertain that one was shot this year, and that by Lord Henry Scott. There are many boasts of crocodiles killed, but the number actually secured is small indeed, comparatively. The Bedoueens, occasionally, after long and patient watching, and an intimate knowledge of the reptile's haunts, contrive to secure an odd one, which they sell to the foreigner, who exhibits him in triumph as the produce of his chase. I need hardly say, that after this want of success we dug no more pits, to lie in wait for crocodiles.

As we floated down the stream this afternoon, our crew, who were in high humour, began to tell robber-stories, which seemed to create the most intense interest. Our interpreter endeavoured to explain, but we certainly lost the most interesting portions by translation. We were at the time going through the country of a celebrated robber chief, *Raggil* by name, who seems to have been a kind of Egyptian Robin Hood—robbing the great, and charitable to the poor. As "Raggil" is Arabic for "man," I imagined that this was not his actual name; but they assured me of the fact, and that he was a great friend of the Howaga, or Europeans, going on board their boats merely to have a smoke, but plundering unmercifully all pashas, and all authorities, and actually meeting them in the field with 1800 good horsemen, when they attempted to suppress him. One of our new sailors then narrated an adventure of his own. When a boy, he was coming up, he said, from Alexandria, in a *dahabieh* belonging to the European physician of the Pasha Mohammed Ali. The physician was, however, not on board, but only a lady who was under his protection. After the boat had been moored by the bank at sunset, and every one had retired to rest, it was boarded by a large body of men. The dragoman was instantly poniarded, and the Reis killed by the heavy blow of a club; our informant rolled overboard at the commencement of the fray, and hid himself in the bushes, where he listened to the proceedings. The robbers first proceeded to strip the vessel, and then, having seized the lady, were about to cut off her hands to get at her rings, but as she fortunately understood Arabic, like the beaver she saved her life by parting with her valuables. One of the marauders, evidently the chief, was so taken with her beauty, that he returned after the robbery with still more naughty intentions, and during the struggle that ensued the lady was enabled to get a clear view of his features. What was the upshot our informant was unable to state, beyond the fact, that they resumed their journey next day, and on arriving at Cairo made an immediate complaint of the outrage to the Viceroy. Old Mahommed Ali by no means approved of these exuberances among his subjects, and the same afternoon sent down four pashas, as the narrator called them, together with the lady to identify the delinquents. On arriving at the scene of action, all the males of the suspected village, which had previously enjoyed rather a bad reputation, were collected together and paraded before the lady, but she was unable to discover the wicked man among them. Subsequent investigation brought to light that the skekh's son was absent; a search was made, and on his being brought up he was instantly identified as the chief offender. It was proposed by the pasha, to soothe the lady's indignation, that this culprit and a reasonable number of other suspected members of the village, should be at once burnt alive; but the sentence, at the intercession of the injured party, was commuted; and every grown-up male of the community, to the number of four hundred, were sent off to Sennaar, there to meditate on the advantages of honesty and continency, until fever and dysentery should have done their work quite as effectually as any *auto-da-fé.*

It was this instantaneous and inflexible infliction of punishment by the old Viceroy, in which example he was followed with equal ruthlessness by his son Ibrahim and grandson Abbas, that has rendered Egypt as secure to travellers as the best-governed countries in Christendom. In return for these and other histories not quite so authentic, of time long ago, I told them some anecdotes of elephants, on which the conversation turned, with which they were enchanted, especially with the known story of the elephant at Delhi bringing home the dirty water in his trunk to souse the sweetmeat-seller, who had run a needle into his proboscis, when passing by his shop on the way to the water-pond. To cap this, a sailor mentioned that there was a beast called a bear, which always came forth to meet the caravan from Osioot to Darfur, at a certain spot, and would infallibly destroy it but that the merchants take care to appease it by always presenting it with a sheep, brought for the purpose, on receipt of which the caravan is allowed to pass. I am afraid Arabs and Christians broke up the *séance* that evening with considerable distrust of the veracity of each other.

The next day we made the best of our way towards a small town called Ballianeh, intending from thence to cross to the old ruins of Abydos, and meet our boat at Girgeh. Abydos possessed some of the most interesting relics on the Nile, and from it came the celebrated tablet of Abydos, the work of Rameses II., which is considered the most valuable historical record of the eighteenth and nineteenth dynasties, and of the highest importance in chronological investigations. It was discovered by Mr. Bankes in 1818, and was considerably mutilated by a Greek in the employment of the French Consul-General Mimant, in sawing it off for removal. By Mimant it was sent to France, and there purchased by the trustees of the British Museum, for £500. After the Karnak tablet of King Thothmes, this is the oldest chronological record in the world. Fortunately, facsimiles of it were taken by Colonel Felix and Sir G. Wilkinson, before it underwent the mutilations of the scientific, in addition to those of time, Copts, Turks, and fellâhs. This representation of ancient kings, with the royal cartouche over them, twenty-six in number, was sculptured on fine limestone, on the wall of a chamber now destroyed, within the temple palace, built, or, more probably, restored by Rameses, in this most ancient royal city. I was anxious to see this famous spot, from a town neighbouring to which, the town of *This*, sprung the royal Thinite dynasty; but as we heard that the sand had completely covered all remains, we hardly thought it worth while to take so long a ride for nothing.

There was, however, but little hope of getting to our destination that night, for as the sun declined a tempest came on, to which all our previous storms were but as fitful puffs. During the night, I fully expected the boat would go to pieces, so violent were the shocks against the low bank, which was fortunately of yielding mud. It was totally impossible to sleep, so I walked about the shore, fully anticipating some catastrophe, while the poor sailors were huddled up in their camels' hair cloaks, shivering under a mound, but ready for any emergency. In a short time the boat of our Belgian acquaintances broke away from its moorings, tearing up its fastenings as if they were twigs. There was a heavy "sea" running at the time in the "river," and something unpleasant was likely to have happened, but that fortunately our crew were able to add their efforts, and by means of a stout hawser to get her in again, and made her fast once more. A more unpleasant night it would be difficult to imagine, whether to the parties ashore with the blinding sweeps of sand coming in on them like pins and needles; or to the parties aboard, from the repeated shocks, after each of which we fully expected to hear the unpleasant gurgling of water, as of yore in Nubia.

All the following day the wind blew hard and foul, so we went ashore with our guns, and for the first time came across the black partridge—*Pterocles exustus*, called by Indian sportsmen the rock-pigeon; and by the Arabs, *gutta*. They are remarkably handsome birds, of the grouse species, with two long furcated tail-feathers; but they fly high, with a flight more resembling that of the pigeon than the grouse, and with a loud harsh call. We subsequently met with another variety of the same shape and cry, but with quite different plumage. This is the sand-grouse—*Pterocles guttatus*, and from its immense numbers in parts of Arabia and Africa, it is supposed by some to be the quail, by which the Israelites were supported in the wilderness. Although quails are common in parts of Arabia where there is tillage, yet it is probable that these are the birds alluded to. Owing to their sweeping and powerful wings, they are capable of a very extended flight, and retire to great distances in the interior of the desert during the daytime, visiting the Nile morning and evening for water, when no other drinking-places are nearer. They came nearly as handy to us as to the Israelites; for we had reckoned on supplying our deficiencies at Girgeh, which the storm prevented; but their extreme wariness made us compliment their quality far more than their quantity on that occasion.

The next day, however, was a bright day in the sporting chronicles of the *Flea;* we had the evening before remarked ducks wending their way inland with a very determined flight, which convinced us there was water somewhere in the interior. Having caught a native, we found our surmises to be correct, and heard that a lake, as he called it, teeming with wild fowl, was to be found under the Arabian hills, apparently about seven miles distant. We departed early, with a guide and our faithful Hammed, and had certainly a fine field-day. We commenced with the black grouse, securing a few in the fields of rough halfeh grass through which we passed; then, arriving at some barley, we laid in a store of quails for the larder; and on the outskirts of a village, despatched, for the sake of his feathers to make pens, an ill-favoured vulture, perched on the back of a dead cow. Shortly after, we arrived at the lake, and for half an hour had grand sport; several ducks of different species, some widgeon, and a fine specimen of the *Anas rutila*, or red goose, were first of all secured; and as the survivors soon found the place too hot to hold them (for, after all, it was only a small swampy piece of water where they had congregated), they retired to safer quarters, and left us to settle our differences with the snipe, which, with other aquatic small birds, were innumerable. The result was, that both guide and Himmed were fairly overburdened with the spoil, and we were obliged to press into the service a Bedoueen, who had joined us, and whom we induced to come to the boat, and carry some of the impediments, on a promise of some powder and shot—invaluable treasure to a Bedoueen.

He was a spare, wiry man, with the bright keen eye and thin features of his race; thorough bred to the backbone, and a most enthusiastic sportsman, though how he contrived to progress at all, shuffling along in an old pair of slippers which looked as if they had been toasted, was a marvel. He had come, he said, from Edfou, with his camels and flocks, roaming about, and so great was his approbation of our shooting snipe flying, that he besecched of us to remain with him, and volunteered

3*

to show us every pass for hyena, wolf, gazelle, and other more ignoble game, within the intervening hundred miles.

His ancient musket, of English manufacture, was without doubt obtained during our occupation of Egypt, and was quite unfitted for anything except the good old conservative system of "potting." According, however, to his own account, he continued to rejoice his little ones with many a plump goose, and delicate gazelle, and to strip divers hyenas of their peltries, in the course of the year. From him we gained a wrinkle as to providing ourselves with wadding for our guns, should our pellets fall short; for on our loading his gun with powder, and attempting to ram some paper down after it with his thin iron ramrod, that implement stuck fast, and was with difficulty removed together with the obstructing paper. Our friend then showed us somewhat superciliously his own superior system of making all secure, which was effected by ramming home sundry goats' droppings, which he assured us was the only wadding he ever employed, and far preferable to any of our civilized inventions.

The inhabitants of this district are of the Howara tribe of Arabs; and I found it almost impossible either to understand their extremely harsh pronunciation, or to make myself understood, but with our Bedoueen we were able to maintain a very lively sporting conversation, the *resumé* of which I have given above. These Howara were, and I believe are, still celebrated for their horses; but I did not see anything remarkable in the very few I met with, although the fine extent of plain is suitable for rearing them. In fact, lovers of horseflesh will not find much in Egypt to reward their researches.

We now at length made some good progress after our long delays. We were getting again into the country where the chalky Arabian range advances to the water's edge, pierced with excavations, some of these the burial-places of great men of the provincial towns of Ancient Egypt, others more modern, the work of that ascetic race of monks who, like the terrible Rajah in Southey's *Kehama*, determined to storm heaven by countless prayers, and to burst asunder the gates of paradise by penance.

> I have seen Indra tremble at his prayers,
> And at his fearful penances grow pale.
> They claim and wrest from Seeva powers so vast
> That even Seeva's self
> The Highest cannot grant, and be secure—
>
> SOUTHEY, *Curse of Kehama.*

Occupants either of the ancient tombs, or artificers of their own eyries perched amid most inaccessible and dangerous crags, they lived, supported by the charity and offerings of devotees, a life little calculated to advance the glory of God or the virtue and happiness of mankind. Forgetting that it is by temptation that purity is proved; by example, that men are led to goodness; by teaching, that the doctrines of their Master's dispensation could alone be promulgated,—these selfish, rude, and unlettered ascetics ignored all the nobler aims of Christianity, the very essence of which is that humanising spirit which impels its votaries to advise and soothe, to mingle with and have its abode in the busy haunts of men.

Hither, in the fourth century of our era, flocked in swarms, that "deluded class of men," to use the words of Gibbon, "inspired by a savage enthusiasm which represents man as a criminal and God as a tyrant. The holy Abbot Pachomius in this region, at the festival of Easter, sometimes collected fifty thousand religious persons who followed his angelic rule of discipline. The Egyptians were disposed to hope and to believe that the number of the monks was equal to the number of the people, and posterity might repeat the saying which had formerly been applied to the sacred animals of the same country, that "in Egypt it was less difficult to find a god than a man." From these holes and cells in the mountain by which we were now floating, have proceeded many of those marvellous tales of personal encounters with the enemy of mankind, of temptations overcome, of visions, of celestial revelations, fertile themes for compilers of monastic legends in the middle ages, subjects worthy of the grotesque pencil of the Flemish, or the nobler conceptions of Italian painters, the buffooneries of a

Breughel, the inspirations of a Domenichino. "The visions of these anchorites, before they attained the extreme and acknowledged term of frenzy, have afforded ample material of supernatural history. It was their firm conviction that the air which they breathed was peopled with invisible enemies, with innumerable demons, who watched every occasion, and assumed every form to terrify, and above all to tempt their unguarded virtue. The imagination and even the senses were deceived by the illusions of distempered fanaticism; and the hermit whose midnight prayer was oppressed by involuntary slumber, might easily confound the phantoms of horror or delight which had occupied his sleeping or waking dreams."

But although the rock-carved chambers are now untenanted save by the jackal and the bat, still the round white cupola of the *santon*, or holy man, standing boldly out on some lofty eminence round which we sweep, and the Arab legends of the austerity of his life, the sanctity of his death, and the miraculous gifts attached to his last resting-place, show how naturally superstition flows on in the same channel, though the Muslim has replaced the Christian—the santon, the anchorite—the Muezzin's call from the minaret, the rustic horn of the monk.

Thus onwards we go with a merry song and measured plash of oars, leaving behind us the mausoleums of old Egypt, the hermit's cell and santon's tomb; villages with mud walls, and square mud houses; white pigeon-towers in gay streaks of red and blue, studded with long outstretching poles, perches for their innumerable inmates; by dervishes' tents with bright flags in front, and drums beating to swell the number of votaries squatting round, all awaiting the oracular responses of the inspired man, until we pull in beneath the high bank, and rest awhile at Echmin, the ancient Chemmis or Panopolis, the city of the god Pan.

To our surprise and pleasure, on nearing this town, the whole space between the walls and river seemed one vast parterre of brilliant flowers, but on landing we found them to consist of poppies of every hue, from which a peasant girl was scraping the soporific exudations which flowed sparingly from incisions made at the bottom of the bud. Poppies were, however, something to eyes wearied so long with the little variety of vegetation in this most unflowery land. This town was one of the most famous of the ancient cities of Egypt; its temples of Pan and Perseus were celebrated for their magnificence; and Abulfeda, writing in the thirteenth century, mentions the ruins of one of these buildings as among the most remarkable in the valley of the Nile. But of these ruins we hardly saw a vestige, nor could we discover the inscription of Trajan mentioned by Sir G. Wilkinson, nor did we meet any of those lovely maidens for whose beauty Echmin has obtained renown; we did not even discover fresh beef, the main object of our researches; so we loosened the rope and proceeded on our way until on the morning of the 22nd of March we arrived at Gow-el-Kebir; where, even at the commencement of this century, a portion of the temple of Antæus was in existence in tolerable preservation. Mr. Hamilton, writing in 1802, mentions its portico as consisting of eighteen columns eight feet in diameter, and with their entablatures sixty-two feet in height; but all these have now disappeared, partly from the encroachment of the river, and partly from the removal of the blocks to build the Governor's mansion at Osioot. We walked up to the caves, which are large, but without inscriptions; there still remains a colossal figure sitting in front of them, but of comparatively modern, and certainly of the rudest execution.

The same afternoon we arrived at our old halting-place, Osioot, where we purchased several specimens of the pretty colored pottery which we had ordered on our way up. We did not, however, hear until we reached Cairo of the terrible tragedy that had been acted about the time of our arrival. To explain this act of bloody tyranny, I must premise that that politic old statesman, Mohammed Ali, during the early period of his viceroyalty, finding it difficult to restrain the predatory inroads of the Bedoueens by foul means, resolved to try what he could effect by fair. He accordingly allowed these migratory tribes to establish themselves on the space of ground lying between the mountains and the cultivated land, where the effects of former unusually extensive inundations had left behind them occasional herbage. This was sufficient to maintain their sheep and camels, and they had the additional promise of being exempted from conscriptions and taxation on condition that they acted the part of border police, and maintained the boundary against all freebooters.

This arrangement was faithfully observed by the old Pasha's successors, Ibrahim and Abbas, nor does it appear that the slightest complaint of infraction of their portion of the agreement was ever urged against the Bedoueens. On the contrary, it seems that they lived on terms of the greatest cordiality with their neighbours, who derived from their camels much service in the conveyance of produce and other goods. That they were approved of and liked by the settled inhabitants, will be shown satisfactorily hereafter.

By this time the Bedoueens had begun to lose a good deal of their wandering characteristics, and had actually settled themselves on certain spots, where by constant labour they continued to cultivate enough of the soil for their maintenance. The present Pasha thought this a good opportunity of adding to his revenue, and to his military array—that pernicious hobby which is doing incalculable injury to the country cursed by his rule. He therefore at once subjected the Bedoueens to taxation and conscription. To any one who knows the wild free character of that race, it is needless to mention that the very atmosphere of towns, not to mention the constraint of discipline and confinement, would have been a calamity worse than death. In consequence they resisted and drove away the emissaries of the Pasha. They then demanded an interview with his Highness. Said, accompanied by five hundred soldiers and two field-pieces concealed behind them, met the whole body of the Bedoueen shekhs at some spot in Upper Egypt. The conference commenced, and the Bedoueens loudly and not politely inveighed against the breach of faith attempted by the Pasha. They urged the fidelity with which they had adhered to their engagements, the efficient manner in which they had protected the frontier from outrage, they adjured him to maintain the pledges of his prodecessors—but in vain. He was inexorable, and would accede to no terms save unconditional submission, taxation, and servitude. At this period of the interview, which was conducted in front of the troops, either purposely, or accidentally owing to the confusion and pressure of a number of Bedoueen chiefs anxious to make themselves heard, the Pasha received a push, and his tarboosh fell from his head.

He immediately ran back to his troops unhindered, which shows that there was no attempt to secure or injure his person, and gave the signal convened on. The infantry opened their ranks, and the two field-pieces were run out, and let fly, at the distance of a few yards, grape and canister among the unfortunate shekhs. Some were taken prisoners, many were killed, and the remainder made off. The matter, however, did not rest here: cavalry and infantry were instantly ordered to attack the Bedoueen haunts. Large numbers of prisoners were taken and conveyed to the Barrage and Alexandria, where, to use my informant's expression, they had died and were dying like flies. In a short time there would not be an individual left alive. The unfortunate survivors, with their families and flocks, made off for the desert, their only refuge. But the wells were few and distant; and the track of the fugitives is still marked by the dry and ghastly skeletons, chiefly of women and children, who were necessarily abandoned to their fate in that fearful race for water.

Now for the last act of this inhuman drama. Injunctions were issued threatening death to any one who should venture to give food or succour to any of these wretches. But there were some in the vicinity of Osioot, who, remembering the kindly relations that existed between them and these poor people, ventured secretly to relieve their wants. They were informed against. Twenty-three were arrested, and the crime brought home to them. They were divided into three gangs, one third of which was hung, another third decapitated, the remainder were blown from a gun in an open space within the walls of Osioot. I was told by a person of undeniable veracity, who had it from an eye-witness, that at the commencement of this bloody work, the kites and hawks, which are innumerable in Egypt, assembled together at the place of execution, and actually swooped at and caught the bits of mangled flesh of the wretches who were blown from the gun, before they reached the ground. And yet these atrocities have been flatly denied by Mr. Lesseps, who, for reasons best known to himself, has constituted himself the approver or encomiast, and, when necessary, the denier of every act of the Pasha calculated to arouse attention and indignation in Europe. There is, however, testimony of the most irrefragable nature as to the truth of the statement, and M—, a Prussian of high rank, and who was at Osioot nearly at the same time as ourselves, saw the mangled remains still lying in the public places, and had ample confirmation of every tittle of this horrible narrative. It is highly probable that we too, had we wandered through the town, might have seen the same, though I am not sure whether the occurrence took place a few days previous to or after our arrival at Osioot. It is difficult in the East to arrive at dates. Not, however, hearing from our sailors anything about the matter, which leads me to suppose it must have happened after our departure, we took a long excursion over the great plain on the opposite side of the river to the town, hunting up quails, and our new friends the gutta, or black partridge. This plain was one vast unbroken sheet of corn, dotted here and there by villages rising out of their palm groves; but we remembered looking over the same expanse on our upward journey from the cave of Stabl Antar, when that which was now all golden was then a sheet of emerald green, and when nothing could be more true than Mr. Stanley's short and graphic description of these plains at that period of the year: "Green, unutterably green lies the land of Egypt —green unbroken, save by the mud villages which here and there lie in the midst of the verdure like the marks of a soiled foot on a rich carpet."

On the 24th we made one of the most remarkable if not most agreeable excursions during our whole voyage. We had heard of the celebrated caves of mummied crocodiles at Maabdeh, from our foreign friends, who had read an account of them in Maxime du Camp's *Recollections of Egypt*, and a very appalling account it is, moreover. Sir G. Wilkinson does not allude to them, except in the remark that he had heard of their existence as extensive caverns cut in the rock, but that he had not himself visited them. Our dragoman was ignorant of their locality, but our second Reis knew of their being somewhere in the neighbourhood of Maabdeh, a small village nearly opposite to the town of Manfaloot. We, therefore, halted at the nearest point, and sent for guides, who presently came down, and presented us with chicken crocodiles, if I may so call little fellows fresh from the egg, to judge from their size, but still carefully mummied; so that it was clear we were in the right direction. It appears however, owing to the dangerous character of these caves, that the very few visitors who inspect them proceed to Manfaloot, and there take a government janissary and an equipment of proper lanterns. Maxime du Camp, I think, speaks of the Arab women rushing forth from their villages, tearing their dishevelled locks, beating their breasts, and casting dust into the air in all the agonies of despair, at the dangers their husbands were about to encounter in performing their functions of guides; but we certainly did not experience any such pathetic interruptions. On the contrary, we made our way merrily enough in paths winding through waving fields of corn, till we came to the Arabian range, about a mile and a half from the shore. Up and along the edge of the mountain, a broad and even path ran easily, evidently once well kept, and befitting the solemn processions that conveyed the mummied remains of human beings and sacred animals to their final abode. Great round brown boulder-stones, like rusty thirteen-inch shells, flanked the outside edge of the road. They reminded me of the enchanted princes in the tale of the *Princess Parizade;* but the Arabs maintained that these stones were once pumpkins, the property of a churlish gardener who refused to receive the prayers of a thirsty holy man, instead of ready money for his goods, in consequence of which his crop, cursed by the exasperated wayfarer, at once assumed this stony form. A like legend exists among the Syrians, where similar round stones at Mount Carmel are supposed to be the melons of Elijah; and a smaller description at Bethlehem, are called the peas of the Virgin Mary.

At last we reached the summit, and found a cool delicious breeze playing over the high table-land which we had to traverse. We had now a good four-mile walk before us, as we subsequently discovered, and a sultry close day would have knocked us up before the chief difficulties had begun. On the way we were surprised at the quantities of alabaster cropping up from the surface of the ground; some of it was extremely beautiful, of a delicate faint pink tinge. To the north of this locality, but in the same hilly range, the Egyptian government discovered some years ago quarries of alabaster, which had been worked extensively in the days of the Pharaohs; but though the authorities at once commenced operations vigorously and successfully, they have since abandoned the undertaking. After about an hour and a half of good walking, we arrived at our destination. A hole about twelve feet deep, not in the side of the hill, but on the top of the undulating table-land over which we had made our way, was pointed out to us as the jaws of the Avernus we were to enter. It was extremely narrow, and looked far more like the entrance of a wild beast's lair than that of the famous place of sepulture to whose recesses thousands upon thousands of bodies, human and animal, have been committed. When we had scrambled to the bottom we found ourselves squatted in a very low and small cave, from whence, however, the blackness visible of one or two outlets gave us a foretaste of what was to come. The guides here requested us to doff our coats and wide-awakes, telling us that both one and the other would be ruined by contact with the rocks, which were inside very black and sticky. They showed us a passage through which we were to grope; it seemed large enough for a good sized dog, and though we did not at all approve of its appearance, still it was now too late to turn tail, so we formed procession, and —forwards. First went one of the guides, then the dragoman, then ourselves, and last of all the second guide, all armed with candles. As the smell began to get sour, we halted and lit our cigars, when the guides, with a cry of horror, shouted to us to put them instantly out, or we should be all destroyed. The reason of these precautions was afterwards sufficiently apparent. A most detestable progress for the next quarter of an hour, now ensued. Almost the whole of it was performed on the stomach, or at best on hands and knees, through a winding hole, along which there was barely room for a single person to squeeze himself; seldom or ever space to raise the head. The rocky walls were black and sticky, and seemed to sweat a thick, fatty, viscous liquor. At last we got into a chamber of the cavern, where there was room to stand upright and look about one, and a more horrible sight I never saw. The whole of the flooring of this cavern was one mass of mummy-clothes, cerements, skulls and skeletons of human beings, with here and there the body of some huge crocodile, either neatly packed and swathed with palm branches, or with his great grinning head emerging as if it had been struggling to get out of the suffocation of this charnel mass. After this, another crawl to another chamber, on all-fours again. Here we found the crocodiles more numerous, but every now and again felt our feet crushing through the chest of some poor relic of human mortality. We passed by an inscription cut in the narrow passage: it read "Spedizione Romana, 1824." That part of the rock where it was inscribed, was still sparkling and bright, so it was clear that the smutty, horrid clothing of the rocky walls was the result of this sepulture of ages—the exhalations from the mummied carcases. Taking my seat on the back of an enormous crocodile, I here protested that nothing should induce me to go further. We had already groped, gasping for breath and streaming with perspiration, apparently a quarter of a mile, and the passage seemed by no means improving. The guides begged of us to go on and see thousands more mummies, as they asserted positively we might do; but we were satisfied. We had seen enough and undergone enough for one day, at all events. They told us that the passage extended an immense way further on, full of crocodile and human mummies; that there were, moreover, passages leading to other caverns where were buried the mummies of birds; and then they explained the reason of their terror at our lighted cigars, which was clearly justified by everything around us. A kind of bituminous substance was the main preservation of the mummies; the heaps of rags and swathings over which we had crept were saturated with this inflammable material. Palm branches, in which as I said before the crocodiles were wrapped, lay about dry as chips; the slightest spark was alone wanting to create a conflagration. And yet, "Good heavens!" shouted we, when we saw our danger, "here we are with five naked candles in our hands, when we ought to have had the best and safest Davy lamp ever invented." "Inshallah!" replied the guides, "please God as we got safe in, we shall get safe out;" and then, by way of making the exit particularly pleasant, we were told how an

American, with his dragoman and guide, went into this cavern, and never reappeared; and how smoke issued from its mouth, and no one could enter it for eighteen months, while this internal and terrible hell-fire raged within, in which thousands of corpses were consumed and whole passages cleared of their contents. They then varied their pleasant story, and narrated how some six Arabs of their own village, no long time ago, went on an expedition to plunder mummies of chance scarabæi, or papyri, and that they never returned alive. Their wives gathered round the entrance, and explorers were sent in search; they found the unfortunates scattered one by one in various parts of the cavern, as they were trying to escape, having perished by suffocation likewise, from some unfortunate falling of their lights. This was really a settler, so we stayed not to listen to more tales of horror, but pressed forward urgently to get out of this ill-omened hole. When at last we emerged, we were really very pretty figures, all blackened with the remains of the former fires, and bathed with perspiration. But we were out, and that was quite enough. Conceive for a moment the horror of an attempted escape from this den of Nox and Erebus, with a fire behind you: you hear the hissing, seething mummies crackling in the flames—you feel the fat suffocating smoke rolling on behind you in fold after fold, you struggle and tear the clothes upon you, and your very flesh, to accelerate your progress; but you must crawl—slowly—slowly—wearily; and now the thick fumes are upon you, they advance quicker than you can grope your way. Like the inexorable tide, they crawl onward, onward, ever onward, from the foot to the knee, from the knee to the chest, from the chest to the mouth, and then—and then we had better say no more on the subject, for fear of dreaming about it; for if we are to dream at all, any subject is better than that of suffocation.

There is so little said of these caves by writers, modern and ancient, that I am not the least aware whether any papyrus or other relic gives a clue to their antiquity. From the date, however, of many of the sculptured grottoes in the neighbourhood, I should be inclined to consider these deposits to have been commenced at an early period. There is one person, and that a lady, who might perhaps be able to give some information on the subject. The guides told us that Miss H., the daughter of Mr. H., a most intelligent and respectable merchant of Alexandria, had descended into this pit for five consecutive days, and had the human mummies brought to her at the first chamber. She then examined them, as they supposed for papyri, or ornaments. Her father, although taking a deep interest in archæology, remained outside during the operation, very wisely refusing to accompany his venturesome young lady. The Arabs asked us why she wore trousers, like male Howaga? We certainly found plenty of signs of ransacking and spoliation, but the mummies seemed to be those of the lower classes, on which there would not be much chance of discovering anything of interest. There were, however, signs of gilding on several skulls, which would intimate that persons well to do were also buried here.

It seems impossible that the entrance to these caves should be the horrible passage through which we groped our way. It is not, as passages in some tombs, blocked up with rubbish, denoting that its original dimensions have been narrowed, but it runs through the living rock, apparently not in the least enlarged, full of abrupt windings, with sharp pieces of stone every here and there protruding themselves, which might with ease have been quarried off and removed; and we know the old inhabitants of the country were not regardful of either time or labor. Besides, it appears almost incredible that the enormous crocodiles which are found in it, could have been transported along this intricate path; and it certainly would have been somewhat undignified for the vulgar eye to have beheld the proud priesthood of Egypt puffing, perspiring, and crawling along upon their stomachs, to install the sacred animals in their appointed resting-places. There must be another entrance somewhere.

It has always struck me, in an amusing point of view, the old Egyptian religious system of potting and pickling their birds and beasts and reptiles. It is quite clear they did not wait for their death, for it would not be an easy job in that land of sacred hawks and kites, to have found the body five minutes after the decease of the illustrious defunct, in a fit condition for mummying. They must therefore, in general, have first of all put them out of the world, and then treated them to posthumous honors. Of course the man of many mummies was the most pious man; and of course too, in order to increase his stock, he laid snares for his neighbour's dog, and trapped the cat of his nearest and dearest friend. His duty to religion was the incentive and the excuse. Conceive the sanctified jealousies that the discovery of a brood of kittens, or a clutch of young crocodiles must have caused—the self-importance of the man skilled in the art of alluring to divine honors the sacred tittlebat, *Lepidotus*. My friend drew a pleasant sketch of Rameses the Great in pursuit of the pet cat of the Queen of the Ethiopians, which he is resolved to mummy. The great monarch, in martial garb, adorned with the crown of Upper and Lower Egypt, is stalking the devoted victim. He is stooping cautiously—already his ponderous mace is raised; in a second more it will fall on the cranium of the innocent mouser, who, with arched back and tail erect, is purring at the lintel of the Ethiopian palace. But the vigilance of the dusky Queen sleeps not; she sees the danger of her favorite—determination alone can save him—she seizes a vase of dirty water—from the royal window she empties it on the head of

Rameses the Great, on the crowns of Upper and Lower Egypt, and puss is saved.

We were now approaching a highly interesting spot, where the monuments tell of the reign of a monarch, Amunoph the Fourth, during whose sway the sacred animals had a reprieve from mummification, and the whole religion of the country was concentrated into an exclusive worship of the sun. These are the grottoes of Tel-el-Amarna, which we hoped to reach in time for a visit the following day. We had, however, first of all to pass our old and formidable enemy, Gebel Aboofoda; but as the day was calm and promised favorably, we determined to row beneath him in our small boat, and take the last chance of bagging a crocodile. It was a fine sight—this venerable old mountain sheering down precipitously into the black, smooth water. No wonder, with its deep shadows and mysterious-looking caverns and rifts, fit abode for the evil spirits who gather storms round its brow, that Aboofoda preserves so evil a reputation. But on this day the wicked Afreets were at rest, and we laid in a fine supply for our larder, of blue pigeons, that looked down on us very demurely from their holes in the rock, and of cunning painted geese, whom we had in vain chased before, but who were now consulting about getting their nests trim and ready. In these domestic arrangements we surprised the poor geese, by suddenly appearing round jutting rocks in front of their abodes. With the great wall of Aboofoda in their rear, these wily birds had now but little chance, and both on that day and the following, when we had a second successful goose hunt at Shekh Timay, giblet soup was the *pièce de résistance* both of the proprietors and crew of the *Flea*. We were so delayed by these operations, that we did not arrive at Tel-el-Amarna till late in the afternoon, much to my disappointment, as I had been anxious to have devoted a whole day to these excavations, which, as I before mentioned, indicate a very remarkable epoch in the history of Egypt.

The character of the decorations of these rock grottoes, which in other respects resemble those of Beni Hassan, differs altogether from all other monuments on the Nile. The grottoes themselves are the sepulchres of private individuals, but the king of the period is represented in one, as borne on a rich throne to the temple; in another he is in his chariot, followed by the queen in hers, his troops are all around him, and the servile adoration of the monarch by the troops, is one of the first things that strikes the attention. Their bodies are all arched, with hands stretched forward to the ground in an attitude of obeisance, quite different from that in any other drawings of processions of earlier or later kings. The royal family here recognize the sun alone in their religious rites. They are represented as praying before him, and the rays of the disc are most curiously devised, terminating in human hands. The cartouches of the king and queen have been defaced, no doubt by the Egyptians themselves, when this sun-worshipping interlude was over, and the religion of Amun restored; but they may be read, and the learned are of opinion that the fourth of the Amunoph family was the monarch in question, while they read his private name as Atinra Bakhan, or Bech-en-Atan. These learned persons suppose that this Amunoph took a start of his own, and altered not only the court ceremonial, but also the religion of the country. This internal revolution seems hardly possible in a body politic so essentially conservative in its usages as Egypt. Others imagine that this was a priestly intruder on the legitimate monarchy, who assumed the title of Amunoph; and others, again, consider him to have been a foreign conqueror. The dates will not allow us to class him among the shepherd kings, although, as Sir G. Wilkinson remarks, the dissimilarity of the features of himself and his family from the usual representations, the erasure of his names and destruction of his monuments, the abject submission required of his subjects, prove him to have been the object of the detestation of the Egyptians; and the peculiar mode of worshipping the sun, and the sun exclusively, shows him to have been of a religion altogether differing from the native. Lepsius mentions having found the shield of this king and his consort, at Gebel Aboo Gush, between Kenneh and Cosseir. The name, as here, was erased, but it had the same distinctive peculiarities of the sun's disc over it, from which rays spread out with hands around it.

The words Tel-el-Amarna, mean "mounds of Amarna;" and the old city that stretched along the hard sandy plain between the hills and the river, must have been of great extent—two miles at least in length, although narrow in depth, and it still shows its vestiges in these mounds. We left this place with some regret, having performed most of our explorings by candlelight, which did well enough inside the grottoes, but was highly unsatisfactory when we endeavoured under a brisk breeze to examine the exterior decorations. There was a good south wind blowing, which we were anxious to avail ourselves of, so we scrambled home in the dark as well as we could, and left the old alabaster quarries for another visit.

For the next three days, until we reached Benisooeff, our progress was monotonous enough; we passed by Ashmouneyn, the ancient Hermopolis, Antinoe, and Beni Hassan, without landing. The only subject that interrupted our satisfaction at the good progress we were making, was the indisposition of our cook, old Hassaneen, the Doubly Beautiful. This good-for-nothing old fellow slept generally about sixteen hours in the twenty-four, and eat copiously and smoked incessantly during the remaining eight. The result was that he struck work, and, being really amiss, insisted on sleeping out the whole period, or all round, as servant maids express themselves. Though this conduct suited his, it by no means suited our arrangements to go without dinner, so, rousing the invalid from under his old cloak, we inspected his condition, and found him with a galloping pulse, an eye suffused with bile, and a most atrocious tongue. A remedy quick, sharp, and decisive, was necessary, therefore, getting the scrapings of the mustard-pot mixed up with warm water, we invited him to drink off the nauseous potion, and then indulged him with the tepid contents of a large kettle, for the succeeding half hour. The effects were so marvellous that the crew, who, like all Arabs, admire the most vigorous remedies, looked on with consternation. When however, the following day, the convalescent, after two powerful pills and a double allowance of seidlitz powder, came forth to make his obeisance, with a regular pulse and a bright eye, and perfect ability to do his work as well as ever, their admiration exceeded all bounds, as to our abilities; but our goodness of heart and charity were much questioned, for it was now clear enough that it was not inability but unwillingness that made us refuse to effect cures, in their opinion quite as easy, both in our upward and downward journey.

This little episode, and many fruitless endeavours to obtain a specimen of the Lybian crane, who accompanied us in a simultaneous migration to the north, are the only matters I find in my notes, but I well remember these cranes, and the amusement they afforded us. Drawn up literally in thousands, on a bank, they looked like an army in regular rank and file, and had their *vedettes* and outposts thrown out as if commanded by the most cautious general. For several days we travelled with these winged hordes, generally interfering with their midday *siestas*, and almost always routing them up in the morning, for they were anything but early risers. We could see them through our glasses, standing on one leg, and evidently sound asleep, but on attempting a surprise, the watchful sentinel, as in Nubia, gave a warning note, and in an instant every drawn-up leg was down, and every lowered beak was up in expectation of danger. It was in vain to attempt a shot with an ordinary fowling-piece, and repeatedly we plumped bullets through their serried ranks, but still none fell, as they rose right up into the clear sky, wheeling and circling with shrill cries, until they appeared no larger than a colony of busy winged ants.

> *ηὕτε περ κλαγγὴ γεράνων πέλει οὐρανόθι πρὸ*
> *αἵτ' ἐπὲι οὖν χειμῶνα φύγον καὶ ἀθέσφατον ὄμβρον*
> *κλαγγῇ ταί γε πέτονται ἐπ' Ὠκεάνοιο ῥοάων*
> *ἄνδρασι πυγμάιοισι φόνον καὶ κῆρα φέρουσαι.*

At last, however, after a shot from my rifle into an

enormous body of them, one remained behind with a dropping wing, looking very foolish and disconsolate. There then commenced between him and the little Nubian from Assouan who was with me, a most tremendous race for an arm of the Nile, about three hundred yards off. The crane, however, won in gallant style, and took the water like a duck. The little fellow, nothing daunted, plunged in after him, and a fine match ensued; any odds apparently at first on the bird. But the boy had rather the best of it this time, for the wind was high and adverse, and caught the feathers of his opponent on the surface of the stream, so that when they reached the opposite shore they were pretty close together. Upon this, with all the pluck inspired by desperation and wet feathers, the brave crane awaited the approach of his foe, like as had his forefathers in the good Homeric days of old, the desperate assaults of the pygmies; and, indeed, he was fully as tall as his pygmæan assailant, who, being naked, received some very severe pecks on the body and arms, ere he rushed in and decided the battle by seizing his adversary by the neck. He swam the broad channel gallantly back, but was so exhausted, poor boy, at last, that I was obliged to run into the water and give him a hand ere he could reach the shore. He was quite a little hero that day, and was greatly lauded and flattered by the crew, who feasted on the crane with *gusto*. The day following, their repast was still more gorgeous, by the addition of a remarkably fine pelican, shot by my companion's rifle. In gratitude for the treat, they brought forward and exhibited to us with pride, the yellow fat of the unctuous bird, which seems to find quite as much favor in the mouth of a Nile-born *vivant,* as turtle green fat in that of a gormandizing London alderman.

On the the 28th we paid a morning visit to Benisooeff, a pretty, clean town, with a cool bazaar and cavalry barracks. We there saw a corps of smart-looking cavalry, armed with lance and sabre. Two or three such regiments, with a couple of batteries of field guns, would be amply sufficient for any emergency likely to arise in Egypt.

And now our Nile journey was near its end, for on the 29th the great Pyramids, one by one, began to disclose themselves; first of all Dashoor, then Abouseer, then Sakara, and in the distance the huge pyramids of Ghizeh; so we landed and ordered our boat to proceed and wait for us at Bedreshayn, the present port of Mitrahenny, the mighty Memphis of old times. After crossing a dyke peopled with innumerable wild ducks, and slinging a dish of them to our donkeys' saddles, we gradually ascended from the plain to the Lybian range, where the vast pyramid of Dashoor towers up 325 feet in height. Its situation is so grand that I am not sure but the impression is more striking than of its loftier brethren of Ghizeh. At a distance it certainly looks more majestic. It still retains a good deal of its original casing, which gives it an appearance of finish and preservation superior to the others; but what makes it very peculiar, is the fact that its sides are not carried up to the top in one regular plane, but at the distance of about two-thirds from the base they incline towards each other with a sharper angle. About a mile to the north-east rises the remains of a brick pyramid, still 160 feet in height, supposed to be the sepulchre of King Asychis. Herodotus tells us that this king, desiring to surpass all his predecessors, erected a brick pyramid on which he engraved this vaunting inscription: "Do not despise me; when compared with the stone pyramids I am as superior to them as Jupiter to the other gods. For men plunging poles into a lake, and collecting the mud thus extracted, formed it into bricks, of which they made me." There is some difficulty to understand this vaunt of the superiority of unbaked bricks over stone, but it may have referred to the beauty of the exterior casing, and the carving upon it. It is, moreover, the only one of all the pyramids in existence which has, like those in Ethiopia, a portico or hypæthral temple on the northern front, remains of which are mentioned in the early accounts. Mr. Perring, in 1839, discovered proofs of the existence of this portico. At the present moment, perhaps, the enormous time that a construction of unbaked brick has endured, may be considered almost as great a subject of curiosity, shapeless though it be, as the pyramids of stone. We are now on the site of the oldest monuments of Egypt, and this pile of bricks never subjected to fire, was erected in the days of King Asychis of the third dynasty, about 3300 years B.C., or 5000 years ago. In this estimation of its antiquity, I believe most of the learned investigators of Egyptian archæology are within a century or two consentient. In fact, the whole range of pyramids are the mausoleums of the very earliest Egyptian kings, who flourished at a period when history was not; and when every now and again they emerge from the superjacent structure of ages, they seem to stand almost in the same relation to history as the Deinornis and Megatherium and Ichthyosaurus to modern zoology. We lingered so long that it was dusk ere we returned to the Nile in search of our boat, and a long and weary search it was; but the discharge of a revolver awakened a salute from the *Flea* afar off, which we found, by some mistake of our Reis, to be moored at least a mile further down than the original destination.

In the morning we were up with the lark, for we had a good fifteen miles before us ere arriving at the village of Ghizeh, and we had to traverse the famed Memphis, and view the pyramids of Sakara, and take one more look at those of Ghizeh. Our boat was to follow, meet us at the ferry of Ghizeh, where we were for the last time to sleep on board, intending the next day to make our triumphal entry into Cairo. From Bedreshayn we went at once to Mitrahenny, the ancient Memphis. Of this enormous city, whose circuit was once seventeen miles, nothing now remains save gigantic mounds ensconced in a forest of luxuriant palms. Desolate indeed it is—as desolate as ever the prophet could have foretold—"and Noph shall be desolate." In a hole, with its face to the ground, lies Abou l'Hôn, the "father of terrors"; a gigantic statue of Rameses the Great, almost perfect, and the property of the British Museum. The material is of white silicious limestone, very hard, and most beautifully polished. It is one of the few Egyptian statues of any note that has the features entirely uninjured; but, as it is of limestone, it will, no doubt, be broken up and converted into cement ere long. The expense of transporting it to England has deterred us from rescuing this noble monument from destruction; and when we estimate the weight of a statue forty-two feet high, without the pedestal, made of a solid block, there is no doubt but that in the present high price of freight its removal would be dear.

Some experiments made in this locality of late years, are supposed to throw a light on the much-contested subject of the antiquity of the human race. In 1852, Mr. Leonard Horner, assisted by Hekekyan Bey, proceeded to sink a shaft close to the colossal statue. He determined, in making this excavation, that the following particulars should be attended to; and he instructed the persons he employed—

To ascertain the height of the surface of the ground at the edge of Caviglia's excavation above the low water of the Nile. Signor Caviglia had uncovered the statue about thirty years previously, by making an excavation of a depth of about five feet.

To search for the pedestal on which the statue stood.

To measure the depth of the soil from the surface of the ground to the upper surface of the pedestal, if found.

To sink a vertical shaft close to one side of the pedestal.

To mark the depth from the surface of the ground to the lowest part of the pedestal.

To ascertain carefully the nature of the ground on which the pedestal rests.

To continue the sinking of the shaft, so long as the soil passed through should consist of alluvial deposit.

If no pedestal were found, that the shaft should be made close to the statue, and that a specimen of each variety of soil passed through should be carefully preserved.

The result of these borings was, that at a depth of thirty-nine feet of alluvial deposit the instrument brought up fragments of what is alleged to be pottery, while traces of human industry are said to have been found throughout the whole of the soil thus traversed. There were nine feet four inches of Nile sediment between eight inches below the present surface of the ground and the lowest part of the platform on which the statue had stood. This eight inches was of sandy earth—consequently there were five feet of true Nile deposit. Taking, then, the date of Rameses II. according to Lepsius, and presuming the statue to have been erected in the middle of his reign, or 1361 B.C., and adding this to 1854, we have 3215 years, during which time nine feet four inches of soil were deposited; and supposing that no disturbing cause had interfered with the regular deposition in this locality, we have a mean rate of increase within a small fraction of three inches and a half in a century.

Below the platform there were thirty-two feet of the total depth penetrated, but the last and lowest two feet consisted of sand, below which it is possible there may be no true Nile sediment in this place, thus leaving thirty clear feet of the latter. If, then, we suppose this amount to have been deposited at the same rate of three inches and a half in a century, it gives for the lowest part deposited a period of 10,285 years before the middle of the reign of Rameses, and 13,500 before A.D. 1854.

The deeper parts of this accumulation of thirty feet of sediment are probably more compact in structure than the upper portion, from the long applied superincumbent pressure, and therefore their age is probably greater on that account than that arrived at by the application of the chronometric scale of three inches and a half in a century, obtained by measuring the superior and specifically lighter part of the accumulated mass.

In the lowest part of the boring of the sediment, namely, thirty-nine feet from the surface of the ground, the instrument brought the supposed fragment of pottery before alluded to. This fragment Mr. Horner holds to be a record of the existence of man 13,371 years before A.D. 1854 (reckoning by the before-mentioned rate of increase in that locality of three inches and a half in the century), and 11,517 years before the Christian era—and 7625 years before the date assigned by Lepsius to the reign of Menes, the founder of Memphis—"of man, moreover, in a state of civilization, so far at least as to be able to fashion clay into vessels, and to know how to harden it by the action of a strong heat."

If these calculations were correct, the Egyptian priests have had some ground for their boast that from Menes to Sethos, contemporary of Tirhaka King of Ethiopia, a period of 11,340 years had elapsed, although they thus claim a lapse of some 3000 years longer than Mr. Horner's experiments warrant. But I believe there is much doubt as to the fact of its being a piece of *pottery* that was brought up. It is represented to have been a piece of burnt brick; and it is contended by the best authorities that burnt brick, anterior to the Roman period, was unknown in Egypt—all the bricks used were sun-dried. If this be the case, these experiments would prove little or nothing; and, moreover, Mr. Horner bases his calculations on the supposition that the Nile mud was deposited round the statue from the time of its erection; but it is perfectly clear that the Egyptians were not the persons to place their great works in so low a position as to expose them to the annual inundation of the Nile. At the time this statue was erected, we cannot but feel confident that it was sufficiently elevated to remove it from the inundation. The discussions on this subject show the importance of the inquiry; and it would be well worth while to institute some more extensive experiments on the Nile deposits, where more reliable data can be obtained.

This is supposed to be, and with reason, the identical statue of the monarch called Sesostris by Herodotus and Diodorus, which, in company with one of his queens and four of his sons, stood in front of the temple of Vulcan, or Pthah. This temple was founded by the earliest king of Egypt, Menes, and was embellished and added to by successive dynasties until it became almost the rival of Karnak. But Memphis was the capital of the whole land when Thebes was but a hamlet. The first shock which this city received, and from which it never recovered, was during the interruption of the Egyptian monarchy by the invasion and conquest of the Hyksos, or shepherd tribe from Palestine. During this period, differently estimated from five hundred to eight hundred years, Memphis was in the occupation of the conquerors—a fierce unlettered race, who laid waste its temples and its monuments. When the kingdom was regained by the warrior princes of the eighteenth dynasty, Memphis was no longer the capital of Egypt. While the lower country was occupied by the shepherd intruders, Thebes and Upper Egypt remained unsubdued, and Thebes became the capital of the whole country. Memphis was, however, not forgotten, although not preferred. Its monuments were restored, and it was, as before, the royal residence of Lower Egypt. Then came the Persians, and the fury of Cambyses was first expended upon this unhappy city. Its existence continued nevertheless, and under the mild government of Darius it was still an important town. The last blow it experienced as a seat of government and centre of traffic was the foundation and rise of Alexandria, which became almost from the day when Alexander traced its foundations with meal, the metropolis of the whole Nile valley; and the last blow to its architectural greatness was the storming of the Egyptian Babylon by Amr, "the sword of Omar," in 638 A.D. and the establishment of the Arab city Fostat on its ruins, now called Old Cairo.

From Memphis and the pyramids up to a very recent period, came the materials of the mosques and palaces of Cairo; and the scientific traveller is tantalized by seeing a hieroglyphical inscription on red granite of Syene, half buried and forming the lintel to some bey's doorway, or the royal cartouche of some early and much-contested monarch built up in the fabric of some modern mosque. Abd-el-Latif, writing in the thirteenth century, speaks of a monolithic shrine called the Green Chapel, then existing, and of the numerous idols and their bright colorings which still remained undestroyed. Abulfeda in the following century, although noticing the fact of the decay of Memphis and her monuments, still records her gay and glowing tints, green and red. But with the exception of the "Father of Terror," "the images have now ceased out of Noph," and its only colorings now are the green palm branches waving over brown heaps of rubbish and Nile mud. Even its very situation has been, until lately, a field for controversy.

The great embankment built by King Menes along the river's edge formerly preserved Memphis from the effects of the annual inundation; but the neglect of Mahommedan rulers, and indeed the inutility of keeping up costly hindrances to prevent the fertilizing stream from flowing over a deserted city, has completely covered whatever remains may exist with a thick stratum of mud. The late discoveries of M. Mariette prove without doubt that Memphis still offers a most remunerative field for the operations of the excavator; that monuments of the deepest interest are still preserved well potted in the Nile mud for the benefit of antiquarians; and an intelligent Arab who was with M. Mariette informed me that his employer had discovered a very large number of fine statues in different localities, but had wisely covered them up again till he should be able to remove them. Perhaps some of the notable monuments that adorned the great temple of Vulcan, or Pthah, may yet be recovered from the embraces of mother earth— to wit, the statues to its north and to its south, twenty-five cubits high, erected by Rhampsinitus, and called Summer and Winter; the twelve Osiride columns, twelve cubits high, of the court of Apis; the strange statue of Sethos with the mouse in his hand, and the inscription issuing from his mouth, "Whoever sees me let him learn to revere the gods," commemorating the repulse of the Assyrians by the gnawing of their bowstrings by this little animal; the immense recumbent statue of Amasis, seventy-five feet long, and two others erect, of Ethiopian stone, flanking it: all these were some of its treasures extolled by Greek historians. There, too, was the habitation of the bull-god, Apis; his gorgeous place of sepulture has been lately discovered; perhaps his sanctuary may still be in existence.

This remarkable animal, in search of whom one might in these degenerate days in vain ransack many a fair at Ballinasloe, was always forthcoming when his predecessor was on the point of being resolved into the original elements of beef, and would have astonished our modern graziers. He was the calf of a cow incapable of bearing another, and his sire was the lightning that descended from heaven and created him. So much for his antecedents, and now for his personal appearance. He was to be jet-black except one square of white on the forehead. On his back he was to bear the figure of an eagle, double hair (whatever that may be) was to be on his tail, and either on or under his tongue was to be impressed the image of a beetle. Such was the deity whom Cambyses in his rage stabbed on the very spot where we are now standing, and whose magnificent mausoleum, a short distance off, was very recently brought to light by M. Mariette, with its enormous black sarcophagi, in which repose a series of these bovine objects of adoration. This is a slight sketch of old Memphis.

The unshapely mounds by which we pass, cover the lofty portals out of which Moses and Aaron went forth from before Pharaoh. The palm branches rustle over the scene of the drama of the Exodus. That flash of shallow water straight in our way, close to which a grizzly baggy-breeched old Turk is squatting, in the vain fond hope of potting some wild ducks, was once the lake over which the judged and absolved dead were transported on their way to the burial-ground of Sakara, whence arose the tale of Charon, that grim Acherusian ferryman. Mr. Stanley's description of this locality and of its pyramids as they rise over the ancient city, of the immense sepulchral plain of Sakara, of the more northern pyramids of Ghizeh and their guardian sphinx, is all so vivid and so true, that if I omitted to quote his words I should omit to convey the best impressions I have received of the ground we travelled that day. "Imagine," he says, "a wide green plain, greener than anything else I have seen in Egypt. A vast succession of palm-groves, almost like the Ravenna Forest in extent, runs along the river-side, springing in many spots from green turf. Behind these palm-forests—behind the plain rises the white back of the African range; and behind that again, even as the hills stand round about Jerusalem, so stand the pyramids round about Memphis. These are to Memphis as the royal tombs to Thebes: that is, the sepulchres of the kings of Lower as well as those of Upper Egypt."

Up this white back we mounted, and first visited the large vaulted tomb which is excavated out of the face of the rock. It is of the time of Psammaticus the Second, highly finished, and covered with the most carefully executed hieroglyphics. Certainly, what Bishop Heber says of the Patans, every fresh monument that we visit seems to render more applicable to the ancient inhabitants of this country, that "they built like giants and finished their work like jewellers." This fine tomb has experienced even more than the usual mutilations: immense pieces, every here and there, of carving have been sawn or broken away; and on turning my eyes to where there was a small tomb-shaped vacancy among the carvings, just over one of these shameful demolitions I read, "In memory of the infamy of Lepsius." We asked our guide if he remembered when this mutilation took place. He remembered perfectly well, he said, when there was hardly a fracture in the tomb, but that one Lepsius had been there and had done it all, and that he had been employed by him, and quite understood how to do it, intimating that *he* was ready enough to recommence this work worthy of the resurrection-men. Is it wonderful, then, that Maxime du Camp, and every other writer, French, English, or American, should mention with such indignation the conduct of this learned Vandal, or that his unscrupulousness should have induced one writer (author of *Village Life in Egypt*) to mention and apparently give credence to the accusation of his having forged a cartouche on the breast of a statue in the front court of the temple of Karnak, for the purpose of substantiating some system of his own?

Leaving this tomb, we made our way to the pyramid, which seems to have been constructed in five stories, but resisting the request of our guide to explore its interior, we put our heads steadfastly to the north, for the citadel of Cairo was gleaming bright and gay, not fifteen miles off, and there were piles of letters and files of newspapers just beneath it, awaiting our return to civilization, to tell us news of home.

And now for miles our course lay over a rough and irregular table-land, made still more gritty than nature had formed it, by the hewings of innumerable tombs, many fathoms beneath our feet: "layers of bones and skulls and mummy swathings were lying all around, or deep down in shaft-like mummy-pits, and amongst these mummy-pits are vast galleries filled with mummied ibises in red jars, once filled, but now gradually despoiled; and lastly, only discovered lately, are long galleries hewn in the rock, and opening from time to time, say every fifty yards, with high arched vaults, under which reposes the most magnificent black sarcophagus that can be conceived—a chamber rather than a coffin—smooth, and sculptured within and without, grander by far than even the granite sarcophagi of the Theban kings; how much grander, then, than any human sepulchres, anywhere else! and all for the successive corpses of the bull Apis. These galleries formed part of the great temple of Serapis, in which the Apis mummies were deposited, and here they lay, not in royal but in divine state." This is the discovery of M. Mariette, to which I have before alluded, and which I heard, when in Cairo, had thrown very considerable light upon the chronology of Egypt. The story there was, that M. Mariette, not having any predilection for the learned spoliator, Lepsius, had determined on keeping secret the results which these monumental documents had furnished him with, until after the publication of Lepsius's expected work on *Egyptian History*; when that is completed, M. Mariette will quietly step forth, and, armed with irrefragable proofs, level the laborious structure to the ground. I can conceive no heavier retribution for his misdeeds to this conceited *savant*, who has, up to this time, lorded it over his erudite compeers, than to know that over his head a sword of Damocles is suspended, and that assuredly it will some day fall;—to know that others too are aware of his apprehensions, and are enjoying them;—to endure the ridicule of Philistines and the literary sneers of Herr Professors, at his being obliged to pause in the middle of his publication, for fear of involving himself in still deeper errors;—not to be certain which of his pet theories or laborious systems is to be levelled by the stroke of the pen of an unsparing foe. There is no torture more poignant than that of wounded vanity to a literary man; and I am confident that few who visit or have visited the scenes of Lepsius's depredations, but will rejoice, whatever be the pangs that ridicule, and the worm that dieth not, the apprehension of loss of literary reputation may inflict on this Prussian Attila—this scourge of ancient Egypt.

But to return to Sakara. We now were evidently in the region where the bull was the sacred animal; as at Lycopolis we found the embalmed remains of wolves; at Beni Hassan, of cats; at Maabdeh, of crocodiles; so here, vast pits were filled with the bones and prodigious horns of this unimproved but sacred breed of cattle. Could Mr. Townley's short-horned Durham, Master Butterfly, have seen the frontal decorations of these his deceased fellows, he would have been rather astonished at the present diminished glories of his race.

We descended into the cave where the sacred ibis was deposited, and there lay literally thousands of pots, all of them rifled of their contents and tossed about, but on penetrating into the interior and groping about by candlelight, we found them arranged neatly in rows, like bottles in a cellar, and got several unopened and sealed up. It is remarkable, that on opening many of these pots the contents appear charred, as if they had been baked previously to having been signed and sealed up; and it is also remarkable, that hardly a single specimen of the real sacred ibis, a bird which must have been common in Egypt in former times, is now found within its precincts, but has receded far away into the inner country, to the shores of the White Nile. The papyrus, also, which is the hieroglyphical emblem of Lower Egypt, is now completely extinct; and if I am not mistaken, is only to be found, and that sparingly, on the brink of a small river in Sicily.

Our guide thought to amuse us by some scandalous stories of a celebrated antiquarian, during the progress of his scientific searches at Sakara, showing that the gravest studies do not banish softer ideas, and that archæologists and excavators can stoop to folly like other simpler men. In other words, he plainly stated that this intrepid European, whom to name would be, perhaps, libellous, had trifled with the affections of all the maidens of the locality who had the slightest pretension to good looks. By having a Government order, and a good supply of piastres, he was enabled to obtain an unlimited amount of female labor; and while apparently devoting his attention to a cartouche or a mutilated inscription, he was in reality selecting his victim from among the little maidens, as they paced to and fro, removing in their baskets the rubbish thrown up by the men. He commenced by the Shekh's daughter, which rendered that dignified official unable to inveigh against the irregularities of other families, without the risk of being reminded to look at home. His ally and assistant on these occasions was a Jew (one of that remarkable race which in every country furnishes for money the ready agent in every rascality), and on any particular girl being pointed out to him, when pay-day came she was delayed to the last, and coaxing and piastres did the rest. This Jew, as may be imagined, does not enjoy a high popularity in this locality. Strange enough, however, my informant did not seem to lay much stress on the matter. He said, that the mothers were generally to blame, as, if there were any reluctance on the maiden's part, the clever Israelite generally appealed to a mother's (Egyptian) feelings for a new dress or gewgaws, and thus got the damsel made amenable to persuasion. He added, that M—— was a very proper man, and never interfered in the slightest degree with the virtue of the married portion of the community. Indeed, like the commander in the old song, "He very much applauded what *he* had done." It was clear I might have dramatically addressed him, "Thou hadst no daughter."

We now descended from the hills, leaving tombs and pyramids above us; and, passing Abouseer, jogged along most comfortably, sometimes on foot, sometimes on ass-back, over a carpet of turf and sand, till we arrived at Ghizeh, where we bivouacked beneath our ancient friend the Sphinx. Coming from the south, we were not for some time perceived by the Bedoueens, who lie in wait for victims on the frequented road from Ghizeh, and thus for a time we escaped the infliction of this annoyance. At last, however, just as we had finished our rest and chibouques, they discovered our snug position, which was immediately invaded, and we were pestered, as before, with offers to run up the pyramid, or to conduct us here, there, and everywhere. Their ardour was considerably cooled by some observations in Arabic, on my part anything but complimentary, especially as we informed them it was not our intention to go either up, down, or into the pyramid; and that, as for their feat of mounting it for a shilling, we had a Nubian boy with us, who had never seen it before, and who would go up it for sixpence, if they would make up that sum for him among them. Here they joined issue both as to the sixpence and our assertion, and said his doing so was quite out of the question, for that no one unacquainted with the road could possibly get up. However, that problem was solved shortly after we got there, by Himmed volunteering, even after his twelve miles' walk, to go up it, commencing his ascent in the middle, quite a novel mode of mounting. He had never seen it before, except from the river; but ran up like a goat, and was soon seen capering and waving his tarboosh on the summit, to the immense disgust of the monopolists. They perceived at last that we were old hands, and ceased to annoy; but an annual bastinado, early in November, to be administered to every adult male of the whole tribe, would be a salutary act, which the representatives of every European nation ought to press on the Viceroy's attention, for the comfort of their countrymen.

We were now enabled to have a good examination of that extraordinary monument, the Sphinx, the greatest mystery in the world. Cuneiform letters and hieroglyphics have yielded to the ingenuity and learning of modern ages, but the Sphinx still remains, as ever inscrutable. To appreciate thoroughly the effect that this mighty animal must have produced on the beholder, the traveller ought to approach it for the first view as we did then, instead of descending upon it from the platform of the pyramids. On advancing from the south, you turn in from the plain upon the rocky edge, and there, looking to the river, it stands the advanced post, guarding, as it were, the eastern portals of this vast sepulchral group. Its immense size, its strange unearthly appearance, its solitary position, strike one with astonishment and awe; but its features are so mutilated, that, although perfectly distinct, I could not discover in them that calm majestic type of oriental beauty so often described as its main attribute. The dimensions may give some notion of it. The height, from the platform on which it rests, between its extended paws and the top of its head, is 62 feet; the paws extend 50 feet, the body is 140 feet long. It is hewn out

5*

of the face of the rock, and is of one solid piece, excepting a small portion of the back and one of the fore-paws, which are constructed of blocks of stone, probably in consequence of some flaw or cavity in the hill's side. It is to Captain Cavaglia, and the support rendered him by our former excellent consul, Salt, that the discoveries were made in 1818, which tell us almost all we know about the Sphinx. After considerable labor the surrounding sand was cleared away, and as you come upon it from the river, the direction towards which its head is turned, you descend towards it by a slope cut in the rock for 135 feet. Here commenced a flight of thirteen steps, which conveyed you to the open paved level space between its feet. "This gradual approach, during which the figure of the Sphinx was kept constantly in the spectator's view, rising above him as he descended, was well adapted to heighten the impression made by its colossal size, its posture of repose, and what was then no doubt the calm majestic expression of its countenance." In this space between the fore-paws, an altar, three tablets, and a lion, were discovered. The altar stood immediately between them, and sacrifices were here performed to this strange deity. A granite tablet was found under the breast, containing the name of Thothmes IV., and the figure of the king is carved upon it, presenting an offering to the figure of a sphinx, who is drawn with the peculiar beard and other attributes that denote a god. On the side there were tablets with similar representations, put up by Rameses the Great. The royal shield of Shafra or Cephren, brother to Shoofoo or Cheops, was found on a fractured part of the first tablet, and seems to indicate a connection with the pyramid supposed to be erected by that monarch, and this its situation also seems to confirm.

But now arises the question, by whom and for what purpose was this Father of Terror, this Abou l'Hôn, as the Arabs call the Sphinx as well as the statue of Rameses at Memphis, erected? From the fact of the tablet of Thothmes the Fourth being found on its breast, Sir G. Wilkinson is inclined to attribute it to his predecessor Thothmes III., in accordance with "the known architectural whims of that monarch;" but it is not likely, had it been the work of any of the kings of the Thothmes family, who, of Theban origin, descended from Thebes and drove the Palestine shepherd conquerors out of Egypt, but that they would have adorned their native and noble city Thebes with equally great monuments of a similar description. It is most unlikely also, that although the Theban king may have been willing to do all honor to the ancient city, Memphis, so gallantly regained, that he should have proceeded to erect at a distance of fifteen miles, a monument of this stupendous nature, to serve as an adjunct to the mausoleum of an extinct and, as Herodotus tells us, deriving his information from the priests, of a detested dynasty of tyrants. It is quite clear from the inscription, which dates from the first year of Thothmes IV., that it is not of his construction; and had it been of his predecessor, would he not have left some dedication or inscription to commemorate so great a work? In all his other monuments he shows any thing but a desire to avoid notoriety; indeed none of the kings of the new monarchy seek to escape posthumous honors. But the rearers of the pyramids seem to have been indifferent to fame, leaving their mighty works to tell of all their greatness, instead of covering them with self-laudatory inscriptions.[1] It seems to me from these reasons, and the whole appearance of the monument, from its intimate connection with these pyramids as adding so much to the grandeur of the approach, that it must have been the work of the powerful kings of the old monarchy, and coeval with the pyramids. What may have been its object it is indeed difficult to surmise. It may have been the symbol of the monarch the architect of the pyramid, for we know that a sphinx is the hieroglyphical sign representing a king—Neb (the Lord) is its name, and forms part of the compounded name of King Nectanebus. The body of the lion denotes strength—the human head, wisdom. Moral and physical power conjoined in royal administration. The offerings of Thothmes and Rameses to

[1] I am aware of there having been representations on the exterior casings, but the internal walls are devoid of ornament or inscription.

the Sphinx with the attributes of a god, do not at all militate against this opinion, it being a constant habit of the Egyptian monarchs to represent themselves as presenting libations to their deified ancestors. Some writers have considered the Sphinx to be merely a monstrous idol, the representation of some imaginary deity, but that cannot be the case: first of all, the hieroglyphic sign denotes it to have reference to "the king," and it is shown that in those rare cases where a female sphinx is represented, that she denotes a female in possession of the supreme power—a queen, in fact. Besides, it is not likely that the representation of a deity should have been used as an ornament for the avenues and approaches to the temples. It is perfectly clear, from the researches that have been made about it, independently of every other argument, that Pliny's story of its being the tomb of Amasis is utterly incorrect, although I believe Amos, Aahmes, or Amasis, to have been the ancestor of the Thothmes family, which may have given some rise to the tradition, coupled with the memorial of the fourth Thothmes presenting libations to the king. The connection with Amasis may also have arisen from Pliny not understanding the meaning of the word "Armachis," which is found on one of the Greek inscriptions upon it, purporting that the inhabitants of the village of Busiris intended erecting a stone tablet to "Armachis." He may have been confused with Amasis. But "Armachis" is derived from, or rather is the Greek mode of expressing, Harem Chu (Horus in the Horizon): that is, the image of the sun-god, the emblem of all kings.

It is remarkable that neither Herodotus nor, indeed, any author before the Augustan age, should have mentioned this wonderful monument. It is a most notable instance, as Mr. Kendrick observes, of the danger of relying on negative arguments merely as proofs of the nonexistence of monuments of antiquity, and shows how utterly futile are the reasonings of those persons who argue that the pyramids were unbuilt during the stay of the Israelites in Egypt, or even in the time of Homer, as not having been mentioned either in Holy Writ, or by the poet. And yet here is the Sphinx unnoticed by that most observing historian, Herodotus, who had personally inspected and was describing the country, and particularly its architectural wonders, with the utmost minuteness. There it has stood as it now stands, assigning it the very latest date, more than a thousand years before his visit, and as he came from Memphis he must have passed by its flanks and inquired into its history, and yet there is not even a mention of its name. Mr. Stanley, I think very truly, takes the same view that I cannot help doing, of its being an accessary, and a noble one, to the pyramids. "For what purpose," he writes, "was this Sphinx of sphinxes called into being—as much greater than all other sphinxes as the pyramids are greater than all other temples or tombs? If, as is likely, he lay crouched at the entrance now deep in sand, of the vast approach to the second, that is the central pyramid, so as to form an essential part of this immense group; still more, if as seems possible there was once intended to be (according to the usual arrangement, which never left a solitary sphinx any more than a solitary obelisk), a brother sphinx on the northern side, as this on the southern side of the approach, its situation and significance were worthy of its grandeur; and if, further, the sphinx was the great representative of royalty, then it fitly guards the greatest of royal sepulchres, and with its half-human half-animal form, is the best welcome and the best farewell to the history and religion of Egypt."

Before departing finally, I took one lasting circuit round the whole group of pyramids, to endeavour to obtain a general idea of what they once were and are. In passing by the pyramid of the good King Mencheres, or Mycerinus, whose mild and equitable sway, after the remorseless tyrants Shoofoo and Shafra, has been handed down even to our days by the acclaim of a grateful people, I was not aware that his estimable remains repose upon British soil, but such is the case. When Colonel Vyse opened this pyramid, he found within it, in the sepulchral chamber, the sarcophagus of Mycerinus. It was made of a brownish-colored basalt, highly polished, which, however, had a blue appearance, wherever it was chipped or broken. The exterior was beautifully carved in compartments of the Doric style of architecture. This fine work was unfortunately lost to the nation, by the vessel that conveyed it foundering off the coast of Spain; the lid, however, was preserved. The supposed body of the king was found in the same chamber, by the side of the sarcophagus, wrapped up in a woollen covering. An account of the whole proceeding which accompanied the invasion of the pyramid, and the desecration of the royal mummy, is preserved by Edrisi, who states that in 1240 A.D. the pyramid was opened by a company. His words are, "After they had worked at it for six months, with axes, in great numbers, hoping to find treasures, they came at last to a long blue basin. When they had broken the covering of it, they found nothing but the decayed rotten remains of a man, and no treasures at his side, excepting golden tablets inscribed with letters in a language nobody could understand. Each man's share of the profits of these amounted to one hundred dinars." Chevalier Bunsen has charmingly commented on these the chequered fortunes of the remains of this ancient monarch. "It is, therefore, a happy fatality, that after the mysterious pyramids have been so frequently ransacked and mutilated, the coffin-lid of this monarch, or that of his successor with the very same name, and the mummy beneath it, and it only, should have been preserved. The bones of the oppressors of the people, who for two whole generations harassed hundreds of thousands from day to day, have been torn from those sepulchral chambers, which they fondly hoped would have preserved their remains for ever from the annihilation they apprehended, and have bid defiance to all search and all demolition. Diodorus, indeed, mentions an Egyptian tradition, according to which, neither of the two kings was buried in his own pyramid, for fear of a perpetual outbreak, but in a secluded spot, as privately as possible. The good and humane king, however, who abolished soccage, and who on that account was immortalized in ballads and hymns, as the favorite of the nation, although his coffin was broken open, has remained down to our days in his pyramid, rescued from the desolation of ages, and has met with a resting-place worthy of his fame. His fate may furnish matter for reflection and thought. The empire of the Pharaohs, of which he was the eighteenth ruler, has perished. Two other empires of Pharaohs have succeeded it, and those who destroyed the last of them have likewise vanished from the stage of history. The gods of Egypt have sunk in the dust. 'Son of Pharaoh' has become a reproach and a byword in the lands of the Pharaohs; even the language is mute among the people, and threatens to disappear from the altar, where, though but partially understood, it still is retained. But the corse of Mencheres reposes at this hour in greater security than it did almost five thousand years ago, in the island, the mistress of the world, whose freedom and free institutions are stronger bulwarks than the ocean which encircles her, among the treasures of all the realms of nature, and the most exalted remains of human art. May it rest, never to be disturbed so long as the stream of history shall roll on!"

This last circuit was a lonely walk, for there is no place to my mind more lonely than these pyramids. It is not like the desolation of the valley of the Tombs of the Kings, or the wide expanse of unpeopled desert, because there you are alone with nature; but here you are alone amid the gigantic works of fellow-creatures, with whose chisel and hammer, with whose laughter or, rather, sighs, the whole of this platform resounded; and who, though now swept from off the face of the earth, have left their mighty recollections all around. You have Cairo, too, in sight, with its gay minarets and mosques, and its teeming population; there are Arab villages on the plain, with peasants moving to and fro; but once up here on this ridge of sepulchres, you seem to be cut off from the present, isolated from the stirring, heaving world below you, perplexed and weighed down by the stupendous greatness of objects which you commence comparing with all you have ever seen and heard of, oppressed by the dead stillness and absence of all life whether of man, or beast, or bird, until as usual, you are wakened from your day-dreaming, and put on your mettle to resist the attempts of the Bedoueens on your purse. So, seeing a white cap approaching, I moved off from my block of Shafra's pyramid, and rejoined my friend at the entrance of that of Cheops. While he went into the interior, I amused myself by looking over the ridiculous inscription which the learned Lepsius has carved in hieroglyphical characters in honor of the King of Prussia. It is just over the entrance passage. Joseph's father-in-law, the good priest of On, would, I think, have rent his clothes, could he have foreseen that the sacred letters would have been so desecrated by commemorating such barbarian rubbish.

In this form runs this delightful memorial:—

"Thus speak the servants of the King, whose name is the *Sun* and *Rock* of *Prussia,* Lepsius the scribe, Erbkam the architect, the brothers Weidenbach, Frey the painter, Franke the moulder, Bonomi the sculptor, Wild the architect. All hail to the Eagle—the Protector of the Cross, to the King, the Sun and Rock of Prussia, who freed his fatherland, Frederick William the Fourth, the Philopator, the Father of his Country, the Gracious One, the Favorite of Wisdom and History, the Guardian of the Rhine whom Germany has chosen, the Dispenser of Life. May the Most High God grant the King, and his Consort the Queen Elizabeth, the Rich in Life, the Philometer, the Mother of her Country, the Gracious One, an ever new and long life on earth, and a blessed habitation in heaven through all eternity. In the year of our Saviour 1842, in the 10th month, on the 15th day, on the 47th birthday of his Majesty, on the Pyramid of King Cheops, in the 3rd year, in the 5th month, in the 9th year of the reign of his Majesty, in the year 3164 from the commencement of the Sothic period under King Menephthes." What a spot to indite such execrable stuff! stuff worthy, no doubt, to be inscribed by a German artist with a huge seal upon his thumb, over some German Glyptothek or Pinakothek. But upon the Pyramid of Shoofoo!!!

I should certainly like to have erased these hieroglyphics, and to have inserted others had I known how, altering the first sentence, which commemorates the servants of the King, into "Lepsius the devastator, Erbkam the mutilator, the brothers Weidenbach the smashers, Frey the scraper, Franke the macadamiser, Bonomi the erasor, and Wild the overthrower. All hail to the Sledge and Crowbar!" &c. &c.

But it was time to be off, and not write hieroglyphics. So, now let us for the last time stand beneath the eastern slope of the Great Pyramid, and, leaning against one of its component blocks, recall Eothen's eloquent description of the impression this scene conveyed to him. "It was not till I came to the base of the Great Pyramid that the reality began to weigh upon my mind. Strange to say, the bigness of the distant blocks of stone was the first sign by which I attained to feel the immensity of the whole pile. When I came and trod, and touched with my hands, and climbed in order that by climbing I might come to the top of one single stone, then, and almost suddenly, a cold sense and understanding of the Pyramid's enormity came down overcasting my brain. Even now, I cannot find words to explain why it is, that the forced contemplation of a mere quality, distinct from matter, should be so terrible. Well, now my eyes saw and knew, and my hands and feet informed my understanding, that there was nothing at all abstract about the Great Pyramid. It was a big triangle sufficiently concrete, easy to see, and rough to the touch; it could not, of course, affect me with the peculiar sensation I have been talking of, but yet there was something akin to that old nightmare agony in the terrible completeness with which a mere mass of masonry could fill and load my brain—and time too—the remoteness of its origin, no less than the enormity of its proportions, screens an Egyptian pyramid from the easy and familiar contact of our modern minds. At its base the common earth ends, and all above is a world—one not created of God—not seeming to be made by men's hands—but rather the sheer giant work of some old dismal age weighing down this younger planet."

Such are the thoughts that rise, even in the mutilated condition of this single monument; but sweep your eye over the whole scene, over its Titanic brothers, and then endeavour to reconstruct, in imagination, what must once have been their aspect. "But it is more easy to conceive Karnak as it was, than to conceive the pyramidal platform as it was. The smooth casing of part of the top of the Second Pyramid, the magnificent granite blocks which form the lower slope of the third, serve to show what they must have been, all of them. The first and second, brilliant white on yellow limestone, smooth from top to bottom, instead of those rude disjointed masses which their stripped sides now present; the third all glowing with the red granite from the cataract. As it is, they have the barbarous look of Stonehenge—but *then*, they must have shone with the polish of an age already rich in civilization, and that the more remarkable when it is remembered, that these granite blocks, which furnished the outside of the third and inside of the first, have come all the way from the first cataract at Assouan. It also seems, from Herodotus and others, that these smooth outsides were covered with sculptures. Then you must build up or uncover the massive tombs now broken or choked with sand, so as to restore the aspect of vast streets of tombs, like those on the Appian Way, out of which the Great Pyramid would rise like a cathedral above smaller churches. Lastly, you must enclose the two other pyramids with stone precincts and gigantic gateways, and, above all, you must restore the Sphinx as he was in the days of his glory."

But the chibouque is finished, and with it our lucubration must finish also. Adieu, then, to stern Shoofoo and Shafra, and beneficent old Mencheres. Our last and best wishes they had, as we turned our backs upon them, "that their shadows might never be less." In a few minutes we were again in the busy haunts of men, in the rich verdant plain of Ghizeh, gay with innumerable tents, with horses, camels, and asses, picketed before them, and at their door black slaves gravely smoking. All the citizens of Cairo, at this time of year, send forth their stud, be it ass, horse, or camel, to pasture on green food, and leave them in the care of trusty servants, who dwell, for the time, in tents. Nothing could be more animated than the scene.

We arrived in due time at Ghizeh, the ferry to old Cairo, but when there we found no sign of the arrival of the *dahabieh*. Neither the gules flag with the flea sable floated amid the forest of masts, nor were any of our crew, as we expected, lounging about the shore. We took refuge in a coffee-shop, and, hoping for some tidings of the missing boat, watched the busy scene. Heaps of oranges, of corn, of beans, of onions, of red "atz," or lentil, were spread all around, watched over by "fierce old hags with long and venomous-looking teeth, and lips distorted by seventy years cursing, morning, noon, and night." Pretty Fellâh girls offered oranges, and failing to sell, asked for *buckshish*. Bold boys were poking up the pariah dogs with palm sticks or any other weapon that came to hand, and were answered with yells or growls, according to the disposition of the animal. Donkeys were galloping down the steep bank and jumping into the boats like sailors, camels were growling and snarling, and resounding with whacks at their refusal to follow so good an example. Soldiers and sailors, Christians and Muslims, Franks and Africans, crowded the shore in all the bravery of their distinctive apparel. The boatmen jostled and adjured the Prophet, and swore as trumpeters alone are said to do. The wordy war seemed never to cease, but fell into a stiff steady breeze, or rose into a hurricane, as the embarkations slackened or increased. Innumerable boats with their white sweeping sails, scudded rapidly to and fro, laden with produce, or with quadrupeds, or human freight.

But busy and amusing as was the scene, at last our patience could endure no longer, so we resolved to cross also, and take refuge in Cairo; and pretty figures we were to make our entrance into the fashionable Ezbekieh at the most fashionable hour of the evening, when Levantine gents come forth and parade in shiny hats and still more shiny boots, accompanied by their dingy partners, dingy only in complexion, but arrayed in all the colors of the rainbow—only not quite so well assorted. Here were we in shooting-coats torn by Nubian thorns, and patched by untailoring hands, with faces smudged by groping into ibis-pits, and dirty turbans round our wide-awakes, to face this rendezvous of swells! We did, however, face them, having met Hubert, my servant, and the second Reis, Hassan, who with his usual forethought and energy, seeing that it was impossible for the *Flea* to make way against the violent north wind, took out the *sandal*, or small boat, and rowed several miles to Cairo, rather than that we might be delayed or inconvenienced. So that evening our Nile pilgrimage ended exactly three months from the day we started, and as it was exactly three months in consequence since fresh or, rather, sweet butter had crossed our lips, the havoc that ensued that afternoon on Mr. Williams's excellent supply may be imagined.

Our journey was indeed over; and, though glad to get back and hear news of home and of our army and of peace, still we were sorry. For the whole three months, with the exception of the indisposition of a few days at starting, I had never been so well in health, and my companion had not even the same drawback to complain of. What little, and really little, occasional inconveniences we had experienced, were all forgotten; they were but specks of dust in the balance of many happy days.

Happy days I may indeed say,—rendered still more happy by the perfect concord or, rather, unanimity that prevailed during the whole period between myself and my comate: to whose invariable good spirits, kindness, and unselfish qualities, much of the charm to me of the past winter may be attributed; much of the longing that comes over me when my thoughts wander back to the old Nile and its glorious climate. May this be but the first time that I shall have quaffed its waters!

The next day was spent in unloading our treasures from the *Flea*, and settling with Hassaneen Effendi, her owner, than whom I am bound to say I never met a more liberal man of business. That vexatious item, to those who have occupied lodgings—breakages to wit—was quickly despatched according to our own ideas of what ought and what ought not to be charged against us. We forgave our Reis his sins of omission, believing them to be more his misfortune than his fault, and begged of Hassaneen Effendi not to forget his second Reis Hassan, but to promote him from the helm to the chief command. A better (Nile) sailor never left Assouan, the nursery of that class —always at his post, well behaved, respectable, and energetic, and withal a wonderful dandy. He will be an acquisition to any one wishing to travel in quiet, and not requiring the excitement of bullying his crew.

On the following morning all the crew came to the hotel to bid us farewell, and we parted the very best of friends. Old Hassaneen the cook also came to make a parting call, but, probably overcome by his feelings, he could not contrive to get up the stairs; and on going out I found him lying supine in the dust at the door of the hotel in a very sad condition. "Booza Master, d—d bad—rompa la testa, Master," was all he could say; and thus ended my connection with the Doubly Beautiful; but I noted, in consequence of this interview among my etymological deductions, that the English word "Boozy" must be derived from the Arabic "Booza"—unfermented beer, in which Hassaneen had been indulging so copiously.

And now having bid farewell to the Nile and to the *Flea*, I think I am bound in justice to say something about our experience of those "rascally Arabs," which is the expression very often applied to them by our countrymen. I have been out at all times and in all places among them, and though by no means an adept at Arabic, I invariably found them civil and obliging, if I asked any question, or entered into conversation with passers-by. This is all I can say of those who were unemployed by us; but of the nine or ten Arabs, whom we had on board as boatmen, I cannot speak too highly,—they were as ready to work as one could possibly expect, and always seemed in good humour. There was not a single instance of any of them being intoxicated with either spirituous liquor, or the very common stimulant of *hashish*, a preparation of hemp. Above all, although there were constant opportunities for theft, and many articles lying carelessly about that were of value in their eyes, yet from the day of our start to the day of our return, the only object missing was a pair of slippers belonging to the Nubian Himmed, which were abstracted by some of the cataract mob that swarmed on the boat. These were their positive good qualities; and I may add that their high spirits and readiness to be amused, whether in singing, telling or hearing stories, or acting as teachers of Arabic to us, would have made me not a little blind to their other faults and failings, had there been opportunities of discovering them, which there were not. The faults they are chiefly reproached with are ingratitude and falseness. I believe both to be defects essentially Oriental. But how can we expect it to be otherwise under the condition in which they have been bred and nurtured? As pointers and setters have hereditary instincts, and set and point almost as soon as they can run about, so have human beings their hereditary instincts—slavish if born of a race of slaves, and independent if of a race of freemen.

The offspring of the one would cringe and deceive even if his lot from the cradle were cast in a land of liberty; the other, if nurtured in a sultan's palace, would sooner or later make manifest to all that to kneel and sue was not the manner of those whose blood ran hot in his veins. The longer the condition, free or servile, the stronger and more difficult to be eradicated is the instinct. Centuries of servitude may require many years of emancipation to remove the inveterate stain and taint; centuries of freedom impress a stamp upon the natural character of a people that conquests and oppression will long be unable to obliterate. But the dawn of independence has not yet even gleamed over the valley of the Nile, and the faults of its inhabitants are the results of a government of tyranny, injustice, and bad faith. There can be but small gratitude where there is but small kindness; no frankness where deception is the only safeguard against violence and wrong. This theory may be met by examples of these vices prevailing among free communities; but even then it will not be difficult to sustain it by accounting circumstances, and on the whole it will remain good. By all this I mean much more than to repeat the old assertion of "fortes creantur fortibus"—"from the brave the brave spring." I mean that there are certain instincts in mankind, as well as in the lower order of animals, that survive and are transmitted long after the circumstances which caused originally these tendencies, have been modified or altogether disappeared.

Of course it would not be very philosophical to argue on the character of a race from the fortunate chance of having met with a well-behaved crew of some eight or ten natives for a few months. But it is just as fair to generalize on the favorable side as to lavish whosesale abuse from a similar contracted observation, which many travellers have done. They fail to recollect that these men whom they employ are the sweepings of the port of Cairo, Boulak; that they well know they are never again likely to behold their employer, a man of different nation, faith, and color, to themselves. Is it wonderful that their conduct should at times be exceptional, and that the *kurbash* should become acquainted with their heels? I question much if an Indian gentleman, not speaking a word of our language, was to hire a mixed crew at Wapping, with an English valet for his interpreter, and to proceed on a yacht excursion about the coast, but that he would have quite as much reason to complain of the natives of this highly favored land, as Europeans have of Arab sailors. The character given by St. John of the Egyptian Arab (and he knows the country well) is so earnest and true, and he seems always to have such a yearning for the poor oppressed Fellâh, that I must invoke his aid to help me to withstand the attacks of the many inveighers against the "rascally Arabs," premising always that I am not alluding to Bedoueens or any other tribe, but merely to the peasants of Egypt. "By the banks of the Nile, the despotism—paternal in nothing but its impartiality, of one man surrounded by a few pampered favorites—has weighed on the unfortunate inhabitants; but these poor people have allies on their side which we have not—as a character of wonderful simplicity, a mind not enlarged by knowledge, desires limited as their means, ignorance, in fact, with all its blessings; and, moreover, they have their climate which in most seasons roofs and clothes them; and the Nile, with the soil it has given; and chief perhaps of all hanging over them, surrounding them, penetrating them, a religious creed which consoles but does not enlighten, which promises but scarcely threatens, which fills them with insolent and bigoted confidence, that never leads them to commune with their own hearts in stillness and melancholy, never bids the tear to start nor the lip to quiver, never lures the adventurous mind into the mysterious regions of contemplation, to send it back in anguish or even hope. Thus the wretchedest Fellâh in his normal state of poverty is a more approachable being than the outcast of European civilization. He is tormented by no theories, never relapses into moody reveries, in which society is conceived under the form of an enemy—never dreams of changing or avenging his condition. It requires a greater degree of cultivation than he possesses to enable him to perceive that the weight which oppresses him is of the earth, and not in the skies." Such is the description of his condition; and as for the working of his faculties, "the Arab is all ears when he listens, all reflection when he writes, all mendacity when he lies, all passion when he loves. His literature is the image of the character; the faith being boundless, no restraint is ever put on his invention. He has worlds of spirits, good and bad, at his command. Nature for him owns no laws but the arbitrary will of God, which operates in a way intelligible and conceivable by no man. He is surrounded, therefore, by infinite miracles, which he believes as sincerely as that the Nile flows or the sun rises; the earth has its ghouls, its jins, its effrits, with indefinite powers of good and evil, which may be controlled and regulated by men or women who have gone through certain studies, subsisted on certain kinds of food, prayed, fasted, and otherwise behaved in conformity with certain formulas."

For the next three weeks we enjoyed the luxury of repose and climate at Cairo. Our occupations were to ride sometimes ere break of day, and while there was yet dew on the ground, and the first sunbeams were breaking through the plane and fig-tree foliage of the Shubra Avenue, to gallop on well-selected donkeys to the narrow passage between the gardens of Shubra and a large island in the

Nile. This passage we crossed in a fisherman's boat, and sitting by the shore, awaited the coming of the desert and black partridge, which invariably made their loud and dissonant cry heard from afar, as they came in panting with thirst from the Arabian desert, between seven and nine o'clock, neither sooner nor later. We might almost have set our watches by the first and last flight. We also shot occasionally some curious aquatic birds, among others the razor-bill and avoset, and finished off the morning by one or more wild ducks—always an acceptable present to friends in Cairo. After nine, the *chasse* ending, we retired to a cool brick-paved *café*, where we had left our bread, butter, and cold chicken, in charge of our attendants. These, and a good cup of black coffee backed with a chibouque, sent us on our way rejoicing, and we generally returned home by a charming long ride, which brought us in by the Gate of Victory, at the other side of Cairo. Our first reason for taking this circuitous route was to endeavour to obtain some specimens of the merops, or bee-eater, a beautiful green bird, which, like the partridge, makes known his whereabouts by loud cries as he floats and skims in the air like a swallow; and his favored haunts were in this locality.

I am sure this bird must have suggested the idea of the green birds in whose crops the martyr of Islam reposes, and whose privilege it is to drink of the waters and eat of the fruit of paradise. But this somewhat confined abode is only to last till the judgment; then, if found worthy, paradise becomes his resting-place. He is waited on by 80,000 attendants. His stature expands to the height of a lofty palm-tree, and seventy-two of the girls of paradise, "hooryas," tall also and slender as the palms, with large black eyes, become his handmaidens. Dishes innumerable, equally delicious but ever varying, are provided for his appetite, which is unpalled as much at the conclusion as at the commencement of the feast. As he rests after the banquet, he listens to the songs of the heavenly Rubini, the angel Israfeel. Wine, too, is allowed, as not affecting his renewed nature, and morning and evening he is permitted to look upon the face of Allah.

But, to leave paradise and return to Cairo: in these excursions we had sometimes a very intelligent companion—naturalist, archæologist, numismatologist: in short, something of everything. His name was Guiseppe Odescalchi, better known in Cairo as Yoossef. He was born in Africa; his father was Roman, his mother German; so he left us, he said, to determine what country should claim him as her own. In his professional pursuits of objects of natural history, he had been in many strange places; almost every summer to the shores of the Red Sea, in search of shells and corals and seaweeds; at another time hunting up birds in Abyssinia; and twice in Sennaar, where he had caught the terrible fever which still showed its traces in his long thin figure, which, as he himself asserted, refused to be fattened or comforted. Then he did business in Egyptian antiquities, and bought and sold coins and vases, and scarabæi and bronzes; and will, I hope, have plenty of success in all his enterprises, for he was a pleasant companion, and a hospitable host, having always ready for his guests the very best cup of coffee I ever tasted. Sir Philip Crampton would have rejoiced in his abode. On entering the yard, a fine bold-looking ibex came forward to receive you, and to make you feel, too, if over familiar, the weight of his great arching horns. A troop of red geese, lately captured, enjoyed themselves in a tub in an outhouse; and putting his hand into a barrel, our friend would pull out some hideous, flat, paunchy, ungainly lizards, kept there till a demand should arise for them by some museum or zoological garden. Then upstairs, in one room, mummies looked gravely at you; in another, skeletons of birds and fishes grinned ghastly; then there were folios of dried plants, and cabinets of dried beetles (for, be it known, that Egypt teems with insects of the *Coleoptera* division, though deficient in that of the *Lepidoptera*); and in his sanctum, apart, a dozen or two recently killed birds are awaiting the preservation of their skins and the cooking of their bodies; for Guiseppe generally consumed most of his specimens, except birds of prey, alleging that stewing got rid of most rank flavors, even those of seagulls, which, among others, he destined for his table, and that a little piquancy of taste did not render them the less desirable.

On our return came the bath; and no one who has not tried it can appreciate the luxury of a fine deep tub, full of cold water, after a morning's ride under an African sun. Then came the pipe, and a read; and in the afternoon a lounge through the bazaars, where we soon became altogether *enfans de la famille*. The long-nosed tobacco-vendor saluted us as ancient customers as we passed, or invited us to a seat on his board, and to sniff his fragrant wares. There was the real Latakia or Gebeli, dark in color, fine in substance, velvety to the touch, and perfume to the nose; this he let you have for about 1*s*. 6*d*. per pound; then next in rank was the Suri or Syrian, much higher in color, costing about 1*s*., and which is, I imagine, the only Latakia our tobacconists expose for sale. The heap on which you lean is the famous "tumbak," which comes across the Hejaz, from El Ajam, or Persia, and is grown in the neighbourhood of Shiraz. This is smoked in the *shishéh*, which answers to the Indian *hooka* and the Turkish *narghiléh*. The tobacco is washed and strained before being lighted and presented to the smoker; therefore, as the smoke passes through the clear cool water it is divested of all heat or acidity, and every sense has a holiday; for the taste is pleasant, and the eye rejoices to see the thin blue smoke curling aloft, and the ear is soothed by the soft gurgling of the water. There is another and an inferior kind of tobacco called *hummi*, with which I was not acquainted. Lieutenant Burton says that it is considered quite *infra dig.* to smoke it,—not merely on account of other demerits, but because it has the evil reputation of producing intoxication. If a man, therefore, tells you that he has known better days, but now smokes *hummi*, it means that worldly matters have gone so badly with him as to have affected his brain.

Although the strangeness, and perhaps the charm, of the first impressions had passed and gone, yet the knowledge of customs and manners which we had obtained, rendered many things intelligible which we before were at a loss to comprehend. Among other things, we became enlightened as to the prominent part which dread of the evil eye maintained in Arab imagination, manifesting itself at every turn of the street, and in every action of daily life. Over the door of this house of bey or pasha, which we are trotting by, swings a huge stuffed crocodile. In my simplicity I imagined it to be a trophy of the owner's prowess, as we suspend in our halls the proud antlers of some stag of many points. Not a bit of it, said old Mahommed. It is against the evil eye. Here comes a grand lady, shuffling along in her yellow boots, with black "habarah" of ample and lustrous silk, spread as a sail before the favoring gale,—look how like Ῥοδοδάκτυλος Ἠώς—rosy-fingered morn—she advances, tinged to the nails with delicate henna; see how those almond-shaped eyes, fringed and arched with the dark shading of "kohl," glance at the passing foreigners; sniff up the balmy gales of Araby the Blest that are dissipated from her comely person, the result of "Zabit soda," or sniff them not, as they may be as offensive to you as they were to me, and only take one's word that the air is heavy with them. Having seen, smelt, and admired all this finery, then turn your eyes on the little dirty, ill-conditioned looking boy, unwashed, umkempt, with flies in his eyes, and clothes in the last extremity of seediness. "Poor little fellow!" we say, he has a nice chance with such a stepmother. Wrong again, would old Mohammed say, if consulted. All this dirt and squalor is the result of maternal affection. The young gentleman is left in this state of uncleanliness, for fear, if smartened up and dandified, he should become the object of envy,—in other words, obnoxious to the evil eye. Very probably the lady has what you would say was a little girl with her, but you would be wrong if you did, for it is a little boy in girl's clothing. The male sex being of so much more importance, there is no fear of envy if the disguise is kept up, for no one envies the possession of a female child; and in this manner, if distrusting filth and ophthalmic flies, the Cairene dame has another resource against the evil eye. If you go to see Il'hamy Pasha, don't ask to see his horses; he will not keep them as close as Colonel P— or Lord E—, to prevent stable secrets oozing out, but he knows you would covet them and envy him, and then would come down on him and his stud the evil eye. Should you pay a visit to a Mahommedan, and delight in the pure lemon tint of his amber mouth-pieces, or some new and glittering chandelier, or other brilliant gew-gaw, you had better keep your encomiums to yourself, for your flattering expressions of delight and pleasure will most assuredly be assigned as the true cause why the mouth-piece has been split in twain, or the brilliant lustre is exhibiting its prismatic colors on the ground, smashed by the clumsiness of some ignorant and careless slave. Your praise has brought on it the evil eye. Besides the crocodile, there is another ornament to the houses which seems to answer the same purpose as the houseleek on the Irish cabins. The aloe is constantly suspended over the doorways, as the emblem of good luck. It is supposed even that the Prophet occasionally honors the abode thus adorned with his saintly presence. Mr. Lane says it will live several years in this manner without earth or water, and even put forth blossoms, whence it is termed "sabr," which signifies patience. The coloring of the houses adds much to the gay appearance of the city. In England, these plain white-washed stone walls, painted with stripes of red, would look rather like Bartholomew fair; but in this sunny climate they are quite in harmony with every surrounding object—the sun's bright beams around them, the glancing palms waving over them.

Then the lace-like network of the lattices—what can be more Oriental? with their delicate and graceful workmanship, looking more as if the wood "were woven in the loom than cut with saw and chisel;" ever open to the breeze and sun, from behind which light sprays of laughter fall upon your ear, and glancing eyes flash merrily upon you, pig-eating Nazranee and Kaffir though you be! Alas! I hear that the proprietors of these beautiful carvings are but too ready to barter them for common venetians —Ay di mi—Alhambra!

Some of the houses are embellished with strange, uncouth-looking frescoes, representing camels, asses, horses, sailing-boats, and even steamers. It was only latterly I discovered that these quaint frescoes were the pictorial honors done to a returning *hadji*, or pilgrim, whose admiring relations have thus portrayed the various conveyances by which their travelled friend has made his way to the tomb and birthplace of the Prophet.

Each day's riding brought with it some new traits of Eastern manners. Sometimes we were blocked up by a marriage, which seems to be a very public affair in Cairo, and a tedious one to the chief performers. The poor little bride, in some instances not more than nine or ten years old, covered with a scarlet Cashmere shawl from head to foot, perambulates the streets, half stifled from the heat and dust. Hired bearers hold over her an awning of silk, very gorgeous no doubt, but which effectually prevents the slightest breath of air from reaching the little victim; but a benevolent old crone was occasionally endeavouring to make up for it by fanning her with a dirty pocket-handkerchief. Before her waddle the married female relations in their black "habarahs"; then follow the virgin bridemaids in white, buffoons tumble and perform feats in front, and the procession is accompanied by an incessant rattle of drums and a horrid ear-piercing dissonance of fifes. Having escaped from this, a funeral, probably, next stops the way, and the body—covered by a scarlet shawl, if of a woman, perhaps the same that served her for her wedding garment; if of a man, with the turban resting on its breast—is borne along for extramural interment; for there are no graveyards in Cairo, nor grasping church dignitaries, like Archdeacon Hale, to extol the propriety of poisoning the living with gases of corruption from the dead, for the sake of his interment fees.

At last we get out of the labyrinth of winding narrow alleys, into the comparatively broad street leading to the citadel, among carriages and loaded camels and ox-drawn carts, and a busy, restless, seething crowd. This is Captain Burton's excellent description:—"O thy right! O thy left! O thy back!" cries a panting footman who runs before the carriage; "Bless the Prophet and get out of the way." "O Allah bless him!" responds the good Mussulman, some shrinking up to the wall to avoid the stick, others rushing across the road so as to give themselves every chance of being knocked down. The donkey-boy beats his ass with a palm cudgel, and curses him at the top of his voice for a Pandar, a Jew, a Christian, and a son of the one-eyed whose portion is eternal punishment. "Out of the way, and say there is but one God," pants out a water-carrier, laden with his skin. "Sweet water, and gladden thy soul, O lemonade," pipes the seller of that luxury, clanging his brass cups together. Then come the beggars, intensely Oriental: "My supper is in Allah's hands—whatever thou givest that will go with thee," shouts some old vagrant. "Naal Abouk—curse thy father, O brother of a haughty sister," is the response of some petulant Greek to the touch of the old man's staff. "The grave is darkness and good deeds are its lamps," sings the blind woman, rapping two sticks together. You answer her, "O lady—O female pilgrim—O bride—O daughter," even if she be the wrong side of fifty. In Arabia you may say, "Y'al mara—O woman;" but near the Nile, if you attempt it, the answer of the offended fair one will be, "May Allah cut out thy heart!" and if you want a real good quarrel, "Y'al agooz—O old woman," pronounced drawlingly, is sure to bring it on—Y'al ago-o-ooz; and high above the hubbub rises the voice of the Muezzin, and rings forth from the balcony of his lofty tower, "Hie ye to devotion—hie ye to salvation—devotion is better than sleep—devotion is better than sleep." The good Muslims piously stand up and mutter, previous to prayer, "Here am I at thy call, O Allah! Here am I at thy call."

A festival in honor of a certain Shekh Bedawee, is held twice annually, at a town called Tanta, in Lower Egypt, and thither from all parts flock in those who are intent on business, devotion, and dissipation, perhaps on all three. We had heard that it was one of the most extraordinary scenes that could be witnessed, and as my Belgian friends were intent on the trip, we hired a tent and all necessary paraphernalia, and proceeded together thither by railway. Our party consisted of the two Belgian gentlemen, their dragoman, and a small boy from Nubia, Abou Zeyd, or Father of Honey, by name. His province was to attend as pipe-carrier. Our starting was signalized by a slight fracas between our dragoman and a sallow-faced, ill-conditioned looking Italian, who had taken his place in our carriage. The poor dragoman very innocently had sat down on a seat which this worthy had retained by placing his umbrella on it. On entering the carriage, instead of requesting the dragoman to remove himself, he commenced abusing him in the most violent manner; and then without any additional provocation, indeed, without listening to the excuses which were freely proffered, he flew like a bulldog at his throat, and proceeded to strangle him. This summary proceeding by no means pleased the dragoman's masters, who released the sufferer, and told his opponent in very clear language, that if he did not at once hold his tongue and sit quiet, they were prepared to eject him from the carriage in a manner more summary than polite. This announcement had a most pacifying effect: the Italian, who was quite unaware of the relations between us and the dragoman, became perfectly livid from rage and fear, but never opened his lips in reply, and for the remainder of the journey sat silent in his corner, looking at us occasionally from under his eye, like a dog that had done wrong, and was suspicious of an impending whipping. I was rather apprehensive that he and some of his friends might play us a trick in the confusion of the fair, but perhaps he had no friends, or that the appearance of a revolver had a deterring effect, for this was our first and last interview.

The train was crowded in all but the first-class carriages to suffocation, and as there are no tunnels or bridges to be passed under *en route*, the tops of the carriages were as closely crammed as the interiors. The first-class carriages, which were beautifully got up, were in a sad state of mutilation; the red silk blinds, very useful with a fierce sun gazing in rudely on the passengers, had been torn away by the ladies of the Pasha's hareem, as we understood, to be converted into handkerchiefs; and the ceilings were all in holes, from the favorite body-guards of the same great man, who generally go in the first class, having beguiled the time by perforating them with their bayonets.

We passed by the palace of the late Viceroy, Abbas, close to the site of the ancient Atribis. It looked sad enough, and deserted, for it was here that wretch met with his deserts, by being murdered by his Memlook slaves. It was reported at the time, that his death was owing to natural causes, but there is now not the least doubt that he was assassinated on coming out of his bath. He was a man of considerable abilities, but his cruelties, and filthy debauchery worthy of Heliogabalus, made him at last perfectly intolerable to those about him; in fact, there is but little doubt that latterly his mind had become affected; he was suspicious of every one around him, and even they who were most in favor one day, could not for an instant feel secure, but that they might be the victims of the next caprice. It was this dread and uncertainty, far more than disgust at his vices, which brought him to an untimely end. He well deserved his fate.

In about a couple of hours we came in sight of Tanta, a large town rising from the middle of an immense plain. It was clear we were approaching the scene of action. By every path along the plain were pouring in turbaned hordes on ass-back, women mounted in boxes were swinging uneasily on camels; and quite regardless of sex and age, in their full blaze of caparison and all magnificence, the men of authority urged their horses through the crowd.

Our first occupation was to pitch our tent, and to obtain a guardian to keep watch and ward, and then we proceeded to see the humors. A gay sight it certainly was: immense herds of magnificent cattle with prodigious horns, droves of asses, patient camels looking around them serenely as they lay and chewed the cud, were gathered together in masses; tents with streamers of gorgeous colors, were spread out in long streets outside the walls; horsemen were galloping madly and for no conceivable purpose, to and fro; processions of santons and dervishes, with banners flying and music scraping one's ears off, were parading round the town; sellers of honey coagulated and twisted round a stick in the form of the caduceus of Mercury, brandished it aloft; apes were performing tricks, and goats climbing on little bits of wood like dice-boxes; and girls with wide trousers and naked feet, and hair encrusted with gold coins, looked gravely at you with bold black undaunted eyes, as they swaggered among the benches of the coffee-shops. Such was the outside of the town.

It was about sunset, when, with the dragoman and the Father of Honey, we made our way with difficulty through the gates. A closely packed incessant crowd occupied every street and byway,—business (and an immense deal is done in all kinds of goods) was nearly over, and in almost every house, the sound of the dharabuka and flute was heard. The coffee-shops were plying an active trade; vendors of roasted doura and pistachio-nuts, which are to the Egyptian as filberts to our wine, were hurrying to the calls of customers hither and thither. Out of each second-floor window were protruded the saucy faces of *ghawazi,* or dancers, inviting all comers to see their performances. The two fairs of Tanta are the harvests of these damsels. It is incredible the sums of money which Egyptians, naturally a most penurious and saving race, lavish on an occasion of this kind. It seems to be their great vent, as far as dissipation goes. I have heard it positively stated that very many of the attendants at these fairs, who would grudge a piastre for ordinary relaxations, think nothing of spending £100 or even £200 in a night's amusement at Tanta. Then it is a night's amusement and no mistake, for the revelling continues from sunset till daybreak; and during that period they are incessantly going from house to house, inspecting with inconceivable delight the performances of the different *coryphées* of celebrity, and making very handsome presents in proportion to their satisfaction. For the life of me I never could see anything in these exhibitions that gave me the slightest pleasure; and I have watched with amazement the ecstasy with which most respectable old Oriental gentlemen have followed every movement. No doubt our enthusiasm at Mario's *Il mio tesoro*, or at Sontag's famous song with Rode's variations, would be equally unintelligible to the Egyptian. After coffee and pipes we prepared to do at Rome as they do at Rome, and certainly went through so good a course of dancing from seven in the evening till four in the morning, that I hope sincerely it may never be my fate to witness a similar *fantasia*. First we paid our respects to Serafia, the great star of the day, who, in the plenitude of her popularity, received us with the *insouciance* of an empress. We there met a gentleman with a superb amber mouth-piece to his pipe, which he sold to one of my friends, on seeing his admiration of it, for about a third of its value, being anxious, as he said, to raise the wind for a merry night of it. The dragoman here got very much excited with *araki* and the dance, and in slow mellifluous accents, as he swayed his body to and fro, kept repeating to himself, "Voila du *b*laisir—Sacré matin—Voila du *b*laisir," to our immense amusement; for he seemed perfectly oblivious of everything except the dance. Serafia's style was slow, dignified, and not without grace, though I greatly preferred the agility of Ayousha, the next lady we visited; but the dragoman thought little of her, his exclamations only being "Sacré matin," without the "*b*laisir." After her we went to the celebrated Kutchook Hanem, whose fame resounded once from Migdol to Syene, the *chère amie* of Abbas Pasha, and whose reputation has been spread by Curtis in his *Nile Notes* through the world, old and new, wherever his charming work is read. Poor Kutchook, a merry laughter-loving dame, had become a thought lusty, but as she warmed to her work, we could well understand how greatly she had once excelled in this peculiar learning of the Egyptians. Thence we went to various other establishments of greater or less degree, Egyptian, Syrian, and Greek, and in one of the last-mentioned *salles de danse*, got into a quarrel which might have been unpleasant. I may prémise that it is the custom, where a dancer has performed her part, for her to advance and sit, until the entertainment recommences, on the knee of the person towards whom she takes most fancy; this is considered a compliment, and the party thus greeted is generally bound to give a slight present in return. The present is made in rather an original manner, by wetting one or more small gold pieces with the tongue, and fixing them on the forehead and cheeks of the young lady. That is true courtesy, and gets you the name of being a thorough gentleman. As the coins are, some of them, not more than about the value of a shilling, it is not expensive to pay the compliment, and I had provided myself with a pound's worth of these little golden fish-scales, but my gallantry was nipped in the bud by some visitor stealing them out of my room at Cairo. I might, however, have followed the example of a little fat Turk, who, by dint of extraordinarily adhesive saliva, contrived to stick five-franc pieces on the forehead and each cheek of a dancer he much admired. To return, however, to the fracas. One of my friends had paid some such compliment to a very pretty little Greek dancing girl, when an Egyptian officer in a marked manner threw himself on the divan where we were sitting, evidently with a view to annoy us; we returned the compliment by pushing him aside with just as little ceremony, and he made no comment on the proceeding except some observation to a brother officer in Turkish, which we did not understand. They then went, as we supposed, from the house. Shortly afterwards, the Vicomte de D——, who sat next me, went out into the anteroom for some purpose; we heard a scuffle, and then a call for assistance. On running out I found that he had been assailed by the officer who had originally offended, while the other stood on the stairs to give assistance. As they were both armed with sabres, it looked rather serious; but Monsieur de D. very quickly disposed of his antagonist, and sent him flying down the stairs most precipitately, while the drunken dragoman roared out from the landing that he knew him well, and that the foreigners would bring him before the Viceroy on the morrow; and then he asked them both how they fancied a pilgrimage to the Soudan and Fazogl, "Sacré matin!" This terrible threat was, without doubt, most potent for good, for our assailants disappeared. The question was, however, now to be discussed as to the best way of getting out of the house, for we had a strong suspicion we were waited for outside, and, as the revolver was unloaded, our chance would have been a poor one. We could not help laughing at being in the predicament of the chickens in the French picture, who are being allured out of their stronghold by a show of oats and the endearing call of "petits," "petits," while a soldier stands on each side with a drawn sword ready to cut down the first straggler. In this emergency I proposed to send forth, first the Father of Honey with the pipe-sticks to be sacrificed, as, if the early brunt of the action fell on a Mahommedan, we should more easily escape. However, there was no obstruction whatever to our exit: the threat of the fevers and black death of Fazogl and the Soudan was quite enough. Our opponents had vanished never to reappear. It was now about four o'clock A.M.; our dragoman had imbibed additional drunkenness after the late affray, and was perfectly useless either as a local guide, or as interpreter. So, although the sport was raging as briskly as ever, we departed to our tent, where the fleas were gathered together in expectation, and feasted on us without hindrance till the day broke.

Such was the last adventure worth recording; for the time had now arrived when we must be homeward bound; the Austrian Lloyd's excellent steamer the *Bombay* was in the harbor of Alexandria, and on the 20th of April, 1856, we rode out of the gate of Cairo with more sincere regret than I ever before experienced at change of quarters. On the 22nd we were on board, on our way to Austrian *espionage* and extortion, by the Lover's Leap of Leucadia and the Gardens of Alcinous.

So now farewell to pylon, obelisk, and colonnade—dromos of sphinxes, pyramid, minaret, and mosque, gaily painted pigeon-towers, and square mud houses of Fellâhs; farewell to the waving palms and carmine-tinted hills; farewell to sailors of Assouan and Berberi Reis; to blue-shirted peasants and green-turbaned Shereefs; to women walking so stately in file from Nile's banks with pitchers on their heads; to herds of lowing buffaloes and flocks of brown and brindled sheep and goats, and processions of solemn camels, and ambling asses with grave riders pipe in hand; farewell to kites floating and whistling in the creamy air over head among the grand acacias, and to doves cooing in every mimosa bush. Farewell to Cairo, ever bright and gay, and to Alexandria and its glare. Farewell to the great red setting sun of Africa.

Such were our last thoughts as we sped by the Headland of Figs.

TUNIS

IN 1857 AND 1858.

TUNIS

In 1857 and 1858.

On the 30th November, 1857, the *Hermus*, bound for Algeria and Tunis, started from the Joliette of Marseilles, taking us in it; its owners, the Messageries Imperiales, took us also in, by promising us a passage of four days and a half to the latter place, together with "nourishment" *en route*. After an excellent passage, with the worst possible set of companions, we reached Stora, the port of Philippeville, in about thirty-six hours, and were informed on getting up that the steamer remained three days in the roads, during which time we might, or rather, must go to Philippeville, and there nourish and amuse ourselves as best we might. In vain we protested at being turned out breakfastless: the command had been given, and there was no gainsaying it. After about an hour's pull, or, more properly speaking, push, we put up at the Hotel des Colonies, in the new and rather pretty town of Philippeville. Besides being well and cheaply nourished during our stay, we had the additional gratification of our grievances to discuss, and these, with walks and drives and a communicative and civil host, enabled us to pass the time pleasantly enough.

Philippeville is exclusively a French town, and is the outlet for the produce of the rich and latest conquered province of Constantine. It is just on the verge of Kabylia, in fact, the border line runs down to Stora. As there had been some hard fighting lately in the neighbourhood between the Kabyles and the French, no one is allowed as yet to enter the mountainous and woody country of these tribes, owing to its unsettled state; but we understand that for hunting it is unrivalled: lions, leopards, and wild boars, composing a very respectable *chasse* for a good eye and a stout heart. This part of Algeria is the most frequented by lions, and they have been seen frequently on the high road between Philippeville and Constantine. With the exception, however, of M. Jules Gerard, who has published his very wonderful feats, I have not heard of any other bold Frenchman who has ventured to encounter these awkward opponents; for it is a desperate hand-to-hand fight, no quarter given on either side; you meet your antagonist on foot, you will look him full in the face; he will stand in the path and bar your way through his domains, like a great unconquered king that he is, and if your hand tremble with anxiety, or your cap fail you, then indeed—then—may the Lord have mercy on your soul. Such, at least, is the language of our French informants, but I am bound to say I do not believe a word of it. From what I have since heard, the lion is far more anxious to avoid than to commence a contest, though when wounded he defends himself desperately, and when attacked by the Arabs he generally puts *hors de combat* more than one of his assailants. The fact of his being of a roaming disposition induces them to submit to his depredations, preferring as they do the visits, which generally occur every other night, and the loss of sundry cattle, to an encounter in which some of their tribe are generally killed. They count on his not remaining more than a fortnight in their neighbourhood, and they hope their neighbour's cow or camel may be the object of his selection. We saw at Philippeville, on our return, the skin of a magnificent lion which had only shortly before been shot. He was killed by a young Arab, who was perched in a tree waiting for wild boars. The lion was apparently on the same quest. He passed under the tree, was shot through the heart by the boy, and fell dead at once. The whole district is peculiarly fitted for the habitation of wild beasts: the coast abrupt, the country hilly, and hill after hill covered with cork-trees, myrtles, and every kind of impenetrable jungle spreading far into the interior. The rich Lybian corn garners are now covered with brushwood; the water-courses and cisterns, evidences of the immense utilitarianism of Rome, are now in ruins and choked up; and civilization has again to begin her work in the former granary of the world. And yet there is a wonderful opening for capital and energy: fine climate, plains of unrivalled fertility, hills pre-eminently fitted for the olive and the mulberry and the vine, heat sufficient almost to ripen the products of the tropics, yet without the moist sultriness that draws up into stalk the hardy vegetables of Europe. When I say fine climate, I must make the reservation of observing that considerable sickness does at times prevail in certain localities, but only such as is ordinarily the case in newly settled countries, arising from the miasma of an undrained, uncleared soil.

In spite, however, of the lessons which French journalists have given us in the art of governing and colonizing India, it seems they have hardly brought it to perfection in a territory not thirty-six hours' distance from their shores. Although Algeria has now been conquered more than twenty years, there are as yet, in spite of the various inducements offered to immigrants, not more than 155,000 Europeans spread over this vast tract. It is still essentially a military government, and viewed as a military possession; and, as a French fellow-traveller remarked, the sabre and commerce are incompatible associates. The French newspapers, it is true, give the most flourishing accounts of the advance and prosperity of the colony; but let any traveller converse with persons who are living in Algeria, and who are neither civil nor military *employés*, and he will soon ascertain that, if we are to seek a model for our future government of India, it will at all events not be found in the French African possessions. Philippeville, as I said before, is prettily situated on the slope of the hills round the Gulf of Stora; there is a charming Corniche road through myrtles and evergreens of about two miles to Stora, the port of the town, and some pretty drives in the environs. We hired a carriage, and drove to the colonies of Vallée and Damrémont, drank some wine the produce of the former place, and walked round it to look at the gardens. The settlers complain of sickness, the result of insufficient drainage, and of great uncertainty in their crops from drought, or from the incursions of locusts. At Damrémont there were evidences, in the shattered tumble-down appearances of several of the buildings not yet restored, of another and very formidable enemy, namely, an earthquake, which last year extended with much severity over a considerable portion of the eastern littoral of Algeria. Roman remains have been found in abundance here, as almost everywhere in north-east Africa. There is a fine quarry of white marble about eighteen miles off in the hills; and the statue of a Roman emperor of that material, dug up in the environs, adorns the "Place" in front of the church of Philippeville; and shattered columns of marble and of stone are to be seen lying about near the port and in the streets.

On the 3rd of November we again steamed forth, passed the Cap de Fer, and about eleven o'clock at night the two remarkable rocks, called the Due Fratelli, which start abruptly from the sea to a height of about 250 feet at some distance from the main land. In the morning we cast anchor for a few hours before the pretty little town of Bona, the ancient Hippo, famed for its great bishop, Saint Augustine, whose tomb is still to be seen in the environs. We had, however, no time to land on this occasion, but reserved our visit for our return, when the steamer remains a whole day.

Early the next morning we found ourselves in the bay of Tunis, and the first look-out was extremely beautiful. On the left, as we faced the town, was a fine range of serrated mountains—in front, Tunis with its white walls running up the gentle slope of a hill, and apparently of great extent—behind the town, at the distance of about twenty-five miles, the bold mountain of Zowan, 4000 feet high, looked down on the smaller ranges; while to the right extended a plain, thickly studded with olive-trees, to Marsa, where the bright white residences of consuls and men of authority gleamed gaily from among gardens, and on the shore two immense red palaces showed us the spot where the ruins of Carthage commenced. Carrying the eye still further back, a white cupola on a hill, in the midst of the site of Carthage, was shown us as the spot where St. Louis of France died in his ill-fated expedition for the honor of Christendom against false Mahound; and still further back was the cheerful white village of Sidi Bou Said, where the religious portion of the Moorish community take refuge from the contaminating presence of the Christian invasion, which in the shape of Maltese, Italians, Greeks, &c., seems interpenetrating the whole of Tunis, even those parts originally strictly forbidden to any but true believers.

The Goelette where we disembarked is about seven miles from Tunis, so we left our servant to get the luggage as best he might through the two custom-houses; for the Bey, to make assurance doubly sure, has two of these nuisances, one at the Goelette, the other at Tunis, to check each other; and yet he is more openly defrauded by smugglers than any potentate I know of.

The Goelette and another fort opposite it, defend the water access to the town, which is approached by a very shallow lagune of considerable extent; the fortifications look smart enough as you come near to them, but, like every thing in the East, it is all makebelief: if you turn away from the main entrance, and that part which is in view, the remainder of the defences will be found to consist of an old crenelated wall, which hardly seems to require the exertions of a twelve-pounder to bring it down about the ears of those it pretends to defend. However, it professes to keep out rogues and robbers, which, considering the number within the town, would appear to be rather a work of supererogation.

Being anxious to avoid custom-house unpleasantnesses, we took a carriage and drove round to Marsa, to the country dwelling of Mr. Wood, our consul-general. Our way lay over a wide plain, evidently of great fertility, but which was now bare, and seemed as if it had been carefully top-dressed with good-sized stones; it was not exactly the style of farming we should have encouraged at home, but they say, and I believe with truth, that the stones preserve the moisture for the roots of the crops. Our way then led through the ruins of the immense aqueducts which in olden times supplied water from the hill springs, some thirty miles off, to the capacious cisterns of Carthage, of which more anon. We then passed through groves of venerable olive-trees, between fences of huge prickly pears, and having completed our business with our representative, returned to Tunis by a drive of about eight miles through olives and over the same flat plains, unbroken save by the black tents of Bedoueen shepherds.

On entering Tunis we were disagreeably surprised by a series of the most villanous odors proceeding from open drains, which, from the number of people sitting in their vicinity, seemed rather to gratify than to offend their sense of smell. To our great astonishment, hordes of filthy lean pigs were rioting in this vile compost, under the very eyes and in actual contact with the Mahommedan passers-by. As Tunis has such a bad reputation in Europe for the fanaticism of its inhabitants, this latitude seemed strange; but, in the first place, there is really but little overt fanaticism, in the town at all events; and in the second, the immense number of European settlers, 20,000, it is supposed, in a population of about 170,000, has resulted in bearing down opposition. If we had any pork-eating tendencies, the sight of these wallowing brutes effectually cured them, and convinced us of the extreme good sense and good taste of the Prophet in proclaiming the pig to be an abomination—the unclean beast *par excellence*. We then passed through a suburb, which gave one the idea that if Dublin is the most car-driving city in the world, certainly Tunis is the most carriage-driving, for it was one line of carriages, the property of Maltese and Italians, who seem to transact a thriving trade, from the number of fat Moors we subsequently saw airing themselves in all sorts of conveyances.

After passing another gate, the threshold of which is formed of a fine white marble column, with an aperture cut in it on each side to let wheels pass over, we found ourselves in what is called the Grande Place of Tunis, which is about the dimensions of a moderately sized court-yard, with a few large houses and a guard-room round about it. We made our way to the Hotel de Provence through some filthy narrow streets, with many forebodings from the uncleanliness around, but were agreeably surprised at being shown into a large clean room, with two smaller rooms leading out of it, and a comfortable divan, for our quarters. M. Francois, the landlord, who had been cook to the late Bey, soon set us to rights on the score of good living by a capital breakfast, and we waited with impatience the arrival of our luggage, which had been landed some five hours previously.

After a long delay it arrived at length, and we found our servant in a state of unspeakable indignation at the treatment our effects had received at the custom-house. Every little package had been opened, as it appears, not the least from a desire to hunt for contraband articles, for they allowed our powder and cigars, which are strictly prohibited, to pass unnoticed—but to satisfy their childish curiosity. They examined the brushes, opened the knife-blades to feel their edges, looked through the opera-glasses, fingered the powder-horns, smelt the pomatum, screwed and unscrewed our wooden bottle-cases, that we were obliged to send them to a vice to get them eventually reopened; inspected the trousers, took views of expanded shirts; in short, for two mortal hours, diverted themselves by putting every thing into a state of confusion, and then, having pocketed a heavy *buckshish*, dismissed them to their own and the bystanders' full satisfaction. It certainly was fortunate for us that we were not there, or probably we should not have been very scrupulous in our language, and might in consequence have had additional trouble.

The next day we devoted to a visit to Mr. Davis, a Protestant clergyman who is employed by our Government in making researches on the site of ancient Carthage. Hitherto, modern excavators have had but little success in their enterprise; partly from ignorance of the proper spot to conduct their operations, but chiefly from the fact that Carthage has been completely gutted of its marbles and remains during the middle ages, to furnish ornaments for the churches of Italy. Edrisi, an Arabian writer of the twelfth century, mentions that there was a regular traffic at that period in marbles, and that there was constant intercourse between Africa and Italy by vessels carrying away the remains of the old town.

Mr. Davis, however, who is most enthusiastic in his enterprise, has been eminently successful. He has thoroughly studied the locality, and from his knowledge of the ways of the people and their language, has had facilities for working beyond others. He has already sent to the British Museum a series of Phœnician inscriptions, chiefly sepulchral dedications, and also some noble mosaics, the finest by far in that collection, if not the finest in the world. There are two heads in mosaic of large size, which cannot be surpassed in spirit and execution.

We were most courteously received by him, and shown over the site of what once was the rival of the mistress of the world. But the tide of ruin has so completely swept over Carthage, that by conjecture alone can we now trace the limits of that great city. Enormous cisterns, with vaulted roofs, still remain in tolerable preservation, some by the sea-side running parallel to each other, and others more inland, which now furnish comfortable habitations to a tribe of Troglodyte Arabs. On the foundations of what was in all probability the temple of Æsculapius, is now built a Moorish fort mounting one cannon, and garrisoned by two soldiers, one of whom is an excavator for Mr. Davis. The traces of steps to the sea from this temple, which now nearly overhangs the water, are still visible, and at its base the wave was rippling over shattered columns, while fragments of masonry emerging from the water show that the sea has encroached considerably on its ancient limits. The lucubrations of some *learned* visitors to Carthage, as to the intention of the huge vaulted cisterns, are rather amusing. Not being informed of the want of water in this locality, and closing their eyes to the remains of the gigantic aqueduct leading to the very buildings themselves, and having heard of Hannibal's array of elephants, they have very complacently set down these buildings as the stables for these quadrupeds, without ever considering the impossibility of getting them either out of them or into them.

With the exception of the structures above mentioned, and a few vaulted arches on the side of the hill, not a vestige remains of the old city, but the innumerable fragments of marbles of all sorts—*giallo, rosso, verde,* white, black, porphyry, serpentine—and bits of mosaic, which are met with all over the surface, prove the wealth and luxury of its inhabitants during the later days of the empire, when Carthage was again one of the greatest cities of Roman dominion. After a walk over the cisterns by the seaside, Mr. Davis took us to see his excavations. We had come at a fortunate time, as he had just laid open a series of chambers paved with the most beautiful mosaic.

What Aubusson and Turkey carpets are to our Northern dwellings, the mosaic pavement in the warmer climates of the South was to the ancients; on it was lavished the taste and caprice of the proprietor. The "pavimentum superbum," as Horace calls it—the "proud pavement," was one of the tests of the wealth and luxury of the day; and when we look into one of these mosaics, and perceive the taste, care, and labor, which were expended on these works of art, it is a matter of congratulation that we shall shortly have some of them transferred to our country in a condition as perfect as when they originally were laid down. We shall then be able really to estimate the value of the epithet "proud" pavement. I wish, however, I could add, that all that have lately been found will be sent over as complete as when they were cleared from their covering of eight or ten feet of earth. Unfortunately, some of them have already experienced the ravages of spoliation; but not at the hands of ignorant Arab, or covetous Bey, or even of Prussian Lepsius, but of English officers—officers of Lord Lyon's fleet, who, armed with pickaxes, and with the view of having some reminiscences of old Carthage, commenced breaking up these beautiful works of art, in spite of the remonstrances of the overseer. The arrival of Mr. Davis alone spared them from complete destruction; as it is, they are in parts hopelessly and irretrievably injured. This act of Vandalism is perfectly inexcusable, as the value of the mosaic depends entirely on the completeness of the pattern. The colors are so insensibly and tastefully blended, that unless a large portion could be taken up complete, it would be useless, and not convey any idea whatsoever. Yet such was the notion on the part of these gallant officers, of carrying away some pleasant recollections of Carthage.

The Pompeian House at the Crystal Palace will have indoctrinated the British public as to the formation of Roman dwellings; the smallness of the bedrooms, which we should consider conducive to much stuffiness, is that which perhaps most strikes the observer for the first time. The chambers in these African houses are constructed with quite as little regard to space; and modern taste would, doubtless, prefer a less "proud" pavement, and a little more breathing room. However, "de gustibus non est disputandum,"—here are the mosaics, most elaborate and tasteful as mere works of art, apart from all antiquarian interest; and the only question is the transfer of them to England. This is no slight difficulty, for so admirable is the old cement in which they are imbedded, that the raising of them is a work requiring the greatest care and personal superintendence on the part of Mr. Davis.

Once raised, the rest of the task is easy. The sea is close at hand, and Lord Clarendon has, in the most praiseworthy manner, given every encouragement to Mr. Davis, and has ordered a ship-of-war occasionally to visit Tunis, in order to transport to London the produce of his labor. And, indeed, Mr. Davis much requires such encouragement, for the success of the investigations seems to have excited the jealousy of the representatives of other nations. By misrepresenting the object of such searches, nothing is more easy than to rouse the cupidity of the native rulers. In fact, urged by insinuations that Mr. Davis was depriving his country, or rather himself, of valuables worth thousands of piastres, the Bey himself in person (a good easy man in general), on one occasion gave orders for the suspension of the works. Mr. Davis had, however, been an old friend and travelling companion of his Highness, when he was Bey of the Camp, and is, besides, on terms of intimacy and friendship with many of the high officials—so much so, that his own representations, without involving our Consul-General in any unpleasant discussions, at once obtained a reversal of the order, and since then every encouragement has been given by the local authorities to his enterprise.

As for the people themselves, they seem hearty, and anxious to be employed—they are docile and well behaved. From a long residence in the country, Mr. Davis is up to their various little tricks; and Mrs. Davis officiates as the lady Tabib, or doctor of the Arab villagers, close to whom she dwells: the inhabitants of the cisterns before mentioned.

Besides the more elaborate mosaics to which I have referred, Mr. Davis has laid bare a chamber of large dimensions, with a pavement of coarser materials; and it has struck me that it would be advisable that it also should be removed and transferred to Europe, to form the flooring of a large room in the British Museum, amid which the mosaics of smaller size might be placed.

With regard to these mosaics, some difference of opinion exists whether they are of Phœnician or of Roman construction. I do not entertain any doubt whatever of their Roman origin. In the first place, mosaics in general were the exclusive product of Roman taste; wherever Roman civilization was introduced, the mosaic pavement followed. I am not aware that the Greeks adopted this ornament for their dwellings. In the next place, the strong resemblance of these mosaics to those of Naples, prove an affinity, both of time, taste, and nationality, which renders it difficult to assign them to a people of a different age, and of a different origin—a people dissimilar in religion, language, and pursuits. I have not a doubt but that these works of art were constructed at the period when, under the Roman empire, Carthage again revived and became a great city. It is true that differences exist in some of the patterns from the mosaics hitherto found: they have represented on them the palm-tree, and another plant to which it is difficult to assign a name—possibly the celebrated silphium; but these differences arise from the difference of locality, from the natural objects of one country being before the artist, which were not to be seen in the other. What is more natural, for instance, than that in Africa the graceful lithe palm, ever a grateful sight to the eyes, should be chosen as one of the objects of representation? How unlikely that it should be so in Italy! Again, we have in the Museum the mosaic of a girl dancing in a costume perfectly oriental; but that is no proof, nor even indication, of Phœnician origin. The dancing girl was one of the attractions of Roman festivity, and she is naturally represented in the costume of the country of which she was a native. The very fact of a dancing girl being represented at all, confirms the impression of Roman design, she being the usual accessary to the Roman feast, just as the same designs of fish, both at Pompeii and at Carthage, denote the site of the dining-room.

If mosaic pavements were the fashion in England, it is probable they would represent objects of general acquaintance—flowers, animals, &c.; but let the same taste be introduced into Anglo-Indian society in Hindostan, and the objects in that case would be borrowed from the products of the East.

Finally, however, if any doubt remains, which does not in my mind, the position of these mosaics convince me they cannot be of Phœnician origin. They are all found about eight or ten feet below the surface, one of the finest so close to it, that it is a marvel the plough has not ere this destroyed every vestige of it. We know that old Punic Carthage was utterly destroyed, and razed to the ground, and a new city built upon it. We must also take into consideration the rapidity with which soil accumulates over ruins. Can one, therefore, imagine for a moment that the Romans, in building their new city, should have built it over these remains, which must, at the time it was being reared, have been uprooted by the foundation of every new house; for that which is now eight feet below the overlying rubbish, must have then been close to the surface? And last of all, if it be said, perhaps these were old Phœnician remains, which survived the destruction of the Punic city, and which were subsequently adopted by the later inhabitants, the answer to that is, that in the sacking of the old city it is not likely that the victorious devastators should have left works of such high art as those in the British Museum, untouched and unmolested: not to mention the utter improbability of the Carthaginians having in use, the same objects of luxury, of almost identical patterns, with those of the later Romans. Besides, there are still remaining some *ex-voto* Phœnician dedications, which at first sight can be distinguished from similar Roman remains. They are quite dissimilar and of the rudest execution, evincing neither taste nor correctness—in short, perfectly uncouth. We have, therefore, only one argument in favor of the Phœnician origin of these mosaics, viz., the arrow-heads, and palm-trees, the so-called silphium plant, and the oriental costume of the dancing girl; while every other resemblance and probability is in favor of the Imperial era. Indeed, I should not have entered into this discussion at all, but that some of my Tunisian friends were bent on affixing a Punic origin to these remains.

Passing from Mr. Davis' excavations, we mounted the hill where the White Chapel, built by Louis Philippe in 1845, in honor of St. Louis, gleams so brightly from afar. It is enclosed by a wall, and garden nicely kept, and commands a fine view of the adjacent country. A small flash of water, now hardly large enough to hold two or three gunboats, was the celebrated Cothon, the harbour of that mercantile nation to which it pleases French writers to liken England: the allusion being, in their view, a peculiarly happy one, as bringing home to the mind the perfidy of Albion, as well as being the prognostication of the ruthless triumph of the Imperial Eagle over a commercial and faithless race.

From this eminence we were enabled to see various spots of more than ordinary interest. It is the highest ground in that great city, which at the commencement of the third Punic war, was 23 miles in circumference, and counted 700,000 souls for its inhabitants. Down below, according to the old legend, the horse's head was dug up by its founder, portending its future warlike greatness; here Æneas came upon the busy throng of Tyrians erecting their future citadel for Dido, the grand-daughter of Jezebel; and from here the smoke of her funeral pyre might be seen ascending, as the perfidious Trojan (who however, unfortunately for the correctness of this early love story, lived two hundred years before the woman he betrayed) steered northwards with his flying galleys. From here the astonished citizens counted the watch-fires of that great Sicilian captain, Agathokles, on some eminence visible both from Carthage and Hadrumetum. And from here too, on the same occasion, might have been seen other and more baleful fires lighting up the Temple of Saturn. The Carthaginians, terrified by the successes of Agathokles, imputed their misfortunes to their neglect of the gods. They made a complete atonement by selecting two hundred children from the most illustrious families in Carthage, and offering them up to Kronus, or Saturn, at a great public sacrifice; besides which, three hundred parents, finding themselves denounced for similar omissions in the past, displayed their repentance by voluntarily immolating their own children for the public safety. The statue of Kronus —placed with outstretched hands to receive the victim tendered to him, with fire immediately underneath—was fed on that solemnity, certainly with two hundred, probably with five hundred, living children. By this monstrous holocaust, the full religious duties being discharged and forgiveness obtained from the god, the mental distress of the Carthaginians was healed. Such is Mr. Grote's account of this fearful propitiation.

At its foot may have passed the procession reconducting Regulus to his prison. To the left, towards the north-east, rose the Temple of Æsculapius, so desperately defended in the last assault, from which the gallant wife of Amilcar reviled her bloodthirsty and traitorous husband. To the right, by the high ground of Gemart, were the two harbours: one from which its hardy mariners issued in quest of commerce to the unknown lands beyond the

Pillars of Hercules, to the gold-bearing regions of Western Africa, and the tin-bearing regions of Britain, the land of murk and darkness; the other, from which went forth the war-galleys to contest the supremacy of the world with Rome. On this low swampy ground were reared the fortifications we read of, each tower with its own gate leading into the city, protecting the spacious storehouses in which were contained the armaments of the fleet, and round which were magnificent galleries supported by pillars.

It was, perhaps, on this very spot, overlooking the smoking ruins of the captured city, that the conqueror, Scipio, in the flush of triumph, pronounced those prophetic and saddest lines—

> *ἔσσεται ἦμαρ ὅτὰν ποτ' ὀλώλῃ Ἴλιος ἱρὴ*
> *καὶ Πρίαμος καὶ λᾶος εὐμμελίω Πριάμοιο·—*

> And the day, who knows, but it may come, when Ilion's sacred wall,
> And Priam of the ashen spear, and Priam's race shall fall—

on the day when his victory left Rome without a rival; and, latest of all, here was consigned to his last resting-place the brave, the pious, the unfortunate St. Louis.

The changes that have taken place on this coast by the retirement of the sea and by alluvial deposits, oblige us to consult with great care the ancient authorities, before we presume to determine any of the most remarkable spots connected with Carthage.

The situation of the port, to which I before alluded as being in the neighborhood of Gemart, and on which much of the rest of the topography depends, can only be gathered from the observations of ancient writers. Shaw has pointed out that we must look for it, not in the Gulf of Tunis, but to the westward of Carthage; and it is pretty clear, from a consideration of the ground, that it may be sought for among the gardens of Marsa. There is no doubt but that it lay to the north-west of the city, and that from it the galleys could at once put out into open sea. The scene of Scipio's operations is now dry ground, and the same fate has attended the port of Utica, which is now seven miles from the sea.

After a well-spent day we dined with Mr. Davis, and were astonished by the enormous dimensions of Tunisian prawns, and Tunisian radishes. The former, *gambri* by name, were of such a size, that I begged of him to send a few to the British Museum, they being certainly, though not objects of *vertu*, quite as curious as the marbles in their way. I can conceive no greater delight than that with which M. Pascal would receive "ces nobles étrangers" at his Café Philippe, preliminary to their conversion into a *bisque*.

On the 9th we proceeded on our first shooting expedition to Bizerta, which is about thirty-five miles to the north-west of Tunis. The first part of our way, after passing the well-wooded Marsa, where a dear old cock robin sat on a bough and piped good morning to us, lay over immense open plains, apparently of wondrous fertility, but, except in patches here and there, abandoned to the Bedoueens and their flocks. The weather had been fine, and as we were obliged to go in a carriage, or rather in two, being unable to obtain riding-horses, we got along pleasantly enough. The soil was dry, and the carriages rolled easily over it. On nearing the small town of Allia, our way, for I cannot call it road, passed over the first range of hills we met with, and dreadful were the joltings and anticipations of upsets, in consequence. We got safely, however, over the ridge, and descended again into another plain, covered with prickly plants, not exactly gorse, but which felt extremely like it to our legs when we subsequently shot over it. From thence we skirted the great salt-water lake of Bizerta, by a Roman causeway, passed through the little town of Bou Shater, the ancient Utica, which witnessed the last hours of Cato; and then, plunging through a morass, entered Bizerta by the Roman bridge, which looks and feels as if it had never known repair since Roman days. On entering the town, we proudly produced our *amr*, or order from the Bey, which we fondly imagined was to create a great sensation, and bring the Governor with a profusion of civilities into our presence. Wishing to give the good man time to make a suitable appearance, we walked to the port and out on the Roman pier; the brisk cool breeze was playing on us, and the waves dashing over the old masonry, which is gradually sharing the fate of every other monument of ancient industry. There we lingered till we imagined that everything was ready for our reception. But to our dismay, there was no sleeve-embroidered *cavass* to conduct us to the palace; no salams, nor salutations, nor greetings in the market-place, for as it turned out, apparently from some mistake, the order, instead of procuring, as is the wont, good entertainment for man and beast, was nothing more than a permit to shoot, which was quite unnecessary, and a recommendation to see to our safety, whereas we were well able to protect ourselves. In general the *amr* of the Bey produces too much civility, and causes too much expense to the parties to whom it is directed, to be agreeable even to the recipients of it. Everything is then to be supplied gratis—food, forage, and dwelling; and the result is, that so burdensome is the imposition, that generally the natives take care, if the visitor be a sportsman, to bring him in a direction where no game can be found, in order to get rid of his unwelcome presence. We wished only for a room, but even that was not in the order, therefore, in our extremity, we had to betake ourselves to Mr. Spezzichino, the Bizertan Anacharsis Clootz, or representative of the whole human race, so many consular agencies does he combine. He placed his house and everything very kindly at our disposal, but seeing him very closely packed, we declined his hospitality, and availed ourselves of that of a Jew, who possessed three rooms in an adjacent house. Hardly had we settled ourselves in our new lodging, when the most fearful row broke forth. I should have mentioned, that our chamber looked out on a kind of terrace, around which other rooms opened. A second Israelite occupied the apartment opposite, and inflamed with dread lest we should be disposed to pay too particular attention to his wife, he assailed our host with very violent invectives, denied his right to admit strangers, and in short created such an uproar, that we were obliged to proclaim that we were English, a nation of singular continence, never looking even out of the corners of the eye at any female, married or single; and that besides, what we saw of his wife by no means suited our taste. The Jewesses, I must premise, all go unveiled, and very comely dames they are, these dusky Miriams and Rebeccas, and by no means so shy of strangers as to take part with their husbands in disturbances of this description. The jealous man was, nevertheless, not appeased, but continued his vociferations, and how it was to end except by kicking him out of his own house, it was difficult to imagine, when, to our delight, a police-officer hearing the wordy war entered on the arena, brought the disputants straight before the judge, who decided as to the perfect legality of our host in his admission of strangers, and effectually cooled the recalcitrant Israelite's ardor by a promise of sundry days' imprisonment on the morrow, which promise we may be assured was fulfilled to the letter, unless the sight of piastres may have induced him to take a more lenient view of the proceedings.

M. Shallum, our Jewish host, styled invariably "Questo Qui" by our interpreter, made us pretty comfortable; and a glass of tea, boiled in the tin case which held my shirt-collars, set all to rights. But then, when the night came on, the mosquitoes, which seemed to have left Tunis *en masse* for a sea-bathing excursion to Bizerta, came down on us in clouds; and what with their buzzing and stinging, and the snoring and scratching of Questo Qui and two servants, right glad were we when the first light told us it was time to be off to the *chasse*.

We were accompanied by a hunter of great renown, and particular sanctity: one of a family of four brothers, all Marabouts, or holy men, who, for religious reasons, neither smoked nor drank coffee, but took snuff instead. Si Morad invited us to his village, situated in the hills, some twelve miles from Bizerta, and promised us even within its holy precincts a warm greeting. On arriving amid some rough ground, covered with prickly bushes, about four miles from Bizerta, we commenced our *chasse*, and had very pretty shooting at the red-legged Barbary partridge for some time. We found the reputation of our friend Si Morad, for once in a way, to be founded on fact, for he shot most creditably with an old flint-lock piece, about two yards in length. We were indulging in hopes of a most creditable day's sport; for although my dog, from extreme good living on board ship, had shut up early, still there were plenty of birds to be found; but the ominous rumbling of thunder all around made our conductor, Si Morad, strongly urge us to make the best way we could to his village. We just arrived in time, for down came the rain in torrents, and for seven mortal hours the thunder was rolling about the hills around us.

The village of Zaowa Daouda, of which our host and his brothers were the chiefs, was evidently a town of Roman construction; the remains of the old buildings were all around, and broken columns were built into and formed the threshold of the Arab dwellings. Our reception-room was apparently an old Christian church, to judge by its appearance; the low-vaulted roof, and pillars supporting arches, dividing the different portions of the church, showed its ecclesiastical intention; but in the present instance it seemed to be used as a carpenter's shop, a shed for agricultural implements, a store for grain, and a hen-house. The wind rushed through its holes and crannies most ominously, but our good hosts tried to do the best they could, by spreading mats and cushions for us in the corner, and by bringing us in eventually a dish of excellent *coscousou* and partridge, some macaroni, and a small pomatum-pot full of honey, of a highly perfumed but rather pleasant taste. *Coscousou* is a simple dish, composed of boiled grains of polenta, about the size of millet-seed, occasionally flavored with onions and capsicums; and it is eaten in a simple manner, by dipping your hand into the wooden bowl and compressing all that it takes up into a ball, which you transfer to your mouth, with a bite *en passant* at any bit of meat you can lay hold of, to give the morsel additional zest.

In course of time, after a long discourse on Egypt and Mecca, where one of our host's brothers had been as a pilgrim, the house was cleared for bed-doings, and then commenced a series of persecutions to which the mosquitoes and snorings of Questo Qui were, in comparison, pleasure. Fleas and bugs, which had congregated in the mats, came forth and revelled on us; the hens endeavored to get in, and were repulsed only by repeated peltings; dogs also scratched and pushed, either to make acquaintance with our dog Trim, or to get repossession of their accustomed kennel; rats squeaked above and around, and raced about us; while some horrid animals, which the heated imagination pictured as scorpions, kept rustling beneath the mats, just in the region of our heads. If the truth were ever to transpire, after all, I believe the rustlers were only a family of feeble young orphan mice, for the movements were too slow to indicate the presence of an active father and mother. At last a *fraças* occurred which completely upset all hopes of sleep, and left us scratching ourselves in wide-awakeness till morning: our dog came into collision with a cat, which, intent on larceny either of partridge or milk, had made its way into our circle through some hole or cranny. It paid the penalty of its crime. The Draconian code was strictly enforced by Trim; but the yells of the cat and the scurry of the pursuit completed that which the bugs and fleas and rats were well able to accomplish alone—namely, the total banishment of sleep. So, up with the lark and off to our shooting, which again promised well, as we were getting in both to partridges and quails; but again the sky foretold the coming storm, and we were forced to give up, just as before, in the middle of the day, and crowd all sail for Bizerta.

The next morning we started for Allia; had some fair shooting at partridges in the brushwood *en route;* and were most agreeably disappointed, after climbing through a dilapidated series of huts and streets excavated by winter torrents, to find an extremely clean little room, with mattresses and cushions around three parts of it, intended for our reception. There was a small terrace in front, where we cooked, and by locking the outside door were able to keep out all interlopers, and so had the place entirely to ourselves. Our host was the Shekh of the village, a most hospitable and courteous old gentleman. The fleas and mosquitoes had departed, and all went well. On closing our habitation for the night, we sent word to some hunters of experience that it was our intention to rout up the wild boars in the morning, and they promised to have everything ready.

A motley assemblage of curs of all sorts greeted our arrival the next day at the foot of the hill, and the party was swelled to a large concourse by a gathering of worthies armed with all sorts of weapons, from portentously long guns, blunderbusses, rusty old pistols, down to simple axes. The scene of the *chasse* was close at hand, amid thick patches of myrtle and evergreens, which seemed impervious to all human beaters. However, what with curs and shoutings of all sorts, the game was soon roused; for the tracks of the cloven feet, and the ground freshly uprooted in every direction, showed that there could be no lack of *haloof* (wild boar). The first symptom was violent barking; then an angry grunting in the thick cover; then an agonizing squeal; when in rushed an Arab and dragged out by the leg a most clamorous little piggy, which had been hardly treated by the dogs.

This was rather an inglorious commencement, still it was something. Another brake, and another violent barking. An Arab beckoned me to hurry on to the end, when all at once out burst, within twenty yards of me, three splendid fellows of great size—the leader quite grizzly from age. A better shot could not be imagined; but, alas! a wretched breech-loading carbine, which I had bought expressly for the occasion, missed fire, and no power could get it to act satisfactorily for the rest of the day. Another shot in another direction, and a loud outcry proclaimed the death of a second boar, considerably larger than the first, but still comparatively small. So away we went after old grizzly and his companions. The old gentleman had not gone far, and was soon routed out by the dogs, one of whom he forthwith ripped up, but was wounded in return by an Arab. The covert he was in extended over a considerable space of ground, and was almost impervious—and from it he would not budge. For two hours there he remained; nothing would induce him to stir We were posted at the far end, where it was supposed he would eventually emerge; but not a bit of it. He was hard hit, had a very strong position, and defied all comers. The dogs barked, the Moors shouted and threw stones, but out, like a very sensible old boar, he would not stir. Our patience was perfectly exhausted; we begged of them to come away, or to show us how to get in; but the first they would not, and the second they could not do. At last, by the intervention, I believe, of a boy who climbed a bush and fired his pistol in the direction where the dogs were barking, the boar thought his quarters invaded, and made off towards Sir S. G.; unfortunately before he reached, or was seen by him, he passed within a few feet of an armed Arab, who shot him dead. He was an enormous beast—so large that we were obliged to send for a horse to carry him home, the donkey which we had for the purpose being unable to support his weight—at least, they said so.

After this, the day being Friday, the Mussulman sabbath, the Arabs protested they must go to their devotions, and our hunt broke up at twelve o'clock without our firing a single shot. Such is the fortune of war, though I am bound to add that I think the Arabs made it a point of placing us in the most unlikely spot for the beast to make his sortie. It was extremely amusing to remark the good care the assistants took of themselves: on the least expectation of a rush, up the olives they scrambled, and from the fork of each tree we saw a red-capped head peeping forth. We had bagged three boars, it is true, but still it was a *chasse manquée,* the dogs were execrable, in fact only two would enter the covert, and the whole thing was managed without any plan or order. There is no doubt but that, with proper system and some good dogs, a grand day's sport might have been had at Allia.

We were anxious to bring our spoils to Tunis,

as a quarter of a wild boar would have been an acceptable present to our friends; but we found that the pious scruples of the neighbors could not be overcome for less than a napoleon. They said it was contrary to their religion to touch the unclean beast, and nothing less than the above-mentioned sum would suffice to satisfy their consciences. We, therefore, embalmed the interior of the small pig with rosemary, and had the larger pair skinned; during which operation the Moors carried off large pieces on the points of sticks, carefully avoiding to touch them, for their dogs they said, but uncharitable people at Tunis declared they had little doubt but that a good deal of pork was quietly digested that night at Allia.

The same night we had another heavy fall of rain, which gave reason to anticipate a tedious journey for the morrow; and tedious it was likely to be, for we had hardly got a mile from Allia, when, in descending the hill, over we went, and, after scrambling out of the window, we found our springs had given way by the shock. The driver, a Maltese, beat his head in despair, and abused the Holy Virgin as being the main cause of the calamity, but by the aid of a rope the conveyance was somehow patched up, and enabled to proceed. On arriving at Bou Shater, we found the great plain we had passed over a few days previously to be nearly a sheet of water from the overflowing of the river Mejerdah, and in consequence we were forced to bear away to the right and make for a hilly road of considerable *detour*. To do so it was necessary to pass over a portion of the low ground, and most pitiable work it was, for the wheels sunk deep in the tenacious mire, and with difficulty the poor horses ploughed their way through it. We did, however, get over the thirty miles in about nine hours, and revelled that night in clean linen, and in other fare than cold partridges—our *pièces de résistance*, excepting the bowl of coscousou—for a week.

We had left Tunis in a state of very tolerable cleanliness, always excepting the open drains; we returned to find it in filth intolerable. All the dirt, refuse of vegetables, and rubbish in general, is thrown into the streets, where it lies till it becomes trampled into the soft soil. In fine weather this is all very well, but when the rain descends and the streets become mud, the horses' hoofs turn up this stratum of decomposition, and most horrible is the smell in consequence. Moreover, as there are no metropolitan commissioners, nor local boards of works, nor Sir Benjamin Halls, to see to the sewerage, because there is no such thing save the open drains aforesaid, it becomes the custom twice a year to open a huge pit in front of each house, to remove the nightsoil. As this operation was going on for a day or two next door to us, we had full opportunities of watching the system, which resulted in blocking up one part of the street, and filling the whole of it with what by rights ought to be pestilential odors. No injury to health, nevertheless, seems to follow from these impurities; the inhabitants all look hale, healthy, and enjoying their stinks, and there is no doubt but that Tunis is anything but an unwholesome residence, in spite of its evil savor.

We had up to this time been undecided as to our future movements; we had thought of going on to Tripoli and thence to Benghazi and Derna, the ancient Cyrenaica, but were strongly urged by Mr. Davis to attempt a journey into the interior, and to the extreme limits of the south of Tunis. We were inflamed by the account of the magnificence of the Roman remains which still exist of the temples of Sbaitla, the ancient Suffetula; of the amphitheatre of El Djem, the Tysdrus of the Romans, said to be one of the grandest in the world. We were told of the beauty of the various oases bordering the Great Sahara, and the vision of lions and leopards and ostriches and gazelles and antelopes floated before our imagination. The stories, it is true, were conflictory as to the possibility of the journey: some alleged that the dangers of marauders and of insurgent Arabs were such that it would be impracticable, or at all events attended with the most imminent peril of life and limb; others objected to the time of year, and said that the rains, which would soon fall, would render the interior impassable, and that neither ourselves nor our horses would be able to endure the hardships we were certain to encounter; others, again, protested that we should meet with much civility, that we were perfectly able to protect ourselves against any party of robbers we were likely to meet, and that, once out of the mountainous districts, we should be in a splendid climate, in which both man and beast would rejoice and flourish. The *timides aris* were overruled, and we determined on a thorough exploration of the interior of the Regency. Our course in the first instance was to be directed westward, and to extend to the extreme limit of the south of the Bey's domains. The route was to be as follows:—First to Zowan,[1] to the south-east of Tunis; thence due west to Keff; then to the south to Kissera, Sbaitla, Feriana, Kafsa, to the oases of Tozer and Neftah, the furthest of the oases in the Great Sahara; returning from Neftah to Tozer, it was proposed that we should strike right across the country due east, cross, if possible, the Chot Nefzouia—or Great Salt Lake, called also the Sea of Marks, from marks placed in it to indicate the only passable track, and make our way to Gabes, on the seashore of the Lesser Syrtis; then ascending northwards by the coast to Sphax, and from Sphax into the interior to El Djem; then to Kairouan, and from Kairouan once more to the seashore, to Susa, to Hammamat, Sulyman, and Tunis. If we could accomplish this, we might say that we had quartered the whole Regency of Tunis as care-

[1] Properly Zaghouan.

fully as a well-trained pointer quarters a large Norfolk turnip-field; and with slight variations we did accomplish it. In this *feuille de route* one unfortunate mistake occurred in orthography, which caused us many weary wanderings, and a loss of time we could little afford. This mistake arose from writing Kissera instead of Kessereen, the place we should have made our way to; whereas Kissera is an insignificant town, perched on the top of a mountain, difficult to reach, and devoid of all interest when reached. The troubles and annoyances entailed by this error have graven for ever the ill-omened name of Kissera on my memory.

To accomplish this journey it was necessary to have an order, or *amr,* from the Bey, for the supply of provisions and proper entertainment, as the Irish signposts express it, for man and beast, and also an escort in the shape of some authorities to enforce the demands. We, therefore, requested of Mr. Wood, our Consul-General, to obtain for us an interview with his Highness. The audience was granted for the hour of ten in the morning, at the Bey's palace at Marsa, about ten or eleven miles from Tunis. In the decorous solemnity of evening toggery we started early, breakfasted with Mr. Wood, and proceeded to the palace, which is only a short drive from the consular residence. There is nothing particular in its appearance, it being much like other Eastern palaces—a large, square, flat-roofed building, surrounding a spacious courtyard. In front lounged a few soldiers, and many geese, both the inseparable attendants on his Highness, who has a slight taste for soldiery, but a strong one for *paté de foie gras* and giblets: in fact, by all accounts, no one understands better or relishes more a good dinner than Mohammed, Bey of Tunis; and, if rumour be true, he is no inconsiderable proficient in the art of cookery himself, but has his own private laboratory for the purpose, where on special occasions he confections ambrosia for himself and favorite *convives*.

In the interior of the courtyard, gazelles were walking independently about, unmolested by many greyhounds and dogs of less degree; on the rim of the basin of a fountain in the middle, some cranes were gravely philosophizing, while thoughtless coots and ducks were diving and disporting themselves in the water. After a short delay in an anteroom, we passed through a small cabinet, where stood a turning-lathe with which the Bey at times beguiles his leisure hours, and thence passing through a garden which the Botanical Society would not think much of, we were conducted to the rear of the palace, and, mounting a staircase, found ourselves in the room of audience and in the presence of his Highness. The room was very beautiful and spacious, exquisitely fitted up with pink satin, comfortable armchairs, tables, much looking-glass, and a magnificent cut-glass lamp. On the chimney-piece, as we advanced, I remarked some huge and excellent apples, which I heard came from Candia, and were greatly cherished by the Bey—so much so that he liked always to have them before his eyes. All the great officers of the court were in attendance, attired in tightly buttoned-up European coats, the red *tarboosh* or cap, and scintillating with diamond decorations. Sitting on the right-hand corner of the divan was the Bey himself, a high-bred-looking middle-aged man, with a particularly kind and prepossessing countenance. His dress was also European, and the same as the rest of his court, except that he wore the coat unbuttoned, and displayed a somewhat loud peach-blossom-colored silk vest; and in his hand he held a string of very fine pearls, for Mahommedans have their rosaries to record their prayers as well as Roman Catholics.

He received us with very great courtesy, and Count Raffo, an old astute-looking Italian, the minister for foreign affairs, acted as interpreter at first, though Mr. Wood subsequently took up the parley, and converted our French into Arabic. We commenced proceedings by expressing our extreme desire of seeing the interior of his Highness's dominions, which we understood, owing to his Highness's firm and parental government, could now be effected without danger. He replied that it would always gratify him to be of use to Englishmen, who were his trusty friends, but that he feared there might be danger in the journey owing to the unsettled state of a part of the country, and to the hardships and privations we were likely to endure at that season of the year. We answered the objection by assuring him that we had no fear of danger, for that his name would be our protection, and that, as for the hardships, we had both of us travelled in other countries where there was more roughness to be endured, both in fare and climate, and that we made but light of them. He then asked us whether we could postpone the journey till February, when he would be himself setting out to visit his domains with his camp, in which case he would be glad were we to accompany him, and he could provide everything for our comfort and security. Alas! we said, time would not permit us to avail ourselves of an offer so eligible and considerate. He then inquired into our proposed route; and on hearing the name of Kairouan, the sacred city, read out, the entrance to which has hitherto been interdicted to Christians and Jews, with the exception of a very favored few, he remarked that he would give us an order that we should enter and see the city and be protected from all affronts, but that he could not give us an order to enter the mosques. "Not," said he, "that I have any prejudices myself on the subject, or any objection, but that it would excite the inhabitants, and probably expose you to annoyance." We were too glad to get the order of admission on any terms, and were by no means anxious to enter the mosques, of which Sir S. had seen quite enough at Constantinople, and I at Cairo.

The conversation then took a wider turn, upon shooting and other matters, and his Highness said he supposed we were anxious to see all old stones with letters on them, which he heard Europeans were curious about, and that orders must be given to our escort to find out and show us the said old stones, and Sir S. quite charmed his heart by a high encomium he paid to the fine appearance and discipline of the Tunisian troops whom he had seen in the Crimean war; and so, having we trust left a favorable impression, we were dismissed with the assurance that everything should be done without loss of time (a most important proviso in the East) to facilitate our journey, and that we should have a tent placed at our disposal.

The allusions which the Bey made to his friendly disposition towards the English were not mere compliments. He is perfectly alive to the fact that France is only waiting for the propitious moment to extend her African frontier to the borders of Tripoli. There is one fixed idea innate and uppermost in the mind of every Frenchman, and that is, that it is a necessity for the glory and destiny of France that the Mediterranean should be a French lake. The possession of Tunis is essential to the realization of this project. Its fine secure bay, in a coast devoid of good harbors from Morocco to Alexandria, would be invaluable to the fleet. Its position would command Egypt, and be a counterpoise to Malta ; its cleared and inexhaustibly fertile plains and excellent climate would attract population and redeem the failure of Algerine colonization. Already quietly and silently everypreparation is being made: two military roads are in course of construction, one from Bona to the frontiers of Tunis near Keff, the other to the south to Tebissa. When these are completed it only remains to march one column to Keff and thence to Tunis, while the other, penetrating the southern part of the regency, can traverse the country, and occupy without impediment the towns along the Mediterranean littoral. Whatever Tunisian forces there may be, would then be taken in the rear. French officers in Algeria do not scruple to open their minds to you upon the subject; with perfect ingenuousness they show you the value of the conquest both in a military and commercial point of view, and they tell you very frankly that Morocco, Algeria, Tripoli, and Egypt, will be a fair set-off to our empire in India.

The position of the Bey, however, as vassal of the Porte, creates a difficulty in the way of the execution of these pleasant schemes of conquest, consequently the policy of France has been, since the occupation of Algeria, to inflame the minds of the successive Beys with charming visions of independence. Every inducement is held out to their vanity and to their fears to induce them to proclaim themselves sovereign princes. At one time they are told, that were they not mere feudatories they would be admitted into the fraternity of the great European powers; at another, they are alarmed by rumours that the Sultan is about to assert a right of appointing and of superseding his vassals, and of converting Tunis into a pashalic, as Tripoli has been converted, the government of which was at one period in much the same position as that of Tunis. Another plan is, by intrigue, to disorganize the country and render the inhabitants ready for a change. A notable example of this creditable mode of proceeding occurred only a few months before my arrival at Tunis. A certain Ghouma, an Arab chief, having revolted in Tripoli, was soon driven out of the country by the Pasha of that district, and took refuge in the south of Tunis. On arriving there he proclaimed that the Bey of Tunis was deposed by the Porte—that he was appointed in his stead, and held the firman of the Sultan. He then warned the inhabitants not to pay taxes, in which they readily concurred, and gave out that immediate assistance was to be sent by France to the Sultan's friend, of which the constant communications with a Frenchman in a high position, but whose name I purposely omit, were the confirmation. The heavy hand, however, of the Bey's energetic minister, Mahommed Hasneddar, fell speedily on him and his dupes: they were literally swept off the face of the earth, fined, confined, and ruined, and he himself fled to Algeria, where, finding that he was of no further use, his French friends had, I understood, given him notice to quit.[1]

The late Bey was unwary enough to be dazzled with the schemes of independence, and in 184– determined on paying Europe a visit, and obtaining from the great western powers a recognition of that independence. The old fox, Louis Philippe, gave him every encouragement, and received him as a sovereign prince; but, fortunately for Tunis, there was one man who had the sagacity to penetrate these well-arranged projects, and who had the firmness to prevent the foolish dupe from becoming the victim of his own shortsighted vanity. Lord Palmerston was at the time Foreign Secretary for England. The Bey notified to him his intention of visiting her Majesty as a foreign prince. Lord Palmerston replied, that he could only come as a vassal of the Porte, and be presented by the Turkish Ambassador. His Highness returned to Tunis in dudgeon, complaining bitterly of the treatment his English friends had given him, but they were, if unpalatable friends, true at all events: it was clear that England was resolved to maintain the Sultan's territorial rights, so that no excuse was sought to pick a quarrel with Tunis in the days of the late Bey, who at last thoroughly

[1] Ghouma has since been killed in action with the Tripoli troops.

understood the wisdom of the course pursued by Lord Palmerston.

On the accession of the present Bey, the same artifices were employed, and it is said that he was disposed to lend too ready an ear to them. Mr. Wood, who speaks Arabic as an Arab, and who knows every twist and turn of the oriental mind, has, however, thoroughly insensed him as to his situation, and he is now convinced that England is his truest and most powerful friend. He is anxious, therefore, to establish relations of the closest kind with England, to obtain investment of English capital in his country, either in mining or in cotton planting—in anything, in short, which will throw a grappling line from Tunis into England; and, from my own personal observation, I believe there is no country in the world where an enterprising Englishman will be able to invest capital with more security and success. It is a country teeming with grain, oil, wool, and dates, and yet, I believe, we have no direct trade whatever with it.

But with this good disposition on the part of the Bey towards us, what is our attitude towards him? Our policy seems to be to sit aloof, like the Tennysonian gods, "careless of mankind," almost ignoring his existence. A few days before our return to Tunis from the interior, a great event took place. A French man-of-war entered the port, bearing a letter from the Emperor, and the Grand Cross of the Legion of Honor, the greatest honor in the power of His Majesty to bestow. Presents were conferred on other officials, the Bey was invested with his decoration in great state, the ship banged away salutes till the air was redolent of powder, and all the bribed adherents cried out, with one acclaim, "See what the French do for you, in spite of your mistrust! See what your English will do for you, in return for your confidence and regard!"

Now, it is curious enough, that if there is one thing more than another which the Bey desires, nay, actually longs for, it is an English decoration. First of all, there is the oriental love of gewgaws and ceremonies; but there is another and a better reason why he so ardently craves this little bit of ribbon and glitter. The partisans of France are perpetually twitting him with the indifference of England to him. "If it were not so," they say, "what difficulty would there be in complying with so moderate a wish in return for all you have done?" And not merely the partisans of France, but independent persons are forced to come to the conviction that there can be no friendly feeling on the part of England to Tunis, when such a trifle is refused. An English decoration, therefore, would not merely be to the Bey a source of momentary or childish gratification, but a strong moral source of reliance to those who wish for the independence of the country, that the Bey has the sympathy and good will of England.

I have used the expression, "All that the Bey

has done." It is not, perhaps, known that Tunis has some claims on England. The last Bey was the first Mahommedan prince who abolished the slave trade in his dominions. He did it at the risk of his life and throne, and through the instigation of Sir Thomas Reid, our consul. His people were most indignant; but a noble example was set, and travellers in Central Africa state that no heavier blow was struck to the slave trade, and to the horrible system of slave hunts in the interior, than by this good act of the Bey of Tunis. He asked for a slight recognition from our country, in the shape of some order or decoration, was refused, and on his deathbed he expressed his regret that he should die without an honor from England. The present Bey, on the breaking out of the late Russian war, behaved most admirably by the allies. With the greatest alacrity and good will he fitted out and sent, free of expense, to the seat of war, 10,000 men well disciplined and appointed. Surely services like these, on his part, and on that of his cousin the late Bey, deserve some notice on the part of England; and, after all, so little is asked for, and would be so thankfully received. It appears that some miserable court etiquette is the obstacle. Is there no Minister bold enough and wise enough to sweep away an obstacle which makes us appear to a really friendly power in the light of ingrates and niggards, and places us at a disadvantage with other nations?

Our occupation during the week preceding our interview with the Bey consisted in the attempted purchase of horses in the morning, and shooting grebes and wild fowl on the sea of an afternoon. We had formed a very profitable acquaintance with a certain M. Bogo, a Frenchman by birth, but Tunisian by education, who is an ardent naturalist and capital sportsman; he very kindly lent us his boat, and a dark-colored mariner to show us sport. Both species of grebe, the small *Podiceps cornutus*, and the larger sort, *Podiceps cristatus*, are found in the shallow water, between the Goelette and the Marina of Tunis. The Goelette is the harbour, about six miles from the city, beyond which large vessels cannot approach, and where they generally consign their cargoes to smaller boats, which land them at the Marina, close to one of the gates of Tunis. The smaller grebe is found in great numbers at no great distance from this Marina; but as they are remarkably good divers, and have a shrewd notion that their skins are in request, it is by no means so easy to secure them as it appeared to be. The larger grebe is still more wary; we saw several, but never could get within shot; their power of diving and speed under water enabled them always, with apparently no efforts, to keep us at a respectful distance. M. Bogo had, however, contrived to get a certain number of peltries; and I subsequently purchased from him, at a very reasonable price, a very beautiful muff, and a bag made of the entire skin of the grebe, with the feet depending from it, and the head forming the opening of the bag. It had an extremely pretty effect, and as the grebe composing it was killed when he was, as M. Bogo styled it, "en habit de noces," that is, in his spring attire, when incubation begins, his graceful chestnut-colored head was highly ornamental. It is curious how so many male birds of different species put on their brightest and most attractive plumage at that period of the year, when they have relinquished a life of celibacy, and taken upon themselves the cares of matrimony. Nature is then most bountiful to them, to enable them to dazzle the imagination and please the critical eye of their little partners. In the human race the process seems different; for, although there are many exemplary exceptions, still, as a general rule after matrimony, however attentive his mate may be to her mantua-maker, the gentleman generally relaxes the *entente cordiale* that prevailed between him and his tailor; and instead of making the grebe his model, and decking himself in the most captivating attire, he exchanges for the *habit de noces* the shooting-coat and highlows. With all our devotion to the *chasse*, we were only able to secure eight of the smaller grebe, which, as it required about eighteen to make a muff, would only suffice for cuffs; and although there were wild fowl innumerable, and flamingoes in plenty, winging their rosy flight at evenfall across the bay, we were prevented by want of wind from doing any execution.

Our mornings were busy enough hunting for horses for the expedition. We determined on purchasing six, four for the luggage and two for riding. The Tunisian Tattersalls is just outside the gate, and conducted on a very proper principle, as far as the theory of the proceedings went; but was, I imagine, not quite so admirable in the practice. All the animals for sale, horses, mules, asses, and camels, are put up to auction, and, after they are bought, are brought before a government official, who examines them carefully and pronounces an opinion as to their soundness. If the opinion be favorable, the purchaser proceeds to another official to whom he pays a tax in the shape of a caroub in the piastre, or one sixteenth of the purchase-money. If the opinion be unfavorable, the animal is returned; but if the horse, after passing, be proved subsequently to be unsound, the official is responsible to the purchaser for the price. Nothing can be more praiseworthy than this custom; but I fear that considerations sometimes intervene which influence the decision of the inspector. I know this much, that on selling the only one of our animals which I believe could hardly be pronounced sound on any point whatever, he passed a triumphant examination, and that there were some little items charged for the expense of the sale by our Moorish servant which we did not care to scrutinize too closely. It was, however, rather amusing to watch the proceedings. On arriving at the scene of action, you looked over a number of horses, all tethered in front of a coffee-house, on a bench before which were squatted the white-burnoosed purchasers and sellers. When the sale commenced, a boy jumped on the bare back of one of the steeds, galloped and trotted him to and fro, while a Moorish auctioneer put him up and received the biddings. When the price reached the culminating point, beyond which the purchaser would not advance, and to which the seller was indisposed to accede, then came into play the real diplomatic talents of the auctioneer: first he took one of the parties aside and whispered in his ear, then bawled up with a voice of Stentor the last bid, *Telata mia oo hamseen*—three hundred and fifty piastres; then the other was taken aside, and owing to his persuasive eloquence, the bidding rose to *telata mia arbaa oo hamseen*—three hundred and fifty-four; then both parties were brought apparently with great reluctance together, and an announcement of *telata mia hamsa oo hamseen*, or three hundred and fifty-five, followed by a general silence, proclaimed that the purchase was completed. Two or three cups of muddy coffee were drunk on the strength of it, and the animal was led off to the den of the inspector. A little wizand, sagacious-looking old Moor commenced the scrutiny; felt the legs, neck, and various points of the horse; made two or three fillips at his eyes, and if he winked pronounced them all right,—and then gave forth his dictum that "Inshallah"—if it pleased God, all was as it should be. Then the payment of the tax succeeded, and a good deal of wrangling as to the auctioneer's and jockey's fee; more coffee was drunk, and the animal at length led off by his new purchaser. Such was the process by which we became possessors of two horses at the rate of about £9 apiece. We bought our other two baggagers by private sale, and the four cost 1400 piastres, or about £37. Sir S. G. had picked up also by private sale, at a very low rate, a remarkably nice horse, indeed I think one of the best-bred-looking horses I have seen in the country. He had the reputation of being somewhat fractious, and accordingly was sold at the low price of 550 piastres, or £14. 10*s.*, and, although on one or two occasions he showed a disposition to have his own way, was invaluable for his pluck and safety, being as steady as a rock to fire from, and never making a mistake in the roughest and most precipitous ground. My investment was not so good, but as time pressed I was forced to take whatever I could get, and consequently found myself possessed of a mealy bay with long weak pasterns and light hind quarters, an animal of amiable disposition, but timorous by temperament, being always in a state of alarm, shrinking back if he felt I was about to shoot, and trembling at any broken ground, stumbling the whole way, but too much afraid of breaking his knees to tumble down. Such was my beast; but he did his best, poor fellow, and it is not well to speak evil of the unfortunate, for the last I saw of him was in harness the day I left Tunis, the property of a Maltese letter of coaches: a worse fate could not have come upon him. The Tunisian horses at one time enjoyed a high reputation for cheapness and goodness, which would be undeserved at present. The close approach of the French has increased the price, and most of the best horses go to Algeria. The Bey in consequence has prohibited the exportation of them, but he has no power to prevent it; any one can ride across the frontier, and come back again with the price of his steed in his pocket. Mules have also become extremely dear—far more so than horses, seven or eight hundred piastres being thought nothing of for even a very ordinary mule.

Then came the bustle of purchasing the necessaries, the *batterie de cuisine*, and the many need-nots which one considers so indispensable, and so soon flings away. We were lent two air-beds by friends, one of which Sir S. occupied, the other became the appanage of my servant. I took for myself a mattress; but, as the air deserted the beds through some insidious orifice which could never be found out, and as my mattress, when the bad weather came on, was generally wet through and always damp, our sleeping apparatus was not satisfactory.

Only one thing now remained, and that was an interpreter. A tall intelligent-looking and grandly attired Moor, Kassim by name, volunteered his services; he produced excellent recommendations from some gentlemen whom he had accompanied into Algeria, and he professed a profound knowledge of the French and Italian languages, and of Tunisian geography. The latter part of his professions was certainly borne out, for he seemed well acquainted with every nook and cranny of the Bey's dominions, and as he had been with naturalists, he was of great use, from his experience of the localities frequented by the different sorts of game. His French and Italian were, however, of a most extraordinary nature: it was a peculiar lingo based upon the two languages, with a pronunciation certainly original, which produced a prolonged conversation hopelessly unintelligible. We did contrive somehow to understand each other on ordinary occasions, and were particularly fortunate in securing him, for he was active and energetic, and did not rob us, as far as we knew; and as activity, energy, and honesty, are not the characteristics of the Moors, it was lucky to have secured an attendant that differed from his fellows in these respects.

On the 25th of November, all our preparations

were finished, thanks to our obliging host of the Hotel de Provence, M. François, who acted as general comprador, and saved us from inordinate extortion. Before starting we went down to the consulate to meet the escort given us by the Bey, consisting of three *hambas* and two *spahis*, and to have the Bey's orders read and translated, and the functionaries duly admonished as to the propriety of their conduct. Nothing could be more flattering than the Bey's *amr*, or order: in it we were called his children, and all his subjects were exhorted to supply our wants; the *hambas* made great professions, and as each paragraph of the order was recited, they exclaimed, as if from their hearts, *Meliyah*—good; and no doubt the prospect was good and pleasing to them, as it held out the certainty for a month or two of free quarters, presents from us, and of squeezing on a notable scale under the shadow of our wings. The *hambas*, I may as well explain, are a class of official the functions of whom it is difficult to elucidate by the illustration of any similar institution at home—inasmuch as they are maintained and exist entirely upon the squeezing process. The French call them *gensdarmes*, and yet they are not *gensdarmes*, for they are but little concerned in the preservation of peace and order. They are men apparently well to do, attired in seemly vesture fashioned according to their own imagination, they are mounted and armed, and yet receive no pay except about £8 for the purchase of a horse, and a piece of cloth annually, to be converted into a garment. If you inquire a little further into their means of existence—squeezing will be the reply. If the Bey is about to visit any portion of his territory, some favored *hambas* are sent in advance, who make demands of a portentous nature on the unfortunate authorities in the different localities on his Highness's route. Much lamentation naturally ensues, but in the end the *hamba* moderates his demand, because he knows the reason why: if the inhabitants of any town have been guilty of conduct which requires investigation, a *hamba* is despatched to the abode of the delinquents; he holds his inquiry, is his own reporter, and is favorable or unfavorable according as he knows the reason why; the ends of justice are, however, answered, for the culprits are squeezed, and it little matters whether what is extracted from their pockets goes into those of the master or the man, the Bey or the *hamba*. If a traveller of any position proceeds on an excursion, a *hamba* is given as an attendant; this is an auspicious event, for he enjoys not only his usual course of squeezing, but has it spread over a wide field, and gets a present into the bargain. So it is not a matter of surprise that the *hambas* found our orders to be extremely good. The *spahis* are in an inferior position: they act as messengers, are sent galloping over the country from governor to governor, officiate now and then as rural police, and do a little squeezing also in their turn. Highly educated, however, as the Moors are in the art of extortion, of which we had many notable examples, still they sink into insignificance alongside the Persians; for though provisions, and even considerable sums of money, were extracted by our attendants, I never heard of their levying a tax on any village for the wear and tear of our teeth, a common enough process in the Shah's dominions, and which the fearfully tough old hens we were condemned to eat occasionally would have fully warranted.

A little after twelve the last pannier was loaded, and amid an admiring crowd we proceeded to start on our expedition; and it is meet here to record the names and characteristics of the wanderers, somewhat perhaps in the style of a Christmas pantomime playbill.

First of all, Sir S. G., a first-rate shot, capital rider, indifferent as to his fare, with a supreme contempt for everything soft.

2. Mr. G., moderate shot, moderate rider, preferring a chicken to an aged and tough hen, and somewhat lazy.

3. Hubert, Mr. G's servant, a Belgian by birth, once a soldier, then a cook, and lastly valet; very honest, very slow, very fond of eating, and detesting exercise; always at war with Kassim.

4. Kassim, the Moor, once a Tunisian soldier, then a deserter to Algiers, then a merchant on a small scale; lastly, servant and interpreter to Europeans; a man of much energy, and disagreeable to speak to either in camping or decamping, but lively in his leisure moments; of lofty stature and pleasant appearance. Given to chaffing Hubert.
5. Trim, a black Norfolk retriever, with good nose and bad education; an amazing glutton, and irreclaimable coward. Not on terms with Azor.
6. Azor, a Tunisian dog, property of M. François, described as *un fameux chien de chasse;* his chief propensity to hunt larks by sight. Of Russian pointer breed, with a bottle-nose, and the hair growing back on it till it nearly covered his eyes; his ancles shaven to avoid dirt, which he disliked; an excellent watch-dog, always barking, and detesting Trim.
7. Nino, a spaniel, also the property of M. François, another *fameux chien de chasse;* good in brushwood, but addicted to pursue the flying game; on good terms with Azor and Trim, but caring for neither, only for himself.

Then came the Hambas.

1. The Oda Bashi, or head man, Kassim also by name, a very high-bred, gentlemanly

looking man; fair in complexion, sedate in manner, timorous in disposition, grandly attired with a diamond decoration gleaming on the breast of his white burnoos.

2. Mahommed El Kaffi, him of Kaff; a burly, good-looking, ruffling, noisy vagabond; always begging cigars or tobacco, with a soul intent on squeezing.
3. Mohammed Tebirski, an ill-favored, downcast, disobliging, disreputable Hamba; also intent on squeezing.
4. Ali, the Spahi, a merry little man resembling a monkey; always active and obliging; the friend of Sir S. G. and Mr. G.
5. Salah, also Spahi, a coarse-featured Arab of the Slas tribe, but honest and obliging; also a friend of Sir S. G. and Mr. G.

Such was the *dramatis personæ* of the expedition.

I had said we proceeded to start, for many were the mishaps and misfortunes before we finally got under way. It was settled that Hubert should ride one of the baggage-horses, and to make his seat comfortable a mattress was thrown from pannier to pannier, affording a luxurious seat. It required, however, a little agility and practice to reach it, and certainly a more unfitting figure for a feat of activity I never beheld, than that presented by Hubert as he issued from the hotel. The weather was warm, but, as it might turn out chilly before evening, he had placed over his morning coat another coat, and over that again a great coat; one pocket bulged out with pipes and stores of tobacco, the other held a double-barrelled pistol, loaded to the muzzle and capped. Round his neck, inside the first integument was a long, sharp dagger, which he had borrowed for the occasion; on his left side were a pair of opera-glasses to look out for the attack, on the right a revolver ready for the fray; and at his back swung my rifle, also loaded, capped, and cocked. He had heard terrible stories of marauders, and had come forth determined to die hard. The difficulty, however, was to get him on his seat with this tremendous armoury; an Italian gave him a back and tried to lift him up, but the horse was, naturally enough, alarmed, and only permitted a partial ascent, contriving to wheel round so deftly that thrice he lodged him in the dust, at the imminent risk of his battery exploding. In fact, so determined was the animal not to accept such a portent as his rider, that Hubert, to his great discomfiture and our great amusement, was forced to uncase himself like an onion from his peels, and, when fairly in his position, to rearrange his attire on the horse's back. I should have mentioned, that he brought from England an English hunting-whip, which he begged hard to be allowed to take with him, and which we found to be a most invaluable weapon in our subsequent daily encounter with Arab dogs. Even this difficulty over, our troubles were not half at an end; the horses were strange to each other, but knew the way to their stables and the roads about Tunis, so one wandered here and the other made off elsewhere; as fast as they were got together they commenced straggling away. Kassim did not despair, but swore the more. The Tunisian dogs, coupled together, were always in the way, and at last twisted themselves round a cow's leg, and were both kicked; in short, we had not advanced a quarter of a mile in two hours, and were forced to hire an additional help as far as Zowan, for the Hamba that accompanied us, Mohammed Tebirski, showed the cloven foot at starting, and refused to aid us in the slightest degree. The other Hambas we had left behind to get orders from the local governors.

All things have, however, an end, even hopeless confusion; we got at last into marching order, and proceeded over a fine open country to our first stage, Oudina, which is about twelve miles from Tunis. The appearance of the landscape reminded both of us of the view of the Roman Campagna; the broad plain intersected by the ancient aqueduct, the distant hills, their form and coloring, all transported us to the prospect we had so often contemplated from the steps of St. John de Lateran, and I find that Sir G. Temple has made a similar observation. About six or seven miles from Tunis, we perceived to our right an apparently extensive and fine range of buildings, but there was no sign of inmates or population about them. We were informed that this place was called the Mohammedia, that it was erected by the late Bey as a residence, but was completely abandoned by the present, who prefers to abide near the sea. This is the general fate of palaces in the East: it is all the same whether at Constantinople, Egypt, or Tunis. Each successive ruler is displeased with the mansions of his predecessor, and very often with his own, and occupies his time and the resources of the country in erecting huge and costly buildings, which are hardly finished before they are abandoned to desolation.

As evening fell, we arrived at Oudina, an Arab encampment on the site of Roman ruins of considerable extent. A battle was fought between the Hamba and inhabitants, on the subject of barley for the horses, and food for ourselves. It seemed as if blood must be shed, for the Hamba was doubtless trying his hand at squeezing, which the Arabs strenuously resisted, and I rather imagine were successful. On the morrow, at all events, everything seemed very serene: they showed us the huge cisterns in which our horses were stabled, and where I subsequently heard some ladies of Mr. Davis's family had passed a very comfortable night, when caught in a storm on their return from Zowan. They showed us also, a large Roman building which looked like a basilica, but we were unable to find any inscriptions which might give us an idea of the date of its construction.

In the morning we started ahead on foot, leaving the tents and baggagers to follow, and got a couple of hours shooting at red legs in the thick brushwood of the plain, before they reached us. Our journey was a short one, about fourteen miles, and we soon came in sight of the cheerful white walls of Zowan, at the foot of the precipitous mountain of that name. I cannot conceive a more lovely residence than Zowan in the summer. It is literally "a land of streams," and teeming with vegetation. Although on the verge of December, the weather was warm and genial, willows shivered in the breeze, palms waved, and the stately cypress rose up with its dark green spire among the gardens. Festoons of parasites ran from tree to tree along the hedgerows; fancy hedgerows in Africa! pomegranates and oranges and lemons, the golden apples of the Hesperides, were in full bearing all around, and streamlets went singing along, and gurgling along unseen amid the oleander foliage that covered them. We were quite surprised that the Bey did not make this beautiful spot his summer residence. Old Zowan hangs over it, shading it from the fierce southern simoon, and catching every passing cloud, to send the shower in rivulets down its furrowed sides. If natural beauty and coolness were not sufficiently tempting, the opportunity of putting thirty miles between him and the European consuls ought to be a sufficient inducement.

The interior of the town is by no means prepossessing. You enter by an abrupt ascent through an ancient gate of Roman construction, with a ram's head carved in the stone over the entrance, and under the ram's head is engraved AVXILIO, as Shaw says, probably denoting that the town was under the protection of Jupiter Ammon. Our way to the Governor's house was through the main street, hardly wider than the narrowest lane of European recollection; then, turning to the right, we scrambled up a deep and dirty by-path, and found ourselves at the door of our abode. The interior very much belied the exterior. First of all we were led into a large and spacious anteroom, floored with tiles; thence into another and smaller room, well carpeted, and with wooden bedsteads for the attendants; and inside this, again, was the sanctum, where a huge bed was sunk into an alcove, which was occupied by Sir S., and below it a sofa or divan large enough for a mattress, which fell to my share. As this was to be our first repast *à la Moresque*, we were curious enough and somewhat nervous to ascertain what dainties we might hereafter expect. Presently a file of attendants stalked in, each bearing a dish covered with basketwork:—first of all the *sherba*, or soup of chicken and rice, highly flavoured with capsicums; then there were divers dishes of mutton stewed with vegetables, others with sweet raisins—very rich and oily; then came chickens, or rather old hens, *au naturel*. An excellent salad of radishes cut in thin slices, with oil and lemon-juice, accompanied the first course, which closed with our old friend, the coscousou; and pomegranates, oranges, and hard eggs, constituted the desert. After this repast, far better than ninety out of a hundred repasts in Spain or Italy—for in fact it was extremely good—we had no further apprehension of being thrown on our own culinary resources.

In the morning they were prepared to give us for breakfast the same *menu* that we had the evening before; but having neither time nor constitutions for such rich dainties, they sent us up some very excellent fried crumpets and highly perfumed honey. I may remark, that throughout our whole journey, wherever we got bread it was of the best quality; even among the Arab tribes, owing to the excellence of the flour, the flat cakes toasted on the embers were, if not very digestible for a fastidious stomach, at all events very good eating. Butter there was none, nor was milk very abundant at that time of year, though what we got was capital—very rich and full of cream. In spring, however, Tunis may really be said to be a land flowing with milk and honey.

After breakfast we went out to hunt wild boars,

but our ride was in vain: we neither found game nor signs of game, though the inhabitants assured us that the unclean beast was in the habit of committing perpetual ravages in their gardens. The country we rode over was very pretty, through thick myrtle and cypress scrub, by the side of water-courses, with oleander coverts. Our chief Hamba preceded us solemnly in front, with his diamond decoration proudly exhibited on the breast of his white burnoos. We ascertained, this first day of our acquaintance with him, that he was of a timorous disposition, being mightily afraid of his horses prancing or stumbling, consequently an excellent guide in rough ground; though an exceedingly bad one to make his way, which he was ever losing, yet always too high and mighty to make inquiries.

In the evening we were honored by a concert of most extraordinary instruments, to judge from their sound; and the dog Azor, after we retired to roost, emulous of the musicians, commenced a solo of barking in the anteroom; in order to expel him I had to pass through it, and the room adjacent to it. On each divan, or what in India would be called *charpoy,* there was a white hillock, which had a very odd effect. The sleepers were all lying on their backs, with their knees elevated, and heads and bodies covered over with their white burnooses. It was a ghastly sight, as the moonlight streamed in on them through the open windows. I subsequently remarked, that whenever we had a house for our covering, our Moors enjoyed themselves in this fashion, instead of having a stretch at full length: in the open air they huddled themselves up in a sitting position.

The next morning rose heavy and lowering, a nightcap of clouds was over Zowan, and the rain presently began to fall heavily, so we were obliged to give up all thoughts of decamping for that day, the 29th; but in the afternoon the sun came forth again, and all was serene and bright. We took a walk underneath the old mountain, and were brought by a little boy to see the Ras-el-Ain, the "head of the fountain," that used in former times to send its waters into Carthage. The source springs from beneath a Roman semicircular temple, dedicated probably to the nymphs: niches are all around it, to hold the statues of the deities; and a prettier spot, or one more appropriate to the rustic goddesses, cannot be imagined. While we were sitting at its side, all at once arose, as if out of the clouds, the music of a shepherd's pipe, the *levis calamus.* It quite transported us to the eclogues and Theocritus; and we almost strained the ear to listen to the rival pipe of Daphnis advancing up the valley to challenge in the presence of the nymphs the Menalcas of the mountain. For it was upon the highest crest of Zowan, among his goats, hardly visible to the naked eye, that our Mahommedan Corydon was beguiling his hours of watching; and the strain fell pleasantly on our ears, as how could it fail to do, sitting as we were by the temple of the nymphs, embowered in bushes of rosemary and myrtle.

The next day we advanced about sixteen miles to the westward, to Bent-es-Saida, another prettily situated Moorish village, under the mountain of that name. We were so eaten up by fleas, that we were forced to waive all delicacy; and telling our host, the Shekh of the village, that human European nature could not stand such attacks, we betook ourselves to our tent, which we always found, except in rain, to be the pleasantest and most independent refuge from men and insects. This town was also a Roman town, and the doorpost of the Shekh's house was formed of a long stone, on which was carved, in large Roman letters,

VVMMVLTIPLICATAASEPECVNII.

The family were much pleased at being informed that the inscription had reference to money, and urgently requested us to find it for them, as they were quite convinced we might do, if we had only the mind. It was in getting to this place that we made the fatal error of our journey, so far as going altogether out of our road, and wandering among the mountains. We had, however, opportunities of seeing places and people new to the world, although we had to encounter some hardships and a good deal of difficulty in doing so. Our course ought to have been to have crossed the ridge of Zowan to the west, where it lies low, and then passing over the great plain to the south, to have made the best of our way to Kairouan, and from Kairouan to Sbaitla and Kessereen. We made however, as I before remarked, the mistake of confounding Kessera with Kessereen; and in order to reach this ill-omened Kessera, which was really the "Ithacæ semper fugientis imago," always supposed to be near, but never to be gained, we wandered to and fro among the mountains for several days without discovering our error. Another mistake that we also found ourselves by this time to have committed, was having horses to carry the baggage instead of camels. The third day of the journey, the unfortunate animal that bore the tent galled his back to such a degree that he was comparatively useless for the rest of the journey; and we soon began to find out that the inroad of so many horses on the Arab's barley rendered our company by no means agreeable. If the journey required extra speed, horses perhaps, lightly laden, would be preferable to camels; but, after all, we found our average of travelling to be not more than eighteen miles a day, which a camel can always accomplish comfortably enough. All our forced marches were for the sake of obtaining water, enough of which to last three horses could easily have been carried by camels, who support without difficulty two or even three days' abstinence.

We remained the 1st and 2nd of December at Bent-es-Saida, in the vain hope of killing a boar, or some *poules de Carthage,* as the lesser bustard is called; we saw some of the latter, but were unable to get within shot. In returning home we heard some plaintive cries among the bushes, and found them to proceed from two unfortunate young puppies, whose unnatural mother had thus abandoned them. We came just in time to rescue them from a large grey falcon, who was swooping ominously over them; and as they looked very pretty in their warm red fur coats, we carried them home in our *gibecières*; and, handing them to the Shekh, offered a gratuity to any messenger who would deliver them when weaned to M. François, in Tunis; but this was the first and last we saw of them; and judging from our subsequent experience of Arab dogs—of their cowardice and utter inutility except to bark—Great Britain has no loss from their non-importation.

On the 3rd we started afresh, passing at first through the same rich myrtle scrub. As we rode along we saw the Roman aqueducts spanning the ravines, and in the plain our route ran for some way by the side of their channel, raised by masonry about a foot or two above the ground. All these constructions were part of the general scheme for the constant supply of the finest water to Carthage and the adjacent towns. The vaulted channel had been broken into in various places, and afforded dry lying for jackals and serpents, but it was still to be traced for miles and miles. We were shown, within a mile of Bent-es-Saida, another temple to the nymphs, embowered in myrtle, with a cistern in the middle where the source of the fountain lay. There was no inscription on the temple, but on a broken stone, which had evidently formed a portion of it, we had—

OIPPDIVIMANTONI;[1]

and a little further on we were brought to another stone at the door of a house, also broken in half, on which was carved—

IREGINAE
ROSALVTE
CIE DIVI NERVAE
VIIF MAXIM
O SVIS IMPENSIS

These inscriptions, as well as most of the others that we met with, show the material prosperity of Rome's African possessions towards the end of the first and commencement of the second century A.D. The "suis impensis" and "sua pecuniâ" of the votive monuments, seem to be a hint very palpably expressed of the immense loyalty of the constructor. These ostentatious flatteries, although quite in accordance with Roman good taste, would hardly be appreciated at present.

The whole of this day's journey was through a beautiful country, through myrtles of every sort,

[1] The first P may be P or R.

narrow-leafed and broad-leafed, by the sides of deep and dangerous water-courses, excavated by winter torrents, on the opposite verge of one of which a wolf stood and watched calmly the cavalcade. We crossed (which we subsequently found we should not have done) the mountain ridge on our left by a wild and beautiful pass, and immediately descended into a vast plain between parallel ranges of hills, the sides of which, as well as the plain itself, were of great fertility, and cultivated carefully: by carefully, I mean that all brushwood was cleared, for the only system of farming that I ever could perceive, was cropping one year and leaving fallow the next. After wandering about this plain in various directions and for some time, we found we had altogether missed our route, and were enjoined to recross, further on, the ridge we had just surmounted. It was a steep ride up, but an ugly ride down, and how the baggagers and the unfortunate animal that carried the tent ever got to the bottom is wonderful. But as we were cautiously picking our way through the bushes and the loose rocks, we heard a clatter behind us, and behold there was galloping madly down this almost perpendicular ravine a handsome black-bearded man, on a remarkably fine grey mare—the very *beau idéal* of Black Hassan, idolized by maidens. He passed us with a shout and a wave of the hand, and presently we saw him sweeping along the opposite heights, with his white burnoos streaming behind him. This was our host Feraj Ben Mansoor, Lord of Caroub or El Hanga, who had been expecting us by the proper route, and, finding we had missed our way, had been in search of us. He was now galloping ahead to have everything swept and garnished for our entertainment in his mountain eyrie. We found his habitation in the midst of the remains of a Roman town of some extent, and it was probably part of the *castellum* of the garrison. We searched in vain for inscriptions, although we were shown gravestones, on one of which were two human figures rudely sculptured. There is a magnificent view from this spot, extending over the vast plains to the north: from it we were shown the lake of Koorseea or Boosha, and we were told it was in the neighbourhood of the Siliana. It is about sixteen miles from Bent-es-Saida, to the W. or, rather, W.S.W. We found our host a fine, generous fellow, passionately fond of hunting. He showed us his grey mare with pride, and his greyhounds—"slogi," as they are called in Tunis—one of which, a very fine dog, had an ugly scar on his haunches, the result of an encounter with a wild boar. We sat in the evening round a sweet-scented fire of myrtle wood, and had a long chat, chiefly about hunting and shooting, and on retiring to our tent, which from recollections we preferred to the chief's house, we presented him with a pair of scissors, which he seemed highly to approve of.

4th.—We advanced twelve miles, still bearing westward, preceded by our friend the Moor, who on the strength of the scissors had conceived a warm affection for us. Our bivouac for the night was to be by the *dowar*[1] of an Arab tribe, for which we hunted for some time, and at last found, again among the mountains. In scrambling over the smooth rocks my horse's legs flew from under him, and I got a fall which by no means improved the symmetry of my nose for a day or two. We had, however, a very good afternoon's sport with the red-legs, which came extremely handy, for our Arab friends, though very well disposed, were poor enough, with only some eggs and milk at their disposal. This was the first regular Arab *dowar* with which we had come in contact, and as henceforth we shall have often to allude to the Arab tent as our resting-place, a slight description will make matters plain. In localities where there is danger from wild beasts the tents are pitched in a circle, in order that the cattle may be in safety. In other spots they generally are arranged in a semicircle, the Shekh occupying the large tent in the centre. They are made of goat's and camel's hair, but are perfectly rain-proof, in spite of their *rara tecta*, or thin roofs. They are extremely low, seldom more than about six or seven feet high in the middle, so that the squatting fashion must be resorted to; and as they are so pitched that there is a wide

[1] Encampment.

interval between them and the ground, they are rather airy habitations for the winter, although their owners fill up the interstices with bushes. Any one who has experienced a bitter northerly blast among the Tunisian hills in the month of January, in one of these tabernacles, will have his ideas of sultry Africa considerably altered. Shaw reminds us that the descriptions of Sallust and Virgil remain perfectly correct to the present day. Sallust compares the Libyan tents of his time to the bottom of a ship turned upside down:—"Ædificia Numidarum, quæ Mapalia illi vocant, oblonga incurvis lateribus tecta, quasi navium carinæ essent."—*Bell. Jug.* § 21. And nothing can be more true, even now, than the lines in the third Georgic :—

> Quid tibi pastores Libyæ, quid pascua versu
> Proloquor, et raris habitata Mapalia tectis ?
> Sæpe diem noctemque et totum ex ordine mensem
> Pascitur, itque pecus longa in deserta sine ullis
> Hospitiis ; tantum campi jacet : omnia secum
> Armentarius Afer agit, tectumque, laremque,
> Armaque, Amyclæumque canem, Cressamque pharetram."

We could this night depose to the truth of their having brought the "Amyclæan hound" with them, for the dogs never ceased barking from sunset to sunrise, indeed some of them had completely lost their voices from their exertions. We had a visit in the course of the night from a white rat, who was so familiar that we could not help supposing he must have been on good terms with the natives, for he sat up, looked at us with his little red eyes, and eat the crumbs as if he had a perfect right to them, and was one of the family.

On the morning of the 5th we descended from the mountains into the plains, after—Oh! such a cold night! and Oh! such a cold bath! We had now left the myrtle forests and the stunted pines, and found ourselves in a wide champaign expanse of immense fertility. It was in the usual course of Moorish farming—fallow and crop; but the amount of barley sown was perfectly prodigious, and how it could ever have been got into the ground I am at a loss to conceive, for of all lazinesses that of the Moors seems to me the most superlative. Their idea of happiness is literally doing nothing except to squat silently like penguins outside their villages. I have passed in the morning, out shooting, an assembly of Moors squatting solemnly in the sun, muffled up in their white garments, and in the afternoon returning, there they were in the same position, having just veered with the sun—

> Sedunt æternumque sedebunt,
> Felices.

The Arabs are, however, certainly much more industrious, and I dare say this cultivation was the work of some Arab tribe the name of which I did not learn.

All along this plain, every quarter of a mile revealed the remains of the former population of this country, once the Regio Zeugitana of the Romans. The sites of former towns, villages, and homesteads, dotted each rising ground, and the very streets were clearly defined by the lintels and the thresholds and doorposts of large blocks of hewn stone; but so it has been ever since leaving Zowan. The houses were constructed of brick, which time and weather destroyed, leaving the stonework as a testimony, to be added to that of shattered columns lying by the outlines of temples, of what Africa was and might be again. We were to be the guests this evening of the Kaïd, or governor, of the Dreed, one of the noblest Arab tribes. He was supposed to be somewhere in the neighbourhood, on his way to Kairouan, where he generally resides. We skirted the mountain of Bargou, leaving it to the left, thence by Gebel Serge, or Saddle Mountain, and thence towards the Gebel Ballota; and as our informants on the road merely pointed in a westerly direction, indicating that the Dreed *dowar* was somewhere in that quarter, we were apprehensive of a supperless evening, when the sun began to sink. At last, however, in the distance we perceived a large body of footmen and cavaliers, and on reaching them found that they were the personages we were in quest of; they were just returning from coursing, and the blue smoke rising over the nearest elevation, showed us that our destination was at no great distance. We calculated our day's journey to be about eighteen miles. On arriving at the encampment, after a desperate fight to preserve the lives of our poor dogs from the attacks of their Arab brethren, we were received at the door of a spacious tent by several Arabs, all of them evidently of high degree; but one in particular was remarkable for his fatness and his finery. This was our host, the Kaïd of the Dreed—one of the greatest, if not the greatest chieftain in the regency. He received us with great cordiality; and, as a preliminary to dinner, he ordered what novelists call a slight refection of French *bonbons,* quince preserve, figs, dates, walnuts, and camels' milk. The milk I thought salt and execrable; but Sir S. was quite of a different opinion, which was fortunate for him, as there were no cows in the encampment. The Kaïd amused us during the repast, by telling us all about himself, and his tribe, who he said numbered 40,000 souls. He was now on an excursion among his people, and returning to Kairouan, the sacred city, founded by his ancestor the valiant Ukba, in the year 670 A.D. In consequence of this distinguished lineage, the tribe of the Dreed have several immunities in the way of taxation; and the magnificent diamond snuff-boxes which he exhibited, one from the Sultan, and the others from the present and the late Bey, attested the exalted position of our entertainer. I am not quite sure, however, but that he exhibited with quite as much pride his boxes of huge French crystallized *bonbons*, of which, as a great compliment, he presented one to each of us. I must do him the justice to say, that he was quite as anxious to inspect everything we had, as to display his own treasures: he examined our guns, then the gun-cases, and was lost in admiration at the revolvers, on which his heart was evidently set. Although he did not signify his wish for anything, still it was clear, that had we offered one of these weapons it would not have been refused. At last dinner came, and we were able to rescue our pistols from having the springs broken by perpetual snapping, to say nothing of the expenditure of copper caps.

In the evening we had a great levée in the outer tent: first of all we were requested to wind up the chief's watches and set them; but a more useless appendage than a watch it is difficult to conceive, for he had not the least idea of the hours, and the time on the dial-plate was marked by European figures. After that we had a long chat on the affairs of Europe. He asked us various questions as to the comparative power of England and France, and seemed quite aware of the maritime superiority of England. The audience was particularly inquisitive about the Queen of England, whom they called by the old Latin name of Regina, not El Regina, or *the* Queen, but simply Regina, as if there was only one queen in the world. There was an old wild-looking Shekh, who, by his odd questions and remarks, created great amusement, and who insisted that England was always governed by queens, and that the women ruled the men. On the Kaïd's asking me what position I held in my own country, I replied that I was one of the Diwan, or counsellors, which was the nearest approach I could make to the functions of M.P. The old Shekh immediately asked if we ever gave Regina bad counsel; and on my replying, that sometimes we were wrong in our advice, he very knowingly closed one eye, and looking round on the company, inquired, greatly to their delight, if on those occasions Regina gave us the stick. We replied, that Regina was a great deal too good to give us the stick, even if she had the power to do so; but that we were governed by laws written out, and that she could do nothing contrary to the laws, which did not permit her counsellors to receive the stick. "Wallah!" said the old fellow; "we have our written law in the Koran, but I should not like to give bad counsel to the Bey for all that." "But," interposed the chief, "Regina must administer the stick when she goes about to collect her money, or you would not otherwise give her any." We had again to explain, through the medium of Kassim, that Regina had a fixed sum paid her by her counsellors, and never went about collecting money. This excited great admiration, and our old Shekh remarked, that the Bey would have but a slender purse if he did not bring his sticks with him in his annual visit to his loving subjects. The next inquiry was, if Regina was married; and on hearing that she was, they wished to know how many husbands she had, and seemed to think it a poor case, that, being so great a Queen, she should be satisfied with one husband all her life. They then were very curious about her Majesty's family, and whether the princesses would be allowed to marry among the *Muslemin;* for, they said, they heard the English were not the same as the French in religion, but worshipped Allah alone, and were friends of the Mahommedans; and they recommended, amid great merriment, the old Shekh to trim his beard, proceed to England, and propose himself to Regina as a son-in-law. We fortunately had a sovereign among us, and great was the satisfaction, in spite of the dislike of the likeness of anything on the earth, at the effigy of Regina, which the old gentleman proposed to keep as a *souvenir* of her Majesty—a proposal to which we did not accede. Of course, being only able to catch a little of the conversation here and there in the original language, and having it translated into the desperate gibberish of Kassim, I lost a good deal of the amusement, for we had a very merry evening of it; and the last and not least part of this Arabian night's entertainment was a trick played by the Kaïd upon the old Shekh, who was evidently but little acquainted with the ways of the gay world. The Kaïd had been playing with a bottle of *eau de Cologne,* which he had produced from among his treasures, and had been indulging his friends with an occasional sniff as a particular treat. As we broke up to retire, he called the Shekh to him, and, by way of special honor, poured some of the spirit into his hands, and made him rub them and his arms with it. He then told him to hold his fingers over the candle. In an instant, of course, hands and arms were in a blaze. I shall never forget the old fellow's look of horror, as if he had been the victim of some foul necromancy. He then jumped up with a shout, danced madly about, and, at last, rushing out of the tent, threw himself on the sand and rolled about, fully under the impression that he was on fire all over. The other Arabs looked on with amazement and fear; but on the Kaïd's repeating the experiment in a smaller way on himself, everybody seemed to think it quite the right thing to do, and crowded round their chief to get a few drops; so the party retired to their tabernacles in great spirits, waving their blazing hands—γέλως τ' ἄσβεστος ἐνῶρτο—"and unextinguished laughter shook the tent."

The next day we went out boar-shooting, accompanied by the Kaïd's brother, a fat youth, very jolly, and all for galloping and sport. We had a large number of beaters, and a large number of curs; but though, from the rooting all about, there was clearly plenty of boars, yet the *chasse* was so badly managed that when we did get the game afoot, which consisted of three very good-sized pigs, no one succeeded in getting a shot, except myself, at a very long distance. It was ineffectual, and we saw no more "Haloof" that day. With a few steady old hounds, and the guns properly placed, we might have had some more skins for our collection, and a really good day's sport.

Our host had, during the evening's conversation, fully enlightened us as to the difference between Kissera and Kessereen, and during the day the first-mentioned place was shown to us. It lay on our left, and is perched on the top of a mountain, and the road to it is so steep, that we should have had to leave the tents and luggage at the foot. We inquired if there was any reason at all why we should go thitherwards, and at last ascertained that not only was there no reason for going there, but every reason, unless we wished to become still more involved in the hills, for avoiding it. The question was now to get to Kessereen and Sbaitla, and, though in a straight direction, we could hardly have been more than about seventy miles from the latter town, yet we occupied a week in going from Kaïd to Kaïd, before we reached it. We bade farewell on the 7th to the illustrious Dreed, and their fat chieftain, Ibrahim; he did me the honor of writing his name, or rather of getting his secretary to write it, in my pocket-book, and requested mine in return, and Sir S.'s, which he looked at very sagely, turned upside down. Kassim, our servant, had a most supreme contempt for this worthy, in spite of his ancient lineage and glorious ancestor, Ukba. He said he was like a woman, lolling on a couch all day; that he could not walk, nor ride, nor shoot, and was only fit to eat quince-jam and *bonbons*; but that he was "bon Arabe," and that we should come across "mauvais Arabe," a very different customer. In fact, as we approached Sbaitla, of dangerous notoriety, it was quite clear that apprehensions of "mauvais Arabe" pervaded not only Kassim, but the magnificent Hamba, and the whole escort. We were brought from one Kaïd to another, whether for the purpose of getting presents, or of staving off the evil day, I cannot tell, but I dare say both reasons were uppermost in the minds of our attendants. Every artifice was employed to prevent us from going there, and, though the bravest of the lot, Kassim generally had some ominous story of murdering and marauding, by way of conversation to beguile the way.

Our march on the 7th was to Mogarowa, about nineteen miles still to the west, but more southward than before. Our course lay during the morning along the banks of a river, probably the Siliana, and was harassing to the baggagers, from the number of dry beds of torrents which we were forced to cross in the course of the day. The tent-horse was completely done up, by reason of his sore back and bad constitution, and henceforth one of our troubles was the extortion of some tent-bearing animal, whether horse, mule, or camel, from the different authorities. A mule was employed on this occasion, who got in every person's way, poled the other baggagers on all occasions, and slipped his burden so often, that we were more than seven hours before we arrived at our destination. The country we passed through resembled for some time that peculiar scenery which is more common in Germany than elsewhere; it was a narrow fertile valley lying between the feet of two high hills, with a river running through the middle. There were some Arabs at work on this rich land, still it seemed almost entirely neglected; and we passed numbers of olive-trees, of great age, but the small size of the berry showed that no fostering care had been applied to them for many a long day. On leaving this valley we passed a village with Roman remains, but, as it threatened heavy rain, I did not dismount to examine them; on a tombstone I read the word Flaccus. As well as I could understand, this village was called the village of the Oulad On, and its inhabitants requested us to stop a little while that they might have a good look at us, as they had not had the benefit of the sight of a Christian before in their lives. The same request was made a few miles further on, coupled with an anxiety to drink our healths, I suppose, for an indigenous lady made a strong appeal to Kassim for a bottle of rum, with which she had heard the Nazarenes quenched their thirst. After leaving these unsophisticated Muslims, we descended into the plain, and inspected the remains of a considerable Roman town, at a place called Hedera by Kassim. There was a large square building still standing, with pilasters, but it had more the appearance of a fort than of a tomb. We asked some natives if there were any inscriptions, but they were not aware of any. I may remark, that this name Hedera, or Hidra, is given in the French map to a town considerably to the south-west, almost on the borders of Algeria. It occupies also the same position on Shaw's map, and he considers it to be the ancient Thunodrunum. It is quite clear these two places are not the same, but whether they both bear the same name, or that my informants were in error about these ruins, I cannot say. The similarity in appearance between them and the Hydrah of Shaw, is remarkable. He says, "Hydrah is situated in a narrow valley, with a rivulet running by it, and appears to be one of the most considerable places in this country, for extent of ruins. For we have here the walls of several houses, the pavement of a whole street entire, with a variety of altars and a mausoleum." The Hydrah, or Hederah, we passed through this day is also in a valley, with a stream (rather a remarkable circumstance) running through it: there are also the remains of the mausoleum. Shaw, however, speaks of a triumphal arch, with an inscription, which we did not see. After surmounting another ridge of hills, we descended to our destination, Mogarowa, which is a collection of square stone hovels, looking rather like small county Galway paddocks, and yet it is the provincial town of these parts. Our host, Setaib Ben Amar, was a hearty good fellow, sent his people flying hither and thither to make everything comfortable, and we passed a pleasant evening enough, round a roaring fire, after a cold showery ride of about twenty miles. Sir S. bought here, from an Arab, a large number of copper coins, some of them Punic or Numidian, which had been dug up by the villagers. I am strongly of opinion, that this town would well repay the visit of the antiquarian. It appears to me, from the coins that we obtained, from the character of the houses, the real Numidian Magalia, and from the fact that Sir G. Temple found at this place a Numidian inscription, and some rude bas-reliefs, that we might here obtain some insight into the Numidian language, by the discovery of other inscriptions which closer investigation and excavations might bring to light. The natives are very friendly, and it would be an excellent central point for examining the numerous Roman remains in the immediate vicinity, and for an excursion to the remarkable cromlechs near Thala, to which I shall refer hereafter.

On the 8th we left Mogarowa, accompanied part of the way by our cheery host riding majestically, with very short stirrups, an ambling mule. On surmounting the hill above our-resting place, we were shown the white houses of Kaff, to the west, but not very much to the north. They told us it was distant about twelve or fourteen miles, and we were shown in the plain some very extensive ruins, which we were unable to visit. Our route lay over an expanse of barren chalky hills covered with rosemary, wild thyme, and a scented grass which, when bruised by the horses' feet, spread perfume all around. After six hours and a half riding, or about eighteen miles, we reached the town of Uksoor, situated amid gardens of prickly pears. It promised well in appearance, but an extremely bad reception awaited us. The inhabitants refused us a house, and offered us a shake-down in a miserable hole full of dirt and vermin. So we stood on our dignity, pitched our tent, although the weather threatened, and promised them faithfully that their heels and the Bey's sticks should form ere long an intimate acquaintance. Even this awful menace, delivered full of dignity through the enraged Kassim, produced nothing more than a few eggs and some bread; but there was always the faithful cold partridge—the true friend in need to fall back on. The cause of this bad treatment did not transpire for some days; all that we remarked at the time was a fierce altercation between Ali, our friendly

Spahi, and the Shekhs of the town, and that the tumult was subsequently appeased by the second Hamba taking the authorities aside, and, after much confidential whispering, informing us that the Governor was absent, and that nothing could be got till his return. We were very green in these early days of Tunisian travelling, but our eyes were soon to be opened to the devices by which starvation was threatened to ourselves and beasts.

During the night it rained vigorously, and we found his Highness's tent to be the reverse of water-proof. A good deal of our time was employed in making canals and water-courses, to carry off the torrents by which we were invaded from below, and in seeking such a position as should relieve us from a slow but sure shower-bath descending from above. It was market-day at Uksoor, and the Zeugitanian farmers, lean, lanky, and white-blanketed, came ambling in on mules and asses. What they came for, I cannot pretend to say, as there was no exhibition of goods for sale, nor did any money appear to change hands. A bowl of muddy water is no great incentive to gossiping, and there was no hot brandy and water in prospect, to induce farmer Ali to mount his ass, and come in to have a chat with farmer Mahommed. We were delayed here some time, endeavoring to get a blacksmith to put a shoe on Sir S.'s horse, which was at last accomplished in so bad a manner, that it came off altogether the next day, and showed us clearly that a slight knowledge of farriery, a few spare horseshoes, and a good pair of pincers, are necessary for an excursion in this country.

Our ride was a short but cold one to the encampment of the Wartan Arabs, about seven miles off. We found them located in a bleak, barren, and stony plain, surrounded by hills, with the mountain range of Smăt to the west. The Shekh insisted on our sharing his tent, which he said was large enough for us all, himself and ourselves, his family and our retainers. With his hand on his breast, he protested that fleas were unknown animals in his abode, and that we should be warm and jolly, in spite of the wide gap between the ground and the borders of the tent. The first part of his representations were true; the latter not quite so correct, for, although the gap was well stuffed with juniper and rosemary bushes, still the bleak north wind would find its way in, and seek us out, in spite of all our attempts at snugness. We might have pitched our own tent, but the ground was so sloppy from the recent rain, that it was a godsend to get a dry resting-place, however cold. We were divided from the family, which, from the squalling of children, appeared large, by a curtain of camel's hair; but the tittering on the other side of it, showed that sundry interstices, what the French would call *trous Judas*, were employed to good purpose by the Arab maidens, and placed us rather in a quandary as regarded the use of our tub next morning.

On retiring to rest, out hospitable chief betook himself to his division, and after two or three battles, which we had to sustain against some hens which would roost on our heads, and a ram which was determined to share our blankets, we made everything right to have a comfortable sleep. And here occurred a somewhat notable adventure, which might have ended more unpleasantly than it did.

The night was now far advanced, the cocks and hens had ceased to persecute us, and canine clamour had sunk into deep silence all around the encampment, when I was suddenly awakened by a terrific outburst of barking, snarling, and fierce objurgation on the part of the dogs in the next partition of the tent. There was evidently something wrong, or some unjustifiable intrusion, to warrant such a disturbance. Presently two shadows stood between me and the dim external light—one was Sir S., the other the Shekh leading him by the hand—not a word was spoken—Sir S. regained his blanket, and the Shekh departed in silence. On asking what had happened, Sir S. informed me that he had fancied the horses were fighting, and had gone out of the tent to have a look after them. It was easy enough to see the way out, but, as all was dark within, he had unfortunately returned by the wrong side of the camel-hair partition. While groping his way, as he thought, to his resting-place, he found himself attacked by the dogs, whom he kept at bay as best he could, with his only weapon of defence, his slipper. He still retreated, until his progress was stopped by a couchant figure, whom he supposed to be myself, and over whom he stumbled. He then perceived, he said, a very pleasant smell of perfume arising from the figure, and as he knew that we had no Ess bouquet or *esprit de Jockey Club* with us, he became rather puzzled, and passed his hand over the prostrate form, still under the impression that it was one of the party. The form remained perfectly quiet, but he found, to his horror, that there was no doubt of its being that of a lady. The dogs were still baying about him, and he was now so far in the recesses of the tent, that he was, in truth, sorely perplexed what to do—to remain was impossible—when he felt his hand suddenly seized, and he was then led out by the tips of the fingers, as formally as if to dance a *minuet de la cour,* by the Shekh his host, who reconducted him without a word to his own portion of the tent, and there left him. The explanations were evidently to be deferred to the morrow. When the morning came, Kassim was summoned, and made acquainted with the whole affair. Presently the Shekh came in, and sat down without making any observation, as much as to say, now let us hear what you have to urge in excuse for your nocturnal intrusion. Of course the proper excuses were made, our want of acquaintance with tent life urged, and the moral character of the English extolled, by Kassim, to the skies. The Shekh's countenance was made white again, and we parted the best of friends. I may mention, incidentally, that we had seen engaged in household avocations, the evening before, a very good-looking Arab maiden, who was perfectly aware of her physical advantages, and had not the slightest objection to our noticing them. Kassim informed us, that if the adventure had occurred with a Moor, instead of an Arab, the matter would not have been concluded so easily, or so amicably.

On December 10th, the sun had a hard struggle with the cold hoar frost, when with numbed fingers and noses, we emerged, after the delicate explanation, from our camel-hair asylum. Our way again lay over a wide plain, and we passed, in the course of the day, several tombs resembling exactly the Celtic cromlechs of the North. They were constructed in the same rough way—with the same huge blocks.

Further on, we came to the remains of a Roman town, with a small roofed tomb, massively constructed, in shape much resembling the Syrian tombs as described by Sir C. Fellowes. There was no inscription on it, but over the entrance were two figures rudely executed, the one to the left holding a trident. Our guides said the place was called Terba. After a ride of about twenty miles with our heads now turned southwards, we arrived at our destination—a small village of the Mejr Arabs, *autre espèce d'Arabes,* as Kassim termed them.

The Kaïd was an old gentleman in bad health, full of years and obesity. He informed us that this town was formerly called Sphay, and he recommended us to go and see some stones with writing on them, among the prickly-pear gardens. We there found an arch, in excellent preservation, with the following inscription on it:—

PRO SALVTE IMP CAES MAVRELIAN . . . ONINI AVG LI.
BEI . . . ORUMQ EIVS COLONI SALTVS MASSIPIANI AEDIFICIA VETV . . . TE
CONLAPSA SVP . . . . ITEM ARQVVS DVOS ASSE IVBENTE PROVIN-
CIALE AVG LIBERDO EODEMQVE DEDICANTE.

This place had a reputation for its mineral waters, and the Governor was here, he said, for the purpose of regaining his lost health. The gardens of prickly pears were strewed with the remains of the old Roman settlement, and from the operations at work in the neighborhood of this votive arch, it seems destined ere long to form the foundation of the next building required.

On the 11th we proceeded about eight miles to the south, to the encampment of the Farasheesh, one of the most powerful tribes of Arabs in these parts. In ascending the lofty hill above our late halting-place, we again met several more of the same Celtic cromlechs we had seen the day before. When we arrived nearly at the summit of the pass, we came upon a town of some size, which we were told was called Thala. There was a tomb in it resembling exactly that which we had passed the day before. We heard, when it was too late, that there was an inscription on its base, which I greatly regret I did not see. The houses were all constructed out of the *débris* of the old Roman dwellings, and it was evidently in former times a place of great strength and importance, commanding the pass by which access might be had to the northern and southern divisions of the Roman province. We were delayed here at least an hour in endeavoring to get Sir S.'s horse, who had thrown his shoe, shod, and, as it was market-day, we were beset and stared at by some hundreds of ill-favored white-blanketed Arabs. It was most unfortunate that we had started unprovided with books, from not having originally intended to make this tour; for a Sallust at that moment would have enabled us to look carefully over the position of Thala, the topography of which has been much discussed, and has occupied more than three pages of Shaw. This traveller was clearly unaware of the existence of the town through which we passed this day, and has labored hard to prove that Feriana is the scene of the siege and desperate defence against Metellus, described by Sallust. Had he been made acquainted with this town, and visited it, he would have seen that it answers in all respects the accounts we receive of its situation from the Roman historian. He says, "that Metellus was aware of the dry and desert nature of the country between Thala and the nearest river, which was distant about fifty Roman miles. He, therefore, had his baggage animals relieved of all their burdens, except provender for ten days, and had them laden instead with skins and utensils necessary for the carriage of water." Shaw is obliged to fall back on the Hataab, or the river of Suffetula, to answer to this river; whereas the Bagradas, the river *par excellence* of that part of Northern Africa, is just about the distance described. Again, it is mentioned by Sallust "that there are certain fountains not far from the walls of Thala." I have no doubt but that it was at these very fountains or wells that we watered our horses just outside the present town. Tacitus also mentions Thala—as a garrison town—a post—"Præsidium[1] cui Thala nomen," and this exactly answers to the present Thala. In fact we ourselves, although oblivious of Sallust, remarked the admirable strategetic position of this place—commanding access to the north and south, whereas Feriana has no such advantage whatever. The name, however, and the vast Roman remains, leave no doubt of its being the old city of Jugurtha, which defended itself for forty days against Metellus, and the inhabitants of which, rather than submit, burnt themselves and all their

[1] Tacitus, *Annal.* iii. 31.

treasures after one last fierce carouse. It became subsequently a garrison town.

After surmounting this high hilly range, we descended into another plain, and found our hosts the Farasheesh, encamped at the foot of the wildest and most rugged mountain that we had yet come across. When we were within a short distance, the Shekh came galloping down to meet us on a fine black mare, in order to escort us in all solemnity to the tent assigned us. He was a fine hale old fellow, with off-hand hearty manners, and very different from our fat friend the Kaïd of the Dreed. The Farasheesh are famous for their breed of horses, and the Shekh's mare was a good specimen; the rest that we saw were poor enough. They have also a high character for their sporting propensities, and the Shekh immediately gave proof of it by introducing us to his hawking establishment. He showed us with great pride three species of falcons: two dark colored, the other nearly white—the peregrine. The white was the falcon of the country, he told us. As to the other two species, one came originally from Constantinople, and was called Stambouli; the other glorious fellows of the darkest hue, with large black wondering eyes, he informed us were Timbucti by name, and derived their lordly origin from Timbuctoo. By this he did not mean that these birds were imported from Constantinople or Timbuctoo, but that the breed came formerly from those parts. We found a capital canvas marquée arranged for us in the middle of his black camel-hair encampment, and while the baggage was being arranged, he volunteered to show us the performance of his falcons. His son, a handsome blue-eyed young fellow with light hair, the image of Lord Elcho, galloped out into the plain swinging aloft a stuffed hare-skin; the old chief followed with one of each species on his shoulder, and Timbucti on his head. When the young man had got far enough, one falcon after another was unhooded and let loose, and away in one long sweep close to the ground they followed in pursuit. On reaching the horseman they rose above him and then swooped, and while one was sweeping downward in attack, the others rose again for vantage-ground to renew it. The young Shekh, with his head on the horse's neck, although well muffled up, had no easy work to keep off his assailants, and at last surrendered the hare-skin, on which they pounced, were fed, and again restored to their perches. The game they chiefly pursued were hares, partridges, bustards, and gazelles. Kassim was extremely desirous of begging one or two, but we discouraged him, by reason of the long journey we had before us, and the difficulty in taking care of them; but for a person anxious for sport in the southern district of the Regency, it would be well worth while to persuade the Shekh, who had about fifteen, to part with one or two, which I am confident he would have readily done had we signified our wishes to that effect. We remarked, on returning to the encampment, that it was surrounded by a huge rampart of thorny brushwood, and, on asking the cause of these defences, learned that for the last fortnight a lion had been in the habit of paying them very unwelcome visits, and levying a toll almost every other night on their flocks and droves. For that reason we and our horses had been considerately placed in the middle of the encampment. We were shown from our tent the mountain over our great present object, Sbaitla, which did not appear more than fifteen or sixteen miles off. The Shekh, however, would not hear of our going there from his locality: he insisted that the country between us and it was most dangerous, from the lawless tribes; and, as the very word of danger or robbers terrified our escort, we were forced, in spite of all our remonstrances, to submit, and proceed to Kessereen, from whence we heard there were fewer dangers to be encountered. We were faithfully promised by our host that he would send the following morning one of his own men to the Arabs at Sbaitla, to make everything smooth with them; but, he said, his head depended on our safety, and he begged hard that we would not place it and ourselves in jeopardy by insisting on going the short way. The matter was discussed till bedtime, and as we closed the canvas door of our tent, we looked forth and saw our camp surrounded by a ring of watch-fires to keep off the ravaging and roaring lion, who generally made his appearance every other night, and, as he had been absent the night before, it was thought probable he might shortly make his appearance. These expectations were partly disappointed: the lion did not come till the watch-fires were burnt out, and all was as dark as Nox and Erebus. We bounded from our mattresses at the tremendous uproar that arose at once: dogs barking for their lives, men shouting, and women uttering shrieks ear-piercing and discordant enough to keep off anything. "The lion, the lion," shouted Kassim, "is on us." We seized our guns and attempted to sally forth; but one fall over the tent-ropes convinced us that bed was the most useful and safe place to remain in, for it was impossible to see a foot ahead. The tumult lasted for about an hour, during which time we heard subsequently, that the king of the beasts was prowling close to the camp, within a few yards of us, but at length the smouldering fires were renewed, lighted brands were tossed about, and hungry and supperless the lion retired to his rocky fortress.

Dec. 12th.—On meeting our friend the Shekh in the morning, we suggested that a hunt would be the proper thing to rid him of his obtrusive and unwelcome guest of the evening before. To our surprise, he replied, that there was no use in attempting a hunt; that the lion had departed, and that they had not the least idea, even if he had not left the locality, where his home might be. On our remarking that he could not have gone far after his visit of the preceding night, he said, it was quite a mistake—that the lion had not been there at all, that he had left the country altogether; and so got rid of the subject, which he was evidently anxious to avoid. In the course of the day, after warming the heart of the guide who accompanied us by a few pinches of snuff, the truth came out that our ears had not deceived us: the lion had been there as usual, but that the Shekh was afraid to attack him, although perfectly acquainted with his lair. The poor man was in an unpleasant predicament: the lion would, of course, show fight, and possibly kill him, or some of his family, which was bad enough; or, what was almost worse, he might kill us, in which case he was confident the Bey would cut his head off. So he thought the easiest and most prudent course was to tell a good lie, and ignore the existence of the beast *in toto*. We departed, therefore, for El Kessereen, or the Castles, about twenty-five miles to the south. Our Shekh accompanied us with his hawks, and escorted us through the hill passes; but we had no flight, as neither hare nor partridge presented itself. The scenery at first starting this day was not unlike parts of the Black Forest:

jagged peaks, covered with low pines and brushwood, started up abruptly, affording capital cover for our friend the lion, and for leopards, which we subsequently heard were not uncommon. This kind of ground, however, did not last long: we soon found ourselves again in the plains, but out of the region of cultivation; it was a wide expanse, covered with stunted juniper and rosemary. To our left rose a high uniform ridge of sandstone formation, and at about a distance of twelve miles to the right we were shown the range of the mountains over Tebissa, on the French territory. On nearing Kessereen, the rain began to descend fiercely, and the plain was heavy and sticky enough, with a strong retentive clay, anything but satisfactory to the poor baggagers. When we arrived at our destination, we found it to consist of a Santon's tomb, round the square *enceinte* of which the Marabouts, or holy guardians, had their apartments. As we had sent on word of our arrival, we expected a roof of some kind over our heads from the torrent of rain which was falling; but were informed that we could not be admitted within the sacred precincts, and the sooner we moved on somewhere else the better; but to move on was impossible: it was now dark night, and there was nowhere to go to. The prospect of the tent was not agreeable either, considering the ground was in a state of mud, and that the experience of the night at Uksoor had destroyed all confidence in the water-proof qualities of our canvas. There was one spot a little elevated above the sheet of mud, and this was the burial-place of departed Santons; but the Marabouts strongly objected to our laying our heathenish and Christian bodies over the remains of the faithful; and the Hambas, instead of taking our part, recommended us to move on, and literally to stick in the mud. While the altercation lasted, which it did for a good hour and a half, we and the poor horses were left standing in the downpour, and in darkness; but at last we insisted on having the tent put up in the only possible spot where it could be fixed, namely, on the burial-ground. The Hambas, of course, cared little where we bivouacked, as they, being of the orthodox faith, were sure of snug quarters, and a good toast before the fire within the building. At last the tent was pitched, but we soon found we had little prospect of shelter within it; and as for thinking of lying down, it was out of the question; one might as well have thought of sleeping in a wet drain. So we got our panniers in the middle, and covered them and ourselves, as well as we could, with our macintosh sheets and water-proof coats, and there sat huddled up together, wet and supperless, till morning. We had a few oranges, a Bologna sausage, and some brandy; and with that simple fare we did as well as we could for supper, dinner, and breakfast. The poor horses, not being accustomed to brandy and sausage, were worse off than ourselves, and tried to refresh themselves and be merry by nibbling each other's tails. This night, however, our eyes were opened to the rascalities of our escort. A violent quarrel took place between Kassim and Mohammed El Kaffi, who seized each other by their garments, and lavished freely the most compromising expressions on the character of their mutual female relations. Kassim openly accused Mohammed El Kaffi and Mohammed Tebirski, the second and third Hambas, of having, since the commencement of the journey, purposely delayed our progress, by bringing us from one Kaïd to another, quite unnecessarily, in order to extort presents from them. This was not a matter of such vital importance, but he also formally accused them of having received 250 piastres at Uksoor, on the stipulation that the inhabitants should be permitted to starve us out, and to refuse us shelter; and that that having turned out such a capital speculation, they were repeating it here, and were sanctioning the bad treatment we were undergoing for a consideration which the pious Marabouts had proffered. Little Ali the Spahi, who had always been staunch, burst into the tent, and openly reiterated the accusation. His indignation was inflamed by having just received a severe blow on the head from El Kaffi, who accused him of peaching, and he showed up most courageously the conspiracy while smarting under the pain and indignity of the blow. I doubt if he would have been so plucky in cold blood.

Our head Hamba, the Oda Bashi, was also implicated as a receiver of illicit contributions; but it did not transpire that he had encouraged or instigated the malpractices of the others, although not disdaining, after all was over, to accept a portion of their earnings. The third Hamba also appeared not to have got much, but only to have taken the part of his comate, and to have threatened Ali with vengeance. We had, therefore, ample opportunities for consultation during the night, and we resolved, on arriving at Kafsa, to send back Mr. Mohammed El Kaffi to his master, the Bey, which was not likely to be an agreeable meeting to one of the parties.

Shaw seems to have been at times in worse predicaments than ourselves, for he travelled without a tent, for fear of the Arabs; and he remarks, "We had now and then occasion enough to meditate upon the same distress with the Levite and his company (Judges xix. 15), when 'there was no man that would take them into his house for lodging,' and of the propriety there was to place (1 Tim. v. 10; Heb. xiii. 2) the lodging and entertaining of strangers among good works."

13th.—The morning turned out fine again, and though, from the night we had passed, I found myself in a feverish state, we announced our fixed and unalterable determination to proceed at once to Sbaitla. This produced more altercation and wrangling; but we quietly told our escort, who wished us to go somewhere else in the neighborhood previously, that if they did not make themselves ready to accompany us, we would go without them; and if anything happened, their heads would be answerable. Our tent was in such a state that it was useless to take it, and there were no houses nor Arab encampments near our destination; but Kassim informed us that we could find some dry lying among the ruins, and, although that was not tempting to a feverish patient, still our characters were at stake: we had said that go we would, and we made it a rule all through the journey to adhere to every determination we expressed. This saved a deal of wrangling and argument; our escort soon perceived it was useless to resist, and after one or two struggles gave in, and never attempted to coerce our movements, although they repeatedly deceived us. The plains over which we went were, except in the immediate locality about Kessereen, altogether devoid of cultivation; plenty of Roman ruins, however, denoted their former fertility. We passed close by one Roman *castellum*, solidly constructed, and saw several others in the distance. While jogging along we were entertained by stories of the lawlessness and rapacity of the Arabs of Sbaitla, and our chief Hamba showed, by his anxious glances ever and anon around him, the internal disquiet that was agitating his mind. We passed one or two very small and apparently very poor Arab *dowars;* but, small and weak as they were, they were objects of distrust to our captain, who seemed to breathe more freely when they were out of sight. At last, after crossing a couple of deep stony ravines, Sbaitla, with its temples and triumphal arch, stood before us. As Gibbon has borrowed Shaw's description of its appearance, I may take the same liberty:—" Sbaitla is pleasantly situated upon a rising ground, shaded all over with juniper-trees. A little brook glides along the north-east side of it, which afterwards, in directing its course towards Gilma, loses itself in the sand. This city, the ancient Suffetula, is one of the most remarkable places in Barbary for the extent and magnificence of its ruins; for there is, first of all, a sumptuous arch of the Corinthian order, consisting of one large arch with a lesser one on each side of it, with a few words of the dedication remaining upon the architrave. From this arch, all along to the city, there is a pavement like that at Hydrah, of large black stones, with a parapet wall raised breast high on each side of it, intended, perhaps, to hinder the populace from incommoding the Emperor in his triumphal entrance into the city. Near the end of this pavement we pass through a beautiful portico, built in the same style and manner with the triumphal arch, which conducts us afterwards into a spacious court. Here we have the ruins of three contiguous temples, whose several roofs, porticos, and façades indeed are broken down; but the rest of the fabric, with its respective columns, pediments, and entablatures, remains perfect and entire. There is in each of these temples a nich fronting the portico, and behind that of the middlemost we have a secret chamber, which might serve as a vestry."

To our great relief, on entering the town we discovered a small hovel, built of mud and stone, hard by one of the ancient buildings; and thither the baggagers proceeded. It was satisfactory to find that our lodging was not to be the cold ground; and, as there was no appearance of there being any of the dreaded Arabs about, we thought we should be comfortable, and have the place to ourselves. Being very weak, from the touch of fever's finger, slight though it was, instead of picketing my horse, I rode down through the deserted town to the triumphal arch, leaving Sir S. behind at the temple. When there I threw the bridle over the horse's neck, and began to copy the inscription on the arch; but while engaged in the occupation, a slight noise occurred, and, on looking round, I found myself surrounded by half a dozen wild-looking Arabs, who had come up unnoticed. As Kassim had pronounced them to be "mauvais Arabes," and as Mr. Davis had given a bad description of them also, saying that all the worst passions were written on their ignoble countenances, it was rather unpleasant being alone, and out of hail of the escort. The best thing was to put a good face on the matter; so, throwing one of them the bridle, I asked them to lead the horse, and to show me all the stones with letters on them. They were quite unaware of the escort until they came within sight of the hut, and the horses picketed before it; but I must do them the justice to say, that nothing could be more civil than they were: they pointed out the different buildings, and the inscriptions, and instead of wishing to cheat, rob, or drive us away, as they are said to have done other travellers, Dr. Barth among the rest, they were particularly anxious we should stop, and hunt for treasure along with them. We were to furnish the science, and they the labor, and to share the profits equally. This was the only request they made; there were no begging demands for anything: so truth compels me to do justice to the much-maligned Arabs of Sbaitla, and pronounce them to be "bons Arabes," in spite of Kassim's assurances of their being "mauvais." Kassim, however, had a decided *guignon* against Arabs in general; he was by no means blind to their errors, or kind to their failings, but pronounced one general dictum on all occasions, which our experience forces us to consider as arising from faulty induction, that "tout Arabe bon avec le baton, tout Arabe mauvais sans baton."

Sbaitla is certainly a remarkable spot, and was worth all the trouble and battling that preceded the visit. You can here see the outline of every street, as I before remarked, when referring to the remains of other Roman towns, by the doorposts and sills of blocks of stone. The streets were extremely narrow, but the marks of the wheels of chariots or carts are still visible on the old stone pavement. One or two streets are exceptions to the rest, being of considerable width—that which sweeps down from the lordly arch to the court of the temples, though not as large as the thoroughfares in Western and Northern cities, is larger than any street I remember in any Eastern city. On the arch Shaw read—

IMP CAESAR AVG . . .
ONIN . . .
SVFFETVLENTIVM . .
HANC EDIFICAVERVNT
ET DD. PP.

I was not well enough to copy the inscription, but I have no recollection of any such inscription as this. I only saw one inscription on the architrave, and I find in my notes that CONSTANT. was on it, and this tallies with a rough copy taken by Mr. Davis, who was greatly hurried, to this effect:

D.D. N
INVIC—SITEM — CONSTAN AIAN
SSIMIS CAES RIB CVS
STIC PROVIN VTO

Over the portico by which you enter into the court of the temple there are some letters, but the stones have fallen out of their position, and the inscription is so much defaced that I could only make out—

IVL PLA
DIV
RVA PRONIR NI
R
TNC A XT H PP

But I have no doubt but that a person giving time to this and the inscription on the triumphal arch would be able to get at the sense.

Although, as Shaw remarks, the porticos and façades of the temples are broken down, still the rear work and the greater portion of the main buildings are perfectly intact; while the fine stone pillars that strew the ground in front, show the wealth and capabilities of imperial Suffetula. There are a number of other large buildings, more or less ruined, and with the usual attention to a supply of water, a small aqueduct spans the dashing mountain torrent which flows to the north of the town. After the dirty muddy water-courses we had been continually crossing, the heart rejoiced in the clear dark stream, and the foam curling in the deep pool at the foot of the aqueduct, as in a Highland burn. Mr. Davis derives the name of Sufetula from the Punic Suffetim, the Carthaginian magistrates who answered to the Roman consuls, and ascribes to it a Punic origin. It however is, most probably, the diminutive of Sufes, a neighboring city, and means Little Sufes. The town of Sufes itself is very likely derived from Sufes, the singular of Suffetim; there are some remains, I understand, on its site, but all of them of Roman appearance. We know, however, that the Carthaginians extended their sway down to the Beled-el-Jereed, and the remark of an American writer, comparing the soil of Italy, covered as it is with the relics of different epochs, to a *palimpsest* on which time has effaced one set of characters to write another, is as true of Northern Africa as of Italy—Etruscans, Greeks, Romans, have stamped their seal of ownership on the one fair country, as Phœnicians, Numidians, Romans, and Saracens, have upon the other. This is, perhaps, the great charm of North African travelling, that while you have the excitement and entertainment of scenes and people little known, and of a state of society which totally dissociates you from Europe, yet during every day's journey some monument—some inscription—recalls your thoughts to the past history of the soil, to famous names, and famous times. You have not the gorgeous vegetation or the fierce hot chase of more Southern Africa; but the triumphal arch, the ruined temple, the half-intelligible inscription, all remind us of old friends, as it were—

> They tell of great old houses,
> And fights fought long ago;

and by the bivouac fire of crackling rosemary, amid keen-eyed, wondering Alis, Kassims, and Mohammeds, it is pleasant to chat over the good old times—of the house of Mago, fertile with great men—of Agathokles, Regulus, Scipio, Massinissa, Syphax, Marius, Belisarius.

Dec. 14.—In spite of the requests of our friends the Mejr Arabs, who invited us to stay and excavate, or else hunt the *nimr* (leopards) on the hills, we returned to our inhospitable quarters at Kessereen. Had we been able to procure any entertainment for man and beast, we should certainly have remained a day, in order fully to examine the Roman remains of this locality. But, as neither menaces nor civil words prevailed to obtain provisions, we shook off the dust, or rather the mud, from our feet, and departed to Feriana. It was a cold raw morning when we started ahead of our cavalcade, and proceeded to copy a very curious inscription of one hundred and nine lines in verse, partly hexameter and partly pentameter, which are still very legible on a handsome three-storied tomb, in the shape of a square tower, almost a mile from our bivouac, on the site of the ancient Colonia Scillitana. I may remark, that the practice which prevailed among foreign towns in the latter days of Roman supremacy, of calling themselves *Colonia*, was by way of a compliment and denoting their attachment to the metropolis, in the same way as we find on Greek coins of the same period the word φιλορώμαιος, to express the same feeling. The tomb seems to have been the mausoleum of one of the principal families of the town. On the third story of it there are eight tablets, recording the names of its inmates, of which I could only read—

—ANDRVS FILIVS
FECIT
PACATAE VXORI PIAE
FLAMINIAE PERP——
VIX AN L

Sir Grenville Temple, who visited this place, read also—

M. FLAVIVS SE
CUNDVS FILIUS
FECIT
Q. FLAVIO SECUNDO
PATRITIO.

All the inscriptions are on the south side of the tomb, and the long poetical effusion would, by its uncouthness, utterly dismay a sixth-form boy of Eton and Harrow. With a little time and attention, every word of it might be read; but I was ill and damp and cold, and could give Sir S. very little assistance in his deciphering. Certain usual allusions to the uncertainty of human life, and a panegyric on the magnificence of the monument, are the objects of the poet, who begins as follows:—

Sint licet exiguæ fugientia tempora vitæ
Parvaque raptorum cito transeat hora dierum
Merget et Elysiis mortalia corpora terris
Assidue rupto Lachesis male conscia penso
Jam jam inventa est blandæ rationis imago.

It is not worth while inserting a hundred lines of extremely bad Latin, and worse versification. There are, however, four lines of such quaint conceit, that I cannot omit them here. They describe a sculptured cock which surmounted the monument, and who, according to the poet, was placed in a position so much more exalted than the loftiest cloud, that if nature had only given him a voice, he would have forced the gods by his matin song to get out of their beds betimes and keep early hours.

> In summo tremulas galli non diximus alas
> Altior extremâ qui, puto, nube volat.
> Cujus si membris vocem natura dedisset
> Cogeret hic omnes surgere mane deos.

Besides this tomb there are other remains and a triumphal arch which time did not allow us to visit. We performed our journey to Feriana over a wild deserted country, occasionally dotted with some of those heaps of stones which here, as in Italy, denote where a murdered corpse has been found. The number of these tumuli we had lately met show that human life has not been held in much respect in these parts: in one short march Hubert counted twenty-two. But we are close to the French frontier, where robbers and murderers resort, as, provided no outrage is committed on French territory, they may always expect a safe refuge from pursuit within it. We are approaching, moreover, the country of the El Hamama, one of the most lawless and predatory Arab tribes, and are, in consequence, looking well to the efficiency of our weapons of war.

No interruption occurred during our six hours and a half ride, which we calculated at about twenty-three miles. We passed a very pretty small Roman intercolumniated temple, nearly perfect. It stood among extensive ruins, and was raised from the ground on a pedestal. I was unable to discover any inscription to throw a light on the name of the spot. As we approached Feriana, we traversed for some space the remains of the old town. It occupies the pass in the chain of hills to the south of which the Arab town at present stands. One of these hills is strongly fortified by a Roman wall which surrounds it, and evidently the citadel stood there. It completely commands the pass, and is quite strong enough to resist the attacks of wandering tribes unprovided with military engines. At the northern entrance of the old town, four columns of sandstone still remain, with a portion of the architrave upon them; but although I had two or three of the native boys with me the following day, and offered them piastres to show me letters on stones, I was unable to discover any record whatever. Shaw considers Feriana to be the ancient Telepte.

The present Arab town is wretched in the extreme; and after some delay, we got possession of a hovel, from which the human occupants were dislodged after considerable objurgation. The Arab proprietress was about the best specimen of a scold we had yet seen, and vented her indignation freely on Kassim and the Hambas, but came in towards evening, and was quite reconciled to us on receiving some needles and thread. So great was her good will, that she even volunteered to kill and make soup of a most aggressive hen that would come in and perch on our heads. We remained the 16th at Feriana; and, as I was not well enough to go the *chasse*, Sir S. made a long excursion to the east, but returned in the afternoon with only one pintail duck. I crawled out in the afternoon to the old town, part of which is very prettily situated by the side of a stream of fresh water, at the head of which is a perfect forest of at least two or three acres of oleanders. Near the stream, which rises from the bottom of a cliff, are the old baths, of great extent, and which must have been of great magnificence for such an out-of-the-way provincial town. The walls are eight feet thick in some parts, with large vaulted halls containing niches for statues and smaller chambers out of them. On the way home I met Sir S. along with the Hamba who had accompanied him, and recommended him to visit the Ras-el-Ain (the head of the fountain) and the baths; he desired the Hamba to go with him, but he point-blank refused to do so, and was very insolent moreover. The strictest injunctions had been given to our escort always to attend us wherever we went, and in the unsettled state of the country, of which we had a proof the same afternoon, it was necessary that a servant of the Bey should be at hand, in case of our meeting ill disposed persons, if only to let them know the danger they incurred by assailing the Bey's children. In the course of the discussion, we were constrained to apply to Mr. Mahommed Tebirski some epithets which his invariable sulkiness and bad conduct deserved, but which so enraged him, that he returned into the town and filled the place with his exclamations and complaints "late loca questibus implet." In the evening, we informed him that he should accompany us to Kafsa on the morrow, but that he should be sent back to Tunis to have a word or two with the Bey along with his worthy comrade El Kaffi, at which threat they were much amused, and laughed heartily. They had yet to learn the truth of the saying, "rira bien qui rira le dernier." On returning to Feriana, we found the town in an uproar: the women were screaming, and the men rushing to and fro, while an occasional shot on the plain denoted that something stirring had occurred. The Hamama, it appeared, had made an incursion, and were at that moment engaged in driving off four mules; they were a small party, but for all that the village braves were unable to prevail against them, and returned crest-fallen, without having rescued any one of the captives. This little incident by no means increased the relish of Kassim and the escort for the morrow's journey.

On the 17th, nevertheless, not having the fear of the Hamama before our eyes, we made an early start, for we had about thirty-five miles to accomplish—a very heavy march—before reaching Kafsa. We were accompanied by a very civil, attentive Negro—Mabrook by name—who had attended to our wants at Feriana, and whom Kassim had allured into our service by a month's wages in advance and a present. This worthy commenced at the start with tales of blood and spoliation; he seemed acquainted with all the murderous reminiscences of the many stony heaps that flanked our path, and by the expiration of an hour he fully convinced our party that we were blessed with special luck indeed if we reached Kafsa that night with our heads on our shoulders. Our first halt was about seven miles from Feriana, at some pits, where we were informed was the last water we should see ere reaching our destination. We had gone ahead, allured by seeing several flights of desert grouse (*Pterocles*) making for that direction, and I had just shot, as he descended to drink at the brink of the pit, a specimen of the rare species *Pterocles coronifer,*[1] when seven as ill-looking

[1] I find there is no specimen of this bird at the British Museum;

scoundrels as one could see in an African summer's day, rode up from behind some oleanders to us. Our head Hamba came forward and had a parley with them, on which they civilly saluted us and sauntered off. They were a regular robber party waiting at the pool for victims, but were wretchedly armed; so wretchedly, indeed, that it would have been almost a treat to have given them a lesson, if they had mustered up courage for an attack; the example would have been useful for future travellers. As we were intent on objects of natural history, our proper course would have been to have taken provisions and to have bivouacked here. It was the only water within eight miles, and we should have provided ourselves with many specimens of the *Pterocles coronifer, alchatus,* and *arenarius,* all of which seemed numerous about. The air resounded with their croakings; but the repeated assurances of "*Yasser godam,*" or "lots of them ahead," from the whole escort, who dreaded a sojourn in this ill-famed spot, brought us again into the saddle and *en route* for Kafsa. The whole of this day's journey was through the finest sporting country; we saw several bustards, and Sir S. brought one down, by a gallant shot on horseback, to the immense admiration of our Feriana guides, who came galloping off to me, waving the poor bird in triumph, till I hardly thought he would have had a feather left

the one described by Temminck is called by him a unique specimen, shot in the vast Nubian deserts.

intact. These bustards are the *Otis houbāra*—*houbāra* being the Arabic name for them. They are beautiful birds, with long black ostrich-looking ruffs fringing each side of the neck, and are the best of eating, but far too wary to be relied on as ordinary *pièces de résistance*, even where they are in numbers. The Arabs secure them with their falcons. Besides the bustards, we met *pterocles* and multitudes of red-legs, and, though we did not see any, we heard that gazelles were in abundance. In short, let me recommend any one who is fond of shooting to devote at least three or four days to this tract of country. Provisions and water should be procured at Feriana, and in all probability some pools will be discoverable in the bed of the river by which we passed. When nightfall came on we were many miles from our destination; we had been now ten hours on horseback, and were all for rest and pitching the tent; but Mabrook had so terrified all his listeners by his tales of horror, that they begged of us to proceed. We continued to pick our way tolerably well along the path, although it had become perfectly dark, when, lo and behold, as we approached the mountain chain which sinks into the plain about three miles to the N.W. of Kafsa, a watch-fire gleamed at some distance off right upon our road, and about half a mile still further on another was seen dimly twinkling. Alarm rose high through the cavalcade—even Kassim's heart sank within him, and our Captain, more frightened if possible than the rest, descended from his dignity, and took Mabrook into familiar, even confidential communication. It was decided that we were to execute a wide and silent *detour* to the left, in which case it was hoped we might escape the robber bands awaiting their prey. It struck us as rather an odd mode of conducting this sort of business to light fires, which I presume would serve the same purpose to others as to ourselves—namely, to show the spots that should be avoided. In solemn silence we left the beaten track, and found ourselves shortly stumbling over stony rough ground, bad enough by day but intolerable by night, with every now and then a precipitate and unconscious descent into the bed of some torrent. Into one of these poor Hubert was deposited over his horse's ears, and the robbers—if they were robbers, and had known their trade—would have had easy work in leading off one or two of the baggagers; for we were so separated, and it was so dark, that the mischief would have been done, and pursuit impossible, before we could have closed up. Sir S. sadly disturbed the Captain and Mabrook, who performed outpost duty, by insisting on finishing his cigar. The light, they protested, would betray our whereabouts; but the cigar was one of the last of Mr. Benson's best and could not be thrown away, and so the sorrowful entreaties and protests went on until it was consumed. At last, after a continuous march of thirteen hours and a half, we found ourselves and our poor steeds marching up a staircase into the Bey's house at Kafsa.

The sun peeped warmly and brightly through our open window on the morning of the 18th, and invited us to take a look over our habitation. It was a large building, not in the best repair, with a number of unoccupied rooms, and not a particle of furniture within it. Pretty little Kafsa sparrows, with their merry song, were flitting to and fro, and seemed as if they had been for a long time the sole proprietors of the building. This bird, called by the Arabs *Bou habibi*, "father of my friend," is, I understand, not found northward of Kafsa. On account of their gay lively note, they have been sent to Tunis, but only survived their departure from the south a short time. Just below our windows, at the foot of the house, was a large square stone basin, of Roman construction, round which were gathered, washing their garments, many of the fair sex of Kafsa. This is the "Jugis Aqua," the unfailing fountain described by Sallust, and, joining with another fountain of warm water at the foot of the citadel, it flows into the plain to the S.W. of Kafsa, irrigating and fertilizing a tract of ground thus won from the encroaching desert. In the morning early this basin was beautifully clear, and seemed well stocked with small fish that looked like carp; but towards midday it became a very disreputable pond, with a fine efflorescence of soapsuds covering its surface. The governor of the town was absent, but his *khalifa,* or right-hand man, was very attentive, and accompanied us in a walk through the streets. It boasts of few buildings of any size, and the best houses, as far as we could see, were occupied by Jews, who have formed a strong and apparently rich colony. They invited us very readily into their houses, treated us to *liqueurs* and spirits made from the date—showed us their gazelles, which were running about the court-yards perfectly tame. Some of the reception-rooms were prettily fitted up, with richly colored blankets spread over the divans, for Kafsa is the headquarters of the blanket manufacture, and very expensive articles they are. In one house we found a young man, the son of the proprietor, lying sick of fever, which his relations informed us he had caught from the deleterious water of the Jereed. Much to Sir S.'s disgust, who prophesied that my drugs would be worse than the disease, I promised to send the sufferer some powders, which promise was apparently received with much thankfulness, and followed by a request that I would visit another fever patient next door. This was more than I bargained for, and I feared I should have to try my therapeutic skill on all the Israelites in Kafsa; but they begged so hard, and seemed in so much real grief, saying that it was a little orphan girl that lay sick, the daughter of their daughter, and the joy of their house, that, in spite of Sir S.'s warning that I should be adding infanticide to homicide, I resolved to do the best I could, and so, with much solemnity and importance, we consented to pay the visit.

After a little delay, during which we were regaled with more *liqueurs* and *anisette*, we were introduced into the sick-chamber. I cannot conceive a finer subject for a painting. On the ground, swathed in the richest shawls and attire, lay the poor child, flushed with fever and moaning in her suffering. On one side of her knelt her grandmother, on the other her aunt. They were both remarkable-looking women—both most handsomely attired. In the celebrated picture by Raphael of the Holy Family, at Naples, called, I think, the Madonna della Culla, Elizabeth is painted at the head of the cradle, and the moment I entered the resemblance struck me. But the old Jewish matron of Kafsa had far higher pretensions to beauty and race. The thin finely shaped nostril—a feature generally coarse in the Hebrew—and the bright, keen eagle eye, which time had not dimmed, and which seemed to be looking us through and through, might have well belonged to the mother of Jehu, or Judas Maccabeus. She never spoke during the interview. On the other side knelt her daughter Miriam, the aunt of the sick child—a perfect type of soft and gentle Eastern beauty. She was plunged in grief, but the old woman's eye was hard and tearless. The light streamed in from the small window just above the child's head, but the end of the narrow confined room where we stood was in deep shade, almost in darkness. Here then is a picture—the light poured in upon the sufferer in her gorgeous array of shawls and finery of attire; the old woman looking at us with keen and steady glance, in grief too deep for tears; the aunt Miriam's sad and despairing face, imploring aid, yet seemingly without hope; and in the dark background, we, in our uncouth European dresses, and by our side one of the Jewish members of the family, and Kassim in his bravest holiday costume.

The poor girl was about seven years old, and had been ill for several days. Her skin was parched and burning, and the pulse in a gallop. She was swathed in clothes, and the room was hot and close from want of ventilation. At first the conversation was kept up in Arabic, through the means of Kassim; but at last, fortunately, a Jew came in who addressed me in Italian. On my replying to him, to my great astonishment, Miriam, the aunt, threw herself at our feet, and, in excellent Italian, implored us, for the love of God, to save the child, the only one of her dead sister—the only little one of the house. She had never left Kafsa, it appeared, but had learned Italian from a brother, who had been engaged in trade at Tunis. My first medical *ordonnance* was to have the room thoroughly ventilated, and the poor child relieved of the load of garments with which it was almost suffocated. The rest of the treatment, having the fear of real doctors before my eyes, must be a secret, except this much, that James's powders was one of the remedies employed. One thing was quite clear, however, that had I been a Brodie or a Ferguson I could not have inspired greater confidence, in which, I regret to say, Sir S. was far from participating. The result of my treatment shall be told hereafter.

After our visit to the Jewish quarter we strolled through the town, followed apparently by the whole population—all, however, perfectly civil. The Khalifa invited us to visit the Kasbah, or citadel, from the summit of which we had a view of the surrounding country; and as there were no troops in it, and the multitude remained outside, we were able to enjoy ourselves at our ease. Shaw seems to have had rather a low appreciation of the appearance of Kafsa, but we thought it very prettily situated: it has three sides, surrounded with gardens, in which were flourishing the finest pomegranate trees I ever saw. To the north of the town, running east and west, is a bold chain of hills of the richest coloring; and the bright white walls shining through the foliage, rendered the whole appearance of the place cheerful in the extreme—anything but a "melancholy situation," as Shaw terms it.

Kafsa, of which Lemprière gives the following valuable account—"Cafsa, a town of Libya, surrounded by vast deserts, full of snakes"—appears to have been, from the earliest times, a place of considerable importance. Sallust says that report ascribes its foundation to the Libyan Hercules, and he calls it in the days of Jugurtha, "oppidum magnum atque valens." It was the treasury—the γαζοφυλάκιον—according to Strabo, of that brave and restless prince, and was taken by a dash of Marius. At the time that his army was supposed to be absent many days' journey, having collected all the skins he could obtain, he filled them with water, and, marching entirely after dark, on the third night he arrived at some elevated ground about two miles from Kafsa, behind which he concealed his army. As soon as the inhabitants had gone forth on their usual avocations, he gave the signal, and ordered his cavalry to charge, and take prisoner every one they could catch. The suddenness of the attack, and the general confusion that followed, together with the fears entertained for the captives, induced the townspeople to surrender; upon which Sallust informs us, that Marius burnt the town, put to death all the grown-up male Numidians, sold as slaves the remainder, and divided the property among his soldiers. He alleges, as an excuse for this atrocity, which he does allow to be beyond the laws of war, that the town was difficult of access to the Romans, though handy to Jugurtha, and that the people were of a fickle, faithless disposition, not to be kept under by benefits or fear. The mountain where the robber-fires caused our guides so much alarm, was probably the spot behind which Marius concealed his army. Kafsa in those days enjoyed a very bad reputation, not only on account of the character of its inhabitants, but from the venomous serpents, which rendered access to it a service of danger. Sallust describes them as haunting the huge solitudes around—their natural venom rendered still more noxious by the rage of thirst. But indeed, according to all old writers, we are in ugly quarters as regards snakes and dragons. We may consider ourselves among the branches of the great ridge of Atlas; and old Father Pigaletta tells us that "Mount Atlas hath plenty of dragons, grosse of body, slow of motion, and in biting or touching incurably venomous." Leo Africanus enters more into particulars, and gives us something of the natural history of the aforesaid dragons. He tells us with much gravity, that "Many affirme that the male eagle, engendering with a shee wolfe, begetteth a dragon, having the beak and wings of a bird, a serpent's tail, the feet of a wolfe, and a skin speckled and partie-coloured, like the skin of a serpent; neither can it open its eyelids, and it liveth in caves." He adds, however, "This monster, albeit I myself have not seen it, yet the common report of all Africa affirmeth that there is such a one." The snakes had, fortunately for us, gone to bed; and as for the dragons, we were not sufficiently lucky to procure a specimen for Professor Owen. They say, however, that in summer there is considerable danger from the multitude of snakes in these parts; and the number of French troops stationed in the south of Algeria who die of snake bites, according to the accounts of the French doctors, is very large indeed.

During our walk through the town we were shown a number of Roman inscriptions on stones built into the citadel and private houses; one of these was a record of the days of Hadrian—

AIANO HADRIA—
LOCVM STATV—
NOB—
COR—

and an Arab, strange to say, brought us a piece of paper, on which he had very ingeniously copied an inscription, which he said was among some ruins in the desert; and of which we were able to make out enough to ascertain that it was a monumental tablet of regret for a departed wife. I could not at all make out what had induced the Arab to this exertion, as I believe there had not been more than two or three Europeans within this century at Kafsa, to inspire the natives with a love of archæological research. In the evening we had more proofs of the Roman occupancy by a levy of Jews and other visitors to sell coins. We purchased several from them, mostly of the time of Constantius and Maxentius; as also two prettily engraved stones, one with the device of the head of Mercury; the other, a huntsman in Phrygian cap, skinning a gazelle suspended from the branch of a tree. Among other of the town notabilities who attended our re-union, was a fat, well-dressed old gentleman, who informed us that in the time of the late Bey he had been either governor or vice-governor of the town. He was very profuse in his civilities and attentions, and brought us coins among the rest; but we discovered, alas! that his friendliness was but a deep-laid scheme to extract 3*s.* for copper coins not worth as many pence.

19th.—Went out shooting, and wended our way to a palm-grove at the foot of the mountain, about two miles from the town. Out of this grove a stream clear as crystal flowed, and we fully antici-pated some snipe-shooting in the marshy ground by its side. Our horses however, generally thirsty souls enough, refused to drink it, and on dis-mounting to ascertain the cause, we found it to be salt; and where it had overflown the hard ground it had left a saline incrustation behind it. We had now got fairly into the district of salt streams and fountains; for after leaving Kafsa, during the whole time we were in the Jereed, we never got a drop of really pure water. We were obliged, in consequence, altogether to dispense with tea, the delicate flavour of which was utterly ruined, as we were not accustomed to drink it *à la Tartare*, with salt and butter; the coffee, however, stood to us, and being much stronger in taste, was not affected. Sir S. shot a couple of brace, in the course of the day, of that beautiful bird the *Pterocles alchatus*; but altogether the prospect of a good *chasse* seemed bad enough. We returned home by the gate we had entered the night of our arrival, and rejoiced that none of us had fallen into the terribly deep pits that flank each side of the way. These excavations are made for the sake of the large blocks of stone left in them, the site of Roman buildings; and as they are never filled in, and some are from twenty to thirty feet deep, they would have been formidable on the pitchy-dark night of our arrival, had we known of their existence. On the outskirts of the town was a large encampment of the Hamama, the robber tribe I before mentioned. They seemed a miserable set, sunk in poverty and squalor, bearing about the same relation to the fine tribes of the Farasheesh and the Beni Zid, as the Digger Indians do to the Comanches and Blackfeet.

At the foot of the hills some distance from the town, to the west, the whole surface of the ground was strewed with curious tubular incrustations; and the only other notable circumstance of our day's excursion was seeing together, browsing apparently on stones, for there was nothing else to eat, the largest collection of donkeys we had ever witnessed, 133 in number.

On the 20th, we announced to the delinquent Hambas, that we had no more occasion for their valuable services, and recommended them to return and pay their respects to their master, the Bey. Hitherto they had taken matters with a very high hand, and professed their intention of accompanying us, whether we wished it or not; but when Sir S. went out shooting, and I had taken out my writing materials, and Kassim had informed them very ominously that I was writing to Regina (the Queen) and the Bey and the Gonsool Jeninar (Consul-General), their faces fell, and they were much perplexed. They first thought to appeal to our fears, and sent the ex-governor to inform us that we were going through such a dangerous country, that we should require even more guards than we had, and that it would never do to send them away; but we replied in their own style, that Allah was great and merciful, and that if it was *mektoob* (written) that we were to be destroyed, it could not be helped; but that go with us they never should. Then they tried to play on our feelings, and got a deputation of Jews to wait on us, who assured us that the unhappy men were contrite, and that, if they were sent back, the Bey would cut their heads off. This had no effect, for we rather unkindly replied, that it was a pity he had not done so long ago; in short, we were pestered the whole evening by different persons coming in on different pretexts, but all with the object of begging off the culprits.

On the 21st, we bade adieu to our very civil friends at Kafsa, and having sent on our tent at early dawn by a Sphax merchant who was going to Tozer with a caravan to purchase dates, proceeded by the southern gate through a series of rather pretty and well-kept gardens, on our destination. We were followed, as we shortly found out, by the dismissed Hambas, and on getting to the outskirts of the town we were apprehensive that something unpleasant would have occurred. We had gone a great deal too far to retract or pardon, and to allow such a pair of scoundrels to dog our heels would have been running a perpetual risk, to say nothing of the annoyance to our future hosts, from the presence of such rogues and extortioners. Kassim's advice was short and decisive—to shoot them both dead, and have no more talk on the matter; and we were obliged to load and threaten them with a volley, before we could drive them back. At last they retired, and thereby fortunately spared us the annoyance of having to fire on them, and henceforth all went pleasantly and serenely, as far as our equipage was concerned.

The squeezing was at an end, and we were no longer starved to fill the pockets of these vagabonds. The captain alone rode moodily ahead, and regretted his deputy and companion, for his dignity would hardly allow him to converse with the Spahi. He made one faint endeavour to remonstrate, but was informed that even his decoration would not save him from a march to Tunis, if he was disagreeable, so he gave in with a good grace, and for the rest of the journey maintained a harmless and dignified, but very useless existence. Our party was thus diminished by three, for Mabrook, after enjoying himself for two days at the Bey's expense, had pocketed his advance and fled away. His nerves had been shaken by the robber fires, and he stood in awe of the Hamama, in whose country we now were, so that whatever became of him it could not be said "Mabrook s'en va t'en guerre."

Kafsa is about fifty-four miles from Tozer, and the country is almost entirely an arid, stony desert, with very little brushwood. It is called the Beled-el-Jereed, known to me as a schoolboy by the somewhat strange appellation of Billidulgerid. Shaw translates it as "the dry country," but the real meaning of the word *jereed* is palm-branch; and the game of the *jereed* was so called from the palm sticks thrown by the Arabs. It takes its name from the palm-forests in the oases. There is no water *en route*, except a few filthy fetid pools, by scratching at the side of which a somewhat clearer fluid, rather saltish and very sandy, may be procured. El Hamma, where there is water, is so close to Tozer that it can hardly be looked on as a watering-place. We came up with the Sphax caravan shortly before arriving at these pools, and, fortunately for us, the merchant who carried our tent had a *jerba*, or skin, which he filled with water, and placed at our disposal in the evening; for although we had bought vessels, and expressly constructed our panniers for such emergencies, Kassim, with usual Moorish improvidence, invariably forgot or omitted to fill our water-jars, and left us to take our chance. There seemed, however, as if there had been a violent action of water at no great distance of time, for we met in the middle of the dry course, of a wide stream apparently, a number of round balls about the size of thirteen-inch shells, composed of clay and pebbles, which had evidently been rolled along, and derived their shape from the rolling.

En route we saw four gazelles on the road at no great distance; shot some specimens of a bird only found in the desert and on its borders;[1] and passed an enormous caravan laden with dates from Tozer. I commenced counting the camels till I arrived at four hundred, and then I had not reached a third of the file. It belonged, as these caravans almost invariably do, to traders from Sphax, who are the

[1] The *Certhilauda bifasciata* or *Desertorum*, found also in the deserts of Scinde and of Arabia.

most energetic and commercial community in the Regency—I may say safely in the whole of North Africa, and, as we met a great number of them, we may add, the most courteous and obliging.

We encamped that night, after a twenty-five miles' ride, in a spot where a quantity of dry tamarisk roots spread about promised the material for a genial cup of coffee. The caravan, by way of society, joined us, and in a few minutes the camels were all sitting in solemn and decorous files growling and blubbering, and their masters squatted on their hams round the fires either doing a little bit of cookery or telling stories. We should have had probably a levy, but for a horrid uproar outside our tent, in which we heard Kassim, amid terrible abuse of some persons unknown, appealing to Regina and the Bey. Presently he entered, and without explanation requested us to put him to death at once; nor was it for some time that we could elicit the cause of this sudden desire to leave this best of worlds, until it at last came out that some one had stolen a cake of soap on which he set much prize. This was a specimen of Mr. Kassim's tantrums, and during these paroxysms he seemed always bereft of his senses; the poor Sphaxis were, however, scared away by his violence, and did not venture to approach, though they must have sniffed the balmy coffee from afar.

The caravan was off and some distance away before we started, but we soon overtook it and had another robber adventure, which illustrates the value placed on human life in these parts. Our party had greatly straggled this day—more than usually. Sir S. had disappeared behind a ridge, and the head Hamba had become uneasy and followed him; Kassim and Hubert were some half a mile ahead, and I had lagged behind with one of the baggagers and little Ali the Spahi. Two men, extremely well mounted on grey horses, rode out of a ravine from behind some tamarisk bushes, and came down on us. Their faces were muffled up in their burnooses, and they seemed well armed. They commenced in a business-like manner by inquiring whether our panniers were full of money, to which our little Ali, as bold as brass, replied that they were, and that they had better come on and try and take them. This response rather disconcerted the two worthies, who first held a little consultation and then proceeded to ask some more questions, as to where we were coming, whither going, and whether there were other travellers on the road. The answers they received evidently did not inspire them with confidence, for they retired to an eminence about one hundred yards off. A sudden inspiration came at once over little Ali, his countenance lighted up

> As when some great thought flashes o'er the brain
> And flushes all the cheek.

"Arfi—master," said he, confidentially—"my horse's back is sore, one of the baggagers is sick, let us call back these men, shoot them, and take their horses." "Shoot them," said I, remonstrating in the best Arabic I could muster, "why, they have done nothing to us." "Ah! master, our horses are galled, and these men are robbers." "Well, then, go out and shoot them yourself." "O, master, they have two guns to my one, and would shoot me, but while I speak to them do you shoot them through the head, one with each barrel." "But what would the Bey say to my shooting his people?" "Master, the Bey would rejoice because they are robbers, and we should all rejoice in their fine horses." "No, Ali—it can't be done at any price." So Ali cast a fond lingering look at the robbers' horses, and the robbers cast a fond look at our panniers, and on we jogged through what Sallust would call "ingentes solitudines"—huge solitudes—till a long, thin, dark-colored line stretched along the southern horizon. The dark line gradually, as we approached, assumed the appearance of a pine forest, and at last we found ourselves on the outskirts of the first oasis of the Great Sahara. Here we were fortunate to shoot three more specimens of the *Pterocles coronifer*, the last we saw of that species. El Hamma was the name of this spot; like the other oases, "An isle of palms, amid a waste of sand," and a waste of stones too, for it is a wrong impression to consider the desert merely an expanse of sand. As we approached, we found, on the whole, the outline nearly as unbroken as when it showed itself from afar, save and except where, in a few instances, some venturous palms seemed to have started forth from the ranks to offer a challenge to their sandy foe. But they are worsted and foiled, and the desert has the best of it; for their green heads seemed ragged and wasted, and bowing with sorrow to the ground. At the foot of a very high rock issued forth the stream, the giver of greenness, the δωτὴρ ἐάων, the formal cause of this garden of fertility. The water was very bad, brackish in the extreme, and not even quite pellucid. My servant, who had had an attack of diarrhœa which chalk powders and *régime* had cured when at Kafsa, in spite of my most earnest warnings and entreaties to refrain from this water, drank copiously of it when my back was turned, and the result was that the disease returned with greater violence, and never left him for six weeks, until almost at the door of death at Tunis. Another hour's ride and Tozer was in sight. Between it and El Hamma we saw large numbers of sheep, and were much perplexed to ascertain what they fed on, except stones, for there was but the scantiest appearance of any herbage. Indeed, poor things, they looked as if stones had been their provender; but their wool, and not their flesh, is sought after. The inhabitants of these parts boast that the wool of the Jereed is the finest and softest in the world, and it commands a very large price.

I am not aware that any of it has ever been exported; in fact, I believe the supply is not equal to the demand, and the burnooses and other garments in which it is employed are made at Tozer and Neftah, and fetch very high prices, far higher than the inferior productions of Susa, which are those that find their way to Europe. We procured with some difficulty a couple of these fine burnooses at Tozer, and they combine warmth, lightness, and softness, in a remarkable degree.

The appearance of Tozer when about a mile distant was curious enough: it looked as if it had been burnt down and was smouldering amid its ashes. I really at one moment imagined that it had been destroyed by a general conflagration. This appearance arose from innumerable fires on which the inhabitants, and the traders with which the town was full, were cooking the afternoon meal, and from the brown-baked color of the mud cabins and brick houses of which the town is composed. It is a place of good size, unwalled, and does a vast amount of business in the date trade, but as, unlike other Oriental towns, there is but little whitewash employed, it looks dull in the extreme. Some of the houses are of good size, and very tastefully adorned with little bricks about the size of cakes of soap, arranged in devices, and in pious sentences in Arabic character. The effect is particularly pleasing—something like lattice-work. It was a busy time when we entered, for the date harvest had commenced, and buyers from all quarters were thronging the market-place in front of the Bey's house. Our appearance created an immense sensation, and all business was suspended until we were lodged in safety from the pressing crowd, within the court-yard of our habitation. The Bey's residence was, like the other at Kafsa, a very spacious building with innumerable rooms, all in bad repair and extremely dirty, nor did it boast of the advantage of a single article of furniture, or even of glazed windows. However, we spread our blankets on the divan, or bench, that ran round three sides of the room, and were presently waited on by the dignitaries of the town, the chief of whom was a very civil, obliging person, who bestirred himself to make our sojourn as comfortable as possible, and as a tribute of respect, I presume, ordered our *sherba*, or soup, to be made more lemony and peppery than ever. We accomplished about twenty-eight miles this day.

The following morning, Sir S. was allured, by the report of there being extensive marshes in the neighborhood, to a shooting expedition; the courteous Kaïd lent him horses, and invited me to a walk through the gardens of the oasis; for the oasis is all a garden. It is apparently about five miles long, and about a mile and a half or two miles in depth; all of it covered with palms, and scrupulously cultivated. Parched as our eyes had been with the glare of the desert, and longing as they had been for the sight of clear water once again, it was inexpressibly refreshing to plunge into the green shade of these gardens, and watch the hundred rivulets, limpid as crystal, singing as they ran along so merrily, as folks sing from lightness of heart when engaged in a labor of love. Up high, high above us, the great lithe palms spread their umbrella tops, and beneath them stretched out the orange-colored boughs bending with the heavy crops of dates, some in hue of gold, others of the darkest plum. From trunk to trunk of palm-trees, vines were trellised, and figs and pomegranates and peaches and almonds and apricots, and oranges and lemons sweet and sour, rejoiced under the hospitable shade that tempered to them the fierce sun of Africa; and below them again were little divisions of ground arranged like patty-pans, wherein rejoiced radishes and onions, and the best turnips I ever tasted, of flavour to render immortal one *purée de navets* from the Jereed, together with other vegetables, the names and use of which were unknown to me. "Here," said the Kaïd, with some pride, "we pitch our tents in the summer, and, leaving our heated houses, enjoy our *keff* beneath the palms." The gardens that day were merry, for it was, to coin a word analogous to vintage, the datage time; the merchants from Sphax had flocked in to buy the great produce of the oasis, and the song of the gatherers formed a curious aërial concert on the tops of the palms. Great heaps of glorious dates lay gathered together on the ground, those that adhered to the branches carefully put aside, for the dainty Tunisian likes to pick his date from off the stem. When the tree was to be attacked, a body of about eight collected below it; at a signal, a boy, armed with an instrument like a small sickle, ran nimbly up the trunk till he reached the summit; he was followed by another, who placed himself below him, so as to be within reach to receive the cluster; another followed him, and so on until the branch could be handed to the ground in safety. When all was ready, the boy wielded his sickle, and burst forth into song, which was taken up by his friends below, as they clung to the trunk with one hand and handed down the branch; and so the oasis was full of cheer and song, terrestrial and aërial. The people were very civil, offering us the best of their produce, and very anxious to know all about us, and about England, and what sort of dates we grew there. I was forced to confess, with shame, that we had not these esculents among us. This *naïve* confession spared all further interrogatories; they concluded that we had come from England to eat dates, whereas the other Arabs were confident we had come to search for gold.

And, indeed, the inhabitants of these oases may be proud of their dates. What Chateaux Margot and Lafitte are to clarets, such is the *digla* to all dates that I have tasted. I have eaten the dates of Nubia, reported excellent in Egypt; the dates of Mount Tor, from the Red Sea, of still higher reputation; and the Tafilet dates of Morocco, which are those we generally see in England: but they are all, in my opinion, a poor fruit. But the rich luscious *digla*, with its pale lemon tint, and almost transparent when not embrowned by the sun, is indeed the king of the dates; a handful, with a biscuit or bit of bread, was, until the bag was exhausted, our subsequent repast during many a long march; and then indeed, when they were no more, we appreciated their merit. They are to be obtained both at Tunis and at Marseilles, but are expensive; for, if I was rightly informed, they are only grown in perfection at Tozer, Loudian, Neftah, and one other oasis, Souf by name, on the French territory. Every one eats dates in this country, and every one that can afford it eats *digla*, so that the amount that crosses the sea to France is very small indeed. Kassim was a perfect connoisseur in dates: he used to run over on his fingers the names of twenty kinds—the *digla*, *hurra*, *aleek*, &c., and could at the first bite, anywhere, pronounce on the origin and tell us the position of the fruit in question among its compeers. In fact, down here the conversation is all of dates; it is the oases shop talk. All the spring they eat them, and discuss their degrees of goodness. All the summer the hopes of the community are on the crop; all the winter the bargain with the exporters and the duties to Government keep them alive and excited. No wonder Arab poets are enthusiastic about their date-trees. Hafard-el-Hadab, describing their leaf-crowned tops, celebrates "the superb date-tree whose head languidly reclines like that of a handsome woman overcome with sleep." And in the poem of Amrelkais occurs this passage:—"Her long jet-black hair decorated her back, thick and diffused like bunches of dates clustering on a palm-tree."

The Kaïd told us that the date-trees paid, each of them, an annual tax generally of 12 caroubs, or about *4d.*; though sometimes, when the Bey was in want of money, it was raised to a piastre, or *6d.* On remarking that that was not a heavy impost, he showed us the number of trees that bore little or nothing, and which were all equally taxed. Should any person be inclined to turn date merchant, here are the statistics of the speculation.

Dates at Tozer, costing from 25 to 35 piastres per cantar of 100 lb, are sold at Tunis at about 12 caroubs the pound, or from 80 to 100 piastres per cantar.

The hire of a camel from Tozer to Tunis is 10 piastres. Each camel is supposed to carry about 2½ cantars; so that the profit would be about £1.5*s.*

per camel, allowing for loss, &c.; and considering one man will own a large number of camels, fair business can be done.

The inhabitants of these two oases, Tozer and Neftah, are extremely well off—indeed, wealthy as compared with other communities in the Regency. Different proprietors own the soil, and they sell the produce of their palms either in retail, or else by the garden, or number of trees. The Governor was extremely polite and intelligent, anxious to show and explain everything; but he had been summoned by the Bey to Tunis, with other local governors, to attend the camp during the Bey's annual tour through his dominions. He offered, however, to remain, if we pleased, until our return from Neftah, which we declined; and he introduced us to his brother, a sullen-looking Moor, who he said would have the same pleasure that he had in making Tozer agreeable. Of all our acquaintances he was the only one we saw again; for, on hearing of our arrival at Tunis, he paid us a visit, and we endeavored to show our appreciation of his civilities by replenishing him with apples, quince jam, and Naples biscuits, and by presenting him with a housewife of Russian leather, containing all sorts of implements for the making and repairing of garments—scissors, knife, needles, thread, silk, cottons of all sorts—which quite delighted his heart, and has, I am confident, produced a permanent *entente cordiale* between Tozer and England.

Tozer being the ancient Tisurus, we inquired for stones with letters on them, as usual; but heard there were none, although we obtained several Roman coins of the emperors, which they said were frequently dug up.

On the 24th we started for Neftah, about fourteen miles to the south-west. Our course lay over the same bleak sterile desert we had traversed two days before, with huge salt marshes extending far to the south. *En route* we met the Governor of the district, a grand-looking dark fellow on a goodly chestnut mare adorned with the most gorgeous caparisons. He had a very well dressed retinue with him, well mounted, and several fine led mules, also decorated regardless of expense. He received us with great courtesy, expressed his regret at being obliged to depart like the chief of Tozer at the summons of the Bey, but said he had ordered everything for us, and that he trusted his brother would make our stay at Neftah so agreeable that we should remain at least a week.

The reception we received did not belie his words: we were saluted by his brother at the door of his house, which he placed at our service, and a most comfortable house it was. The divans were not, as elsewhere, merely bare boards, but were covered with well-stuffed comely mattresses; a profusion of cushions for lolling on, lay about; there was a table that had once upon a time witnessed finesse and revoke, for it was an ancient whist-table, and—more wonderful still—there were actually chairs. These we did not appreciate, for after a month's squatting they appeared hard and stuck-up implements of discomfort. All the rest of the establishment was equally well mounted, and a most excellent dinner produced a very favorable impression of this *ultima Thule*—this last island of the desert; for to the southward of Neftah lies the boundless space of the Great Sahara, without water or vegetation. Occasionally an ostrich-hunter provides himself with a small supply of water, and ventures some distance within its precincts; but there is no track over its pathless expanse, which has probably never been trod by foot of man or beast. Our friend the deputy-governor informed us of a rumour that a Frenchman had made his way from the nearest French oasis of Souf to Gadames; that the story was that he freighted fifteen camels with water and a scanty supply of provisions, and arrived in the last stage of exhaustion at his destination, with one surviving camel, on the fifteenth day. In the evening we had several visitors: besides our obliging host, his nephew, the son of the Kaïd, a good-looking young fellow about eighteen, also came in, and henceforth never left us. He did not add much to the feast of reason or flow of soul, for his education had not advanced to writing or reading, and his conversation was not very lively or instructive. His was a passive civility; but it was meant for civility, this continual attendance, so we could not complain. Some Jews also dropped in, hearing we were amateurs of ancient money; they brought a gold coin of Honorius, and two silver coins, one of Gordian and the other of Constantius, all in good preservation, and dug up in the neighborhood. The owner informed me that it was a sad misfortune we had not come sooner, for that he had had a large nnmber of gold coins, which he had lately melted down. We heard, in the course of conversation, that these oases, though charming residences in winter, are extremely unhealthy in summer, and that almost all the inhabitants suffer more or less from fever. We told our host that his brother, when he went to Tunis, should visit our Cousul-General, and be recommended to a European doctor, who would give him medicines, and instructions how to use them, which would be of vast service to his community. He acknowledged that it would be a good plan, but seemed to think they had got on, upon the whole, pretty well with the good old orthodox fever, and that it was hardly worth while to make any such strange innovations, as to dose a whole townsfolk. On retiring for the night, he very considerately observed that our horses must be tired, from their long journey, and requested us to let him mount us on the morrow, should we feel any desire to go out shooting.

On the morrow, two very good-looking greys stood at the door for the *chasse*, the one I rode—a mare—being about the best-looking animal I had seen in the Regency. We started in the direction of the marshes, but soon found ourselves pounded by the complete inability of the Arab horses to get over the smallest drain; so Sir S. made off for the desert in search of Gutta (*Pterocles*) and Habara bustards, while I returned, and, having put up the mare, got a guide and proceeded round by the western extremity of the oasis towards the marshes, with a view of making a complete circuit of it. My guides were two grown-up boys, in some way connected with the Governor; one of them, a remarkably fat youth, whose bare legs suffered terribly among the short prickly plants and broken reeds of the swamp; but all our labor met with no reward except a solitary duck. There was not an appearance of any game, though we saw hiding-places for fowlers, who lay in wait there by night for geese and ducks. I met Sir S. also returning at the other end of the oasis; he had seen nothing; and as time pressed, and there was neither shooting nor remains of the antiquities of the ancient Negeta—the present Neftah—we notified to our host our regret at being obliged to leave him the following day. He seemed really sorry for our departure, which, considering that we had nine horses in his stable, and that each consumed two shillings' worth of barley *per diem*, to say nothing of the feeding of their seven masters, showed him to be a really generous, hospitable fellow, of which we had more ample proof in the evening. When our dinner was over he came in, and, turning the conversation on horses, he asked us if we approved of those we had ridden in the course of the day, of which, of course, we expressed ourselves in high encomiums. Upon this he requested that we would take them with us as a present; that they were fresh and hearty, while our own were rather tired and heavily laden for so long a journey as we had before us. We expressed our great obligations, but added that it was the custom of the English never to accept a present. He again pressed them on us, observing that they were his brother's, but that his brother had left him full authority, and that he would be grieved at our refusal. Still however, with many protestations of gratitude, we were forced to decline the offer. Shortly after he went away, but soon returned, and producing from underneath his burnoos two very handsome *haïcks*, a garment that bears the nearest resemblance to a very long shawl, fabricated of the Jereed wool and silk, insisted on our acceptance of them. As they are worth a good deal, we still demurred, but he was evidently determined we should not go empty away, saying that he was sure we should not like him to remain in our room all night, and that he could not leave it until we took them. It was clear that any further refusals on our part would have given great offence, so we accepted his handsome present, with many thanks for his really genuine and disinterested kindness, for on my pressing a large hunting-knife upon him, he was quite unwilling at first to receive it, saying that he knew travellers only took with them things they absolutely required, and that he feared we might feel the want of it afterwards. He then turned to Kassim, who was grinning in the corner at our extreme softness in not taking all we could get, and, placing on the table a pile of five-franc pieces, he told him that he wished him to receive them as a recollection of our lucky visit to Neftah. Had Kassim, he said, given the people of Neftah a bad character, we should not have come among them; but it was clear he had spoken well of them to induce us to take so long a journey to visit them, and that he should always consider our visit as a happy incident and of good omen to Neftah. Kassim did not say that he never received presents, but with a profusion of salaams thrust the pile into his pocket. We found that the present amounted to one hundred and twenty francs, which was a pretty good day's work for Master Kassim. We asked our entertainer how French silver money had penetrated there, and he told us they obtained it from the French Arabs in the purchase of dates.

He seemed to bear no great love to the French, notwithstanding their fine silver pieces, and evinced the greatest horror at the thought of being annexed to Algeria. He said they were a cruel, faithless people, and treated the Muslims with great cruelty and contempt. He then wrote his name in my pocket-book, and his lineage at full length, and begged of me on my return to show it to Regina, and to tell her that the people of Neftah had heard of her greatness and goodness, and that they were her friends, and would always receive and treat with hospitality any of her children. These good people are changed since the days of Leo Africanus, who accuses them of being rude and inhospitable, for we found them without exception civil and polite; there were no crowds to suffocate us, no expressions about Christians which sometimes reached our ears elsewhere, and when we left Neftah on the morrow it was without one unpleasant reminiscence.

26th.—On the 26th we returned to Tozer, and met *en route* large numbers of laborers from Morocco, who were returning from the date-picking. These fellows are the *spalpeens* of Tunis: they crowd in from their own country for the harvest, and are looked on by the more polished inhabitants of the Regency in pretty much the same light as the Irish harvest laborer is looked on by the better-dressed and better-fed Englishman. These Marokeens bear also a strong resemblance, besides, to the Irish reapers—they are very dirty, very ignorant, and very quarrelsome. They wear nothing on the head, which is shaved, with the exception of a scalplock, by which they are to be raised to heaven. They are employed in guarding gardens and crops and olives in the neighborhood of Tunis, and are generally ready to do a little business in the robbery-accompanied-with-violence line, so that for their sakes we were recommended to take a friendly revolver, should we feel inclined to take solitary rides. Kassim's observations on these folks were very sarcastic: though the Arabs were "mauvais sans baton," but "bons avec baton," these were "pas bons sans baton, pas bons avec baton"—their badness overcame all beatings; and he intimated, notwithstanding, as each successive party passed, how much he would like to give them the *baton* all round. But, indeed, Kassim's placidity was much ruffled that morning, for the head Hamba had laid claim to half the present that was given by the Kaïd's brother, and had appealed to us to enforce the partition. We, however, stolidly ignored every particle of Arabic, and left the parties to fight it out. Kassim, therefore, was angry with the Hamba, and wished to bastinado the Marokeens, as a relief to his feelings; the Hamba being eager to defraud and injure Kassim, was angry with him, and with us for our pretended ignorance of his claims; and little Ali was out of humour because there had been some good pickings in which he had been forgotten. The consequence was, a sulky ride back to Tozer, where we were met by additional sulkiness. The good Kaïd had gone, and his sullen, down-looking, ill-conditioned brother soon showed us that he preferred our room to our company. We were desirous of purchasing some *burnooses*, in which this fellow threw every impediment, and it was only by informing him very decidedly, that we should remain at Tozer for a fortnight if everything we required was not furnished, that we succeeded in getting any article we were in search of; and so changed was the attitude of the people, influenced by his example, that when we left the town on the following morning, we were hooted and cursed, and demonstrations of throwing stones were quite apparent. Sir G. Temple mentions, that the inhabitants of this place were extremely uncivil to him, but certainly, as far as we had seen of them in our first visit, they were particularly well behaved.

Our journey on the 27th was to Loudian, lying to the east of Tozer; and after a ride of a couple of hours we found ourselves making our way under its lofty mud walls to the Governor's house. Loudian is under the Kaïd of Neftah, which was soon apparent from the hearty reception. Among other visitors that dropped in to salute us was a Jew, whose face we remembered to have seen at Kafsa, and who informed us that both our patients had perfectly recovered, and that Kafsa was filled with the glory of the English strangers, who had, by their miraculous powders, effected such miraculous cures. He gave us an additional bit of information, the facts of which, if true, must have rather damped the spirits of the Israelites on the recovery of their offspring, namely, that the vice-governor had administered three hundred blows of the stick to the heels of the heads of the families that had invited us into their houses, and had thrown him and others into prison for three days. The pretext of this was the apprehension, lest, on our seeing the beauty and wealth of the interior life of Kafsa, we, the English, should send forth an expedition to conquer it, or else join with the French in doing so.

The Governor came into our room in the evening, and was very chatty and communicative; he told us various stories of the perils and dangers of the great salt Sea of Marks, the Shebkah-el-Lowdeah, that we should have to traverse on the morrow. How there were quicksands on each side of the path, in which we might, as were many before us, be instantly swallowed up; how we should get into the Nefzouia country, consisting of one hundred villages, and that they were bad, treacherous people, not to be depended on. He also told us how the rebel Ghouma had been down in the Nefzouia, and had raised all the turbulent spirits to join his plundering and insurgent forces, and how Mahommed Hasneddar had come down on them with an iron hand and had utterly crushed them—selling off some entire villages to new proprietors, and exterminating the old, and doing altogether the best bit of squeezing in the remembrance of the oldest inhabitant. There was a terrible disturbance in the town that night, so that we really thought Ghouma had taken fresh heart and come down on us; but it was only the fantasia of a marriage in high life, in which frequent discharges of firearms are part of the ceremony and of the pleasure. The Governor's brother had been killed the day before by the explosion of a pistol on the joyous occasion; but, as it had been written that he should be so killed, our host's spirits did not seem at all lowered in consequence.

The next day, the 28th, we had a long and heavy ride of about thirty-two miles to accomplish, crossing the great Salt Marsh of the Shot Nefzouia and thence to Tebabshé, one of the small Arab villages of the district called Nefzouia. The oasis we were leaving was different from the compact oasis of Tozer and Neftah—it was rather a dissipated erratic kind of oasis. It formed itself into peninsulas and isthmuses, and vagrant palms ran out here and there into the desert, very rakish-looking, and with the seedy appearance of having been up all night. We crossed towards the eastern extremity of the palm forest, and for the next six hours had a very nasty journey of it. First of all, we were some hours sliding and sinking in the slush of the Salt Marsh; after that, we got on a hard bed of salt, the moisture of which had evaporated, and there it lay several inches thick; then, again, we had to traverse an expanse of slushy salt which looked like dirty thawing snow—all was salt, far, far into the dreary desolate distance; and the only objects to intercept the range of sight were the palm trunks, fixed to mark the way (hence its name the Lake of Marks), and the many skeletons of camels that had perished on the journey. We had a curious instance of optical delusion this day, arising from the state of the atmosphere. While crossing the salt expanse, we saw at no great distance two palm-trees which rejoiced our hearts; for at length, we said, we are out of this desolation, and again mid groves and greenness; but as we advanced, the tall palms gradually diminished and came together till they assumed the appearance of a camel, and then at length, on nearer approach, the camel split in twain and became two foot passengers; and the same appearance followed, as we sent on two of our retinue to make the arrangements for the bivouac. We were ten hours and a half on the road, and before we arrived at our destination, night had come on, and we lost our way; and as Arabs, for fear of spirits, do not wander much after dark, we had great difficulty in reaching Tebabshé. Our entry into the oasis was amid perfect silence: no friendly Shekh to greet us, or messenger to show the way. The few miserable huts were closed, nor was there any possibility of getting their occupants to open them to us. After a long search, at last Ali was discovered in a hovel where he had obtained admittance, and Kassim announced to us the pleasant intelligence, "il Shekh e scapato"—that the Shekh had bolted, and there was no provender for either man or beast. It was the old story again of brandy, sausages, and oranges, for ourselves; and a feed on their own tails for the horses. After about an hour, however, when our tent had been put up, and the horses picketed, the Shekh made his appearance—and his excuses. We got some eggs and bread for ourselves, and some straw and a handful of barley for the horses, and then informed the village potentate that his conduct had been marked with great inhospitality, that he ran away from us instead of coming to greet us, and that when hungry and thirsty, our souls were fainting in us, every door in the village was shut in our teeth, to say nothing of our nearly having broken our baggage and necks in the dark, for want of a guide. For these errors on his part, we had resolved on recommending him to the animadversions of Mohammed Hasneddar, who was reported not far off. We thought this word of fear, at which men elsewhere trembled, would have produced an awful impression—but not in the least. The Shekh replied very briskly that Mohammed Hasneddar's troops had been there already, and had carried off everything worth having, and that all that was left for them was to mount the date-tree and eat the fruit, during which period he would retire into the desert. In fact, the force of plundering could no further go, and the poor man, with empty pocket, could sing before the spoliator. We parted, however, very good friends; for seeing that we required very little, and had no sinister intentions, he was disposed to do all he could to make amends for his previous want of hospitality.

I must now refer back to the remarkable salt lake we had traversed this morning—the Lacus Tritonis of the ancients, called at present the Shebkah-el-Lowdeah, or Sea of Marks. It was from here that the goddess Minerva was supposed to have sprung, "the Τριτογένεια born in Libystic spots," by the waters of Triton,[1] loving Africa more than all her other haunts from its proximity to heaven, "as its heat clearly indicates";[2] the Tritonia Virgo, who, when she sprang from her father's head, first saw her face in the waters of the Shot Nefzouia. As being the birthplace of so illustrious a divinity, a good deal has been written by the ancients on the subject of this lake. Herodotus refers to it, without doubt, when he writes of the "Great lake Tritonis, in which the island of Phla is situated;" but he makes the Triton, a considerable river, to fall into it. Shaw mentions an island of some extent, well stocked with dates, which he supposes to be the Phla of Herodotus, the Chersonesus of Diodorus Siculus. Ptolemy makes the river Triton to pass through this lake on its way to the sea.

[1] Æsch. *Eum.* 282. [2] Lucan ix. 350.

Shaw on this remarks, that the river which falls into the sea at Kabes is undoubtedly the Triton, and yet that it has no communication with the lake; but Ptolemy is altogether abroad as regards this river, for he speaks of it as taking its rise in Mount Usaletus, and flowing in a northerly direction, passing through three lakes, Libyæ Palus, Lake Pallas, and Lake Tritonitis, after which it falls into the sea near Tacape, or Kabes. This would, however, clearly place Mount Usaletus as the range bordering the desert to the south, but Mount Usaletus is the Gebel Waslaat; and it would almost appear as if Ptolemy was confounding the Triton river with the river Nibhana, which, taking its rise in that mountain, flows through the plain of Kairouan, and empties itself into the Mediterranean at Susa. Scylax gives this lake a circumference of 1000 stadia, and describes it as connected with Syrtis by a narrow spring, and he alludes to the island of Phla, mentioned by Herodotus. Shaw's map is erroneous, as far as the extent and shape of the lake go; and he seems to confound the lake to the west of Neftah with the lake to the east: whereas they are separated by a tract of desert, not very wide it is true, but still quite apparent to any one who has ridden in the environs of Neftah. Ptolemy is perfectly right with regard to the three lakes; for there is still to the east the Shot Nefzouia; between it and the Shot Shebika lies Neftah; and again to the west, the Shot Hamza: all connected by a small river. As the river of Kabes flows from the direction of these lakes, and as there is water, salt and brackish, from El Hamma, at intervals, to the Shot in the great plain between Gebel Ayousha and the southern range bordering the Sahara, it was very easy for a person to be deceived as to the extent of the river's course. Moreover, the formation of the ground between Kabes and the sea would appear to have been much influenced by the encroachments of the sea and by deposits of mud; so that what is now but a small stream might have been a considerable river two thousand years ago.

On the 29th we had a short ride of about seven miles to Minshia, another village of the Nefzouia, passing many small villages *en route*. The inhabitants were generally squatting under their walls enjoying the sun, and the land looked ravaged and untilled. Mohammed Hasneddar had paid them a visit, and paid them off for many a long day of unchecked insubordination and bloodshed. We were accommodated in a room at the entrance of the village, and had considerable difficulty in getting anything: not so much from the incivility of the inhabitants as from the disputes of the Shekhs of the adjacent villages, who were each endeavoring to throw the burden of our entertainment on his neighbor, while all were equally bound by the Bey's command. One village, at last, sent a few eggs, another a couple of tough old hens, another a jug of milk, and last of all arose a desperate fight about barley, which we only obtained by declaring we would go round and stop a day or two with every village in succession.

Minshia lies at the foot of a detached sandstone sugarloaf hill, one of a range which extends from this place, running east and west, to near El Hamma, a distance of about fifty-five miles. The vast plain through which we were about to travel, is bounded by this ridge of conical upstarting hills, to the south, separating it from the Great Desert; and to the north, Gebel Ayousha runs also parallel to this range, to near El Hamma, sloping off, when arriving at its eastern extremity, to the north. Kassim told us terrible tales of the inhabitants of Gebel Ayousha, how they would come down on us in a body of five hundred and destroy us, if they discovered us in their vicinity; and how they laughed at the Bey's beard, and did many other unreasonable things. He said he had been among them trading, and was rather puzzled to account for his survival, when we asked how he contrived to escape from their hands.

On the 30th we started without any fixed idea where we were to bivouac, probably in the open. We were told that we could take in a supply of water at Mags; but on arriving there, we found the village to be merely a very small oasis, perfectly deserted, half of the palms were cut down, and the two or three cabins of the original inhabitants tumbled and destroyed. It was rather a pretty place, naturally, but was now the abomination of desolation. We subsequently heard that the inhabitants had died every one of them from the badness of the water, and it certainly was detestable, and capable of doing any bad act that water might do, but not of tumbling houses and cutting down palm-trees. So we made on to Zouia, another very small oasis, inhabited by one individual, a Marabout, or holy man. We found the saint to be an old ill-favored Negro, who dwelt all alone, save with a female saint, a Negress, who well deserved the Arabic denomination of *om el kabahet*, or "mother of ugliness." But if their faces were black and ugly, their hearts were white and open, for they received us, poor as they were, with the most genuine kindness: giving us everything they had—dates, forage for horses, and the milk of their one cow, to the great detriment of the calf, who complained lustily at being separated from its mother for our accommodation. This little oasis is very prettily situated, quite an African "Auburn, sweetest village of the plain," with fine palms and figs; and had evidently seen much better days and been carefully cultivated, but now the fences were all broken down, the irrigation suspended, and the little patty-pans dry and caked, and no good radishes or turnips or onions the joy of man. The Beni Zid and the Hamama had made the place too hot for any one except a saint, to live in; and though the water was very drinkable and in plenty, and the ground apparently productive, yet to be a kind of half-way house between the haunts of these two desperate marauding tribes, was too much for any nerves, even those used to a good deal of plundering and ill usage. Our friend the Marabout told us that we were now in a famous hunting country, in which bustards, gazelles, ostriches, and the *oudadh*, or wild sheep (*Ammotragus tragelaphus*) abounded, and that there were leopards galore in Gebel Ayousha. He gave us as a present, two pair of horns of the wild sheep which haunt the southern chain, and which had been killed by some Arab sportsman. We were unfortunately dissuaded from an expedition into the hills by the cowardice of our escort, by our ignorance of the locality, and by the want of proper means for carrying water, for we were assured that not a drop was to be found. Here is the real country for a person fond of his gun; we got during the day some red-legs, and saw some of the lesser bustard; but with camels able to support themselves we might have encamped at the foot of the hills, and have had wonderfully good sport.

I could not help remarking the similitude between the names of the places we had visited this day, namely, Mags and Zouia, and those of the African tribes which Herodotus, in his fourth book, places somewhere in this neighborhood. He says, "To the west of the river Triton, certain Libyans, who plough the land and are accustomed to live in houses, called Maxyes, border on the Ausenses;" and in a subsequent chapter he adds, "next adjoining the Maxyes, the Zaueces are situate."

The oasis of Mags, as it is pronounced, or Ma*k*s, as it is written, would quite answer the description of the position of the Maxyes, to the west of the river Triton. It lies, in fact, exactly to the west of the Triton, and I have no doubt but that at one period a large portion of the land, now wilderness, was cultivated. All through the vast plain there are stumps and shoots of palms, and every appearance of its having been inhabited, although we traversed upwards of fifty miles without meeting a living soul. With regard to the Zaueces, who adjoin the Maxyes, we have the district bearing the name of Nefzouia, which would be the country probably inhabited by them, and of which Herodotus would hear, comprising as it does, and probably did, so many communities. The Zouia is clearly the name of the district, the Nef being an adjunct, and connected with the word Neftah. The small oasis we stopped at, which I have called Zouia, would be out of its place, and to the east instead of the west of Mags; but I have doubts whether Zouia be its real name, or, rather, whether it be not included in the district of Zouia, which, as Mags has been destroyed, would include all the oases in these parts. The reply of the Arabs to my question, "Aish ism Beled hadeea?" "What is the name of the place," or "country?" would naturally be Zouia, supposing the locality to have had no distinguishing name, from there being no inhabitants; or, what is more likely, that they imagined I was asking the name of the district. I find in my notes, that in regard to both places where we stopped to the west of Mags, I have written them as Minshia of the Nefzouia, and Tebabshé of the Nefzouia.

I should not lay much stress on the coincidence of the modern and ancient names, but for the fact, that throughout this country one can so frequently, indeed generally, connect the past with the present by the similarity of names—Mount Usaletus, Gebel Waslaat; Cafsa, Kafsa; Thala, Thala; Tisurus, Tozer; Negeta, Neftah; Tacape, Kabes; and many other examples. And as Rennel, from similarity, makes the Gindanes of Herodotus to correspond with the modern Gadames, I think we have far stronger reasons to connect Maks and Zouia with the Maxyes and Zaueces of the same historian.

The Zouaves, although French soldiers, derive their name from the Algerian tribes of Kabyles, called Zouaoua, from whom that force was first recruited. The word Zouaoua, in the Kabyle language, signifies the "possessions or territory of the Zoua;" and as these Kabyles are the African aborigines, or rather, the early Semitic settlers, driven from their settlements in the plains to mountain fastnesses by different invaders, it is probable that they are the descendants of the Zauecces of Herodotus, who once inhabited the country we have just traversed, but who migrated into the more secure territory of Algeria, and have retained their name until this day. It is strange to find the ancient Zauecces reappearing and becoming famous through the modern Zouaves.

Herodotus refers to many other stories of this part of Africa, that salt, for instance, is found in large lumps on the hills. This is the case in the ground we traversed on the 28th, where a large extent of the surface of the ground, when it rose above the lake, was covered with thick cakes of salt. And Shaw mentions an entire mountain of salt, called Gebel Had-deffa, as being situated near the eastern extremity of the lake. This I did not see, nor did I hear of it. Another story Herodotus tells of a fountain possessed by the Ammonians, which tallies with the condition of the hot wells of El Hamma and Kafsa, namely, that in the morning it is tepid, and grows cool about noon, and again it becomes warm towards sunset, increasing in heat till at midnight it boils and bubbles up. I understood at El Hamma, that early in the morning and in the evening the water was hotter than during the day, when it cooled considerably; and certainly at Kafsa we had opportunities of knowing that early in the morning the water was tolerably warm, but in the daytime cool. All these stories which Herodotus picked up from report, are interesting enough, and many of them day by day are found to be grounded on fact. Minutoli stated, that he saw the spring of hot water at the oasis of Siwah, the Ammonium which may have appeared cooler in the day than in the morning and after sunset. When one reads the wonderful hearsays and tales of mediæval travellers, one cannot but admire the discretion of old Herodotus, who must have exercised incredible self-restraint in those early days of adventure, when the "antres vast and deserts wild" were peopled by even stranger monsters, and stocked with greater marvels than Othello had to tell of.

Dec. 31st.—This day rose pregnant with terrors for our escort. We were this night to camp with the Beni Zid, those terrible marauders whose firerceness, and plunderings and bloodshed had been the theme of many an hour in the wilderness. Their fame had spread even to Tunis, where more than one friendly voice was raised to bid us beware of the Beni Zid, and give them a wide berth. It was, however, impossible to avoid them, as their encampment, we were informed, lay between us and El Hamma, at a distance of about thirty miles. The Hambas would have run into a rat-hole to escape the meeting, but it was impossible; there was Mount Ayousha to the left, teeming with cutthroats, according to Kassim's account; to the right was the Desert, and no water. Their terror was not so much excited by the tribe *en masse,* for they hoped that Mahommed Hasneddar had exercised a salutary influence over them, but detached parties doing a little spoliation on their own account, was the real danger they apprehended. We made an early start, and bid adieu to the old Marabout, who, inspired by a handsome present, prayed for every imaginable blessing on our heads, and promised to keep all the horns and skins of every sort of animal that should come in his way, until our return. The attendants wondered much at our generosity to the old saint, and seemed surprised that we had not been equally profuse when among great people. Kassim, with great self-sufficiency, expatiated on the character of the English, who, he said, cared nothing for the mighty and rich, but were always liberal to the poor. I regret to say that this explanation did not produce the admiration we expected, for they remarked, that they did not see any use in giving presents when you could take by force, and that as the Marabout had no friends save the "mother of ugliness," we might have hit him hard, and eaten up all he possessed, without even paying him in thanks.

We had now got into a real fine country for game, bustards, and gutta, and occasionally red-legs, in number. The immense plain was covered with low brushwood, and a few good pointers or falcons would have been invaluable. At mid-day we reached a well, and in its neighborhood we should, had we been a little more experienced, have camped, for it was evidently the resort of all the *feræ naturæ* of the neighborhood, and some excellent shooting might have been had by establishing an ambush. We found an ostrich feather which had been deposited there by its owner the same morning; and we found, what was much more useful, a grey mare enjoying her liberty. She was a perfect godsend, for the ass that had conveyed our tent from Minshia, was done up, and we had little hopes of getting it to the Beni Zid. Sir S. shot a magnificent eagle this day, who had been making havoc among the bustards, but our guide looked askant at it, and said we had done an unlucky thing, for that the eagle was a Marabout, or holy bird. This was a grand ride to-day, weather glorious, and a fine plain seventy miles long and thirty broad, to ride over, and lots of elbow-room, for we met no one. The baggage horses and guards proceeded decorously in the middle. Sir S. acted as *vedette*, about half a mile on one side, and I on the other. There is something which always appeared to me most strange in the ride through these vast and noiseless solitudes: with nothing to interrupt the attention, the mind is thrown back entirely on itself, and recalls scenes and sensations which had apparently long since vanished. So vividly have arisen these impressions of past time, that I have fancied them to be rather hallucinations than recollections, and have often been amused by finding myself suddenly recalled to circumstances around, when I have been gravely arguing and debating with myself, "Can these things have ever been?" The words traced in lemon-juice have been warmed, and have reappeared.

Towards evening, as the sun was sinking behind us, the black tents of the Beni Zid appeared afar, and presently immense flocks of sheep and goats, and innumerable camels, showed, if the palpable terror of our Hamba was not sufficient index, that we were now within the grasp of these redoubtable warriors. The Oda Bashi and myself rode on ahead into the semicircle of tents to the large one, that denoted the presence of the Shekh. Out of it there stalked a magnificent Arab, considerably above six feet high, but looking quite a son of Anak, in his white *burnoos*. He advanced to my horse, and, taking him by the bridle, gave not the usual salutation of peace and welcome, but sternly put the question to me, "Enta Franzoui?" —Are you a Frenchman? I replied, "No! that I was an Englishman." On this his manner at once changed; he immediately gave the salutation of peace, told us that his tent was at our disposal, ordered his people to and fro, to get food ready for us and provender for our horses, and held the horse while I dismounted. The other magnates of the tribe soon came flocking around, and all welcomed us with the greatest cordiality. The faces of our escort were now as short as they were long and moody before, and they whispered to us that the Beni Zid were the best people in the world. As to their goodness, we can only speak from experience, that we never got a heartier welcome from any tribe; and they were certainly, as a body, the finest set of men I ever saw. They were taller, and with much more appearance of pure Arab blood, than the men of any of the other tribes we had mixed with. In the evening, after discussing the sheep and *coscousou*, we had a great bonfire, for it was very cold, and a great chat round the bonfire. We asked the Shekh why he had demanded whether we were French or not, before he gave us his greeting; to which he replied—that had we been French he would have given us a very different reception—that he had never seen any English or French in his life, but that he had heard from the people who had come from the sea, that the English were people of one word, but that the French were double-tongued; and that the French were the enemy of the Muslims, while we were their cousins. I did not, as may be supposed, make any reference to Delhi and Indian doings, but told him that we were always well disposed to the Mahommedans, and that Regina had numbers of them for her subjects. He told us that Mahommed Hasneddar had paid them a visit, and, as he had come with cavalry and artillery, that they were unable to resist his importunities, but had been forced to pay him a prodigious sum of money, which had completely impoverished them; in fact, that he had carried away everything they had, except their flocks. They admitted that they had taken part with Ghouma against the Bey, but alleged that it was in consequence of his having produced a firman which stated that the Bey was deposed, and that he was appointed by the Sultan in his stead. They were evidently very much depressed by the squeezing they had suffered, and attributed their non-resistance to the artillery, which it was impossible to oppose. We tried to get some tales from them of their feuds with the Hamama; but my knowledge of the language was so circumscribed, and Kassim's interpretations so unintelligible, that all we could make out was, that they alleged that the Hamama were a set of cowards who attacked in superior numbers, and ran away if resisted, while the boast of the Beni Zid was never to retreat, but always to die fighting. Of course we applauded this martial spirit, and did not believe one word of it. They spoke a great deal about hunting and shooting, and gladly acceded to our proposal for a *chasse* next day. They were to show us lots of bustards and gazelles, and would bring their greyhounds for a course. The *chasse* opened with rather an untoward incident. After going a little way, Sir S. had to return to the encampment for something he had left behind, and his horse, rather a fiery little fellow, being excited by the other horses about him, became restive and commenced rearing. The girths were, as usual, left loose by neglect, and the saddle was slipping round, when, to avoid the indignity of a fall, Sir S. dropped off. The Arabs, to make the horse advance, pitched into him with sticks, which had not the desired effect, but made him retrograde till he actually backed into the Shekh's tent, one pole after another of which he deliberately knocked down, and the whole tent fell prostrate to the earth. The Shekh was greatly disconcerted, not from the fall of the tent, for that was speedily arranged, but from the evil omen. He said that when a chief's tent fell, it always was a warning to him of speedy death, and that it and the dead eagle which he had seen with us, clearly prognosticated some impending evil to his tribe. Kassim, however, consoled him by saying that men's fates were in Allah's hands, and that our horse had kicked down a tent in every Arab encampment since we left Tunis; and as for the eagle, we had killed so many, that if men's lives depended on them, half Tunis would be depopulated. So the Shekh's forehead brightend, and we went forth. We found some bustards, and in the course of the day came right into the middle of a flock of gazelles. They were on the brink of a very steep water-course, which they were unwilling to face, and made a bolt right through dogs, men, and horses. Sir S. had unfortunately discharged his gun when they were too far off, and I was mounting the water-course, and was too late; but if ever dogs had a fair chance, the Beni Zid greyhounds had, for they were not more than a few yards off, and yet the gazelles beat them to a stand-still. We longed that day for the hawks of the Farasheesh, for there was plenty of game, and fine ground for a gallop. Sir S. made a grand shot at a falcon, high in the air, as he rode along, which immensely pleased our Arab friends, and one of them, not to be behindhand, descended from his horse, and, creeping along the banks of the ravine, took a long and deliberate shot at something we could not see, (for he waved us back), on the other side. It took effect, and he shortly returned very much elated, and exhibiting a little owl, *booma,* as they call it, which he thought would be a valuable adjunct to our collection. Kassim made it a point to inform the natives, who wondered much at the trouble we took in skinning birds, that Regina always desired her subjects to bring her from every country, specimens of the birds and animals and stones, that she might know about the country as well as if she visited it herself. The Beni Zid begged and prayed us to stop another day, which, as we did not know when we were well off, and inspired by Kassim and the rest, who were anxious to get to Kabes, we refused to do. They said there were lots of game ahead, the old story of "yasser godam,"—"plenty before us," for they were anxious to shift their quarters where they were afraid to bully and extort money; and Kassim, having relatives at Kabes, was in a hurry to exhibit himself, and have fantasias, and spend his money. We rather astonished our Tunisian friends, when asked by them had we really been among the Beni Zid, by assuring them that not only had we been among them, but found them the heartiest and most sporting of our entertainers, and that their country was the only part we were particularly anxious to revisit. Finding us determined to be off, the Shekh sent an escort with us, which accompanied us half way to El Hamma; and as a proof of the cordiality of the tribe, the next day the Shekh sent in a messenger to know how we were, and left word that he had punished the escort for not conducting us to our destination, as he considered us under his care until we had altogether left the country.

El Hamma, where we put up, is about fourteen miles from the Beni Zid *dowar;* it is a large date village, or oasis, which has evidently known better days. The cultivation is extensive, but slovenly enough, and from the number of ruined houses and ruined Marabout tombs it seems to have received rough treatment at no very distant period. El Hamma was the Aquæ Tacapitanæ of the ancients, or the Baths of Tacape, now Kabes; and as we entered the part of the town where we were to lodge, a dense steam hung over the vicinity of the hot wells. A fort with a small garrison is close to them, in which we were invited to put up; but Kassim had a comfortable room for us elsewhere, and little Ali whispered significantly, *Beraghit ya arfi*—"Fleas, my master," so we declined the favor, and passed on. We visited the baths the next day: they were of Roman construction and very clean, the water beautifully limpid. The heat was considerable—about 98; and Kassim and our escort revelled in it, and washed themselves and their clothes preparatory to astonishing the citizens of Kabes with their greatness. We went out shooting the next day, and got some wild fowl. A salt river runs by the town from north-west to south-east; we traced this river to its source a few miles to the north-west of the town, and beyond it at some distance was a large sheet of water extending considerably westward. There was also water in the bed of a river, flowing from the west when filled, between the Beni Zid and El Hamma. All these appearances of a water connection with the Lake of Marks might have easily persuaded the ancients that a large river flowed into Lake Triton, which is the account heard by Herodotus, though Ptolemy makes the river flow from the lake to the sea. In fact, as Shaw observes, "the errors about this river were easily accounted for, as it seemed that few or no curious persons had hitherto the hardiness to traverse over these deserts, the abode and resort of cuthroats and assassins, and, consequently, where there could have been no opportunity of rectifying mistakes."

On the 3rd we marched to Kabes, or Gabs, as it should be pronounced. During the ride the swaggering of Kassim and the Hambas was very grand indeed, as to the great reception we were about to get. They abused the Arabs and their tent life, and extolled the comforts of the Bey's house, and all the good things we were to enjoy. In this agreeable conversation we soon got over the fourteen miles between El Hamma and Kabes. On entering the oasis—for we are still among oases—we found it very carefully tilled, and with pretty gardens all green with henna,[1] for the production of which this place is famous. It resembles in leaf the box-tree, and grows about three feet high. There are three distinct villages in this town, which is about one mile from the sea, and we betook ourselves first of all to that in which the Bey's house was situated. We found, however, anything but the flattering reception we anticipated. They said they knew nothing about us, and did not want to make our acquaintance. We protested, and showed the Bey's

[1] The dye with which the Arab ladies color their fingers, and the Arab gentlemen their horses' tail and legs. It comes out a rich orange color.

order, giving us the absolute command of all his habitations. While the wordy war was raging, the Kaïd's son, a good-looking young fellow of about eighteen, came down and informed us that we had better be off, for that we could not stop there—that his father was with the camp of Mohammed Hasneddar, and that he did not care for any order of the Bey. The Shekh of the village consoled us by telling us that he had prepared a delightful residence for us in the other village, where we should be quite as well off—in fact, rather better. So we crossed the river Triton, and were led in state to a most filthy and disreputable house, in such a rickety condition that I have not a doubt but that, had we been induced to occupy it, we should all have been buried in its ruins. "There," said the Shekh, "there is a beautiful abode for you, where you can enjoy every privacy and take your *keff*." We cut short his eulogiums very quickly by informing him that we did not care where we roosted that evening, but that to-morrow morning we should be off to the Hasneddar, and that, Inshallah! his sticks and the Shekh's back would make acquaintance for such gross neglect of the Bey's commands. This threat so alarmed Shekh Haj Boubukr, that he instantly led the way to the house of a Jew, whom he forthwith dispossessed of the best portion of it, and placed him and his dwelling at our service. This arbitrary proceeding we found to be justified by the fact that the Jew was employed as custom-house officer of the port, and as a servant of the Bey, and had this house lent him in consequence. We found the Jew's family obliging enough; but Kassim and the escort were in terrible dudgeon, after all their boastings, at the reception they had met with, and declared confidently to the awe-struck listeners, that certainly the Bey would cut off the Governor's head when he heard of his son's misconduct. For the first day the Shekh behaved very well, lending us his horses, and supplying us with tolerable liberality. He sent us also in some vessels of *lagmi* or palm juice, which is obtained by cutting a nick into the head of the palm-tree, and allowing the sap to flow into a jar placed there to receive it. This liquor is sweet, but very insipid, and is chiefly prized for its intoxicating qualities, which are produced after it is kept for a few days and allowed to ferment. It is in that state particularly nasty; but still we saw more than one of the villagers who gave evident tokens of recent revel on these, to us very colicky, and anything but jolly potations. The Shekh was, however, a cunning fellow—very obsequious while under the influence of fear, but that once removed, most parsimonious and disobliging. His fear was removed by a letter we wrote to Mahommed Hasneddar, in which we complained of the demeanor of the Governor's son, but mentioned that the Shekh's conduct was everything we could approve of. When this letter was despatched, he felt quite secure, and henceforth his sole object was to circumvent us and cut off the supplies. Every morning there was a fierce battle for bread, and a still greater disturbance for milk. One day we found an unfortunate man tied by the leg in the yard, who they said was the keeper of the cows, and was handed over to us as a hostage for milk, which still did not come. Then there was a fight for barley, and at last the Shekh pretended he had departed on some urgent business, and we were left to our own resources. We remained altogether five days at Gabs, for the sole purpose of shooting the *Pterocles arenarius,* that were in thousands in the neighborhood. Yet so wild were they, that we only succeeded in getting five brace and a half; indeed, I could make no hand of them at all with my little 16-bore gun: they all fell to the unerring aim and heavy metal of Sir S. They generally came in at about eight o'clock in the morning from the desert to the flashes of water that lay beneath the sandhills on which the tomb of a celebrated saint, Sidi Bul Baba, a contemporary and friend of the Prophet, is placed. They gave notice of their approach by the croaking note peculiar to this species of desert grouse. This was the time to catch them; for, their thirst once satisfied, it was next to impossible to approach them on the plain. We made an excursion one day into the wild country to the south, passing through Bibo and two other smaller oases by the seaside, till we came to the course of a river which, although at the time with very little water, must from the width of its banks be, during floods, of considerable size. We met bustards and gazelles, and I have no doubt but that good shooting might be had among the wild and uninhabited hills to the south.

I have been much amused with an extract quoted by Heeren in his *Historical Researches.* It is from Tully's *Narrative of a Residence in Tripoli,* of which the date only goes back as far as 1820. "The woods," he says, "on the road from Tunis to Tripoli, are so infested with savage beasts, that even numerous caravans cannot pass them without great danger. As the darkness comes on, the woods resound with the howling of the jackal, and the dreadful roar of the lion seeking his prey: even large watch-fires will scarcely keep them off." This is truly ridiculous; for, though there may have been more wild beasts thirty years ago than at present, yet the country is totally unfit for harboring the larger animals. The woods spoken of by Mr. Tully are perfectly mythical—as mythical as the lions: they do not exist, and have certainly not been in existence this century. The jackals are the only formidable monsters, and the worst they do is to make an occasional foray on a henroost.

It seems, however, to be a vestige of the old Carthaginian tradition to make the Regency formidable by accounts of its wild beasts, dragons, snakes, and other monsters. The Carthaginians wished to keep out intruders; but, as we have no such object, it is as well to tell the truth.

Dr. Arnold remarks, that it seems to have been the policy of the Carthaginians to spread abroad tales of the venom of the serpents, the ferocity of the wild beats, and the multitude of astounding monsters haunting their territory, while they were silent as to its great fertility. It was so inaccessible to foreigners that these exaggerations were readily received; and a good proof is given of the success of their policy by the extraordinary account that Herodotus (who had previously been giving a detailed and most remarkably exact narration, not only of all the African tribes on the coast from Egypt to the Lesser Syrtis, but also of those in the interior) has sent forth of the monstrous animals and preternatural creatures infesting the territory of Carthage.

On our return we heard that an Englishman had paid us a visit, and that he was staying in the town; and the next morning he presented himself. He was dressed in European costume, and told us he was the doctor of the 32nd Bengal Infantry, enjoying his leave. He had come, he said, from the island of Jerba, in a native boat, accompanying a Jewish gentleman whom he had met in Tripoli, and whom he was curing from the effects of a very severe wound. He said he had travelled all over the world, through Persia and Asia Minor, through Egypt and the Soudan, and had been at Khartoom. He certainly had been all through Egypt, but tripped very considerably in his geography when beyond the first cataract. He had not the appearance of an Asiatic, but he evidently knew little of Europe, and seemed to speak English with considerable difficulty. It certainly was strange how the doctor of a native regiment could have found leisure and means for the vast amount of travelling he had unquestionably gone through. He said, however, that he made more by his profession during his leave than he did when with his regiment, and that he was to get £80 in hard cash for curing the Jew. He was of use to us, for he spoke Arabic extremely well, and so terrified the Governor's son by expatiating on the rage of the Bey when he should hear of the bad reception Regina's children had met with, that that bumptious young man shook in his shoes and came down to beg pardon. But it was our turn now to be saucy, and we refused to receive him, which the more increased his alarm; and the report spread through the town that the English Consul-General would insist, as reparation, that the young man's head should be cut off. Then flocked in deputations, and the Jews put in a good word, and the Shekh urged extenuating circumstances, and the youth himself sent to say that he was young and foolish, and should therefore be excused. But knowing that a hot struggle was impending for barley for the road, we refused to be appeased, making the youth's fears ancillary to obtaining forage. The evening before we started, the Jew with whom our Anglo-Indian ally was staying, begged so earnestly for a visit from us that I went to see him. His house was on the other side of the river, and reached with some difficulty, for it was very dark, and there were deep holes on each side of the winding path, from which the inhabitants had been extracting the foundations of Roman buildings. It was very clean and very nicely furnished, and I was received with much *empressement* by the occupiers, a pretty Hebrew girl among others. The invalid was a most intelligent middle-aged man; he had received a terrible slash across the face, having been cut down by some unknown hand while returning one evening to his house after dusk. He insisted that I must break bread in his house, and would have served up a fine dinner, but time did not permit more than a slight collation of walnuts, figs, dates, and bread, and some excellent arraki. He very kindly insisted on sending us down for the morrow's journey some bottles of this spirit, and two large home-baked loaves of excellent bread, which were valuable adjuncts to the future short commons which it was our lot to experience. I had a good deal of conversation with this Jew through the means of the doctor; he complained very much of the absence of any settled and defined system of administration in the country, that the local governors committed most arbitrary acts, and that no one was sure of enjoying the fruits of his industry. He wished greatly, he added, that England would take possession of the Regency. I asked if France would do equally well; and he replied, that it was quite indifferent which of the European great powers took it, for that it then would be under fixed laws: and as for the French, he believed the natives in Algeria were happier under them than under their former cruel squeezing rulers. He was the only person I met in the Regency who did not express a horror of the French and their rule. He said the present Bey was a mild well-meaning man, but that he was surrounded by a set of robbers and extortioners, and never heard the truth. While this conversation was going on, in came the delinquent youth, the Governor's son. He shed some tears, professed great sorrow, and begged so hard for forgiveness, in which he was joined by our host, the doctor, and all the lookers-on, including the pretty Jewish girl, that I was obliged to say that I was ready to forgive and forget, provided Sir S. was of the same opinion, and that we would not apply to the Consul-General to lay the matter before the Bey. The doctor congratulated the youth on the prospect of his being allowed to keep his head on his shoulders a little longer, and we all parted the best friends. As a matter of sentiment this was all right; but, as a matter of worldly wisdom, it would have been better to have remained stern to the last; for, on the morrow at starting, the Shekh, that most cunning of rogues, evidently treating us as good, easy, forgiving creatures, had neither barley nor bread nor anything ready for our journey. In vain we protested. He said he would write a letter to the Shekh of Woodriff, our halting-place, and desire him to furnish everything; and as time pressed we were forced to depart with panniers empty of corn but full of promises.

Woodriff, another date village, is about ten miles from Kabes, not far from the sea. We had a pleasant ride over the hills with the blue Mediterranean spread out at our side. It was the last but one pleasant ride we were to enjoy for many a day, and we all rejoiced at leaving Kabes—men, dogs, and horses. On reaching Woodriff we found a very different Shekh from cunning old Boubukr; our host was a rough hospitable fellow, and seemed only too pleased to oblige us. To our very great surprise, he said, we should have all the barley we required in case we wished to camp out, and that he wanted no letter from Kabes, as he was his own master and knew what was right. The poor fellow had lost his hand, and was in great danger of his arm going also, in consequence of the bursting of a gun some short time before in resisting an excursion of the Hamama. This oasis is persecuted by these scoundrels, who even gallop through the town in search of spoil. The Shekh said he prayed they might come during our stay, that they might know the effect of pistols that never ceased going off and required no loading, our revolvers to wit, and that, if he could only see a few of them knocked over, he would be amply revenged. We had another very civil friend here also, a merchant from Sphax, who had met us somewhere, and who was very obliging, giving us a supply of tobacco, which we sadly needed, as, in spite of Kassim's magniloquent eulogies of Kabes, everything we bought there was very bad, the tobacco execrable. This Sphax merchant had been buying the dates of El Hamma and these villages: we tried some of them, but they were nasty woody esculents, very different from the delicious *digla*, whose loss we so much deplored, and our own shortsightedness in not bringing a large stock with us. The Sphaxi said very wisely, that it was not every man who could eat *digla*, tantamount to drinking claret and champagne, therefore it was necessary to provide for those who could not, and that he could get a very good market for the inferior article.

On the 9th we marched for about nine miles through a fine country for game, until we reached the banks of the river Lakarīt. This is a small stream which runs about four or five miles inland. Towards the sea it is deep and muddy, and fringed with reeds; but its bed further inland is a mass of jungle, just the very spot for wild beasts and a *chasse*. We ordered the tent to be pitched at a little distance from the river, much to the annoyance of Kassim and the escort, who had always been throwing every obstacle in the way of this camping out, and who swore we should be all attacked and killed before morning, as soon as our fires denoted our whereabouts to the marauders. Then came appeals to our compassion: the escort had no bread, no provisions; but as we had that very morning given strict orders to each man to have enough bread to last him a day, on the very ground of our likelihood to camp out, we were not deterred by this difficulty. We soon found we were in a first-rate place for game. There were pterocles and red-legs and bustards, and the ground was rooted up by wild boars, and there was a probability of leopards in the fine lying in the river's bed; so we contemplated at least two or three glorious days. On coming home in the evening, we found the encampment in consternation: all protested they had seen a large body of men in white *burnooses*, galloping up and down on the shore; and that they were the Hamama, who no doubt had seen a ship in distress, and were waiting to wreck her, and who would infallibly discover and wreck us also. But we too had come homeward not far from the sea, and had seen the same appearance, and certainly it appeared as if persons were running to and fro, but on approaching cautiously within sight, the formidable party turned out to be nothing more than a number of huge cranes, which were dancing and performing the odd evolutions that cranes at times perform. We laughed in consequence, heartily, at their fears; but when men are determined to be frightened, it is not easy to reassure them, and they predicted, that though the Hamama might have been cranes, we should find before long the rogues from Gebel Ayousha and Telj to be stern realities. During the night it began to blow hard, and in the morning there was a full gale of wind, a clouded sky, and every appearance of foul weather, so that all our hopes of a couple of days' bivouac in the open were at an end. The horses had no shelter, and we already had experience of the instability of our tent as a protection against rain, so with many a groan at our hard luck, we sent on the baggage with the intention of having a couple of hours' shooting, and catching it up; and certainly we had every reason to regret our forced departure. We made for the sea, and had first-rate wild-fowl shooting for a short time; ducks of several sorts were flying to and fro up and down the stream, and ensconced in the reeds we very soon had more than we could carry, so we galloped on with the ducks slung to Ali's saddle, and regained our party. We remarked on the way a number of thorn bushes profusely decorated with shreds of clothing, which had the exact appearance of the trees in the vicinity of Holy Wells, in Ireland, which are similarly decorated. We were told that when a native lady was anxious for a child, or for the recovery of some dear relative, she invoked some particular holy man, and, tearing up the whole of her dress, fastened it in shreds on the thorn trees in question. This is much the same course of proceeding as in Ireland: the saint is invoked for recovery, or for the son and heir; but the Irish are more economical, and only deposit a portion of their garment. I should have mentioned, that yesterday I was taken to see a spot connected with an Arab story. One of the Arabs of the country led me to a piece of ground about a rood in size, which was perfectly bare, without a particle of herbage on it, although surrounded by the brushwood of the country. He told me a long story about Zazia and a dog and *coscousou*, and Kassim tried to explain it afterwards, but neither Sir S. nor myself could obtain the slightest idea of the tale. On reaching Tunis, we got Mr. Davis to extract the story from Kassim, and it was to this this effect:—Once upon a time, a long while ago, the tribes of the Hallaleea, or Ben Hillal, and of the Zenata, dwelt in these parts. The Ben Hillal were very powerful, and held all the territory about Gabs. Their Cadi was handsome, young, and gentle. He heard of the beauty of Zazia, the daughter of the Shekh of the Zenata, and sent an embassy to ask her in marriage. The embassy extolled his openhanded generosity and goodness of heart; but the Shekh, who was a magician, in order to try his generosity, disguised an evil spirit as a dog, and sent him to the tent of the Ben Hillal Cadi. When he saw the dog he spoke courteously and kindly to him, and then fed him with his own hands on mutton and *coscousou*—an unusual act of condescension on the part of an Arab chief. The dog had departed the next day when the chief arose to feed him, but it was to tell the tale of his goodness. So the marriage took place, and by it the Ben Hillal and Zenata were united. The good Cadi died, and his wife became the ruler; she governed so well, that they all became rich and powerful under her sway. It was the custom of the women of her tribe, when any person died belonging to them, to betake themselves to the particular spot pointed out to me, and there to tear their hair, beat their breasts, and lacerate their bodies, until at length the soil became so saturated with blood that nothing would ever grow henceforth upon it. My informant evidently was ignorant of the fertilizing properties of blood. After the death of their female ruler, the tribe dwindled away, and moved off towards the confines of Egypt, where it dwells to this day.

There was not much to interest or induce remarks, during our canter of sixteen miles over the wildest and bleakest country we had yet traversed. The wind was piercingly cold, and the bitter, bitter blasts went through us like swords; at last we arrived at the tomb of Sidi Maddhab, an eminent saint, close to which was a low, square mud enclosure, in the yard whereof the tent was pitched. Lucky it was for us that we had even these low walls for shelter, for had we been in the open, tent and all would have been blown right out to sea. This sanctified spot was inhabited by three or four grizzly old saints and their partners, real mothers of ugliness, and not an atom of food for ourselves or horses was obtainable. We purchased some barley for the poor half-starved quadrupeds, at an exorbitant price, for the pious men insisted that their holy calling relieved them from all compliance with the Bey's orders. Very early in the morning the rain came down in torrents; all our engineering efforts to construct canals were fruitless, we were driven out of the tent in no time, and forced to take refuge in a recess of the porch of the enclosure. During the whole day of inexorable rain, we were huddled up in this hole, occupying our time in skinning birds, cooking the wild-fowl of the day before for future emergencies, and hunting innumerable fleas. The damp soon penetrated everything, as we found to our cost; and the poor horses, with heads and ears down, without a dry spot to sleep out their troubles, added much to the melancholy, which was only varied by the ferocity of one of the female saints, who rated her pious mate in a style that astonished even me, accustomed as I was to the revilings of the old hags of Ghizeh, near

Cairo—the most emphatic Billingsgate I wot of. After these onslaughts, the African Xanthippe used to betake herself to the porch, and, grinning with a row of fierce white teeth, laugh lustily at her old mate, and tell us stories evidently to his disfavor, could we have understood them. One little incident rather refreshed us: when dinner-time arrived, we asked for something in the shape of a table to place the saucepan on. I must premise that the Eastern table is a small round piece of furniture not more than a few inches from the ground To our great amusement, when these highly orthodox Mahommedan Marabouts produced their table, it turned out to be the top of a barrel, on which was inscribed

I W LEWIS PRIME PORK—200.
N. YORK
CITY

Fancy these godly men daily feeding off the lid of the vessel that had enclosed the pickled unclean beast, the touch of which would have been unspeakable pollution. They said they had picked it up on the shore, where a vessel had been wrecked some time previously. The piety of these cenobites did not relieve them from the constant infliction of the Hamama, a body of whom a few days previously drove off the only two cows they possessed.

At last the long day passed, a weary one to us

and a sad one to the unfortunate half-drowned horses; and as the morning was fine, we made an early start of it, to get over the thirty miles to Maharas, our next station. There was a dense vapor steaming up from the moist ground, which prevented us at first from seeing much, but it was still the same wild and utterly desolate country of the day before. When we had got about half way, a great black cloud rose up before us, and out of it came the most tremendous shower of rain I ever in my life experienced; it more resembled a sheet of water poured out of a bucket on our unhappy heads. The ground we were crossing at the time was low, and apparently at all times marshy, but from the rain of the day before it had become a regular morass. We had the satisfaction of seeing our superb captain march ahead with his usual dignity into a hole, and be extricated with some trouble and much dirt. Then came down the unfortunate baggagers, and our effects with them, into the morass, which diminished our amusement. There was an immense caravan proceeding from the date country, on the same way as ourselves, but its guides had very wisely taken some high ground to the left, where they were on *terra firma*, and our object was to reach this. This was no easy matter, for the tremendous shower was now flowing over the ground like a river, and all vestige of track had disappeared. Poor Kassim was, therefore, sent ahead, a shivering pioneer; and at length, after many a mishap and many a ducking, we got to firm ground. But our troubles even now were not fated to be over. We had scarcely got the baggage to rights, and were jogging along congratulating each other on our escape, when all at once our best and bravest baggage-horse, hitherto particularly good tempered, whether stung by something or pricked by his harness, became suddenly possessed as if by the devil. He commenced kicking furiously, then proceeded to galloping about and charging the other horses. The three dogs, excited by the row, flew at him, which of course only increased his terror. Sir S. jumped off his horse to flog off the dogs, and hardly had he left him when he also went at the fugitive with teeth and heels. The Bey's people were at first too much alarmed by the kicking and fighting to approach, but the affray was now so serious that they also ran to the rescue; upon which, their horses, generally good sober beasts, became inspired with the general fury, and commenced fighting like incarnate fiends. The drenching of the preceding night, and starvation at Sidi Maddhab, instead of cooling their courage, seemed to have roused it to fever heat. At last, the author of all the mischief, the baggager, in the midst of his gallopings and kickings, came down with such a fall, that, impeded as he was by his panniers, he found it impossible to rise. The dogs ran in on him and worried him, Trim inflicting a severe wound on the poor brute's thigh. This settled the business; the other horses were soon tranquillized, the dogs were flogged all round, and our decorous march continued. We passed by Unga, a deserted town with some considerable remains. It stands close to the sea, and was of course, according to our escort's account, infested by robbers, and a harbor for the Hamama. We met two of these worthies, fine looking young men, probably after no good; our intercourse was highly amicable: we mutually deplored the state of the weather, inquired as to the condition of the track, and Kassim cursed them when they were out of ear-shot. Just before nightfall, we crawled into the small and dilapidated fishing village of Maharas, where our accommodation was wretched in the extreme. In vain we demanded a house, or even a room, stanch against the rain; the head man declared there was not such a dwelling in the whole town; so we passed the night under a pleasant drip, and had ample occupation in shifting to and fro to try and get as dry lying as could be accomplished.

The next day's journey was about twenty-one miles, to Sphax, and the morning looked again promising as we skirted the bleak stony hills that guard the shore. It was a low coast, dotted every here and there with stake-nets, which extended far out into the angry, dirty, shallow sea. We passed one or two dreary watch-towers, but, as they were situated in salt marshes and out of the line of road, we had no opportunity of examining them: indeed, there was little enough energy among us for exploration, for the rain came down again in gusts, and the cold north wind blew a gale in our teeth. Right joyful was the sight, when at last the white walls of Sphax, and its white pleasure-houses in green gardens extending many a mile, gleamed on our sight; for we were wet to the skin, and our appearance when we entered the town was as the appearance of so many bundles of unclean moist rags. We rode through the streets to the Kaïd's house, where we were received with the greatest civility by a host of gorgeously dressed attendants, Assyrians in purple and gold, who looked doubly imposing to our eyes, so long accustomed to dirty-white blankets and dingy *burnooses*. We were ushered into most comfortable rooms, with chairs and tables, and well-cushioned divans; a huge brazier in the anteroom gleamed ruddily to dry our effects; and a very nice-looking youth desired us to consider him our particular attendant, and that his master's orders were, that we were to ask for everything we could possibly require. He added, that his master, having heard of the sad condition we were in, would not trespass on us till we were recovered from our fatigue on the morrow, and begged of us to accept some refreshment until dinner could be got ready; and it was a refreshment indeed—some screeching hot rum-punch and sponge-cake, with a host of cigars, most acceptable after smoking dirt for a fortnight, and gorgeous *chibouques* fit for a pasha. In due time came the dinner, and it was worthy of the preliminaries: several dishes of fish, and made dishes, and all sorts of good sweet things; and two bottles of excellent, really excellent red *vin de pays;* and plates, and actually glasses, and coffee coming in on all occasions; and a huge bowl of *coscousou* for the dogs—nothing forgotten. So that night we got our clothes off us, and slept drily and cleanlily, though we had not eschewed sack; and dogs, horses, and men, all blessed the good Governor of Sphax.

The next morning we were waited on by the English consular agent, Mr. Carleton by name, a most pleasing gentlemanly young man, very like Lord N. in appearance. He proposed showing us the lions before the Governor's visit, and accompanied us round the town. It was in a filthy state from the rain that had fallen, but especially filthy was the European quarter, as is always the case in Oriental towns. This part of the town, although within the walls, is separated from the Mahommedan part by an inner wall and gate, and judging from the specimens of Christianity which we saw, the Faithful have certainly no loss by the demarcation. There is hardly anything of a port, but the roadstead is well protected by a headland from the wind most generally prevalent, the northern, and though it was blowing hard, and a heavy sea running outside, the ships in the roads, among them a Tunisian steamer, were riding very snugly at anchor. The Governor was busily employed levelling and embellishing the esplanade by the port: a very unusual act of neatness on the part of a Muslim, and one that will be duly acknowledged by the dingy Levantine ladies, as they flaunt along it of a Sunday afternoon in all the bravery and color and discordance of the peacock. Some noble columns of red granite lay by the water's edge, which the sailors said had come from Benghazi to be cut up and converted into crushers for oil-mills. To the north of the town is a large inclosed space within which the townspeople boast of there being three hundred cisterns. Each of these cisterns is built by some pious Moor for the benefit of the community, and, considering the want of water in this locality, is a gift of great utility. A space of ground round the cistern is smoothed and made stanch with mortar, and as it inclines towards the centre, under which is the reservoir, all the rain that falls upon it flows into it and is preserved. Want of good water is one of the great drawbacks at Sphax. The name of this town is derived from *fakus* (water-melon), from the quantity of that fruit which used to be grown there. It is celebrated in the Regency, as I before remarked, for the mercantile tendency of its inhabitants; and Mr. Carleton informed us that they were a most active go-ahead community, with very great toleration, and desire for improvement. There is a brisk trade between this town and Malta; and on my expressing a surprise that a direct trade was not established with England, our Vice-Consul remarked, that the whole course of business had hitherto been on two months' bills, about which occasionally there arose troubles, owing to the irregularity and uncertainty of Moorish tribunals. English merchants, he said, would not stand this, and the trade was therefore in the hands of Maltese and Italians, who were quite a match for any Oriental roguery. He hoped, however, to see the time erelong, when Sphax would import direct to England her immense supplies of oil, barley, and wool, and receive English goods direct in return. The quantity of oil produced in this neighborhood is very large: to the north of the town, for seven or eight miles, there is a succession of gardens, in each of which gleams whitely the country house of the citizen, who goes every day to look after his agricultural produce and fruits, and returns in the evening to the city. We were shown an oil-mill just established close to the town, which was being completed, and of considerable size, the property of a Jew, and the greatest care seemed to be taken in the manuring and culture of the olives. In an account, however, of Tunisian produce, by M'Gill, in 1811, he says, that the oil of the Regency is divided into six qualities, of which the oil of Sulyman obtains first rank, and that of Sphax fifth. The wine we drank was made by the Jews, and is of very good quality—better than that of Bizerta; it reminded us of red Rhenish wine, and was not acid or heady. After making the circuit of the town, we returned and paid our respects to the good Governor, who had come to see us. He was a shrewd, short, kind-looking elderly man, and is, according to Mr. Carleton, an excellent specimen of a governor, as governors go. We remarked his improvements on the esplanade, which greatly pleased him, and congratulated him on his desire to make the people under his sway happy and contented. He said it was a difficult task to govern Arabs, who were a hard-headed race, and could only be governed by stern and prompt measures; that he understood that we, in Europe, did not resort to such extremities, but that it was impossible to maintain order without them. He then spoke at large about the Russian war, and said that he heard that the Russians were violating the stipulations of peace, and endeavoring to raise the ships and reconstruct the harbor of Sebastopol. There was sitting with him his adviser and head man, a Georgian by birth, who has the character of being a person of great ability, and of influencing the conduct of the Kaïd. He was a remarkable-looking man, tall and gaunt, with a thinking serious face, and an eye like an eagle. He seemed evidently well up in all the incidents of the war, and took the greatest interest in that part of the discussion. After a good deal of talk about France and England, and their comparative power, the Kaïd bade us good morning, with the request that we should make ourselves perfectly at home, and have no scruple whatever in asking for everything we might require.

Shaw speaks of Sphax as "a neat thriving city, where, by the extraordinary indulgence of their Kaïds, the inhabitants enjoy the fruits of their industry, carrying on a good trade in oil and linen, and know little of that oppression which is severely practised in many other places in Barbary." To judge by our friend, Sphax is fortunate in its Kaïds.

In the evening again we had another walk, and came into a large gathering of townspeople outside the walls, who were attending a camel-fight. The "function" was over before we reached it, but we saw the victor and the vanquished. The latter was proceeding into the town amid the hoots, jeers, and chaff of the young Moors, while the former was growling and blubbering and stalking about proudly, awaiting any new comer. These fights are the custom always of the afternoon at Sphax, and, as they are attended with nothing worse than disgrace to the beaten animal, they may fairly be classed as innocent amusements. The country about Sphax, with the exception of the gardens, is not particularly picturesque; but the high white crenelated walls of the town, with their old-fashioned bastions, give it a very cheerful, gay appearance, and the more so as they are not blocked up with excrescences and buildings. There is a wide space of land at the foot of this wall, whereon the cavaliers exercise their steeds and exhibit their dexterity; but from the fact that only a few months previous, thirteen of the Beni Zid rode up to the foot of the walls, and, having discharged their firelocks in derision of the whole population, drove off thirteen camels without let or hindrance, I should not be inclined to attribute any excessive courage to the good citizens of Sphax. We remained another day to recruit ourselves and the poor horses, and to lay in stores, as there was likely to be some rough work and very little provender before arriving at Kairouan.

On the 16th with great difficulty we dislodged my servant from the good things of Sphax, his last speech being an outcry for *haloo,* or "sweet thing," in spite of his diarrhœa and my warnings, and reached an oil-mill about fourteen miles distant, called, as well as I could catch the name, Masara Abd Jowat. The weather was again cold and dreary, and the poor almond-trees, the "*awakeners,*" as the Hebrews called them, in full bloom, looked sadly like victims of misplaced confidence. There were a few miserable Arab tents near the oil-mill, and from their inhabitants we in vain endeavored to extract either eggs or milk. A fierce battle, as usual, ensued; one of the heads of the tribe was seized and put in irons till either eggs or milk should be produced. The irons were, however, only Trim's chain, a wrinkle derived from the Boots at the Swan. Even this had no effect; so Kassim and the Hamba stalked forth with guns, and swore destruction against hens which were useless to produce eggs. Two had already fallen amid the screams and execrations of the women, when one egg was produced. They would willingly have given us more, they said, but how could they do so, when a fat man who was in the oil-mill sucked all that were laid every day? The fat man shortly appeared; he was steward of the Governor of Zowan, and was sent by him on an oil speculation; he looked exactly the man to suck the eggs of a whole community of hens, nor did he make any secret of his propensities. We warned him, on pain of extermination, to put on the muzzle till our departure; but, as no eggs appeared the next morning, it is probable he had friends at the henroosts, and also among the cowkeepers, for not even the threat of the dog-chain nor the offers of piastres could obtain either one or other commodity. For the sake of our just and gentle characters, I am bound to add, that the chorus of execration and sorrow which greeted our razzia on the ancient hens, was changed into blessings and a pæan of exultation by a noble remuneration to the dusky dames who owned the fallen fowls; and I will venture to say, that if hereafter any pale-faced bearded men in Knickerbockers arrive at Masara Abd Jowat, eggs and milk will not be wanting to their reception.

We were six hours and a half the next day in doing about twenty-two miles and reaching El Djem, the ancient Tysdrus. The first view we got of the magnificent amphitheatre, for which this place is famous, was very grand indeed. The day had been, like all the days of late, cold, gusty, and fraught with showers. As we rode up the ascent which leads to this great building, a huge black cloud, coming up from the north, stood opaquely behind it, but the sun's says played brightly on its front. The situation of this edifice is superior to any other that I have ever seen. The Egyptian remains, except the Pyramids and Kom Ombo, lie low, and are comparatively low, owing much of the impression they produce to the sense of enormous weight. The Roman monuments are choked up with adjacent buildings, and even the Pyramids themselves do not force their greatness upon you till you come to them and lay your hands upon the huge stones of which they are composed; but at El Djem, this noble building stands out so objectively, at the summit of a gentle ascent looking over a vast plain to the north, almost as far as the eye can extend, encumbered by neither trees nor buildings to interrupt the view and spoil the effect, that I cannot help thinking that those who have seen the amphitheatre of old Tysdrus will pronounce it to be one of the most imposing edifices in the world.

As Sir Grenville Temple has devoted some time and observation to this place, I will avail myself of a portion of his remarks. He writes of it as "an edifice which, though yielding in magnitude and splendor to the Coliseum, is still one of the most perfect, vast, and beautiful remains of former times that exist, combining in itself more of those united properties than any other building which I can at this moment bring to my recollection. The amphitheatre at Nismes I have never seen; that of Pola in Istria is perfect in its exterior, though completely the reverse interiorly; whilst, on the contrary, the one at Verona is diametrically the opposite, possessing the range of seats as entire as at the time when admiring citizens witnessed the sports performed in the arena for their gratification, but, with the exception of four arches, completely deprived of its exterior façade—the principal and most beautiful feature of these stupendous edifices." Sir G. Temple proceeds to compare the sizes of the most remarkable amphitheatres. "The length of the amphitheatre of Tysdrus, which extends nearly east and west, is 429 feet by 368 feet, and that of the arena, 238 feet by 182 feet. The height of the level of the first gallery is 32 feet, and to the summit of the edifice 96 feet.

	Length.	Breadth.	Height.
Coliseum	613	510	164
Verona	506	405	—
El Djem	429	368	96
Nismes	430	338	76

It possesses four ranges of pillars and arches, sixty in number, on each range, or, rather, on the three lower ones; for the fourth is a pilastrade elevated on a stylobata, with a square window in every third interpilaster. The capitals are of the species of the Composite order which we see on Diocletian's Pillar at Alexandria, with a slight variation in the second range from those composing the first and third. At each extremity was a great entrance; but the west one, together with an arch on each side of it, was destroyed, together with the same portion of the whole superstructure, about a hundred years ago, by Mahommed Bey. The interior of this magnificent building is in a far more dilapidated state than the exterior, which, with the above-mentioned exceptions, may be stated to be in excellent preservation. Great part of the vaulted and inclined plane which supports the seats, the galleries, and vomitoria, are still left Under the surface of the arena, like those of the Coliseum, and Amphitheatre of Capua, are seen the same sort of passages, little chambers for containing the wild beasts, as well as square apertures opening upon the arena, up which were raised the lions and tigers enclosed in boxes made on the principle of the pigeon-traps used at shooting matches, whose sides on reaching the summit, being unsupported by the walls of the tunnel, fall to the ground, and working on the hinges which joined them to the bottom of the box, left the ferocious monsters at once exposed to the view of the spectators."

Although some of the stones have been removed from the Amphitheatre, to make a few small buildings in the town, yet fortunately there is no great resident to construct a palace with the spoils. Moreover, underneath and round the walls are the hovels of the greater portion of the few inhabitants of the village, who have therefore a vested interest in the integrity of the superstructure lest some windy night it might come down about their heads. We had some experience of what the power of the wind is in that exposed situation, for so violent was it, that we were afraid to ascend to the top, in spite of the temptation of a magnificent view. This fine structure is supposed to have been built during the period of the most material prosperity of the Roman provinces, about the era of the Antonines. It was at this city that the elder Gordian was proclaimed emperor; and Shaw surmises that in gratitude to the place where he received the Imperial purple, he might have been the founder of it. This is, however, hardly likely to have been the case, considering that Gordian's reign was something under six weeks. Shaw seems to consider that the coins of the younger Gordian, which have an amphitheatre on them, have reference to this monument of Tysdrus. We were lodged in what was once a powder magazine, and, as the wind was blowing the fire about the courtyard, were uneasy until assured that the last barrel of the combustible had been for some time removed.

El Djem is not merely famous for its amphitheatre, but it also enjoys a high reputation for the size and ferocity of its fleas. To the truth of this we could bear the strictest testimony, more especially as one was so pleased with my society, that he established himself in the lining of my trousers; and for many a long day I had perpetual reminders of Tysdrus, and was able to distinguish (or at least thought so) the inhabitant of that ancient town among the onslaughts of his many busy comates.

I must strongly recommend the neighborhood of El Djem to any one who wishes for a real good day's partridge shooting. The red-legs are literally swarming, and on any fine day a fair shot, with very little walking beyond the olive groves to the south of the town, ought to pick up his twenty brace.

Before leaving El Djem, we held a council as to our future route, our original intention having been to proceed to Mehdia, thence to Susa, and from Susa to Kairouan. Influenced, however, by Kassim, who had been telling us marvellous stories of the bustards, gazelles, and gutta, in the desert country between Kairouan and El Djem, we determined to proceed that way: more especially after the remorseless wettings we had experienced on the seacoast, which we were informed was a moister district than the interior.

On the 19th, therefore, we made for an encampment of the Suasi Arabs, about fourteen miles off, who were unanimously represented to be the most blameless of mankind. The country was highly tilled by their industrious tribe; but Courage! cried Kassim: to-morrow we shall be among improvident Arabs, among whom the *feræ naturæ* abound. We found the Suasi to be as virtuous and as hospitable as they were represented to be, and apparently the wealthiest tribe we had yet visited. In consequence of the virtues of a holy man, one of their number, whose white tomb we passed in the plain, they have certain remissions from taxation, and their general good behaviour relieves them from the squeezings that fall periodically on their more turbulent brethren elsewhere. Kassim, during our evening chat before the fire, had his heart so warmed by the good fare and civility, that he relaxed his severity towards Arabs in general, and made some profound moral reflections on the excellence of virtue, remarking that the peaceable and unaggressive Suasi were enjoying all the good things of this life, its purple and fine linen, while the robbing Hamama were always poor, hungry, and wore seedy, ragged old burnooses. These observations were extremely well received by our hosts, and Kassim afterwards observed with a grin, that the horses obtained an extra feed in consequence.

On the 20th we marched about twenty-one miles to a place called El Haj, where some Roman ruins still remain, but without inscriptions. The Slas Arabs were our hosts, very poor, but very civil. Our Spahi Salab was one of this tribe, but failed to produce any sensation by his arrival. We were greatly disappointed in this day's journey, for instead of the wild country teeming with game which we had been promised by Kassim, almost the whole of it was under cultivation, chiefly by the Suasi Arabs. We were at first disposed to be wroth with Kassim, attributing his representations to have arisen from an anxious desire to remove us from the dreaded territories of the Hamama and other evil-minded parties, but he assured us positively that only three or four years before he had passed over this ground, and that there was then not a vestige of the ploughshare, and, moreover, that it was full of game. We found, on subsequent inquiry, that Kassim was correct, and that the altered state of affairs was referable to the increased security of the country under the present Bey. This fact enabled us, on leaving Tunis, to pay a suitable and well-deserved compliment to his Highness on the large spread of agriculture throughout his dominions, the effect of a just and moderate government, which Mr. Wood was confident would be a pleasing topic, as well as a salutary one.

20th, to Kairouan, distant about eight miles from El Haj. This was a morning of considerable importance to us, as we were by no means sure of the reception we were likely to get in this sanctuary of pure, undefiled Islamism. It is one of the seven sacred cities of Islam, and it boasts proudly that neither Jew nor Christian is allowed to dwell within it, nor even to enter it, except as a special favor on the part of the Bey, which has been exercised only in rare instances, and never in the case of a Jew. The bones of Sidi Sabi, the barber of the Prophet, here repose; and to dwell within its holy walls is the very next thing, indeed almost an approximation, to being actually in heaven, in Moorish estimation. The approach to this paradise was anything but heavenly: the path was almost impassable, and it was with great difficulty we crossed a very insignificant watercourse just outside the walls; the baggagers, we heard, were completely bogged in it, and Kassim's crossness on arrival was quite proof of the trouble he had had in extricating them. The view, however, of Kairouan was extremely pretty: the sun shone out upon it, and its white walls and domes and minarets made a gay and gallant appearance; it lies in the middle of a large plain, and as it has no dingy, disreputable faubourgs, you embrace the whole circuit of the town within the clasp of its lofty white setting. This once famous city, the name of which is at present hardly known in Europe, was at one time the seat of Arab power in North Africa, the metropolis of Sardinia and Sicily, and even of Spain for a short period. From it proceeded those brave and genial Moors that covered Southern Spain with the monuments of Saracenic art, and by their industry and politeness rendered it the garden and the glory of Europe. It was founded by the gallant Ukba, about the year 670, near the ruins of the ancient Vicus Augusti, to be a secure point for the extension of his conquests in Western Africa. "In its present decay," says Gibbon, "Cairoan still holds the second rank in the kingdom of Tunis, from which it is distant about fifty miles to the south; its inland situation, twelve miles westward of the sea, has protected the city from the Greek and Sicilian fleets. When the wild beasts and serpents were extirpated, when the forest, or rather wilderness, was cleared, the vestiges of a Roman town were discovered in a sandy plain. The vegetable food of Cairoan is brought from afar, and the scarcity of springs constrains the inhabitants to collect in cisterns and reservoirs a precarious supply of rain-water. These obstacles were subdued by the industry of Akbah: he traced a circumference of three thousand and six hundred paces, which he encompassed with a brick wall. In the space of five years the Governor's palace was surrounded with a sufficient number of private habitations, a spacious mosch was supported by five hundred columns of granite, porphyry, and Numidian marble, and Cairoan became the seat of learning as well as of empire." Gibbon is somewhat in error in this description: Kairouan is more than twelve miles from the sea, and more than he states from Tunis. As far as the vegetable supply goes, the rich loam of the plain to the south ought to afford it in abundance; and though there are cisterns to contain the rain-water, yet, within the walls is the celebrated and unfailing fountain, Baroota, which communicates, as the holy men of Kairouan relate, with the sacred well Zem Zem, in Arabia, and is held equally sacred in consequence. It is curious that they have here precisely the same story with regard to their Holy Well that the Cairenes have with regard to theirs in the Mosque of Amr. In both places it is stated, that a pilgrim had dropped his wooden drinking bowl into Zem Zem, and on returning to his native country, discovered the identical bowl floating on the surface of his own fountain: a fact which of course clearly proves the undoubted connection of the two sources. A messenger had been despatched early in the morning to warn the Governor of our approach, and to claim, in pursuance of the Bey's order, his special protection. When just outside the walls, we were urged vigorously by our escort to remove our European garments, and to put on our *burnooses*, in order to avoid observation. As it was very cold, I complied with the request; but Sir S., like a true Briton, would not lower his flag nor cover his shooting-coat and knickerbockers for all the Mahommedans in Kairouan. Thus we proceeded solemnly under the guidance of a servant who had been sent to show us the way, and at a turn of the path, squatted underneath a garden-wall, sat the notabilities, the captains and the shekhs, as Kassim called them, commissioned to conduct us through the town. Three of these worthies placed themselves in front, three marched behind, and in that formation our cavalcade passed through the gate. Few persons seemed about, but the escort determined that even those few were too many, for directly we entered a street the guards behind halted and allowed no one to follow, and those in front pushed on and cleared away every one before them. It quite recalled the procession of Lady Godiva through the streets of Coventry, in the good days of Peeping Tom. At last we reached a capital house, where the Bey is usually entertained. The stables occupied the basement, and were of large extent, supported by a number of ancient columns of white and red marble and porphyry, evidently the spoils of some ancient structure. The house was got up with good taste, chiefly floored with encaustic tiles, and the walls lined with the same material. In summer it would have been cool and comfortable enough, but now it was cold and damp, and as there was no outlet for the fumes, it was impossible to bear the brazier in the room we occupied for more than a short time. The Kehaya, or great man of the city, called immediately, accompanied by a grave *cortège* of elders. He was a very handsome man, magnificently dressed, very civil, but very ignorant and very stupid. He inquired into our travels, and Kassim gave us the character of perfect Nimrods, the exterminators of ferocious beasts, and wound up with some wonderful anecdotes of railways, and of Englishmen flying hither and thither on the wings of steam. He told them also of the powers given us by the Bey, and of the splendid treatment we had received *en route* from all the governors, and how we had dismissed and treated as nothing the Bey's Hambas who had misbehaved. This last was an excellent stroke of diplomacy, as the news had reached Kairouan that our refractory Hambas had been put in prison, and, as no tale loses by telling in the East, that they were in hourly expectation of being deprived of their heads. On asking Kassim why he told such lies, and talked such nonsense, he excused himself on the ground of his audience being asses, and, as he wanted many things from them, it was necessary to talk big, and astonish their very weak minds. The Kehaya evidently was astonished, and, in order to be more astonished, kept paying us repeated visits, which we could well have dispensed with, for, as he was a grandee of the highest order, it was necessary to be civil. However, in return for his company he gave us excellent fare, and a capital supply of necessaries for the road, and promised that the next day we should see the town without any molestation. When the next day came it was so wet that we could not emerge till the afternoon, and were then quite surprised at the cleanliness and comfort of the town. The streets through which we walked were strictly guarded, and a boy who commenced shouting and abusing us was instantly seized and lodged in a guardhouse, but we begged off the castigation that was to follow. We walked about for some time, and could not help drawing a strong contrast between the neatness of this town, its excellent private houses, which flanked the streets, and its general air of respectability, with the filth, squalor, and disreputable appearance of the Moorish towns inhabited by Europeans. There was certainly very little sign of business going on; it was sleepy enough to all intents, but it really seemed generally inhabited by people who had ideas of propriety and neatness. It was a kind of Mahommedan Bath, or, rather, Oxford, to which Tunis and Sphax would play the part of Wapping. I attribute this to the fact of the number of Moors who, from finding themselves jostled by the inroads of Christians, determine to remove themselves from the contagion, and retire here to live and die in the odor of sanctity. These will be most of them men of easy circumstances, whose means enable them to spend a life of what they call contemplation, but what we should call intense indolence, and hence the opulent well-to-do appearance of the streets and houses. We were conducted to the walls, and thence to the office of the collector of taxes, who received us with great *empressement*, gave us coffee, and wished to be very communicative, but Mr. Kassim had just bolted, and we were not in a position to realize much of what he said. He was, however, very particular in his inquiries after Regina, whose good health and prosperity were apparently a matter of much concern to the municipality. The walk wound up by a visit to the famous well, Baroota. We were shown a seedy old camel, a very sacred animal indeed, who is perpetually engaged in drawing water for the Faithful. The elders professed much gratification at our telling them that we had come from far to drink this celebrated water, and to do honor to their celebrated saint, Sidi Sabi, about whom they were curious to hear if his name was known in England. Having, when at home, read Mr. Davis's *Evenings in my Tent*, I was able to answer in the affirmative, which was another satisfaction, and they were most *empressés* in handing us the water from the holy well, and in bidding us quaff it into our bodies, and with it Islam into our souls. On great occasions, the poor seedy old camel plays a conspicuous part; he is exhibited to the Faithful clothed in magnificent velvet housings, and is regarded by them with infinite respect. In the evening we had again a long chat, chiefly about the Queen, and the way she treated her husband, and squeezed money and administered the stick; to all which queries our answers rather puzzled the not very intelligent Kehaya. He told us in return, some stories about the saint, Sidi Sabi, and that the present saint of the town was a female Marabout, as is also the case at Tunis and in Morocco. We endeavored to argue, that, as they had female saints, we might have female rulers; the difficulty, however, that chiefly affected their minds was, that a female governor would never be able to squeeze with near as much efficiency as a male. The late Marabout, that had not long died, was a man of extraordinary sanctity, and had performed the most wonderful miracles. M. François, our landlord at Tunis, when accompanying the late Bey, as cook, through his provinces, had the misfortune at Kairouan, to lose his horse, and was in despair, as he could find no one to sell him another. In this emergency, some one advised him to consult the Marabout, as to what was to be done. He accordingly went to his abode, and as he was about to state his perplexities, before he had time to open his lips the holy man said to him—"Return to your tent, and you will find standing before it what you require." The saint then shut the door in his face; but on M. François arriving at his habitation, he found there a man holding a horse, who handed him the bridle, without a word, and went away. The conversation then became again more secular, and we were informed that the women of Susa were famous for the beauty of their eyes; those of Tunis, for their good taste and knowledge of the becoming in dress; while those of Kairouan, bore away the palm for the symmetry of their legs. As in these matters we were profoundly in the dark, as far as experience went, we must take our informant's word for the accuracy of these characteristics.

The 23rd was a remarkable day indeed to us, and marked in our annals with the blackest tints. It was cold and raw and damp when we left Kairouan, and were bid the farewell words of peace by the captains and the shekh and the elders who escorted us out of the town. The plain was in a state of mud inconceivable, except to those who have watched around Sebastopol, and, strange to say, in the vicinity of this large city there is not a single made road. A few beaten paths formed by mules and camels, are the only approaches to the second city of the Regency. At last, after ploughing our weary way over about seven miles of ground, we arrived at a small stream called the Wady Bougal. It was muddy, but apparently quite insignificant—not more than a couple of yards wide. The guide we had taken with us hinted there was trouble in store for us, but got over; Sir S. followed gallantly, and my poor cowardly nag did contrive, after a desperate struggle, to emerge from the tenacious mud which constituted the bed of the brook and of its bank. Then came my servant on one of the most active of the baggagers, but with all his endeavors the poor animal could not extricate himself, and down he came on his side, sinking deep into the slush, with Hubert under him. The same fate befell two more horses, and the unfortunate camel bearing the tent stuck fast midway, and was in imminent danger of being split up. It was on emergencies like these that Kassim showed his worth: he plunged in like a man, and, though hardly able to move in the mud, still, with the assistance of a couple of shepherds, dragged and hauled the unfortunate camel to *terra firma*, extricated the horses, and put Hubert on his legs again. As we had no wish to be involved in the same "fix," we were obliged to remain passive spectators of the scene, which was not a pleasant one. Unfortunate Hubert had all the appearance of a statue modelled in clay; beds, baggage, guns, panniers, everything was covered with the same material, and when we resumed our march we were certainly as dirty and wobegone a lot as had crossed the Wady Bougal for many a day; of course, under the circumstances, any refuge was an object, and we were shown on the side of the hill an Arab *dowar*, for which we made. They told us the Shekh was absent at another *dowar*, about a mile off, and requested us to go there and hunt him up. When we arrived, the guide who conducted us, Kassim, and the Hamba, were all assailed with the most violent outcry by such a set of horrible hags, that we were glad to beat a retreat to the first encampment. Here we endeavored to make a little fire, to dry our miserable beds and baggage, and thaw poor Hubert; but, except to cook some coffee, there were not enough dry sticks in the encampment. All the brushwood was wet and clammy, and, as our tent was a mass of mud, we were obliged to avail ourselves of that of one of the Arabs; and through the interstices the north wind poured in that night, and the sheep and goats trampled on us and befouled us, in a manner which will not readily let the adventures of Wady Bougal escape from memory.

Oh! the bitter, bitter day—Oh! the cruel, cruel wind—of the 24th of January, on the plains of sultry Africa! Old Zowan, at whose back we were passing, and Bent-es-Saidah, were covered with snow; and over them the blasts came and cut into us like swords. Ice lay on the pools half an inch thick, and eagles and vultures were rejoicing on the carcases of cattle and camels which lay dead and dying among the bushes. I never remember such piercing cold as we endured all that morning, and the poor Arabs seemed to suffer from it more than we did. The events of yesterday had quite overcome my unfortunate servant. For five weeks he had been suffering from diarrhœa, and, though nearly well at times, yet his total incapacity of self-restraint, and eagerness for rich unwholesome food, always caused a relapse. The immersion in the mud yesterday, and the severity of the weather, now completely overcame him, and it was with difficulty he could continue his journey: there was, however, no stopping-place between where we were and Sulyman, where he could possibly be deposited. Shortly after leaving our bivouac we remarked a curious geological formation: two parallel lines of rocks, some hundred yards asunder east and west, extended for several miles. At first they only emerged from the ground and appeared artificial—so much so that we supposed they were Roman remains. Gradually, however, they increased in height, and at last became tolerable elevations of about a hundred feet, formed of huge crags tossed about in a remarkable manner. They were tenanted by vultures and eagles, one of whom I much feared was inclined to make a meal of our spaniel Nino, so resolutely did he follow and soar over him. I fired at him, and heard the shot rattle on his great wings, but it had no effect whatever, not even to disturb him. Seeing this, Sir S. galloped up and with a green cartridge brought him to the ground, and thus put a stop to his designs on our merry little companion. Kassim informed us that the people of the country accounted for the formation of these rocks, owing to the intervention of the holy man, Sidi Sabi. When that great saint was building Kairouan, as his foundations were sunk in a sandy plain, he naturally required stones; but, as they were afar off and beasts of burden scarce, this Mussulman Amphion ordered the ridge of rocks we passed to rouse themselves up and run down into the plain; and without doubt they obeyed his bidding; but—"Chi sa," said the sceptical Kassim, with a knowing look, at the conclusion of the story.

In the course of the day we passed the small town of Takroura, situated on an isolated height, a thorough eagle's nest, and renowned for its honey.

> There the blithe bee his fragrant fortress fills,
> The free-born wanderer of the mountain air;

and thither Kassim used to betake himself, when engaged in mercantile pursuits, in search of honey. On asking him why the inhabitants of this eyrie had chosen such a spot, which must give them a hard climb to reach after their daily avocations, he replied, that if it was hard for them to clamber, it was much harder for other people, tax-gatherers especially, and the difficulties in the path much impeded the course of squeezing; so that, on the whole, he thought them a wise community. After a ride of twenty-five miles, we reached a square enclosure containing a few small chambers, where dwelt the young Kaïd of the Feetha Ouled Saïd—Plain of the Ouled Saïd, one of the minions of the late Bey. We were offered the choice of a large room just built, or a small receptacle, and chose the latter and the prospect of suffocation, rather than the probability of being buried beneath the ruins of the new edifice, which, we were warned, would likely enough be the case. The Kaïd was confined to his bed with fever; he had been here for three months in this out-of-the-way miserable place, with only a cook and a young fellow for servant: squeezing was his object, and, though an invalid and very young, he was reported to be a proficient in the business, and had amassed during his short tenure of office a considerable sum. He was one of the wretches of the court whom the late Bey was in the habit of rewarding for their vices by governments and situations; but most of them have been sent adrift by the present sovereign, who has altogether set his face against the foul immoralities of his predecessor.

In the morning, ere we started, the Kaïd begged us to visit him in his sick-room. We found him in bed, in a miserably small though very neat and orderly apartment. He was rather good-looking, but seemed wretchedly ill and worn. On our expressing surprise that he had not sent for a doctor from Tunis, he said he was expecting every day to be better, and to be able to go there himself, and that he knew of no doctor who would come to him. So we recommended him to keep up his courage and do a little in the perspiration way, and bade farewell without much regret to the Ouled Saïd and their precious Kaïd.

Our march next day was sixteen miles, in view of and by the coast to Burlubeyta-a-Fendik—or "place of public entertainment." Barth writes Burlubeita as Bir-el-Bebita, "the little chamber"; but the word is certainly pronounced as I write it. Fendik is a corruption of the Italian *fonduca*, and is the term applied to places where horses and camels are put up. In the present instance the building consisted of two large courtyards, one of which was entirely devoted to the animals of the traveller, the other was surrounded by chambers in which the occupants took their *keff* and did their cooking. These two yards were approached by a gateway, where dwelt a roaster of kabobs and dispenser of coffee; and on the other side, up a steep staircase, was an extremely neat and inviting suite of rooms belonging to Mahommed Hasneddar, the owner of the place which we occupied. Poor Hubert was so weak that he could hardly keep up with the party, and was made in consequence a prisoner by some irate Arabs, with whom the van had had an altercation. We were riding quietly along with our dogs by our sides, and passing some Arab tents several hundred yards from our path, when five powerful dogs rushed out and flew on Nino without the smallest provocation. The owners of the dogs were standing by, and, though we begged of them to call them off, they remained perfectly indifferent, with a placid smile enjoying the sport. Having no help for it, I shot one dog dead, and another retired from the fray minus his leg, which execution so discouraged the others that they beat a precipitate retreat. The Arabs now made a terrible outcry at the destruction of their watchful guardians; they demanded compensation, and would have proceeded to extremities but for the appearance of double-barrelled guns, and the august Oda Bashi with his diamond decoration. Hubert however, being some distance behind, was seized and made prisoner. He was too weak to resist, and by no means at any time of a remarkably intrepid disposition, so that most fortunately we were within hail, and the Hambas rescued him. Kassim was particularly rejoiced at the occurrence, and was jocose at the expense of the Arabs and their dogs. After calling them sundry names, he congratulated them on the good supper we had furnished them, meaning the dogs, for the Arabs are accused by the Moors of a strong predilection for canine flesh, which impeachment, although I believe it to be perfectly true, they strenuously deny. This taste may probably be a legacy from the Carthaginians, who were notoriously addicted to this dainty, as I do not remember its being laid to the charge of the Eastern Arabs.

As we rode along we were rejoiced, in spite of

the severity of the weather, with the sight of the prettiest wild flowers. Wherever a bush of thorn remained in the cultivated ground, it was surrounded by the brightest tints of flowers, which seemed to be nestling under its protection; and the plain was all dotted with these gay spots. This was the first day we had seen them, and they seemed to say, as we rode shivering along, "Lo the winter is past, the rain is over and gone, the flowers appear on the earth, the time of the singing of birds is come, and the voice of the turtle is heard in our land." But Tunis is famous for its spring carpeting; nothing, I hear, can be more beautiful than the vicinity even of the town—rich in vegetation of every hue. But these bright hues are, like most things fair, shortlived—the gods love them, and they die young. The fierce sun strikes them, and they wither away.

Our path to-day was over the same ground that Belisarius traversed in his campaign against the Vandal Genseric; but we were not fortunate enough to meet with the reception experienced by the Roman veterans. According to the account of Gibbon, "The weary Romans indulged themselves in the refreshment of shady groves, cool fountains, and delicious fruits; and the preference which Procopius allows to these gardens over any that he had seen, either in the East or West, may be ascribed either to the taste or the fatigue of the historian." In the course of the day we passed a round tower of considerable dimensions, where Shaw found a Latin inscription. It is a tower dedicated to L. Æmilius Africanus, C. Suellius Pontânus, and Vitellius, and is called by the natives the Menarah, or "lamps," from several small altars on the cornice in front of it, and which were supposed to be intended for placing lamps to direct mariners.

Just opposite Burlubeyta is the town of Hamamat, under the lee of the rugged promontory which shelters it from the north wind. It had apparently a good pier, and seemed a snug town; but the illness of Hubert, and his increasing weakness, made us anxious to hurry on without visiting it. This place has given rise to much learned disquisition as to its classical name. It was probably constructed out of the remains of a Roman town—the Civitas Siagitana, and the inscriptions found at Hamamat containing this word corroborate the opinion. The similarity of sound induced the belief that it is the original Adrumetum, which, however, Shaw maintains to have been Herkla, more to the south; other geographers place it at Susa. The advocates of Hamamat rely on the narrative of Diodorus relating to the campaign of Agathokles. He, speaking of the stratagem whereby Agathokles released himself from his perilous position, mentions that the Sicilian general chose a certain mountainous spot—*τόπος ὀρεινὸς*, where he lighted fires, which were visible to the inhabitants of Adrumetum and of Tunis. The inhabitants of the former town supposed that Agathokles had received reinforcements, and capitulated, while the Carthaginians, who were besieging Tunis, imagined that he was marching straight on them with his whole army. Hamamat is about forty odd miles from Tunis, and there are places where fires might be lighted so as to be seen both from it and Tunis, but Herkla and Susa would be quite out of view.

The name of Hamamat is derived, says Shaw, from the wild pigeons which frequent the cliffs under which the town is situated; and he certainly adduces sufficient reasons to dissuade one from considering it to be the imperial Adrumetum, though it is difficult to get over the story of the τόπος ὀρεινὸς of Diodorus, unless we were to take the crest of Zowan as that mountainous spot, and even then I am not sure that it can be seen from Herkla.

26th—From Burlubeyta to Sulyman, twenty-five miles, the road at first very pretty and very good, so good that carriages can get along it; but, indeed, what cannot Tunisian carriages and charioteers surmount! We were passing the eastern shoulder of Zowan, once more through shining fragrant myrtles, and every here and there, high banks flanked the way, and heath in flower brushed us as we jogged along. This was all very well while we kept the road to Tunis, but when we turned off to the right, in the direction of Sulyman, we found much difficulty in making our way, for the ploughed ground was impassable from softness, and the rest of the plain had been converted by the rains into a morass. Hubert, moreover, had become unable to sit up on his horse and guide him, which added to the difficulties. We arrived fortunately before dark, had a cordial welcome from the head man of the village, and were given a very comfortable small house for our exclusive occupation. Shaw says that the inhabitants of Sulyman are of Andalusian origin, who still retained in his time the Spanish language, and were noted for their courtesy to Christians above their brethren.

We rested until the 30th at this place, to enable Hubert to recover his strength as far as possible; and, fortunately, the ground was sufficiently dry to enable us to send him by carriage on the 29th, in company with a Moorish gentleman who had business in the metropolis. They must have had a pleasant communicative drive. We had heard a great deal of the amazing number of snipe in a marsh hard by, but, strange to say, there was not one to be found when we searched it, although we were informed the same evening by an Italian gentleman, a resident at Sulyman, that last year we might have shot till we were tired. This Italian is a famous sportsman, and most courteous to all comers, being always ready for a *chasse;* so we agreed to make up a party to shoot wild boars on the 28th, in the jungle by the banks of a river a few miles off, and notorious for harboring the unclean beast. We had made all our preparations, and were retiring for the night, when news arrived that his Highness the Bey, who was residing at Hamam Lif, had resolved on shooting over the ground, and had sent orders to all the bakers to bake bread, and all possessors of dogs to attend and do their worst. Sir S. did not augur well of the sport, and remained at home; but I got up early and joined the party. At about eight o'clock, loud and shrill *Lou lou lous* from the women, betokened the loyal reception they were giving their ruler, and presently advanced persons bearing flags and pennons to wave over the road by which he passed; then came led-horses in gay caparisons, then carriage after carriage, broughams, cabs, cuckoos—in short, every kind of vehicle jolting and splashing through the muddy lane. We followed the party, and on reaching the head of the lane, the carriages were dismissed and the horses mounted. All the great dignitaries of the court were there: the Bey, and his son, and his brother; the Bashhamba, head of the police, a man who can squeeze and no mistake; Mustapha Hasneddar, who rules the Bey; Haireddin, and Shekhs and Kaïds without end. The Arab portion of the gathering was picturesquely dressed, but the officials in their fezzes and tightly buttoned blue coats looked what they were—fat, frowzy, and apoplectic. The Bey himself, however, was every inch of him the lord of men: he was altogether attired *à l'Arabe:* a burnoos of black and white stripe, and of the softest material, covered a peach-colored dress within; on his high maroon boots gleamed the long formidable steel spike used as a spur; his shovel-shaped stirrups were of burnished steel; and the housings of a noble iron-grey horse, who seemed conscious of the dignity he bore, were of scarlet velvet incrusted with gold. By his side rode two servants to load and hand him his guns.

The rest of the *cortège* was most incongruous. Arabs on foot, Arabs on ass-back, fat officials ambling on mules; more adventurous spirits galloping bravely in all directions, and for no conceivable purpose; hordes of dogs of every description, shepherds' dogs, broad-sterned pottering old pointers, greyhounds, lurchers—in fact, every conceivable specimen of the canine race raised in Barbary was summoned for the occasion. It was indeed the ἀνδρῶν ἠδὲ κυνῶν κολοσυρτός of Homer. The first game afoot was a jackal, which all the dogs pursued and all the riders galloped after, and at which every gun, whether discharging bullets, slugs, or shot, was let off. It was a mercy no one was killed, for predestination was the order of the day. "Allah kerim," "God is merciful." Bang-bang went the fowling-pieces, ping-ping went the bullets; the unhappy jackal was cut off from all retreat by the bold riders; he died without a chance being given him, and the first man up had the honor of galloping back and exhibiting the carcase to his Highness.

Then we beat the bed of the river, but in a most unsporting manner, for, instead of keeping any line or order, one person beat one way, another another way, and the dogs were permitted to do as they pleased, wandering at their own sweet will, though indeed very few of them cared to enter the covert at all. At last a moderately sized boar was flushed, who, having ripped up a pertinacious dog, had the good taste to bolt about twenty yards before the Bey. I never saw a finer or a quicker shot than that made by his Highness: with a single bullet he shot him through the heart, and the animal fell with hardly a kick left in him. Immense applause, *wullahs* and *inshallahs* innumerable, followed this feat of dexterity; the boar was dragged out and surrounded by an admiring circle, who pointed at the hole below the shoulder in admiration of the shot, and in their enthusiasm I believe some actually stuck their fingers into it, despite of the polluting contact with the unclean beast. The Bey, seeing me outside, very considerately ordered room to be made that I should have every opportunity of contemplating the result of his prowess. Unfortunately I did not know sufficient Arabic to ask for the skin, and to express, in the most complimentary language of which the English language is master, the pride and pleasure I should have had to exhibit to friends in Europe the spoils which I had myself seen gained so adroitly by his Highness. I subsequently heard from one of his people, that I could not have paid him a greater compliment, for that he piques himself on his dexterity in the *chasse*. There was no further opportunity that day of displaying it, for, with the exception of a few hares that perished in the same manner as the jackal, we were not fortunate enough to meet with more game. Some of the scenery was very beautiful that we went through this afternoon—by far the prettiest I had seen in Tunis. The hills, of considerable height, approached one another closely in some spots, and formed valleys with a river running through them. The sides of these hills were neither rugged, bare, nor austere, as in the south; nor were they a mass of myrtle and brushwood, as in the neighborhood of Zowan; but every here and there, clumps of myrtle and trees were growing; in other spots huge masses of rock cropped out boldly like old castles, and the sward (for all was sward) was green and elastic, and in sheltered nooks already beginning to gleam with wild flowers. I can conceive nothing more delicious than a spring ride along these glorious mountain sides, with a brisk sea-breeze blowing across the peninsula, for it is peninsula from Sulyman to Cape Bon, and the innumerable flowers and shrubs for which Tunis is famous, scenting the air and painting the glades with color. I rode home through the immense olive forests to the east of Sulyman, and by Menzel. They were at least seven miles in depth, and extended as far as the eye could reach; but Sulyman stands to oil as Kent does to hops in England—oil is the great speculation, the great topic of conversation.

30th.—After a ride of sixteen miles through roads so heavy as to be nearly impassable, by Hamam Lif with its somewhat Vauxhallish appearance, where the Bey was residing, and where his geese as usual occupied a conspicuous position, we reached Tunis in great health and spirits, all but Hubert, who gradually recovered, thanks to the kindness and attention of Dr. Heap, an American physician, whose skill and courtesy I shall ever remember. We found the Tunisian world complaining of the desperate severity of the weather, such as the oldest inhabitant could not recollect. Mr. Davis had in consequence been unable to do much, and there was therefore little inducement to plough our way to the Dowar-es-Shat; still less inducement was there to wander through the filthy streets now reeking with mud and abomination. We, therefore, made the best haste to dispose of our steeds, and were of course cheated in consequence of the haste. We paid our Hamba, and recommended friendly, worthy little Ali and the respectable Salah to the Bey; we wrote a complimentary letter to his Highness, to thank him for his kindness, and to congratulate him on the increasing prosperity of his country; and bid farewell to Tunis on the 11th of February, with fewer regrets than we should have had if the same bright warm sun that was standing over double-peaked Boo Kurnain had cheered us a little more with his presence than he had done for the last thirty days.

As I mentioned at the commencement of this book, it was our original intention, on leaving Europe, to make merely a wandering excursion, chiefly for the sake of change of scene, exercise, and shooting. We had no prospect, at the time, of being able to penetrate into the interior of the Regency. The general impression that prevailed of the insecurity of travelling, and the fanaticism of the Moors, forbade the hope of being able to see much of a country so interesting from its historical recollections. We had, therefore, neglected to brush up old classical reminiscences, or otherwise, from the perfect ease with which we travelled, we might have been enabled to throw some additional light upon several disputed points of geography. I have no doubt but that we passed at no great distance from the field of Zama, and that, had we been provided with the proper authorities, we might have accurately fixed the main topographical features of this famous battle. But under the auspices of the present Bey, the country is open, and the scholar and the botanist will find an excursion in the spring well deserving the little trouble it will require. I say in the spring, because at that time the heat is not too great, and the country, by all accounts, is a tapestry of flowers. In autumn, when the heat is again diminished, the flowers have disappeared; and in the depth of winter, except in the extreme south, where the climate is delicious, the cold and constant rains are terrible drawbacks to a traveller. But in the spring, by all accounts, it is a land flowing literally with milk and honey; and a tent-life is enjoyment in itself. The inhabitants of the country, especially the Arabs, are disposed to be civil and obliging, and a few presents will ripen that good disposition into friendliness. The Tunisian Moors, too, have always had a better reputation than their Algerine neighbors, and the insolent and fanatical inhabitants of Morocco. Shaw, writing of them in 1738, gives them an excellent character. "The Tunisians are the most civilized nation of Barbary. They have very little of that insolent and haughty behaviour which is too common at Algiers. All affairs, likewise, with the Regency are transacted in such a friendly, complaisant manner, that it was no small pleasure to attend Mr. Consul Lawrence at his audiences. This nation, which for many years has been more intent upon trade, and the improvements of its manufactures, than upon plunder and cruising, has always had the character and reputation of living, not like their neighbors, in open war or perpetual disputes with the Christian princes, but of cultivating their friendship, and coming readily into their alliances; but the late revolution and change of government may have introduced a new system of policy."

The insecurity of travelling has hitherto arisen not so much from the general bad disposition of the inhabitants, as from the impunity which attended the evil practices of outlaws, robbers, and insurgent Arab tribes. The precarious position of most of the Beys depending on a mutinous and capricious soldiery, has paralysed their power over the distant portions of their dominions; and indeed, even in the vicinity of the capital, outrages have until lately remained comparatively unpunished, when committed by the troops, for the fear of incurring their displeasure. The history of the successive rulers of this country, as of Algiers, might be tracked, as Judge Jebb remarked of Ireland in the statute book, "as you would follow a wounded man through a crowd, by blood." Their annals are ever-recurring scenes of insubordination, family feuds, perfidy, and assassination. A good deal of this was caused by the perpetual interference of the Algerines in Tunisian quarrels, taking part with children against their parents, and usurpers against the legitimate sovereign. But Algiers being now in French hands, and the authority of the last two Beys being supported by the influence of European powers, matters seem in a fair way of settling down permanently, and Tunis of becoming as safe and as open as any Christian country. The fact of a large district being only a few years ago a perfect desert, and now entirely under cultivation, namely, the tract of country between El Djem and Kairouan, to which

I before alluded, shows how rapidly security is taken advantage of. There is a strong commercial spirit in the towns of Susa and Sphax, which only requires the encouragement of safe transit, good roads, and moderate and fixed taxation, to extend itself throughout the Regency.

Mahommedanism must not be encountered solely with 32-pounders and Congreve rockets: we must endeavor to break down its arrogance and prejudice by other means than by bombarding towns over the heads of ignorant fanatics, however richly they may deserve it. No doubt the inhabitants of the East must be kept down with a strong hand at first—with the same inflexible determination with which old Mohammed Ali trampled under his heel Egyptian intolerance; with the same determination which has influenced the two last Beys of Tunis in repressing the insolence of their subjects. But there should be some other ingredient besides fear, in the endeavor to bring the Mahommedan within the usages and pale of civilization. Commerce may do it, at all events it is the only thing that can; and of all Mahommedan countries, perhaps Tunis is the most fitted to be put on its trial. It is readily reached, it has a commercial class and commercial instincts; the Sphaxi is found wherever Islam has penetrated Africa. The climate, with its rough hard winters, has not the enervating effect of the glowing temperature of other Mahommedan countries nearer the tropics. To obtain the necessaries of life, work is necessary, and work is done.

I have much confidence in the capabilities of the Arab race, although I may have little in the future of the Turks. It is impossible, however they may be sunk, to forget that these are the descendants of the famous men who, in the darkest ages of Europe, were the founders of science, literature, and architecture at Damascus, Bagdad, Cairo, Kairouan, Granada, and Cordova; that among them there was an eager, passionate spirit of inquiry, although it has now degenerated into subtle disquisitions on theology; that commerce was esteemed, and not, as in the West, deemed derogatory; and that merchants were the chosen friends, associates, and advisers of the great. There is no doubt but that this anxious spirit of inquiry, this thirst for knowledge, still exists, however latent it may seem. Dr. Barth is a witness to the venturous love of traffic, which, as well as of conquest, brings the Arab to central Africa; he testifies to their eagerness for information, to the value they attach to a book printed in their own language; that they have even offered to come from the central regions of that continent to England, solely for the sake of obtaining that inestimable treasure—knowledge conveyed to them in their own tongue.

Security—by that I mean the certainty that every man shall enjoy the fruits of his industry—and justice, by which I do not mean the quirks and subtleties and delays of English administration of the law—these are the first requisites for Tunis. It is not the regular taxation that depresses that country, but the irregular taxation, the bribing, and the squeezing. The present Bey has placed the taxation of the country on a far lower and fairer basis than it enjoyed before, and so far he has done well; but it is the inflictions of the Kaïds and their Khalifas that render it impoverished and insecure. The words that John the Baptist spake, nearly 1900 ago, on the banks of the Jordan, are just as applicable now on the banks of the Mejerdah:—"Then came also publicans to be baptized, and said unto him, Master, what shall we do? And he said unto them, Exact no more than that which is appointed you. And the soldiers likewise demanded of him, saying, And what shall we do? And he said unto them, Do violence to no man, neither accuse any falsely, and be content with your wages."

We are apt, in my opinion, to take a view too desponding and unphilosophical as to the future of the East. With that anxious, eager spirit which animates our efforts at amelioration at home, and which is generally rewarded by early fruits, we regard the progress of civilization in the East. We are disappointed that it has not grown into a goodly tree ere it has begun to spread its roots, and, like children, are almost disposed to pluck it up, to see if these roots have made any shoot at all. The best and truest answer to these expectations and to this despondency is in the admirable speech of Lord Stratford de Redcliffe on laying the foundation stone of the railway station at Smyrna. "Take the whole list of great discoveries, of great institutions, of great reforms, of great transitions from one state of society to another, and show me where there are those which have not been born in sorrow, nurtured in hardship, and established with difficulty. As years pass away before the child grows up into a man, or the acorn expands into the oak; as for one offspring that reaches maturity, a thousand perish at their birth or in their growth, so can time alone, with all appliances of mind and body, convert a great conception into a system of fact, or give coherence and stability to an empire disordered in all its parts, and hitherto saved by foreign alliances from the dissolution which threatens it. What Turkey stands most in need of is a vigorous determined will in high quarters to awaken the dormant energies of the population, and to carry out, by means of capable agents, the reforms which have been proclaimed with so much appearance of good faith." This is the answer Lord Stratford gives to "the language of despondency and disparagement which of late have too often characterized the language of diplomacy and of the press."

That there are immense difficulties in the way of the restoration of these Mahommedan countries to civilization, cannot be denied. Ignorance, fanaticism, the retaliatory spirit of the code of law, and, above all, the abominable and pernicious results of polygamy, are fearful obstacles to contend against; but to obtain the moral improvements, we must commence with the material. Before despairing of Tunis, let us not forget how many persons despaired of Ireland before 1847, and prophesied that its redemption could only arise from an extermination of the Celt and the religion of the Celt.

In Tunis, thanks to the indefatigable exertions of our Consul-General, Mr. Wood, who never loses an opportunity of enlightening the rulers of the country as to their true interests, these improvements are commencing; an admirable currency has been established, and those who have changed gold pieces in the East know the value of it. A bank, too, is about to be set on foot, with the full concurrence and co-operation of the Bey; concessions of land for cotton-growing and for mining purposes will, erelong, be readily obtained by Englishmen; the Bey is most anxious for direct commerce with our country. All this shows how much may be effected by an intelligent and active representative thoroughly understanding the language, the feelings, and the prejudices of those he has to deal with.

If the natives can be induced to have confidence in the bank, and to understand its value, it is impossible to over-estimate the good it may effect. The deposits of an individual would be unknown to the rulers and squeezers, and would be safer and more readily transferable than when buried under a tree, or hid in the roof of a house. The value of money-orders to merchants travelling through an insecure country, instead of carrying specie offering inducements to rob, would also much facilitate commerce. There will, of course, be great suspicions at first, and the success of the bank will mainly depend on the tact and local knowledge of its managing directors. If these suspicions were overcome, the fame of the institution would rapidly spread, and there would be a desire throughout the interior of Africa for similar advantages, which would be organized and directed by natives. It would be, of course, an absurdity to expect such an advance for many a long day, but still everything has a beginning.

From the many advantages which it possesses, I cannot help thinking that Tunis, if not disorganized by French intrigues for French ends, might become the point from which a Mahommedan civilization might proceed as far as Islam has penetrated into Africa. But a ruler who is encountered at every step by ignorance, fanaticism, and corruption within, and by foreign intrigue without,—who, though a well-meaning man himself, has not the energy and talent to beat down every obstacle by force of will and superior abilities—such a man requires not merely urging, but every encouragement.

We who have so deep an interest in overcoming Mussulman prejudice, and in opening a vast continent for the paths of commerce and of peace, should make some more effort to obtain the attachment of the ruler of this country than we seem disposed to do. I have already alluded to the difficulties which attend every step taken by the representative of British interests at Tunis, and when I say British interests, I include the interests of the country to which he is accredited; for British interests are—that Tunis should be peaceful, independent, well governed, and civilized. Very little is required to conciliate the entire confidence and good will of the Bey: even those recognitions of which France is so generous and England so niggardly, would go a long way, and will, I trust, be not long withheld. It appears, from the proceedings of France, to be French policy that this country should not emerge from its present position, but the greater the discontent and disorganization, the more plausible will be the pretext for its annexation, and the less resistance will be experienced by the invading army. This is a sad and wicked policy—but not the less, I fear, that which actuates French diplomacy at present. But what can be expected from a nation that has relapsed into the slave trade—that, for the sake of one miserable colony, has outraged the sense of Europe by its conduct toward Portugal; that is reviving slave hunts, massacre, and misery, in unfortunate Africa, and that glories in its violence and shame?

THE END.